MAXIM GORKY

Selected Short Stories

With an Introductory Essay by
STEFAN ZWEIG

FREDERICK UNGAR PUBLISHING CO.
NEW YORK

Stefan Zweig's essay, written for Gorky's sixtieth
birthday, was first published in 1929. It is reprinted
in this volume by permission of the *Virginia Quarterly Review* and the author's estate.

Second printing, 1966

Printed 1959
in the United States of America

Library of Congress Catalog Card Number 58-8959

Contents

MAXIM GORKY
An essay
By Stefan Zweig

ALEXANDER PUSHKIN, the father of Russian literature, came of princely blood; Leo Tolstoy of very ancient lineage; Turgenev was a landed gentleman; Dostoevsky an official's son but of noble extraction—artistocrats all. For literature, art, all forms of intellectual achievement within the Russian empire in the nineteenth century were prerogatives of aristocracy, as were all other privileges—the land and palaces, rivers and mines, woods and fields, and the living human beings, the enthralled peasants, who tilled them with their sweat. All power, all wealth, all influence, all learning and position were reserved for a scant hundred noble strains, ten thousand individuals in the midst of millions. These alone depicted Russia to the eyes of the world, her wealth, her racial stock, her power and her soul.

A hundred families, ten thousand individuals. But beneath this thin superstratum heaved and moved an infinite, limitless mass of millions, a misshapen, gigantic being: the Russian people. Scattered millionfold over the huge plains of Muscovy, they toiled with millions of hands day and night for the wealth of the great land. They cleared forests, they leveled roads, they pressed out wine and brought up ore from the mines. They sowed and reaped on the black or snow-laden earth, they fought the Czar's battles and, like other European peoples at the same time, they served and evermore served their princes in abnegating toil and steadfast fealty. But one thing distinguished this Russian people from its brother folk: it was still mute; it had no speech. Long ago the other peoples had sent out spokesmen from their midst, orators and scholars, speaking tongues. These millions, however, were not yet able to express their desires in written words; they might not voice their thoughts in the councils of their land; they could not explain themselves, could not express that great and wild spirit which animated them. Stolid, full-lunged but voiceless, impotent with its monstrous strength, this oceanwide mysterious being of the peo-

1

ple stirred on its Russian earth, spirit without speech, being without self-conscious thought. It was only their masters, the aristocrats, the powerful, who spoke for these silent ones. Until the twentieth century we knew of the Russian people only through the voices of their high-born writers—Pushkin, Tolstoy, Turgenev, and Dostoevsky.

This will, however, be for all time to the glory and honor of these nobles—that, notwithstanding its speechlessness, its enforced silence, they never despised the Russian folk, its peasants and laborers, the insignificant man, but, on the contrary, as if from a feeling of mystical guilt, each of them passionately reverenced the greatness and the spiritual force of the lowly mass. Dostoevsky, the visionary, lifted the conception of the people to a Russian Savior, symbol of the ever-returning Christ, and, bitterly resisting the bourgeois revolutionaries and anarchistic nobles, reverently bowed his head to the Russian earth before the lowest criminal as the representative of a divine power. And still more passionately did Tolstoy, the other aristocrat, humble himself before the silent multitude; he abased himself only to raise the oppressed. "The way we live is wrong, their way is right." He laid aside his noble's dress and donned the muzhik blouse; he tried to copy their simple picturesque speech, their dull religious humility, to submerge, to dissolve himself in this immense life-giving force. All the great writers of Russia with one voice declared their awe in the presence of the great company; they all felt the defenselessness, the speechlessness, of their brother millions in the shadow of their own illumined lives as a monstrous, mystical soul-guilt. They all saw the high significance of their mission in the task of speaking for this dumb, unformed, voiceless being and interpreting to the world its thoughts and ideas.

But suddenly the miracle comes to pass, the unexpected, the unhoped for; suddenly this being, dumb for a thousand years, himself speaks. He creates lips from his own flesh, a spokesman from his own speech, a man from his midst, and this one man, the poet—his poet and witness—he suddenly thrusts out from his giant body that he may give to the whole of humanity tidings of the Russian people, of the Russian proletariat, of the lowly, the downtrodden and the oppressed. This man, this human being, this messenger, this poet is suddenly here, come into this world

2

sixty years ago, and for thirty years with unswerving fidelity the spokesman and painter of a whole tragic generation of the disinherited and the downtrodden. His parents call him Maxim Peschkov; he names himself Maxim Gorky—the bitter—and, with this self-made name, he is gratefully hailed today by the intellectual world and all who feel themselves truly as people among the peoples, because his bitterness has become healing for a whole race, his voice expression for a whole nation, and his advent happiness and blessing to our spirit today. Fate has taken this one unknown human being, Maxim Gorky, from the waste and chaff of humanity to make him a witness for the life of the thwarted, a portrayer of all the misery of the poor of Russia and of the whole world. And that he might be a true and faithful witness, it gave him for his portion every task, every torment, every renunciation, and every test in his own being so that he might painfully experience each in his own body before he shaped them and further revealed them in literary form. It sent him out to every kind of labor so that he might represent each fairly before the invisible parliament of humanity. It made him for a long time apprentice and bondsman of all suffering before he dare become lord of words and master of form. It was his lot to go through all the chances and changes of proletarian destiny before he became triumphantly the all-transmuter, the artist. So, in addition to artistic greatness, his rich and powerful work has the peculiarity that nothing was given by life to this poet, but everything was struggled for, was wrested from a miserable existence, and the pure and glorious result appears to have been wrung with bitterness from a malevolent reality.

What a life! What depth before this ascent! A dirty gray suburban street in Nizhny Novgorod gives birth to a great artist; poverty rocks his cradle; poverty expels him from school; poverty tosses him into the turmoil and into the world. The whole family lives in two cellar rooms, and in order to bring home a little money, a few pitiful kopecks, he, a schoolboy, must crawl around in sewers and dumpheaps, collecting rags and bones in the foul stench, so that his classmates avoid sitting beside the dung collector and sewer-crawler because of the bad smell. Although greedy for knowledge, he cannot finish primary school, but must with his slight childish figure become helper in a shoe factory, then house-

3

boy for a draftsman, scullion on a Volga steamer, porter at the docks, night watchman in a fishery, a baker, a letter carrier, a worker on the railroad, in the country, printer's devil, an eternally hunted day laborer beyond the pale of law, unhappy, homeless— vagabond on all roads, now in the Ukraine and on the Don, now in Bessarabia, now in Tiflis and in the Crimea. Nowhere can he stop, nowhere is he held. Scarcely has he found shelter under some foul roof when fate like an evil wind lashes him on and again, winter and summer, he scours the streets with burning soles, hungry, ragged, ill, and always, always hunted by poverty. Again and again he changes his work, but it is as if fate had willed these shifts with intention so that he could, with knowledge and experience, bear witness to all sides of the life of the proletariat, the Russian land in its entire breadth, the Russian people in its vast diversity and multiplicity. It was laid upon him—and nobly he stood the test—to know all forms of poverty in order to become the just and proper advocate for all misery; laid upon him also was the fate of all those in Russia who rebelled against the injustice of this scheme of things: to sit in prisons, to be watched by the police, to be spied upon, beset, suspected and hunted by the *gendarmerie* like a rabid wolf. This poet of the Russian people must endure in his defiant soul the lash of spiritual bondage, misrepresentation, for he is called to endure every single form of suffering of his class and kind. He must experience all forms of injustice and despair, even that ultimate and most frightful—the deepest and supreme despair of mankind—when he can no longer endure life and spews it from him like a bitter draught. Even this last abyss is not spared him. In December, 1887, Maxim Gorky bought with his last money a wretched revolver and fired a bullet into his breast. It remains in his lung and has threatened his life for forty years, but—happily—he was saved for the huge labor, which singlehanded he has accomplished, of witnessing for his people before the tribunal of humanity.

When this vagabond, this humble day laborer, this street waif and penniless fellow became a writer no scholarship will ever be able to figure out. For Maxim Gorky was always a poet by right of the alert vision and clear spirit of his generously receptive nature. But to express this poetic material he must first learn speech, writing and spelling, and how laborious was this

4

necessity. No one helped him in it; only his own tenacious will and the unyielding, unshakable primitive force which urged him on. As baker and street cleaner he eagerly collected by night whatever came into his hands in the way of books, newspapers, printed matter. But his real lesson book was the highway, his real guide his inner genius, for Gorky was a poet long before he had read anything and an artist before he had learned to spell correctly. At four and twenty he published his first novel; at thirty he is suddenly discovered, already the best known and, by the people, the most loved artist of Russia, the pride of the proletariat and a glory of the European world.

The effect of Gorky's first works was indescribably portentous, like an upheaval, an alarm, a wrench, a breaking. Every one felt that a different Russia from that of the past had here spoken for the first time, that this voice came from the gigantic anguished breast of a whole people. Dostoevsky, Tolstoy, and Turgenev, to be sure, had long before in noble visions given some inkling of the Russian soul in its breadth and power. But here suddenly the same thing was presented differently, more vividly— not the soul merely, but the whole naked man, the pitilessly clear, authentic Russian reality. In those others Russian destiny floated in a spiritual element, the stormy spheres of conscience—this widespread suffering, tension to the breaking point, the tragic knowledge of the course of world history. In Gorky, however, the Russian man arises not in the spirit but in flesh and blood, the shadowy, nameless one takes definite form, becomes compelling reality. Gorky, in contrast to Tolstoy and Dostoevsky and Goncharov, has no comprehensive symbolical figures of world literature like, say, the four Karamazovs, like Oblomov, like Levin and Karatejev. It is no diminution of his greatness that Gorky has never sought to form a single symbol of the inward nature of the Russian soul, but has instead placed before us, so that we can seize and touch them, ten thousand living figures of individual men and women with penetration and detail, with incredible veracity and verisimilitude. Born of the people, he has in himself made visible a whole people. From all stages of misery, from all stations in life he has invoked figures—each one of unsurpassed fidelity to life—dozens, hundreds, thousands, an army of the poor and diseased. Instead of a comprehensive vision this

glorious eye gives back to the living again in a thousand individual forms each man who met him in life. Therefore, for me,
this remembering eye of Gorky belongs to the few genuine mar-
vels of our present world, and I do not know what in the artcraft
of our time can be even approximately compared in naturalness
and exactitude to his art of observation. No shadow of the mys-
tic dims this eye, there is no distorting flaw in this wonderful
crystalline lens which neither enlarges nor diminishes, which
never sees things obliquely or distorted, never falsely perceives
them too bright or too dark. This eye sees only truly and clearly,
but in unsurpassed truth and unexcelled clarity. What has once
passed before this candid and just eye, this clearest and truest
instrument of our newer art, remains undistorted, for this eye
of Maxim Gorky forgets nothing—it gives purest and justest
reality. When Maxim Gorky describes a man I am ready to swear:
such was he exactly as Gorky saw and depicted him, exactly so,
no greater and no more insignificant; here is nothing added and
nothing taken away, nothing glossed over and nothing subtracted;
here is caught pure and undistorted the uniqueness of a human
being divined and forced into a portrait. There is no picture of
Leo Tolstoy among his ten thousand photographs, no account
among the ten thousand by his friends and visitors, which to the
same degree illuminates his being, discriminatingly, vividly, truly,
as the terse sixty pages which Maxim Gorky has dedicated to him
in his recollections. And exactly as this greatest of all Russians
whom he met, he has depicted with equal truth and justice the
most wretched vagabond, the lowest gypsy whom he met on the
road. The genius of Gorky's vision has only one name: veracity.
    Europe is indebted to this incorruptible, magnificently honest
vision of Maxim Gorky for the truest picture of the present Russian world—and when has there been more need of truth between the nations than at the present hour, and what people
among all the peoples has such sore need of it as the Russian in
this epoch-making instant? What a momentous event, a provi-
dence, a gift of fortune for this nation to possess in its crucial
hour a portrayer from its own blood, who shows in black and
white to each his own image unembellished, who is not sceptically contemptuous, who with the unerring and unconfused justice
of the artist brings appreciably nearer to the whole of humanity the

need and hope, the peril and greatness of an infinitude of people. Tolstoy and Dostoevsky in their deep, penetrating, solicitous love —confused, but none the less nationalistic—made the Russian people into a kind of Savior; so that in spite of the wonder the Russian man appeared to us somehow as other-worldly, strangely great and dangerous, but always strange—a different nature, different motives. Gorky, however—and this is his undying service— shows the Russian people not only as it is Russian, but above all as people, one and the same kin with all the poor and oppressed, the people as proletariat. He appears to belong more to mankind than to a nation, he is more humanistic than political, a revolutionary from sympathetic love of the people and not from monstrous hatred. He did not, like Dostoevsky and Tolstoy, see the coming revolution as the product of a few overexcited and anarchistic intellectuals, as the realization of exactly thought out theories, but in him and in him alone will future history be able to read the chapter and verse that this uprising and revolt in Russia was organically an affair of the people. He has shown how in the masses, in millions of individual details, the tension grew to the unbearable. In his masterpiece, "The Mother," one sees exactly how from the humblest men, from peasants, workers, from the uncultured and illiterate, the will concentrates in countless nameless sacrifices, and becomes tense before it bursts furiously forth in monstrous storm. No single man, but always the multitude, always the mass appears in his works as the holder of power; for because he himself was framed from a multitude, from the fullness of people, from the breadth of fate, this man perceives all that happens as universal experience. Even in this abnormal development of the people Gorky knew also, eternally and unshakably, the invincible power of his people. He trusted them as they had trusted him. While the great seers, Dostoevsky and Tolstoy, trembled before the revolution as at a pestilence, he knew that the sturdy health of his nation would outlast it. Just because he understood the Russian people as a son his mother, through nearness or by blood, Gorky never shared the frightful apocalyptic shudder of anxiety of Russia's great poet-prophets; he knew his people and all peoples strong enough to overcome all crises, to survive all dangers. So his presence during the Czarist years gave to the great masses more faith in them-

7

selves than all the shrieks of Dostoevsky for the Russian Christ, than all Tolstoy's calls for atonement and preachings of humility. In his person the people took courage and became confident because of him. Maxim Gorky's unhindered rise from the depths of the people has become a symbol for millions and his work witnesses the determination of a whole people to lift itself and find spiritual expression.

Today every one acknowledges that Maxim Gorky has generously rendered this service of testifying; a pure, true man, a great creative artist, never setting himself up as leader, never usurping authority as judge and clothing himself as prophet, but ever a steadfast witness for the rights of his people, for its spiritual complexity and for its moral force. As behooves an honest witness, he has never embellished and never denied the truth, he has never pleaded but reported. Without pessimism in the dark years and without exuberance in those that followed, strong in the hour of danger and without pride in success, he has called to life man after man in his work until they themselves formed a multitude, a people and a picture of the eternal people, this basic material of all form and all creative power. Thus his great epic has become no wavering myth of the Russian soul, but irrefutably true, reality itself. It is because of his works that we can understand Russia as a brother, near and neighborly to our world, without enmity, without antagonism; and in this is the highest obligation of the poet fulfilled—to destroy all enmity between men, to bring the distant near, to unite people with people, class with class, until at last all mankind are one. Whoever knows Gorky's work knows the Russian people of today and in him the need and renunciation of all the oppressed; he knows with comprehending soul its rarest, most passionate emotion even as its wretched day by day existence. We can shudderingly experience in Gorky's books as in no others all the sorrows and trials of the transition period. And since we have learned to feel with the Russian people in its most tragic hours, so now we can share the pride of Russia and experience its joy as our own, the proud joy of a people who have created out of their own blood such a blameless and true artist. We recognize in him two who are one—Maxim Gorky, the people-made poet, and the Russian people become poet through him.

MAKAR CHUDRA

A COLD wet wind blew from the sea, wafting over the steppes the pensive melody of the splashing surf and the rustle of shrubbery on the beach. Now and then its gusts brought shrivelled yellow leaves and whirled them into the flickering flames of the campfire. The gloom of autumnal night around us quivered and receded apprehensively, disclosing for a brief moment the endless steppe on the left, the boundless sea on the right, and opposite me the figure of Makar Chudra, the old Gypsy, who was looking after the horses of his Gypsy camp pitched within fifty paces of where we sat.

Heedless of the cold blasts that blew open his Caucasian coat and mercilessly buffeted his bared hairy chest, he reclined in a graceful vigorous pose with his face towards me, drawing methodically at his huge pipe, emitting thick puffs of smoke through his mouth and nose, staring out over my head into the deathly hushed darkness of the steppes, talking incessantly and making not a single movement to shield himself from the cruel gusts of wind.

"So you're on the tramp? That's fine! You've made a splendid choice, my lad. That's the way: trot around and see things, and when you've seen all you want, lie down and die—that's all!

"Life? Other people?" he went on, having lent a sceptical ear to my protest about his "that's all." "H'm. Why should that worry you? Aren't you Life? Other people live without you and'll live their lives without you. Do you imagine anybody needs you? You're neither bread nor a stick, and nobody wants you.

"To learn and teach, you say? But can you learn how to make people happy? No, you cannot. You get grey hairs first before talking about teaching. Teach what? Every one knows what he wants. Those that are cleverer take what there is to take, the sillier ones get nothing, but every man learns himself.

"They're a curious lot, those people of yours. All herded together and treading on each other's toes when there's so much
room in the world," he waved a sweeping hand towards the steppes.
"And toiling away all the time. What for? Whom for? Nobody knows. You see a fellow ploughing, and think—there he is
sweating out his strength drop by drop on that land, then he'll
lie down in it and rot away. He leaves nothing after him, he sees
nothing from that field of his and dies as he was born—a fool.

"D'you mean to say he was born to dig the earth and die without having managed to dig a grave for himself? Does he know
what freedom is? Has he any idea of the vast and glorious steppe?
Does the music of the steppe gladden his heart? He's a slave,
from the moment he is born, a slave all his life long, and that's
all! What can he do for himself? All he can do is to hang himself,
if he learned a little sense.

"Now look at me; at fifty-eight I've seen so much that if
you'd write it down on paper it would fill a thousand bags like
the one you've got there. You just ask me what places I haven't
been to? There aren't such places. You've got no idea of the places
I've been to. That's the way to live—gad about the world, and
that's all! Don't stay long in one place—it's not worth it!
Like day and night that chase each other around the world, you
keep chasing yourself away from thoughts of life, so as not to
grow sick of it. Once you stop to think you'll get sick of life—
that's how it always happens. It happened to me too. Humph! So
it did, my lad.

"I was in prison, in Galicia. What am I living on this earth
for?—I started to mope, feeling sort of dreary—it's dreary in
prison, my lad, ever so dreary! And I felt sick at heart when I
looked out of the window at the fields, so sick as though some
one were gripping and wrenching my heart. Who can say what
he lives for? No one can say it, my lad! And it's no use asking
yourself about it. Live, and that's all. Go about and look around,
and you'll never be bored. I very nearly hung myself by my belt
that time that's a fact!

"Huh! I spoke to a man once. He was a serious man, one of
yours, a Russian. You must live, he says, not the way you want, but
according to the word of God. Obey the Lord and he will give

you everything you ask for. He himself was all in rags and holes. I told him to ask God for a new suit of clothes. He fell into a rage and drove me away, cursing. And he'd just been telling me that one should forgive and love his fellow creatures. He might have forgiven me if what I said offended his lordship. There's a teacher for you! They teach you to eat less, while they themselves eat ten times a day."

He spat into the fire and fell silent, while refilling his pipe. The wind moaned plaintively and softly, the horses whinnied in the darkness, and the tender passionate strains of the *dumka* melody floated up from the Gypsy camp. The beautiful Nonka, Makar's daughter, was singing. I knew that deep throaty-toned voice of hers, that always sounded so strange, discontented and imperious, whether she sang a song or said "good day." The warm pallor of her dark-skinned face was fixed in a look of queenly hauteur, and the deep pools of her dark brown eyes shone with a realization of her own irresistible loveliness and disdain for everything that was not she.

Makar held out his pipe.

"Take a smoke! She sings well, that lass, eh? I should say so! Would you like a girl like that to love you? No? That's right! Never believe girls, and keep away from them. Girls find kissing better and more pleasant than I do smoking a pipe, but once you've kissed her say good-bye to your liberty. She'll bind you to her by invisible strings which you'll never be able to break, and you'll lay your soul at her feet. That's a fact! Beware of the girls! They're all liars! She'll say she loves you more'n anything in the world, but you just prick her with a pin and she'll break your heart. I know a lot about their kind, I do! Well, my lad, d'you want me to tell you a story, a true story? Try to remember it if you can, and it's a free bird you'll be all your life.

"Once upon a time there was a young Gypsy, a young Gypsy named Loiko Zobar. All Hungary and Bohemia and Slavonia and all around the sea everybody knew him—he was a fine lad! There wasn't a village in those parts, but where a half-dozen or so of the inhabitants didn't swear to God they'd kill him. But Loiko went on living, and if he took a fancy to a horse, Zobar'd be curvetting about on that horse even if you was to put a regiment of soldiers to guard it! Ah! He wasn't afraid of anybody, not likely! Why, if the prince of devils with all his pack came to him, he'd as likely as not stick a knife in him, and he'd certainly curse him roundly and send the whole pack off with a flea in its ear—you can take that from me!

"And all the Gypsy camps knew him or had heard of him. All he loved was horses, and nothing more, and even then not for long—he'd ride 'em a bit then sell 'em, and the money was anybody's for the asking. He had nothing that he cherished—if you wanted his heart he'd tear it out of his breast and give it to you, as long as it made you happy. That's the kind he was, my lad!

"Our caravan was wandering at the time through Bukowina— that was about ten years ago. Once, on a night in spring, we were sitting around—myself, the old soldier Danilo who fought under Kossuth, and old Noor and all the others and Radda, Danilo's daughter.

"You know my girl Nonka, don't you? A beautiful maid she is! Well, you couldn't compare her to Radda—too great an honour! There aren't any words to describe that girl Radda. Maybe her beauty could be played on the violin, and even then only by a person who knew that violin as well as he did his own soul.

"She seared the hearts of many of fine lad she did, aye, many a fine lad! In Morava a magnate, an old, shock-headed man saw her and was struck all of a heap. Sat on his horse and stared, shivering as with the ague. He was pranked out like the devil on a holiday, in a rich Ukrainian coat embroidered with gold, and the sword at his side all set in precious stones flashed like lightning whenever his horse stamped its foot, and the blue velvet of his cap was like a bit of sky—he was a big lord, that old gent! He stared and stared, then he says to Radda: 'Hi, give me a kiss, I'll give you my purse!' She just turned away without a word! 'Forgive me if I've offended you, can't you look at me more kindly?' said the old magnate, immediately coming down a peg, and he threw a purse at her feet—a fat purse, brother! And she spurned it in the dust, casual like, with her foot, and that's all.

" 'Ah, what a maid!' he groaned, and flicked his horse with his riding crop and was gone in a cloud of dust.

"The next day he came again. 'Who's her father?' he went thundering about the camp. Danilo stepped out. 'Sell me your daughter, take whatever you want!' And Danilo, he says: 'Only the nobility sell everything from their pigs to their conscience, but I fought under Kossuth, and don't traffic in anything!' The other became furious, made a snatch for his sword, but one of the boys stuck a lighted tinder in the horse's ear and he made off with his rider in a flash. We struck tents and moved off. We hadn't been travelling two days when up he dashes again! 'Hi, you,' he says, 'before God and you my conscience is clear, give that maid to me in marriage. I'll share all I have with you, I'm mighty rich!' He was all on fire and swaying in the saddle like feather-grass in the wind. That set us all thinking.

" 'Well, daughter, what do you say?' Danilo muttered under his moustache.

" 'What would the eagle be if she went into the crow's nest of her own free will?' Radda asked us.

"Danilo laughed, and so did we all.

" 'Well said, daughter! Hear that, Sir? Nothing doing! Look among the doves—they're more docile.' And we moved on.

"That gentleman seized his cap, threw it to the ground and galloped away so furiously that the very earth shook. That's the kind of girl Radda was, my lad!

"Yes! Well, one night as we sat around we heard music floating over the steppe. Fine music! It set your blood on fire and lured you into the unknown. That music, we all felt, made one yearn for something after which, if you got it, life would no longer be worth living, unless it was, as kings over all the earth, my lad!

"Well, a horse loomed out of the darkness, and on the horse a man sat and played as he approached us. He drew up at the campfire, ceased playing and smiled down at us.

" 'Ah, why, that's you, Zobar!' Danilo cried out to him joyfully. Yes, that was Loiko Zobar!

"His moustaches lay on his shoulders and mingled with his locks, his eyes were as bright as stars and his smile was like the sun so help me God! He and his horse might have been forged of a single piece of iron. There he stood red as blood in the

firelight, his teeth flashing in a smile! Damned if I didn't love
him then more than I loved myself, even before he had spoken
a word to me or had as much as noticed my existence!

"Yes, my lad, that's the kind of man he was! He'd look into
your eyes and captivate your soul, and you wouldn't be the least
bit ashamed of it, only feel proud about it. With a man like that
you feel nobler yourself. Such men are rare, my friend! Perhaps
that's better so. If there'd be too much of a good thing in this
world it wouldn't be looked on as a good thing. Aye! Well, let's
get on with the story.

"Radda she says: 'You play well, Loiko! Who made you such
a sweet-toned delicate fiddle?' He laughed—'I made it myself! And
I made it not of wood, but from the breast of a young girl whom
I loved dearly, and the strings I play on are her heartstrings. The
fiddle plays a little false, but I know how to handle the bow!'

"Our breed, you know, tries straight away to befog a girl's
eyes, so they be dimmed with sad yearning for a fellow without
kindling his own heart. That was Loiko's way too. But Radda was
not to be caught that way. She turned away with a yawn and said:
'And people said Zobar was clever and adroit—what liars!' With
that she walked away.

" 'Oho, pretty maid, you've got sharp teeth!' said Loiko with
a flashing eye, getting off his horse. 'How do you do, brothers!
Well, here I am come to you!'

" 'Welcome, guest!' said Danilo in reply. We kissed, had a
talk and went to bed. . . . We slept soundly. In the morning we
saw that Zobar's head was tied up with a rag. What's that? Oh,
his horse accidentally hurt him with its hoof while he was asleep.

"Ha-a! We guessed who that horse was and smiled into our
moustaches, and Danilo smiled too. Well, wasn't Loiko worthy of
Radda? I should think so! However fair a maid may be, she has
a narrow, petty soul, and though you'd hang a pood of gold round
her neck she'd never be any better than she was. Well, anyway!

"We lived a pretty long time on that spot, things were going
well with us and Zobar was with us. That was a comrade for you!
Wise like an old man, informed on everything and knew how to
read and write Russian and Magyar. When he'd start speaking
you'd forget about sleep and could listen to him for ages! As

for playing—well salt my hide if there's another man in the world could play like that! He'd draw his bow across the strings and your heart'd begin to flutter, then he'd draw it again and it'd stop beating while you listened, and he just played and smiled. You felt like crying and laughing one and the same time when listening to him. Now you'd hear some one moaning bitterly, pleading for help and lacerating your heart as with a knife; now the steppe telling the heavens a fairy tale, a sad tale; now a maid weeping, bidding farewell to her beloved! And now a valiant youth calling his beloved to the steppe. Then suddenly—heigh-ho! A brave merry tune fills the air, and the very sun, it seems, bids fair to start a jig up in the sky! Yes, my lad, that's how it was!

"Every fibre in your body understood that song, and you became its slave, body and soul. If Loiko had then cried out: 'To knives, comrades!' we'd have snatched up our knives as one man and followed him blindly. He could do anything he wanted with a man, and everybody loved him, loved him mightily—only Radda had no eyes for the lad. That wouldn't have been so bad, worse was she mocked him. She smote that lad's heart sorely, aye sorely! He'd gnash his teeth, Loiko would, pulling at his moustache. Eyes darker than an abyss, and sometimes with a gleam of something fit to harrow up the soul. At night he'd go far out into the steppe, would Loiko, and his fiddle would weep till morning, weep over the death of Loiko's liberty. And we lay listening and thinking: what's to be done? We knew that if two stones are rolling down on each other it's no use getting between them—they'd crush you. That's how things were.

"Well, we all sat assembled, discussing affairs. Then things got dull. So Danilo asks Loiko: 'Sing a song, Loiko, something to cheer the soul!' The lad glanced at Radda who was lying at a little distance with her face looking up into the sky, and drew his bow across the strings. The fiddle spoke as though it were really a maiden's heart, and Loiko sang:

> *Hey-ho! A flame the heart doth feed,*
> *Vast the steppe and wide!*
> *Fleet as the wind my gallant steed,*
> *Strong-armed rider astride!*

"Radda turned her head, and rising on her elbow, smiled mockingly into the singer's eyes. He reddened like the dawn.

> *Hey-ho-hey! Up comrade arise!*
> *Onward let us race!*
> *Where steppe in deepest darkness lies,*
> *To waiting dawn's embrace!*
> *Hey-ho! We fly to meet the day,*
> *Soaring above the plain!*
> *Touch not thee in passing, pray*
> *The beauteous moon with thy mane!*

"Did he sing! Nobody sings like that any more! And Radda says, letting the words drop:

" 'You shouldn't fly so high, Loiko. You might fall and come down on your nose in a puddle and wet your moustache, be careful.' Loiko glared fiercely at her and said nothing—he swallowed it and went on singing:

> *Hey-ho-hey! Lest daybreak's flush*
> *Overtake us in idle slumber,*
> *Away, away, ere for shame we blush,*
> *And men begin to wonder!*

" 'What a song!' said Danilo, 'never heard anything like it before, may the Devil make a pipe out of me if I lie!' Old Noor twitched his moustache and shrugged his shoulders and everybody was delighted with that brave song of Zobar's! Only Radda didn't like it.

" 'That's how a wasp once buzzed when he tried to imitate the cry of an eagle,' said she, and it was as if she had thrown snow over us.

" 'Maybe you'd like a taste of the whip, Radda?' Danilo said, starting up, but Zobar threw his cap on the ground and spoke, his face as dark as the earth:

" 'Stop, Danilo! A spirited horse needs a steel bridle! Give your daughter to me as wife!'

" 'Now you've said something!' said Danilo with a smile. 'Take her if you can!'

" 'Good!' said Loiko and spoke thus to Radda:

" 'Well, lass, listen to me a while and don't put on airs! I've seen a lot of your sisterhood in my time, aye quite a lot! But not one of them ever touched my heart like you have. Ah, Radda, you have snared my soul! Well? What's to be must needs be, and ... the steed does not exist on which one could escape from one's self!... I take you to wife before God, my conscience, your father and all these people. But mind, you are not to oppose my will—I am a free man and will live the way I want!' And he went up to her, his teeth clenched and eyes flashing. We saw him holding out his hand to her—now, thought we, Radda has bridled the horse of the steppe! Suddenly we saw his hand go up and he fell, hitting the ground with the back of his head with a crash!...

"Good heavens! It was as if a bullet had struck the lad in the heart. Radda, it appears, had swept the whiplash round his legs and pulled it, sending him off his feet.

"There she was lying back again without stirring, with a mocking smile on her face. We waited to see what would happen next. Loiko sat on the ground clutching his head as though afraid it would burst. Then he got up quietly and walked off into the steppe without a glance at anyone. Noor whispered to me: 'Keep your eye on him!' And I crawled after Zobar into the darkness of the steppe. Yes, my lad!"

Makar knocked the ashes out of his pipe and began refilling it again. I drew my coat closer about me and lay looking at his old face, blackened by the sun and winds. He was whispering to himself, shaking his head sternly; his grizzled moustache moved up and down and the wind stirred the hair on his head. He was like an old oak tree seared by lightning, but still strong and sturdy and proud of its strength. The sea still carried on a whispered converse with the shore and the wind still carried its whispers over the steppe. Nonka had stopped singing, and the clouds that had gathered in the sky made the autumn night still darker.

"Loiko dragged his feet wearily along, his head bent and hands hanging nervelessly by his sides, and when he reached a ravine by the stream he sat down on a boulder and groaned. It was a groan that made my heart bleed for pity, but I didn't go up to him. Grief won't be comforted by words, will it? That's just it! He sat on for an hour, then another, and a third, just sat without stirring.

"And I was lying on the ground nearby. It was a bright night the whole steppe was bathed in silver moonlight and you could see far away in the distance.

"Suddenly, I saw Radda hurrying towards us from the camp.
"That cheered me up! 'Ah, splendid!' I thought, 'brave lass,
Radda!' She drew close, but he hadn't heard her coming. She put
her hand on his shoulder; Loiko started, unclasped his hands and
raised his head. Then he leapt to his feet and gripped his knife!
'Ah, he'll knife the maid, I thought,' and I was just going to shout
out to the camp and run to them when I suddenly heard:

"'Drop it! I'll smash your head!' I looked—there was Radda with a pistol in her hand aimed at Zobar's head. There's a
hell-cat for you! Well, I thought, they're now matched in strength,
I wonder what'll happen next?

"'Look here!'—Radda thrust the pistol into her waistband—
'I didn't come here to kill you, but to make up—drop the knife!'
He dropped it and looked sullenly into her eyes! It was a sight,
brother! There were two people glaring at each other like animals
at bay, and both such fine, brave people. There were just the
shining moon and I looking on, that's all.

"'Now, listen to me, Loiko. I love you!' said Radda. He merely shrugged, as though tied hand and foot.

"'I've seen brave youths, but you're braver and better in face
and soul. Any of them would have shaven their moustache had I
so much as winked my eye, all of them would have fallen at my
feet had I wished it. But what's the sense? They're none too brave
anyway, and I'd have made them all womanish. There are few
brave Gypsies left in the world as it is, very few, Loiko. I never
loved anybody, Loiko, but you I love. But I love liberty too! I
love liberty, Loiko, more than I do you. But I cannot live without you, as you cannot live without me. So I want you to be mine,
body and soul, do you hear?' He smiled a twisted smile.

"'I hear! It cheers the heart to hear your speeches! Say some
more!'

"'This more I want to say, Loiko: no matter how you twist
I'll have my way with you, you'll be mine. So don't waste time—
my kisses and caresses are awaiting you, and I shall kiss you
sweetly, Loiko! Under my kisses you shall forget your adventur-
ous life ... and your lively songs which so gladden the hearts
of the Gypsy lads will be heard no more in the steppe—you shall
sing other songs, tender love songs to me, Radda.... Waste not

time then—I have spoken, therefore tomorrow you shall obey me like the youth who obeys his elder comrade. You shall bow the knee to me before the whole Gypsy camp and kiss my right hand—then I shall be your wife.'

"So that's what she was after, the mad girl! It was unheard of! It had been the custom once among the Montenegrins, so the old men said, but never among the Gypsies! Well, my lad, can you think of anything funnier than that? Not if you racked your brains a year, you wouldn't!

"Loiko recoiled and his cry rang out over the steppe like that of a man wounded in the breast. Radda winced but did not betray herself.

" 'Well, good-bye till tomorrow, and tomorrow you will do as I bade you. Do you hear, Loiko?'

" 'I hear! I will,' groaned Zobar and held his arms out to her. She went without even turning her head, and he swayed like a tree broken by the wind and dropped to the ground, sobbing and laughing.

"That is what the accursed Radda did to the poor lad. I had a job bringing him to his senses.

"Ah well! Why the devil should people have to drain the cup of misery? Who cares to hear a human heart moaning in pain and grief? Make it out if you can!...

"I went back to the camp and told the old men all about it. They thought the matter over and decided to wait and see what would happen. And this is what happened. When we all gathered next evening around the campfire Loiko joined us. He was gloomy and had become terribly haggard overnight and his eyes were sunken. He cast them down and, without raising them, said to us:

" 'I want to tell you something, comrades. I looked into my heart this night and found no place therein for the old carefree life of mine. Radda alone dwells in it—and that's all! There she is, beautiful Radda, smiling like a queen! She loves her liberty more than me, and I love her more than my liberty, and I have decided to bend my knee to her, as she bade me, so that all may see how her beauty has conquered brave Loiko Zobar, who until he knew her used to play with the girls like a gerfalcon with the ducks. After that she will become my wife and will kiss and caress me, so that I will have no more desire to sing you songs

and will not regret my liberty! Is that right, Radda?' He raised
his eyes and looked darkly at her. She silently and sternly nodded
her head and pointed her hand to her feet. And we looked on,
understanding nothing. We even felt like going away, not to see
Loiko Zobar prostrate himself at a maid's feet, even though that
maid were Radda. We felt sort of ashamed, and sorry and sad.

"'Well!' cried Radda to Zobar.

"'Aha, don't be in a hurry, there's plenty of time, you'll
have more than enough of it ...' he retorted with a laugh. And
that laugh had a ring of steel in it.

"'So that's all I wanted to tell you, comrades! What next? It
remains next but to test whether Radda has so strong a heart as
she showed me. I'll test it—forgive me, brothers!'

"Before we could fathom these words Radda lay stretched on
the earth with Zobar's curved knife sunk to the hilt in her breast.
We were horror-struck.

"And Radda pulled out the knife, threw it aside, and pressing a lock
of her black hair to the wound, said loudly and audibly with a smile:

"'Farewell, Loiko! I knew you would do that! ...' and she
died. ...

"D'you grasp the kind of maid that was, my lad? A hell of a
maid she was, may I be damned to eternity!

"'Oh! Now I'll kneel at your feet, proud queen!' Loiko's loud
cry echoed all over the steppe, and throwing himself to the ground
he pressed his lips to the feet of dead Radda and lay motionless.
We took off our caps and stood in silence.

"What do you say to that, my lad? Aye, that's just it! Noor
said: 'We ought to bind him!. . .' No hand would lift to bind Loiko Zobar, not a hand would lift, and Noor knew it. He waved his
hand and turned away. And Danilo picked up the knife which
Radda had cast aside and gazed long at it, his moustache twitching. The blade of that knife, so curved and sharp, was still wet
with Radda's blood. And then Danilo went up to Zobar and stuck
the knife into his back over the heart. For he was Radda's father,
was Danilo the old soldier!

"'There you are!' said Loiko in a clear voice, turning to Danilo, and he followed on the heels of Radda.

"And we stood looking. There lay Radda. pressing a lock of

hair to her bosom, and her open eyes stared into the blue sky
while at her feet brave Loiko Zobar lay stretched. His face was
covered by his locks and you couldn't see his face.

"We stood lost in thought. Old Danilo's moustaches trembled
and his bushy brows were knitted. He stared at the sky and said
nothing, while Noor, grey old Noor, lay down with his face on
the ground and all his old body was racked with sobs.

"There was something to cry over, my lad!

"... So you're going on the tramp—well, go your way, don't
turn off the road. You go straight on. Maybe you won't go to
the dogs. That's all, my lad!"

Makar fell silent, and putting the pipe into his pouch, wrapped
his coat over his chest. Rain began to fall in a drizzle, the wind
was rising, the sea growled and rumbled angrily. The horses one
by one came up to the dying campfire and regarding us with their
big intelligent eyes stopped motionless around us in a dense ring.

"Hey, hey, ho!" Makar cried to them kindly, and patting the
neck of his favourite black horse, said, turning to me:

"Time to go to sleep!" and, drawing his coat over his head
and stretching his great length out on the ground he fell silent.
I did not feel like sleeping. I gazed into the darkness of the steppe
and before my eyes swum the queenly beautiful image of proud
Radda. She was pressing a lock of hair to the wound in her breast
and through her delicate swarthy fingers the blood oozed drop by
drop, falling to the ground like flaming-red little stars.

Following close on her heels there floated the vision of the
brave Gypsy lad Loiko Zobar. His face was screened by thick
black locks from under which big cold tears fell fast. . . .

The rain grew heavier and the sea was chanting a mournful
solemn dirge to the proud pair of Gypsy lovers—to Loiko Zobar
and to Radda, the daughter of the old soldier Danilo.

And they both hovered silently in the misty darkness, and the
dashing Loiko, try as he may, was unable to catch up with the
proud Radda.

OLD IZERGIL

I

I HEARD these stories at a place on the Bessarabian coast, near Akkerman.

One evening, having finished our day's grape picking, the group of Moldavians with whom I was working, went off to the beach. I remained behind with old Izergil, reclining on the ground, in the shade of a thick vine, silently watching the silhouettes of the people who were going down to the sea merge with the falling shadows of night.

They strolled down to the beach singing and laughing. The men in short tunics and wide pantaloons had bronzed faces, thick black moustaches and heavy locks of hair that reached down to their shoulders. The women and girls, merry and graceful. had dark blue eyes, and their faces too were bronzed. Their black, silky hair hung loose down their backs, and the warm, light breeze, that blew through the tresses, caused the ornamental coins that were plaited into them to tinkle. The wind blew in a broad, even stream; but now and again it seemed to leap over some invisible obstacle, and heavy gusts caused the women's hair to spread in fantastic manes around their heads, giving them the appearance of having walked out of some strange legend. As they receded further and further away from us, the night and my imagination clothed them with increasing beauty.

Someone was playing a fiddle.... A girl was singing in a soft contralto. The sound of laughter was heard....

The air was impregnated with the pungent odour of the sea and of the greasy exhalation of the earth, which the rain had thoroughly saturated just before sundown. Even now fragments of clouds wandered across the sky in grotesque shapes and colours—here soft. like wreaths of smoke, blue and ash-grey, and there ragged, like fragments of rock, a dull black or brown. Between them fondly peeped dark blue patches of the sky, dotted with golden stars. All this —the sounds and smells, the clouds and the people—looked strangely beautiful and sad, like the beginning of a wonderful tale. And everything seemed as though it were checked in its growth, as if it were dying. The sounds of the voices, receded further into the distance, subsided, and became nothing but mournful sighs.

"Why didn't you go with them?" old Izergil asked me, nodding in the direction in which the people had gone.

Time had bent her double; her once shining black eyes were dull and bleary. Her dry voice sounded strange; it crackled, as if she were crunching bones.

"I didn't feel like it!" I answered.

"Ekh!... You Russians are born old. You are all as gloomy as demons.... Our girls are afraid of you.... But you are young and strong...."

The moon rose, large, round and blood-red, seemingly out of the bowels of this steppe, which had absorbed so much human flesh and blood in its time, and probably for that reason had become so rich and fertile. And as it rose it threw upon us the lace-like shadows of the vine leaves, and the old woman and I appeared to be covered with a net. To the left of us the shadows of the clouds flitted across the steppe; and the clouds themselves, lit up by the bluish rays of the moon, seemed brighter and more transparent.

"Look! That's Larra!"

I looked in the direction in which the old woman pointed with her trembling hand and crooked fingers, and I saw shadows floating, many of them; but one was darker and thicker than the rest, and it moved faster and lower than its sisters—it fell from a clump of cloud which was floating nearer to the ground and was moving faster than the others.

"I can't see anybody," I said.

"Your eyes are worse than mine, an old woman's! Look! Over there! The dark one, running across the steppe!"

I looked again, and again saw nothing but shadows.

"That's a shadow! Why do you call it Larrà!"

"Because it is he. He is now no more than a shadow. No wonder! He has lived thousands of years; the sun dried up his body

his blood and his bones, and the wind blew them away like dust.
You see what God can do to a man for being proud!"

"Tell me how it happened!" I begged of the old woman, expecting to hear one of the wonderful stories that are composed in the
steppes.

And she told me the following story.

"This happened many thousands of years ago. Far beyond the sea,
where the sun rises, there is a country with a big river; and in
that country every tree leaf and blade of grass gives as much shadow
as a man needs to shelter him from the sun, which is very hot there.

"That's how bountiful the earth is in that country!

"In that country there lived a powerful tribe of men. They herded their cattle and spent their strength and manhood in hunting,
in feasting after the hunt, singing songs and frolicking with the girls.

"One day, during a feast, one of the girls, black-haired and tender like the night, was carried away by an eagle, which swooped down
from the sky. The arrows which the men shot at the eagle, pitiful
things, failed to reach it and dropped back to earth. The men then
went out to search for the girl, but they searched in vain. They failed
to find her. And then they forgot about her, as everything on earth
is forgotten."

The old woman sighed and paused. Her grating voice had sounded like the complaints of all the forgotten ages which had revived
in her breast in shadowy recollections. The sea had softly accompanied the opening of one of those ancient legends which had probably been composed on its shore.

"Twenty years after, the girl came back herself, worn and haggard. With her was a young man, handsome and strong, as she herself
had been twenty years before. When they asked her where she had
been, she said that the eagle had carried her away to the mountains,
and she had lived with him there as his wife. The young man was her
son; his father was dead. When he grew feeble he soared for the last
time high into the sky and, folding his wings, dropped heavily onto
the jagged crags of the mountain and was killed. . . .

"Everybody looked in wonder at the eagle's son and saw that
he differed in no way from themselves, except that his eyes were
cold and proud, like those of the king of birds. When they talked

to him he answered if he had a mind to, or else remained silent; and when the elders of the tribe came and spoke to him, he addressed them as an equal. They regarded this as an affront. They upbraided him and said he was still an unfeathered arrow with an unsharpened point, and told him that they were honoured and obeyed by thousands like him, and by thousands twice as old as he. But he looked boldly at them and answered that he had no equal, and if others honoured them, he did not wish to do so. Oh! ... Then they became really angry with him, and angrily they said:

" 'There is no place for him among us! Let him go wherever he wills!'

"He laughed and went where he willed—to a beautiful girl who had been gazing intently at him; he went up to her and embraced her. But she was the daughter of one of the elders who had rebuked him; and although he was so handsome she pushed him away, for she was afraid of her father. She pushed him away and walked off; but he struck her, and when she fell to the ground he stood upon her chest, so that the blood spurted from her mouth to the sky. The girl gasped, writhed like a snake, and died.

"All those who witnessed this were petrified by fear—this was the first time a woman had been killed among them in this way. They stood silent for a long time, now looking at the dead girl lying on the ground with open eyes and bloodstained mouth, and now at the young man standing beside the girl, proudly facing them all—he did not hang his head as if asking to be punished. When they recovered from their surprise they seized and bound him, and left him there; for they thought it would be too simple a matter to kill him off-hand, that would not satisfy them."

The night grew darker and became filled with strange, soft sounds. The marmots whistled mournfully in the steppe, and the metallic grating of the grasshoppers was heard in the leaves of the vine; the leaves sighed and whispered to each other; the full moon, blood-red before, was now pale and grew paler as it rose over the earth; the bluish haze spread more widely over the steppe. . . .

"And so they gathered together to devise the punishment that would fit the crime. . . . Some suggested that he should be torn apart by horses, but this was thought too lenient. Others proposed that each one should shoot an arrow at him, but this too was rejected.

Somebody proposed that he be burnt at the stake, but this was rejected because the smoke from the fire would prevent them from
seeing how he suffered. Many proposals were made, but not one of
them seemed to be satisfactory. And while they were discussing this,
his mother knelt before them in silence, unable to find either the
tears nor the words with which to plead for mercy. They talked and
talked for hours until, at last, one of the wise men, after long reflection, said:

" 'Let us ask him why he did it!'

"They asked him, and he answered:

" 'Unbind me! I will not speak while I am bound!'

"And when they unbound him he asked in a tone as if he was
speaking to slaves:

" 'What do you want?'

" 'You have heard', answered the wise man.

" 'Why should I explain my conduct to you?'

" 'So that we may understand. Listen, proud one! You will die....
Make us understand what you have done. We shall remain alive,
and it is useful for us to know more than we know now.'

" 'Very well, I will tell you, although I myself do not quite understand what happened. I think I killed her because she rebuffed
me.... But I wanted her.'

" 'But she was not yours!' he was told.

" 'Do you use only that which belongs to you? I see that every
man possesses only speech, arms and legs... but he owns cattle,
women, land ... and many other things.'

"In answer to this he was told that for every thing a man takes
he pays with himself: with his wisdom, his strength, and sometimes
with his life. But he answered that he wanted to keep himself whole.

"They talked to him for a long time and at last realized that he
regarded himself as the first in the land and had no thought for
anybody but himself. They were all horrified by the isolation to
which he had doomed himself. He belonged to no tribe; he had not
a mother, nor cattle, nor a wife, and he wanted nothing of the kind.

"When the people realized this they began to discuss again what
punishment to inflict upon him. But this time they did not debate
for long. The wise man, who had remained silent up to now, spoke
up and said:

" 'Stay! I have a punishment. A terrible punishment. You would not have thought of one like it in a thousand years! The punishment lies in himself. Let him go. Let him be free. That will be his punishment!'

"In that instant a wonderful thing happened. A loud clap of thunder burst in the sky, although no clouds were visible. The celestial powers thus signified their approval of what the wise man had said. All bowed low and dispersed. But the young man, who was now given the name of Larra, which means outcast, laughed loudly at the people who were leaving him. He laughed as he remained alone, as free as his father had been. But his father had not been a human, whereas he was. And so he began to live as free as a bird. He stole up to the tribe's encampment and carried away their cattle, their girls, everything he wanted. They shot arrows at him, but his body was protected by the invisible armour of his supreme punishment— he could not die. He was agile, rapacious, strong and cruel, but he never met men face to face. He was seen only at a distance. And so he hovered alone, round the habitations of the tribe, for a long, long time, for many scores of years. But one day he came very near to the habitations of the tribe and when the men ran out to seize him he did not run away, and made no signs that he intended to defend himself. One of the men guessed what was the matter and shouted out loudly:

" 'Don't touch him! He wants to die!'

"And all halted at once, not wishing to ease the lot of the one who had done them evil, not wishing to kill him. They halted and jeered at him. He stood trembling, listening to the jeers, and seemed to be searching for something in his bosom. Suddenly he stooped, picked up a rock and rushed at the men. But they, avoiding his blows, did not strike him; and when, at last, he fell to the ground with a despairing cry of weariness, they stood aside and watched him. He raised himself, picked up a knife which one of the men had dropped during the fray, and plunged it into his own breast. But the blade snapped as if it had struck a stone. He fell down again and beat his head on the ground, but the ground yielded to the blows and only dents were left in it.

" 'He cannot die!' the people shouted gleefully.

"They went away and left him. He lay face upwards and saw mighty eagles soaring high in the sky, like black dots, and his eyes

were filled with bitterness, enough to poison all the inhabitants of
the world. Since then he has remained alone, free, waiting for death.
And so he roams and roams around, roams everywhere. . . . Do you
see? He is already like a shadow, and so he will remain forever.
He understands neither the speech of men nor their actions, he understands nothing. He does nothing but roam and roam, searching
for something. . . . He knows not life, nor does death smile upon him.
He has no place among men. . . . That is how a man was punished
for his pride!"

The old woman sighed and stopped speaking, and her head,
which had drooped to her breast, swayed to and fro several times,
in a very queer way.

I looked at her. It seemed to me that sleep had overcome her,
and for some reason I felt very sorry for her. She had ended her
story in such an exalted and admonitory tone, but for all that, there
was a furtive, slavish note in it.

The people on the beach began to sing, and to sing in a strange
way. First the contralto voice was heard. It sang two or three bars
and then another voice started the song from the beginning while the
first continued . . . and then a third, a fourth and a fifth voice began
the song, one after the other. Suddenly, the same song was started,
from the beginning, by a chorus of male voices.

The voice of each woman was heard distinctly from the rest,
and all their mingled voices sounded like a rainbow-coloured mountain stream that comes tumbling from ledge to ledge, leaping and
gurgling as they merged with the deep tones of the male voices
which floated upward to meet them, separating from them, drowning
them, and again rising high, pure and strong, one after another.

Because of the voices, the sound of the sea could no longer
be heard.

II

"Have you ever heard singing like that anywhere else?—Izergil
asked me, raising her head and smiling, revealing her toothless gums.

"No, I haven't, I've never heard anything like it anywhere. . . ."

"And you never will. We are very fond of singing. Only handsome
people can sing well, handsome people, who are fond of life. We are

fond of life. Aren t the people who are singing over there tired after
their day's work? They worked from sunrise to sunset, but as soon
as the moon rose they began to sing! Those who don't know how to
live would have gone to bed, but those who find pleasure in life—sing."

"But health. . . ." I began.

"One always has enough health to live. Health! If you had money, wouldn't you spend it? Health is the same as gold. Do you
know what I did when I was young? I wove carpets from sunrise
to sunset, almost without getting up. I was as lively as a sunbeam, and
yet I was obliged to sit all day long, as motionless as a stone. And I
sat so long that all my bones ached. But when night came, I hurried
to the one I loved, to fondle and embrace him. And this I did for
three whole months, while love lasted; I spent all my nights with
him. And yet I have lived right up to now—I had enough blood in
my veins, didn't I? And how much I loved! How many kisses I
took, and gave!..."

I looked into her face. Her black eyes remained dull, her recollections had roused no spark in them. The moon lit up her dry, cracked
lips, sharp chin with the grey hairs on it, and her wrinkled nose,
which was drawn up, like the beak of an owl. Her cheeks were dark
hollows, in one of which lay a strand of ash-grey hair which had
straggled from under the scarlet rag which she had wound about her
head. Her face, neck and hands were wrinkled, and every time she
moved I expected the dry skin to crack and break and fall away in
pieces, leaving before me a bare skeleton, with dull, black eyes.

She began to talk again in her grating voice:

"I lived with my mother near Falma, on the very bank of the
River Birlat; I was fifteen years old when he first came to our farm.
He was tall and graceful and had a black moustache, and he was
so jolly! He was in a boat, and he called out in a ringing voice, so
that we heard him through the window: 'Hey! Have you any wine ...
and something to eat?' I looked out of the window and through the
branches of the ash tree I saw the river, all blue from the moon.
And he, in a white tunic with a broad sash round his waist with the
ends dangling at his side, was standing with one foot in the boat
and the other on the bank, swaying and singing to himself. When he
saw me he said: 'What a lovely lass lives here!... And I didn't
know!' As if he knew all the lovely lasses in the world but me. I

gave him wine and some boiled pork.... Four days later I gave myself to him, entirely. We used to go rowing together, at night. He used to come and whistle softly like a marmot, and I used to leap out of the window into the river like a fish. And then we would go rowing, on and on.... He was a fisherman on the Prut, and later, when my mother learned about everything and beat me, he tried to persuade me to go with him to Dobruja, and further, on to the branches of the Danube. But by that time I had already ceased to love him—all he did was sing and kiss, and nothing more! I got tired of it. At that time a gang of Huzulians roamed those parts, and they had their lovers there.... Now, those girls had a merry time! One of them would wait and wait for her Carpathian, wondering whether he was in prison, or had been killed in a fight somewhere, and suddenly he would turn up alone, or with two or three of his comrades, as if he had dropped from the skies. He would bring her rich presents—after all, they came by everything so easily! And he used to feast at her house and praise her to his comrades. This pleased her very much. I asked a friend of mine who had a Huzulian for a lover to let me see them.... What was her name? I have forgotten.... I have begun to forget everything now. This was very long ago. No wonder I have forgotten it! Well, she introduced me to one of those lads. A handsome fellow.... He was red-haired, all red—moustaches and locks! A fiery head! But he looked so sad. Sometimes he was tender, but at other times he used to fight and roar like a wild beast. Once he slapped my face ... and I sprang at him like a cat and dug my teeth into his cheek.... After that he had a dimple in that cheek, and he used to like me to kiss the dimple...."

"But what became of the fisherman?" I enquired.

"The fisherman? Oh, he ... he joined that gang of Huzulians. At first he kept begging with me to go with him and threatened to throw me into the river if I didn't, but he gave it up after a time. He joined the gang and got himself another girl.... They were both hanged together—this fisherman and the other lad. I went to see them hanged. It was in Dobruja. The fisherman went to the gallows weeping, he was as pale as death; but the other lad calmly smoked his pipe. He went along smoking, his hands in his pockets, one moustache lying on his shoulder, and the other dangling over his chest. He saw me, and taking his pipe out of his mouth he called out: 'Good-bye!...' I grived for him a whole year. Ekh!... This happened just as they were about to leave for their homes in the Carpathians. They had a farewell party in a Rumanian's house, and there they were caught. Only two were taken. Several were killed, and the rest got away.... They paid the Rumanian out for this, though, ... they set fire to his house, to his windmill and his cornfields. He became a beggar after that."

"Did you do it?"—I asked.

"Those Huzulians had lots of friends, I was not the only one.... Whoever was their best friend, that one said these prayers for the dead...."

The singing on the beach had stopped by now, and the old woman's voice was accompanied only by the sound of the surging sea— that pensive, restless sound was indeed a splendid accompaniment to this tale of a restless life. The night became milder, made brighter by the pale light of the moon, the vague sounds of the restless life of the night's invisible inhabitants gradually died out, they were drowned by the increasing sound of the waves ... for the wind was rising.

"There was also a Turk that I was in love with. I lived in his harem, in Skutari. I lived there a whole week. It was not so bad.... But I grew tired of it.... Nothing but women and women.... He had eight of them.... All day long they did nothing but eat, sleep and talk nonsense.... Or else they'd quarrel and cackle at each other like hens.... He was no longer young, that Turk. His hair was almost grey, and he looked so pompous. He was rich too. He talked like a bishop.... He had black eyes ... and they looked straight at you ... right into your soul. He was very fond of saying his prayers. I first saw him in Bucharest ... in the market place. He was walking about like a king, looking ever so important. I smi'ed at him. That same evening I was seized in the street and carried to his house. He was a merchant who traded in sandal and palmwood, and he had come to Bucharest to buy something. 'Wi'l you come with me?' he asked me. 'Oh, yes, certainly!' 'All right!' And so I went with him. He was rich, was that Turk. He had a son—a dark little boy, and so graceful.... He was about sixteen. It was with him that I ran away from the Turk.... I ran away to Bulgaria, to Lom-Palanka.... There a Bulgarian woman stabbed me in the chest because of her lover, or her husband, I have forgotten which.

"I lay sick for a long time in a nunnery. A Polish girl nursed me. She had a brother, a monk in a monastery near Arzer-Palanka, and he used to visit her. He wriggled like a worm in front of me. . . . When I got well I went away with him . . . to his country, Poland."

"Wait a minute! What became of the little Turk?"

"The boy? He died. Whether it was from homesickness, or from love, I don't know, but he withered, like a newly-planted tree which gets too much sun. . . . He simply dried up. . . . I can almost see him now, lying all transparent and bluish, like a piece of ice; but the flame of love was still burning in him. . . . And he kept on begging me to bend over and kiss him. . . . I loved him and, I remember, I kissed him a lot. . . . Then he got very bad—he could scarcely move. He lay on his bed and begged me pitifully, like a beggar asking for alms, to lie next to him and warm him. I did so, and as soon as I got next to him he would get as hot as fire. Once I woke up and found he was quite cold. . . . He was dead. . . . I wept over him. Who can say? Perhaps it was I who killed him. I was then twice his age. And I was so strong and full of vigour. . . . But he, he was only a boy!"

She sighed and—for the first time that I saw—crossed herself three times and mumbled something with her dry lips.

"Well, so you went to Poland"—I prompted her.

"Yes . . . with that little Pole. He was a mean and despicable thing. When he wanted a woman he used to sidle up to me like a tomcat and speak to me with words that flowed from his lips like hot honey; but when he did not want me he used to snarl at me, and his words sounded like the crack of a whip. Once we were walking along the river bank and he was arrogant and offensive to me. Oh! Oh! wasn't I mad! I bubbled like boiling pitch! I took him up in my arms like a child—he was only a little fellow—held him and squeezed his sides so hard that his face became livid. And then I swung him round and threw him into the river. He yelled. It was so funny to hear him yell. I looked down at him struggling in the water and then went away. I didn't meet him again after that. I was lucky in that way: I never met again the men I had loved. Meetings like that are not at all pleasant. It's like meeting the dead."

The old woman stopped speaking and sighed. I pictured to myself the people she had resurrected: the fiery-red, bewhiskered Huzulian going to his death, calmly smoking his pipe; probably he had cold blue eyes which had looked upon everything with a firm and concentrated gaze. At his side is the black-whiskered fisherman from the Prut, weeping, not wanting to die. His face is pallid in anticipation of death, his merry eyes are now dull, and his moustaches, now moist with tears, dangle disconsolately from the corners of his contorted mouth. And the old, pompous Turk, probably a fatalist and a despot, and by his side his son, a pale and tender flower of the Orient, poisoned by kisses. And the conceited Pole, polite and cruel, eloquent and cold.... All are only pale shadows now, and the one whom they had embraced was sitting beside me alive, but withered by time, without a body, without blood, with a heart without desires, and with eyes that lacked the glint of life—also almost a shadow.

She began to speak again:

"I had a hard time in Poland. The people who live there are cold and false. I could not understand their serpent's language. They hiss when they speak.... Why do they hiss? God must have given them this serpent's language because they are false. I roamed about the country not knowing where I was going, but I saw that they were preparing to rise in revolt against you Russians. I reached the town of Bokhnia. A Jew bought me, not for himself, but to trade with my body. I consented to this. To be able to live one must be able to do something. I couldn't do anything, so I had to pay with my body. But I thought to myself: when I get enough money to enable me to go back home on the Birlat I will break my chains, no matter how strong they may be. What a life I led there! Rich gentlemen used to come to my house and feast there. That cost them a pretty penny, I can tell you. They used to fight over me and ruin themselves. One of them tried a long time to get me, and this is what he did. One day he came to visit me, accompanied by his servant who carried a bag. The gentleman took the bag and spilled its contents over my head. Golden coins poured from the bag, hitting my head, but the ringing sound they made as they struck the floor was delightful to my ears. For all that I drove that gentleman away. He had a fat, moist face and a belly like a big pillow. He looked like a well-fed pig. Yes, I drove him away, although he told me that he had sold all his land, his house and his horses to be able to be-

sprinkle me with gold. At that time I loved a worthy gentleman with
a scarred face. His face was criss-crossed with scars, from wounds
inflicted by the Turks, with whom he had recently been fighting on
behalf of the Greeks. Now that was a man! He was a Pole, so why
should he bother about the Greeks? But he went to help them fight
their enemies. His face was slashed, he lost an eye, and also two fingers from his left hand. ... He was a Pole, so why should he bother
about the Greeks? The reason is that he admired brave deeds, and a
man who admires brave deeds will always find an opportunity to perform them. There is always room for brave deeds in life, you know.
And those who find no opportunity to perform them are simply lazybones or cowards, or else they do not know what life is, because if
people knew what life is, they would all want to leave their shadow
in it after they have gone. And then life would not devour people
without leaving a trace. ... Oh, that man with the scars was a really
good man! He was ready to go to the end of the world to do something worth while. I suppose your people killed him during the rebellion. Why did you go to fight the Magyars? All right, all right, don't
say anything!"

Commanding me not to say anything, old Izergil fell silent herself and became lost in thought. After a little while she said:

"I also knew a Magyar. One day he left my house—this was
in the winter—and he was found only in the spring, when the snow
had thawed; they found him in a field with a bullet through his head.
What do you think of that? You see, love kills no fewer people than
the plague does; I'm sure you'll find it so if you counted up. ...
What was I talking about? About Poland. ... Yes, I played my last
game there. I met a squire there. ... Wasn't he handsome! As handsome as the devil. I was already old, oh, so old! Was I already
forty? Yes, I believe I was. ... He was still proud, and still spoilt
by us women. It cost me a lot to get him. ... Yes. He wanted to take
me like a common woman, but to this I would not agree. I was
never anybody's slave. I had already settled with the Jew. I gave
him a lot of money, and I was already living in Cracow. I had
everything then, horses, and gold, and servants. ... He used to come
to me as proud as a demon and wanted me to throw myself into his
arms. We quarrelled. ... I remember I even lost my good looks because of it. This dragged on for a long time. ... But I won in the

end; he went down on his knees to me.... But soon after he took
me, he gave me up. Then I realized that I was already old.... Oh,
how bitter that was! Oh, so bitter! You see, I loved that devil....
But when we met he used to jeer at me.... Mean fellow! And he
used to make fun of me to others, I knew that. That was hard to bear,
I can tell you! But I had him near me, and after all I loved him.
When he went off to fight you Russians I was sick with longing for
him. I tried to fight the feeling down, but couldn't.... And so I
decided to go to him. He was stationed in the woods, near Warsaw.

"But when I got there I found out that your people had already
beaten them ... and that he was a prisoner in a village, not far away.

"That means that I won't see him any more, I thought to myself.
But oh, how I longed to see him! So I tried to get to him. I dressed
up as a beggar, pretended to be lame, and tying up my face I went
to the village. It was filled with Cossacks and soldiers.... It cost
me a lot to be there! I found out where the Poles were. I could see
that it would be no easy task to get there. But I had to get there!
So one night I crept up to the place, through a vegetable plot, between the furrows, suddenly a sentry barred my way.... But I could
already hear the Poles singing and talking loudly. They were singing a song to the Mother of God, and I could hear my Arkadek's
voice. I couldn't help thinking bitterly of the time when men used
to crawl in front of me, and here I was, crawling on the ground
like a snake for the sake of a man, and perhaps crawling to my
death. The sentry heard me and stepped forward. What was I to do?
I got up from the ground and went towards him. I had no knife
with me or anything, only my hands and my tongue. I was sorry
I had not taken my dagger with me. I whispered: 'Wait!' But the
soldier pointed his bayonet at my throat. I whispered to him: 'Don't
stab me, wait! Listen to me, if you have a soul! I have nothing to
give you, but I beg of you....' He lowered his rifle and said to
me, also in a whisper: 'Go away, woman! Go away! What do you
want here?' I told him that my son was a prisoner here. 'Do you
understand, soldier—a son! You have a mother, haven't you? Look
at me, then—I have a son like you, and he's over there! Let me
have a look at him, perhaps he will die soon ... and perhaps you
will be killed tomorrow. Won't your mother weep for you? Won't
it be hard for you to die without having seen your mother? So it

will be for my son. Take pity on yourself, and on him, and on
me—a mother!'

"Oh, how long I pleaded with him! It was raining, and we were
both drenched. The wind raged and roared, buffeting me, now
in the back and now in the chest. I stood swaying in front of that
stony-hearted soldier, but he kept on saying: 'No! No!' And every
time I heard that cold word the desire to see my Arkadek flared
up still hotter in my breast.... While I was talking I sized up the
soldier—he was short and thin, and he coughed. I dropped to the
ground in front of him and embraced his knees, pleading with him
with burning words to let me pass. Suddenly I gave a hard tug
and the soldier fell to the ground, into the mud. I quickly turned
him over face downwards and pressed his face down into a puddle
to prevent him from shouting. But he didn't shout, he only struggled, trying to throw me off his back. I pressed his face deeper into
the mud with both my hands, and he was suffocated. Then I dashed
to the barn where the Pole was locked up. 'Arkadek!' I whispered
through a chink in the wall. They have sharp ears, have those Poles.
They heard me and stopped singing! I could see his eyes opposite mine. 'Can you come out here?' I whispered. 'Yes, through
the floor!' he said. 'Come out, then.' And four of them crept out
from the barn; three, and my Arkadek. 'Where's the sentry?' Arkadek asked me. 'He's lying over there!' And we crept along quietly,
ever so quietly, crouching low on the ground. The rain was pouring down in torrents, the wind roared. We left the village and entered a forest. We walked for a long time in silence. We walked
quickly. Arkadek held my hand; his hand was hot and trembling.
Oh! I felt so good walking by his side, he not saying a word. Those
were the last moments—the last good moments of my greedy
life. At last we came out on a meadow and halted. They thanked
me, all four of them. Oh, how long and how much they talked,
something I didn't understand! I listened to them, but kept my eyes
fixed on my gentleman, wondering what he would do. Suddenly he
embraced me and said in such an important tone.... I don't remember what he said exactly, but what he meant was that he would
love me now out of gratitude for having helped him to escape. And
he dropped down on his knees in front of me and said with a smile:
'My queen!' False dog! I was so mad that I kicked him and

wanted to slap his face, but he staggered and jumped to his feet. He stood in front of me pale and threatening.... The other three also stood frowning at me. And nobody said a word. I looked at them and felt—I remember it quite well—only a feeling of disgust and apathy. I said to them: 'Go!' Those dogs asked me: 'Will you go back there and tell them which way we've gone?' Weren't they mean, eh? Still, they went away, and I went away too.... Next day your people took me, but they soon let me go. Then I realized that it was time for me to build myself a nest. I'd had enough of living like a cuckoo! I had become heavy, my wings were weak, and my feathers had lost their sheen.... Yes, it was time, high time! So I went to Galicia, and from there to Dobruja. Since then I have been living here, nearly thirty years. I had a husband, a Moldavian. He died about a year ago. And now I am living like this! Alone.... No, not alone. With them."

With that the old woman waved her hand in the direction of the sea. It was all quiet on the beach now. Now and again a brief, deceptive sound was born, only to die again.

"They are fond of me. I tell them such a lot of interesting things, and they like that. They are all still young.... It feels good to be with them. I look at them and think to myself: 'I was like them once.... Only in my time people had more vim and vigour, and that was why life was merrier and better.... Yes! ...'"

She fell silent. I felt sad sitting next to her. But she dozed, nodding her head and whispering to herself.... Perhaps she was praying. A cloud rose up from the sea—black, heavy and with rugged contours, like the peaks of a mountain range. It crept over the steppe; and as it moved fragments of cloud broke away from its summit and speeded on in front, putting the stars out, one after another. The sea surged more loudly. In the vines, at a little distance from us, the sounds of kissing, whispering and sighing were heard. Far away in the steppe a dog whined.... The air irritated the nerves with a strange smell which tickled the nostrils. As they crept across the sky the clouds cast on the ground numerous shadows, like flocks of birds, which disappeared and appeared again.... Of the moon only a blurred, opal patch remained, and now and again even this was blotted out by a grey clump of cloud. And far away in the steppe, now black and grim, as if hiding and concealing something within itself, tiny blue lights flashed. They appeared for an instant, now here and now there, and vanished, as if a number of people scattered over the steppe, at some distance from each other, were searching for something, and lighting matches, which the wind at once blew out. They were bluish tongues of flame, and there was something weird about them.

"Can you see any sparks?" Izergil asked me.

"What, those blue ones?" I said, pointing into the distance.

"Blue? Yes, that's them.... So they are flying after all! Well, well! I can't see them any more. There's lots of things I can't see now."

"Where do those sparks come from?" I asked the old woman.

I had heard something about those sparks before, but I wanted to hear what old Izergil would tell me about them.

"Those sparks come from the burning heart of Danko," she said. "Once upon a time there was a heart, which one day burst into flame.... Well, those sparks come from that flame. I will tell you about it.... This too, is an old tale.... Old. All old! You see what a lot of things happened in the old days! There's nothing like it nowadays—no great deeds, no men, no stories.... Why?... Well, tell me! You can't tell me.... What do you know? What do any of you young people know? Ekh ... ekh! If you looked into the past well enough, you would find an answer to all your riddles.... But you don't look, and that's why you don't know how to live.... Don't I see how people live? Oh, I see everything, although my eyes are not as good as they used to be! And I see that people don't live, but grub for a living, and spend all their lives on that. And having deprived themselves of everything worth having, having wasted all their time, they begin to bemoan their fate. What's fate got to do with it? Everybody decides his own fate! I see all sorts of people nowadays, but I don't see any strong ones! What's become of them?... And there are fewer and fewer handsome ones."

The old woman became lost in thought, wondering what had become of the strong and handsome men and women; and she gazed into the dark steppe, as if seeking for an answer there.

I waited for her story in silence, for I feared that if I asked her anything she would go off at a tangent again.

At last she began to speak and told me the following story:

III

"Once upon a time, long, long ago, there lived a tribe of people who lived in the steppe, surrounded on three sides by a dense forest. They were a merry, strong and brave people. But one day misfortune befell them. Alien tribes appeared out of the unknown and drove them deep into the forest. The forest was dark and swampy, because the trees were very old, and their branches were so closely entangled that they shut out the sky, and the sun's rays could scarcely pierce the dense leafage and reach the ground. When the sun's rays did reach the ground, they raised such a stench that people died from it. And then the women and children of this tribe wept and the men became despondent. They realized that they must leave the forest if they wanted to survive, but there were only two ways by which they could do this: they could go back, to their old habitations, but there they would meet their strong and wicked foes; or they could push forward, but here their way was barred by the giants which embraced each other so closely with their mighty branches and clung so tenaciously to the swampy ground with their gnarled roots. These trees stood silent and motionless in grey gloom in the daytime, and at night they seemed to crowd still closer around the people when they lit their fires. Day and night these people—who had been accustomed to the broad open spaces of the steppe—were cramped in this dark, evil-smelling forest, which seemed to want to crush them. It was still more frightful when the wind blew through the treetops and the forest was filled with a sinister humming that sounded like a funeral dirge. These people were strong and could have gone out to those who had vanquished them, but they dared not die in battle, because they had traditions to preserve, and if they were killed, their traditions would perish with them. And so they sat through the long nights in mournful reflection amidst the humming of the forest and the poisonous stench of the swamp. And as they sat the shadows cast by their campfires leaped around them in a silent dance; and it seemed as though these were not shadows that were dancing, but the evil spirits of the forest and swamp celebrating their triumph.... And so these people sat and pondered. But nothing—neither hard work nor women—wears out the bodies and souls of men as much as mournful thoughts. And so these people grew feeble because of their thoughts.... Fear was born among them and it fettered their strong arms. The women gave birth to horror by their wailing over the bodies of those who died from the stench, and over the fate of the living who were fettered by fear. And cowardly words began to be heard in the forest, at first softly and timidly, but later more loudly and loudly.... The people were already willing to go to the enemy to make him a gift of their freedom; all were terrified by death; not one was afraid of a life of slavery.... But just then Danko appeared and saved them all unaided."

Evidently the old woman had often related the story of Danko's burning heart, for she spoke in an accustomed singsong tone, and her voice, low and grating, vividly conjured up in my mind the noise of the forest amidst which the unhappy hunted people were dying from the poisonous breath of the swamp.

"Danko was one of those people, young and handsome. Handsome people are always brave. And so he said to his comrades: 'You can't remove the rock from the path by thinking. Those who do nothing can achieve nothing. Why are we wasting our strength in thinking and grieving? Rise up! Let us hew our way through the forest, it must have an end—everything in the world has an end! Let us go! Come on!'

"They looked at him and saw that he was the best one among them, for great strength and living fire shone from his eyes.

"'Lead us!' they said.

"And he led them...."

The old woman stopped speaking and gazed into the steppe where the darkness was growing more intense. Far away the sparks from Danko's burning heart flashed every now and again, like blue flowers which bloomed only for an instant.

"And so Danko led them. All followed him like one man, for they believed in him. It was a hard road! It was dark; at every step the swamp opened its greedy, putrid maw and swallowed men; and the trees barred their road like a solid wall, their branches intertwined and their roots stretching in all directions like snakes. Every step cost those people much sweat and blood. They fought their way on for a long time.... The forest became thicker as they went, and their strength was giving out! And so they began to murmur against Danko and say that he was young and inexperienced, and did not know where he was leading them. But he went on in front of them, cheerful and calm.

"One day a storm broke over the forest and the trees whispered to each other in a sinister and threatening way. The forest became so dark that it seemed that all the nights which had existed since it arose had gathered together in this one place. And these little people pushed their way through the giant trees amidst the frightful din of the storm; they pushed on, and the mighty swaying trees creaked and hummed in anger, while the lightning flashed over the treetops, illuminating them with its cold blue light, only to vanish as quickly as it had appeared. The people were frightened. The trees, lit up by the cold flashes of lightning, looked as if they were alive, as if they were stretching their long, gnarled arms, intertwined in a close net around them, in order to detain them, to prevent them from escaping from their dark captivity. And out of the gloom among the branches, something frightful, dark and cold stared at them. It was a hard road, and the people, wearied by it, lost heart. But they were ashamed to confess their weakness, and so they vented their anger on Danko, the man who was marching in front of them. They began to complain that he did not know how to lead them. What do you think of that!

"They halted amidst the sinister sounds of the forests, amidst the quivering darkness, tired and angry, and upbraided Danko:

" 'You, wretched man,' they said, 'are the cause of our misery! You led us and wore us out, and now you shall die for this!'

" 'You said: "Lead us!" and I led you!' exclaimed Danko, facing them proudly. 'I have the courage to lead, and that is why I led you! But you? What have you done to help yourselves? You have only walked, and have not been able to preserve your strength for a long journey! You only walked, and walked, like a flock of sheep!'

"But these words only enraged them all the more.

" 'You shall die! You shall die!' they shouted.

"The forest hummed and hummed, echoing their cries, and the lightning tore the darkness into shreds. Danko looked at those for whose sake he had toiled so hard and saw that they were like wild beasts. They crowded around him, not a human expression in any one of their faces, and no mercy could be expected from them. Then anger flared up in Danko's heart, but out of pity for the people he subdued it. He loved these people, and believed that they would perish without him. And so he yearned to save them, to lead them out on to an easier road, and the light of this mighty yearning shone in his eyes. . . . But they, seeing this, thought his eyes were burning with rage, that it was rage that caused them to shine so brightly; and they stood alert, like wolves, waiting for him to attack them; and they closed in around him to be able to seize and kill him. He guessed their thoughts, and this made the fire in his heart burn still brighter, for their thoughts saddened him.

"The forest continued to hum its mournful dirge, the thunder roared, and the rain poured down in torrents. . . .

" 'What can I do for these people?' shouted Danko in a voice that drowned the thunder.

"Suddenly, he clutched at his breast, tore it open, plucked out his heart and held it high above his head.

"It burned as brightly as the sun, even brighter. The whole forest fell silent, and became lit up with this torch of human love. The darkness fled from the light deep into the forest, and quivering, fell into the putrid maw of the swamp. The people were petrified with amazement.

" 'Let us go!' shouted Danko, dashing forward and lighting up the path with his burning heart.

"They surged after him, as if enchanted. Then the forest hummed again, the trees swayed with astonishment, but the noise was drowned by the tramping of the feet of the people as they ran. They all ran quickly and boldly, drawn on by the wonderful spectacle of the burning heart. Now, too, people perished, but perished without complaints or tears. And Danko was still in front, and his heart blazed and blazed.

"Suddenly the forest opened before them, let them out, and remained behind, dense and silent; and Danko, and all the people, plunged into a sea of sunshine and pure air, which had been purified by the rain. Behind them the storm raged over the forest; but here the sun shone, the steppe heaved as if it were breathing, the grass sparkled with the jewels of rain on their blades, and the river glistened like gold. . . . Evening had fallen, and the river, reflecting the rays of the setting sun, looked red, like the blood that flowed in a hot stream from Danko's torn breast.

"Danko, proud and brave, scanned the vast steppe stretching before him; he gazed joyfully at the free land and laughed, and pride rang in his laughter. And then he fell down and died.

"The people, overjoyed, and full of hope, did not see that he was dead, and they did not see that his brave heart was still burning beside his dead body. Only one of them, more observant than the rest, saw this and, moved by fear, he stepped upon the proud heart. . . . And the heart burst into sparks and was extinguished. . . .

"That's what causes the blue sparks which appear in the steppe before a storm!"

Now that the old woman had finished her beautiful story, a great silence reigned in the steppe, as if it too was amazed at the strength of will displayed by the brave man Danko, who for the sake of men had plucked his burning heart out and had died, without asking for any reward for himself. The old woman dozed. I looked at her and asked myself how many more tales and recollections remained in her mind. And I thought of Danko's great burning heart, and of the human imagination which had created such beautiful and thrilling legends.

Izergil was now fast asleep. The wind blew aside the rags she wore and exposed her withered breast. I covered her old body and stretched out on the ground next to her. The steppe was dark and silent. Clouds still floated slowly and despondently across the sky. . . . The hollow, mournful sounds of the sea reached my ears.

CHELKASH

THE BLUE southern sky, darkened by dust, bore a leaden hue; the hct sun, looking down onto the greenish sea as if through a fine grey veil, was barely reflected in the water, which was chopped by the strokes of boats' oars, ships' propellers, the sharp keels of Turkish feluccas and of other vessels that ploughed backwards and forwards in the congested port. The granite-fettered waves, borne down by the immense weights that glided over their crests, beat against the ships' sides and against the shore, growling and foaming, befouled with all sorts of junk.

The clang of anchor chains, the clash of the buffers of the railway cars that were bringing up freight, the metallic wail of iron sheets slipping onto the cobble-stones, the muted sounds of wood striking wood, of rambling carts, of ships' sirens rising to a shrill, piercing shriek and dropping to a muffled roar, and the loud voices of the dock labourers, the seamen and the military Customs guards —all mingled in the deafening music of the working day, and quivering and undulating, hovered low in the sky over the port. And from the land, rising to meet them, came wave after wave of other sounds, now muffled and rumbling, causing everything around to vibrate, and now shrill and shrieking, rending the dusty, sultry air.

The granite, the iron, the timber, the cobble-stones in the port, the ships and the men, all breathed the mighty sounds of this fervent hymn to Mercury. But the human voices, scarcely audible in this tumult, were feeble and comical; and the very men who had originally produced these mighty sounds were comical and pitiful to look at. Their grimy, ragged, nimble bodies, bent under the weight of the merchandise they carried on their backs, flitted to and fro amidst clouds of dust and a welter of heat and sound. They looked insignificant compared with the steel giants, the mountains of merchandise, the rattling railway cars and everything else around them which they themselves had created. The things they themselves had created had enslaved them and robbed them of their personality.

The giant steamers, lying with steam up, shrieked and hissed and heaved deep sighs; and every sound they emitted seemed to breathe scorn and contempt for the grey, dusty, human figures that were creeping along their decks, filling the deep holds with the products of their slavish labour. The long files of dock labourers carrying on their backs hundreds of tons of grain to fill the iron bellies of the ships in order that they themselves might earn a few pounds of this grain to fill their own stomachs, looked so droll that they brought tears to one's eyes. The contrast between these tattered, perspiring men, benumbed with weariness, turmoil and heat, and the mighty machines glistening in the sun, the machines which these very men had made, and which, after all is said and done, were set in motion not by steam, but by the blood and sinew of those who had created them—this contrast constituted an entire poem of cruel irony.

The overwhelming noise, the dust which irritated one's nostrils and blinded one's eyes, the baking and exhausting heat, and everything else around, created an atmosphere of tense impatience that was ready to burst out in a terrific upheaval, an explosion that would clear the air and make it possible to breathe freely and easily—after which silence would reign over the earth, and this dusty, deafening, irritating and infuriating tumult would pass away, and the town, the sea and the sky would be tranquil, serene and magnificent. ...

A bell struck twelve in slow regular strokes. When the last brassy vibrations died away, the savage music of labour sounded softer and a moment later sank to a muffled, discontented murmur. Human voices and the splash of the sea became more audible. It was dinner time.

I

When the dock labourers stopped work and scattered over the port in noisy chattering groups to buy the victuals that the market women were selling, and had squatted down on the cobble-stones in shady corners to eat their dinner, Grishka Chelkash turned up, an old timer, well-known to the people in the port, a confirmed drunkard, and a skilful, daring thief. He was barefooted; his legs were encased in a pair of threadbare corduroy trousers; he wore no hat, and his dirty cotton blouse with a torn collar, which exposed the brown skin drawn tightly over his lean collar bones. His matted, black, grey-streaked hair and his sharp crinkled, rapacious face showed that he had only just got up from sleep. A straw was entangled in his brown moustache, another was sticking to the bristle on his left cheek, and he had a freshly plucked linden twig stuck behind one ear. Tall, gaunt, slightly round-shouldered, he strode slowly over the cobble-stones, wrinkling his hawk-like nose and casting his keen, grey, flashing eyes around, looking for somebody among the dock labourers. Now and again his long, thick, brown moustache twitched like the whiskers of a cat, and his hands, held behind his back, rubbed against each other, while his long, crooked, grasping fingers nervously intertwined. Even here, among the hundreds of rough hoboes like himself, he at once became conspicuous by his resemblance to the hawk of the steppe, by his rapacious leanness, and by his deliberate gait, outwardly calm and even, but internally agitated and alert, like the flight of the bird of prey that he reminded one of.

When he drew level with a group of bare-footed dockers who were sitting in the shade of a pile of coal-laden baskets, a thickset lad, whose stupid face was disfigured by scarlet blotches and his neck badly scratched—evidently the results of a recent scrap—got up to meet him. Walking by the side of Chelkash, he said in an undertone:

"The sailors are missing two bales of cloth.... They're searching for them."

"Well?" asked Chelkash, looking the lad up and down.

"What do you mean, well? I say they are searching for them. That's all."

"What? Have they been asking for me to go and help in the search?"

Chelkash smiled and looked in the direction of the warehouse of the Volunteer Fleet.*

"Go to hell!"

* A merchant shipping company.—*Trans.*

The lad turned to go back, but Chelkash stopped him with the ex-
clamation:

"Hey! You do look a sight! Who messed up your shop front
like this?" And then he enquired: "Have you seen Mishka about
here anywhere?"

"Haven't seen him for a long time!" retorted the other, leaving
Chelkash to rejoin his mates.

Chelkash proceeded on his way, greeted by everybody as an old
acquaintance; but today he was obviously out of sorts, and instead
of replying with his customary banter, he snarled in answer to the
questions put to him.

Suddenly a Customs guard appeared from behind a pile of merchandise, a dark-green, dusty, and truculently erect figure. He stood
in front of Chelkash, defiantly barring his way, clutched the hilt
of his dirk with his left hand and put out his right to take Chelkash by the collar.

"Halt! Where are you going?" he demanded.

Chelkash stepped back a pace, raised his eyes to the guard's
good-natured but shrewd face and smiled drily.

The Customs guard tried to pull a stern face; he puffed out his
round, red cheeks, twitched his brows and rolled his eyes ferociously, but he succeeded only in looking comical.

"How many times have I told you not to go prowling around
these docks. I said I'd smash your ribs in if I caught you! But here
you are again!" he shouted.

"How do you do, Semyonich! We haven't met for a long time!"
Chelkash answered serenely, proferring his hand.

"It wouldn't break my heart if I didn't see you for a century!
Clear out of here!"

Nevertheless, Semyonich shook the proferred hand.

"Tell me," continued Chelkash, retaining Semyonich's hand in
his tenacious fingers and familiarly shaking his hand. "Have you
seen Mishka anywhere around here?"

"Who's Mishka? I don't know any Mishka! You'd better
clear out, brother, or else the warehouse guard will see you, and
he'll. . . ."

"That red-haired chap I worked with on the *Kostroma* last time,"
persisted Chelkash.

"The one you go thieving together, you mean, don't you? They took that Mishka of yours to the hospital. He met with an accident and broke his leg. Now go along, brother, while I'm asking you quietly, otherwise I'll give you one in the neck!"

"There! And you say you don't know Mishka! You do know him after all! What are you so wild about, Semyonich?"

"Now then, now then! Don't try to get round me! Clear out of here, I tell you!"

The guard was getting angry, and looking round from one side to another, he tried to tear his hand out of Chelkash's close grip. But Chelkash calmly gazed at the guard from under his thick eyebrows and keeping a tight hold on his hand went on to say:

"Don't hustle me! I'll have my say and then go away. Well now, tell me, how're you getting on? How's the wife, and the children? Are they well?" With flashing eyes, and teeth bared in an ironic smile, he added: "I've been wanting to pay you a visit for a long time, but I've been too busy ... drinking. ..."

"Now, now! None of that! None of your jokes, you skinny devil! I'll give it to you hot if you don't look out!... What! Do you intend to go robbing in the streets and houses now?"

"Whatever for? There's plenty of stuff lying about here. Plenty I tell you, Semyonich! I hear you've swiped another two bales of cloth! Take care, Semyonich! See you don't get caught!"

Semyonich trembled with indignation, foamed at the mouth, and tried to say something. Chelkash released his hand and calmly made for the dark gates in long, regular strides. The guard kept close on his heels, swearing like a trooper.

Chelkash brightened up and whistled a merry tune through his teeth. With his hands in his trouser pockets he strode along unhurriedly, throwing biting quips and jests to right and left and getting paid in his own coin.

"Hey, Grishka! Look how the bosses are taking care of you!" shouted a dock labourer from a crowd of men who were sprawling on the ground, resting after dinner.

"I've no boots on, so Semyonich is seeing that I don't step onto something sharp and hurt my foot," answered Chelkash.

They reached the gates. Two soldiers ran their hands down Chelkash's clothes and then gently pushed him into the street.

Chelkash crossed the road and sat down on the curbstone opposite a tavern. A file of loaded carts came rattling out of the dock gates. Another, of empty carts, came from the opposite direction, their drivers bumping on the seats. The docks belched forth a howling thunder and clouds of biting dust. . . .

Chelkash felt in his element amidst this frenzied bustle. Solid gains, requiring little labour but much skill, smiled in prospect for him. He was confident of his skill, and wrinkling his eyes he pictured to himself the spree he would have next morning when his pockets were filled with bank notes. . . . He thought of his chum, Mishka; he would have been very useful to him that night if he had not broken his leg. He swore to himself as doubt crossed his mind as to whether he would be able to manage alone, without Mishka. He wondered what the weather would be like at night, and looked at the sky. He lowered his eyes and glanced down the street.

A half a dozen paces away, on the cobbles, leaning back against the curb, sat a young lad in a coarse blue homespun blouse and trousers of the same material, bast shoes on his feet, and a dilapidated brown cap on his head. Beside him lay a small knapsack and a scythe without a haft, wrapped in straw and carefully tied with string. The lad was broad-shouldered, thickset, fair-haired, and had a sunburnt weather-beaten face and large blue eyes, which looked at Chelkash trustfully and good-naturedly.

Chelkash bared his teeth, poked his tongue out, and pulling a horrible face, stared at the lad with wide-open eyes.

The lad blinked in perplexity at first, but soon he burst out laughing and shouted between his chuckles: "Aren't you funny!" And then, scarcely rising from the ground, he shifted awkwardly over to Chelkash, dragging his knapsack through the dust and rattling the heel of his scythe over the cobble-stones.

"Been on the booze, eh, brother?" he asked Chelkash, tugging at the latter's trousers.

"Yes, baby, something like that!" confessed Chelkash with a smile. He at once took a fancy to this sturdy, good-natured lad with the bright childish eyes. "You've been out haymaking, eh?" he enquired.

"Yes! . . . But it was plenty of work and little pay. I made nothing by it. And the people! Hundreds of them! Those people from

the famine districts came pouring in and knocked the price down.
The job was hardly worth taking. In the Kuban they paid only
sixty kopecks. Something awful!... And they say that before they
used to pay three, four and five rubles!"

"Before!... Before they used to pay three rubles just to look at
a Russian! I used to do this job myself about ten years ago. I
would go to a stanitsa* and say—I'm a Russian! And they'd look
me up and down, feel my arms, shake their heads in wonder and
say: 'Here, take three rubles!' And then they'd give you food and
drink, and invite you to stay as long as you like!"

The lad listened to what Chelkash was saying with mouth wide
open and amazement and admiration written on his round, tanned
face; but soon he realized that the hobo was pulling his leg, and,
smacking his lips, he burst into a hearty laugh. Chelkash kept a
straight face, hiding his smile under his moustache.

"I'm a boob! You talk as if it was all true, and I listen to it
and believe it.... But, still, so help me God, things were better there
before!"

"Well, and what am I saying? Ain't I saying that before things
were...."

"Stop kidding!" interrupted the boy with a wave of his hand.
"What are you, a shoemaker? Or a tailor? You, I mean."

"Me?" asked Chelkash in his turn, and after thinking for a
moment, he said: "I'm a fisherman."

"A fish-er-man! Is that so! So you catch fish?"

"Fish! Why fish? The fishermen here don't only catch fish. Mostly
it's drowned bodies, lost anchors, sunken ships—things like that.
They have special hooks for this work...."

"Yah! It's all lies!... They must be the fishermen they sing
about in the song:

> *On arid shores*
> *We spread our nets,*
> *And barns and sheds we trawl....*

"Have you ever met fishermen like that?" asked Chelkash with
a smile, looking hard at the boy.

* Cossack village.—*Trans.*

"Met them? No, where could I have met them? But I've heard about them...."

"What do you think of them?"

"That kind of fisherman, you mean? Well ... they're not a bad lot. They're free. They have freedom...."

"What's freedom to you?... Do you like freedom?"

"What do you think? Be your own master. Go where you like, do what you like.... I should say so! You can keep yourself straight and have no milestone round your neck. Have a good time, and nothing to worry about, except keep God in mind. What could be better?"

Chelkash spat contemptuously and turned his head away.

"With me it's like this," continued the boy. "My father's dead. We've only a patch of a farm. My mother's old. The land's all dried up. What can I do? I've got to live. But how? I don't know. I thinks to myself—I'll go and be a son-in-law in a good house. But what's the use? It would be all right if the father-in-law gave his daughter a share of his property, and we could set up for ourselves. But do you think he'd do that? Not a bit. The devil wants to keep it all for himself and expects me to slave for him ... for years! You see what I mean? But if I could earn a hundred or a hundred and fifty rubles, I'd be independent, and I'd say to the father-in-law—you can keep your property! If you give Marfa a share, all well and good. But if you don't ... thank God she's not the only girl in the village! I'd be quite free. On my own.... Y-e-s!" The boy heaved a deep sigh and went on to say: "But what can I do now? Nothing. I'll have to go and slave for a father-in-law. I thought I'd go to the Kuban and earn a couple of hundred rubles, and then everything would be all right. I'd be able to live like a gentleman. But I didn't make anything. So I'll have to go as a labourer after all.... I'll never have my own farm now! Ah, well!"

It was quite evident that the lad was extremely reluctant to go as a son-in-law, for as he finished speaking his face became beclouded with grief and he squirmed as he lay on the ground.

Chelkash asked him:

"Where are you bound for now?"

"Home, of course! Where else?"

"How do I know? You might be bound for Turkey...."

"T-u-rkey!" drawled the boy in astonishment. "What Christians go to Turkey? That's a nice thing to say!"

"You're a fool!" said Chelkash, heaving a sigh and turning his head away again. This sturdy peasant lad stirred something in him. . . .

He became conscious of a vague, but steadily growing feeling of vexation gnawing at the pit of his stomach which prevented him from concentrating his mind on the task he had before him that night.

Offended by the snub which had just been administered to him, the boy muttered something under his breath and now and again cast a sidelong glance at the hobo. He pouted his lips, puffed out his cheeks, and far too rapidly blinked his eyes in the most comical fashion. He was obviously disappointed at the conversation with this bewhiskered tramp having been brought to such an abrupt close.

But the tramp paid no more attention to him. He sat on the curbstone engrossed in thought, whistling softly to himself, and beating time with his dirty, bare heel.

The lad wanted to pay him out for the snub.

"Hey, fisherman! Do you often go on the booze?" he began, but the "fisherman" suddenly turned his face towards him and asked:

"Listen, baby! Do you want to do a job of work with me to-night? Tell me quick!"

"What kind of job?" the lad asked suspiciously.

"What do you mean, what kind? Any kind I give you. . . . We'll go fishing. You'll row the boat."

"Oh, all right. Not so bad. I don't mind taking a job. But . . . I won't get into trouble with you, will I? You're a dark one. . . . There's no understanding you."

Chelkash again became conscious of a feeling like heartburn rising in his chest. In a low voice of cold anger he said:

"Then don't chatter about what you don't understand. . . . If you're not careful I'll give you a crack over the head that'll make you understand."

His eyes flashed. He jumped up from the curbstone, twirled his moustache with the fingers of his left hand and clenched his right hand into a hard brawny fist.

The boy was frightened. He glanced round rapidly, blinked timidly, and also sprang to his feet. The two stood looking each other up and down in silence.

"Well!" asked Chelkash sternly. He was burning and trembling with rage at the insult he had received from this callow youth whom he had despised when talking to him, but whom he now hated because he had such a healthy, tanned face, bright blue eyes and short sturdy arms, and because he lived in a village somewhere, had a home there, and some rich farmer was asking him to be his son-in-law; because of his whole past and present, but most of all because this lad, who was only a baby compared with himself, dared to love freedom, the value of which he did not appreciate, and which he did not need. It is always unp easant to see a man whom you regard as being inferior to and lower than yourself love or hate the same things that you love and hate and thereby resemble you.

The lad glared at Chelkash and felt that the latter was his master.

"Oh ... I don't mind," he said, "I'm looking for a job, ain't I? It's all the same to me who I work for, you or somebody else. All I wanted to say was ... you don't look like a working man, you're ... er ... so ragged. Of course, I know it might happen to anybody. Lord, haven't I seen enough drunkards! Lots of them! And some even worse than you."

"All right, all right! So you agree?" Chelkash interrupted in a milder tone.

"Me? Why, of course! With pleasure! But how much will you pay me?"

"I pay according to results. It depends on the results. ... On the catch. D'you understand? You might get a fiver. Will that be all right?"

Now that it was a question of money the peasant wanted to be definite, and he wanted his employer to be definite too. Again distrust and suspicion awoke in his mind.

"No, that doesn't suit me, brother!"

Chelkash also began to play the part.

"Don't argue. Wait! Let's go to the pub!" he said.

They walked down the street side by side. Chelkash twirled his moustache with the important air of an employer. The lad's face expressed complete readiness to obey, and at the same time complete distrust and apprehension.

"What's your name?" Chelkash asked him.

"Gavrila," the boy answered.

When they entered the dingy smoke-begrimed tavern, Chelkash walked up to the bar and in the familiar tone of a frequenter ordered a bottle of vodka, some shchi, roast meat, and tea. When all this was served, he curtly said to the barman: "On tick!" The barman silently nodded his head. This scene impressed Gavrila and roused in him a profound respect for this man, his master, who was so well known and enjoyed such credit in spite of his disreputable appearance.

"Well, we'll have a bite now and then talk business. But wait here a moment, I have somewhere to go," said Chelkash.

He went out. Gavrila looked around him. The tavern was in a basement; it was damp and dismal, and a suffocating smell of vodka fumes, stale tobacco smoke, tar, and of some other pungent substance pervaded the place. At a table, opposite Gavrila, sat a red-bearded drunken man in seaman's dress, covered from head to foot with coal dust and tar. Hiccoughing every now and again, he sang a song in twisted and broken words that sometimes sounded like a hiss and sometimes were deeply guttural. He was evidently not a Russian.

Behind him sat two Moldavian women, ragged, black-haired and sunburnt, and they too were drunkenly singing a song.

Out of the gloom other figures emerged, all strangely dishevelled, all half drunk, noisy and restless....

Gavrila began to feel afraid and longed for the return of his master. All the noises of the tavern merged in one monotonous tone, and it seemed as though some enormous beast was growling, as though, possessing hundreds of different voices, it was angrily and blindly struggling to get out of this stone pit, but was unable to find the exit. Gavrila felt as though his body was absorbing something intoxicating and heavy, which made him dizzy and dimmed his eyes, which were roaming round the tavern with curiosity mixed with fear....

Chelkash came back and they began to eat and drink, talking as they proceeded with their meal. After the third glass of vodka, Gavrila was drunk. He felt merry and wanted to say something to please his master, who was such a fine fellow and had given him this splendid treat. But the words which welled up in his throat in waves could not, for some reason, slip off his tongue, which had suddenly become so strangely heavy.

Chelkash looked at him and said with an ironic smile:

"Half seas over already! Ekh, you milksop! What will you be like after the fifth glass?... Will you be able to work?"

"Don't ... be ... afraid ... brother," stammered Gavrila. "You'll! ... be ... satisfied. I love you! Let me kiss you, eh?"

"Now then, none of that! Here, have another drink!"

Gavrila took another drink, and another, until everything around him began to float in even, undulating waves. This made him feel unwell and he wanted to vomit. His face looked foolishly solemn. When he tried to talk he smacked his lips in a comical way and mooed like a cow. Chelkash gazed at him absently, as if recalling something, thoughtfully twirling his moustache and smiling sadly.

The tavern rang with a drunken roar. The red-haired seaman was sleeping with his head resting on his elbows.

"All right, let's go," said Chelkash, getting up from the table.

Gavrila tried to get up too, but could not. He swore, and laughed idiotically as drunken men do.

"What a wash-out!" muttered Chelkash, resuming his seat at the table opposite Gavrila.

Gavrila kept on chuckling and gazing stupidly at his master. The latter stared back at him, keenly and thoughtfully. He saw before him a man whose life had fallen into his wolfish clutches. He felt that this life was in his power to turn in any direction he pleased. He could crumple it like a playing card, or could help place it in a firm peasant groove. He felt that he was the other one's master, but through his mind ran the thought that this lad would never have to drain the cup of bitterness that fate had compelled him, Chelkash, to do.... He both envied and pitied this young life, he despised it, and was even conscious of a feeling of regret as he pictured the possibility of it falling into other hands like his own.... But in the end all these feelings merged into one that was both paternal and practical. He was sorry for the lad, but he needed him. He took Gavrila under the armpits, lifted him up and gently prodding him from behind with his knee, he pushed him out into the tavern yard, laid him in the shade of a wood-pile, sat down beside him and lit his pipe. Gavrila wriggled about for a while, moaned, and fell asleep.

II

"Are you ready?" Chelkash in an undertone asked Gavrila, who was fumbling with the oars.

"In a minute! This rowlock's loose. Can I give it just one bang with the oar?"

"No! Don't make a sound! Force it down with your hand and it will slip into its place."

Both were noiselessly handling a boat that was moored to the stern of one of a whole flotilla of small sailing barges laden with oak staves, and of large Turkish feluccas laden with palm and sandal wood and thick cyprus logs.

The night was dark. Heavy banks of ragged clouds floated across the sky. The sea was calm. The water, black and thick, like oil, gave off a humid, saline smell and lazily lapped against the ship's sides and the beach, gently rocking Chelkash's boat. Far from the shore loomed the dark hulls of ships, their masts pointing to the sky, tipped with different coloured lights. The sea, reflecting these lights, was dotted with innumerable coloured patches, which shimmered on its soft, black, velvety surface. The sea was sound asleep, like a labourer after a hard day's work.

"We're off!" said Gavrila, dropping his oars into the water.

"Aye, aye!" said Chelkash, pulling hard with his steering oar to bring the boat into the strip of water between the barges. The boat sped swiftly over the slippery water, and with each stroke of the oars the water was lit up with a bluish phosphorescent radiance that trailed like a long, soft, fluttering ribbon from the boat's stern.

"Does your head · still ache?" Chelkash asked in a kindly voice.

"Something awful!... It's ringing like a bell.... I'll splash some water over it in a minute."

"There's no need to do that. Take this. It'll help your inside, and you'll soon get better," said Chelkash, handing Gavrila a flask.

"I doubt it. . . . Well, God bless us. . . ."

A soft gurgling sound was heard.

"Hey, you! That's enough!" said Chelkash, stopping the boy from drinking more.

The boat pushed ahead again, noiselessly and swiftly winding its way among the ships. . . . Suddenly it shot out from among the crowd of ships, and the sea—infinite and mighty—spread out before them into the blue distance, where mountains of clouds towered out of the water—some violet and grey with puffy yellow borders, others greenish, the colour of sea water, and others of a dull, leaden hue, of the kind which throw heavy, mournful shadows. The clouds moved slowly, now merging with and now skirting each other, mingling their colours and forms, absorbing each other and again emerging in new shapes, majestic and frowning. . . . There was something sinister in the slow movement of this soulless mass. It seemed as though over there, on the edge of the sea, their number was infinite, and that they would eternally creep across the sky in this indifferent manner with the malicious object of preventing it from shining again over the slumbering sea with its millions of golden eyes—the multi-coloured stars, living and dreamily radiant, exciting lofty desires in men to whom their pure radiance is-precious.

"The sea's fine, isn't it?" asked Chelkash.

"Not bad! Only it makes me feel afraid," answered Gavrila, pulling strongly and steadily at the oars. The water was barely audible as it splashed under the strokes of the long oars and shone with the warm bluish light of phosphorus.

"Afraid! You boob!" exclaimed Chelkash contemptuously.

He, the thief, loved the sea. His vibrating nervous nature, thirsting for impressions, could not contemplate enough the dark, boundless, free and mighty expanse. He felt hurt when he heard this answer to his enquiry about the beauty of the thing he loved. Sitting in the stern, he cleaved the water with his oar and calmly gazed ahead, feeling that he would like to glide far away over its velvety surface.

The sea always gave him a warm expansive feeling which filled his whole soul and purged it somewhat of the dross of

everyday life. He appreciated this, and loved to see himself a better man, here, amidst the water and the air, where thoughts of
life, and life itself, always lose, the former their painful acuteness,
and the latter all value. At night, the sound of the sea's soft,
breathing as it slept floats evenly over its surface, and this limitless
sound fills a man's soul with serenity, and gently subduing its
evil impulses, rouses in it mighty dreams. ...

"Where's the tackle?" Gavrila suddenly asked, looking anxiously into the bottom of the boat.

Chelkash started.

"The tackle? I've got it here, in the stern."

He felt ashamed at having to lie to this boy, and he also
regretted the thoughts and feelings that had been disturbed by
this boy's question. It made him angry. The familiar sense of
burning rose in his breast and throat, and this irritated him still
more.

"Now look here!" he said to Gavrila in a hard, stern voice.
"You sit still and mind your own business. I hired you to row.
Do the job I hired you for. If you wag your tongue too much,
you'll be sorry for it! Do you understand me?"

The boat shivered for a moment and stopped. The oars remained
in the water, causing it to foam. Gavrila wriggled uncom-
fortably on his seat.

"Row!"

A foul oath shook the air. Gavrila swung back his oars. The
boat shot forward, as if with fright, and sped on at a rapid,
jerky pace, noisily cleaving the water.

"Steady now, steady!"

Chelkash stood up in the stern, and keeping hold of the steering oar, he glared coldly into Gavrila's pale face. Bending forward, he looked like a cat crouching for a spring. In his rage he
ground his teeth so hard that it could be distinctly heard, and
Gavrila's teeth, chattering with fear, were no less audible.

"Who's that shouting?" came a stern cry from the sea.

"Row! Row, you devil!... Quieter!... I'll murder you, you
dog!... Go on!... Row!... One! Two! Make a sound, and I'll
tear you limb from limb!" hissed Chelkash. And then he went on in
a jeering tone: "Afraid! Booby!"

"Mother of God.... Holy Mary ..." whispered Gavrila, trembling with fear and exertion.

The boat swung round smoothly and returned to the docks, where the ship's lights crowded in multi-coloured groups, and the tall masts were visible.

"Hey! Who's that shouting?" came the voice again, but it sounded more distant this time. Chelkash became calmer.

"It's you that's shouting," he said in answer to the distant voice, and then he turned to Gavrila, who was still muttering his prayers, and said: "Well, brother, you're lucky! If that devil had come after us, it would have been all up with you. Do you understand what I mean? I'd have put you over to feed the fishes!"

Chelkash now spoke calmly and even good-humouredly, but Gavrila still trembling with fear, begged of him:

"Let me go! I ask you in the name of Christ, let me go! Put me ashore somewhere! Ay-ay-ay!... I'm lost! I'm a lost man! Remember God and let me go! What do you want me for? I'm no good for this sort of job.... I've never been on one like this before.... This is the first time.... Lord! I'm lost. I'm lost! Christ, how you fooled me, brother, eh? It's a sin.... You are damning your own soul!... Some business...."

"What business?" Chelkash asked sternly. "What business, eh?"

The lad's fear amused him, and he delighted in it as well as in the thought of what a terrible fellow he, Chelkash, was.

"Shady business, brother!... Let me go, for God's sake!... What do you want me for?... Please.... Be good...."

"Shut up! If I didn't need you, I wouldn't have taken you. Do you understand?... Well, shut up!"

"Lord!" sighed Gavrila.

"Stop snivelling, or you'll get it in the neck!" snapped Chelkash.

But Gavrila, unable to restrain himself any longer, sobbed quietly, wept, sniffed, wriggled on his seat, but rowed strongly, desperately.

The boat shot forward like an arrow. Again the dark hulls of the ships loomed before them, and soon the boat was lost among them, winding like a shuttle in and out of the narrow strips of water between them.

"Now listen! If anybody asks you about anything, you're to keep
mum, if you want to keep alive, that is! Do you understand me?"

"Ekh!" sighed Gavrila resignedly in answer to this stern command. Then he added bitterly: "I'm done for, I am!"

"Stop snivelling, I tell you!" said Chelkash in an angry whisper.
This whisper robbed Gavrila of all capacity to think; his mind was
benumbed by a chill foreboding of evil. He mechanically dropped
the oars, leaned far back, raised the oars and dropped them again,
all the time keeping his eyes riveted on the tips of his bast shoes.

The sleepy murmur of the waves sounded angry and terrify-
ing. They entered the docks. . . . From beyond its granite walls
came sounds of human voices, the splashing of water, singing and
shrill whistling.

"Stop!" whispered Chelkash. "Ship your oars! Hold on to the
wall! Quieter, you devil!"

Gavrila clutched at the wall and worked the boat along; the
thick coating of slime that covered the masonry deadened the sound
of the gunwale as it scraped along its side.

"Stop!. . . Give me the oars! Come this way! Where's your
passport? In your knapsack? Give me your knapsack! Look sharp!
That's to prevent your running away, my friend. . . . You won't run
away now. You might have bolted without the oars, but you'd be
afraid to run away without your passport. Wait here! Mind! If
you blab—I'll find you even if you're at the bottom of the sea!"

Suddenly clutching at something with his hands, Chelkash leaped
upwards and vanished over the wall.

Gavrila shuddered. . . . All this had happened so quickly. He
felt the accursed burden of fear which weighed upon him in the
presence of this bewhiskered, skinny thief, dropping, slipping off
his shoulders. . . . Here was a chance to get away!. . . He breathed
a sigh of relief and looked around. On the left towered a black,
mastless hull; it looked like an enormous coffin, deserted and empty. . . . Every wave that struck its side awoke a hollow, muffled
echo that sounded like a sigh. On the right, the grey stone wall of
the mole stretched above the surface of the water, like a cold,
heavy serpent. Behind him loomed some black piles, and in front,
in the space between the wall and the coffin, he could see the sea,
silent, desolate, and the black clouds floating above it. The clouds

moved across the sky slowly, large and ponderous, spreading horror out of the darkness and seeming ready to crush one with their
weight. All was cold, black and sinister. Gavrila grew frightened
again, and this fright was worse than that with which Chelkash
imbued him; it gripped his breast in its powerful embrace, reduced
him to a helpless clod and held him fast to the seat of the boat.

Silence reigned all around. Not a sound was heard, except for
the sighing of the sea. The clouds still crept across the sky slowly and lazily, but they rose out of the sea in infinite numbers. The
sky too looked like a sea, but a restless one, suspended over the
calm, smooth and slumbering sea below. The clouds seemed to be
descending upon the earth in grey, curly waves, into the chasms
from which the wind had torn them, and upon the newly-rising
waves, not yet crested with angry greenish foam.

Gavrila felt crushed by this gloomy silence and beauty and
yearned to see his master again. Suppose he didn't come back?...
Time passed slowly, more slowly than the clouds creeping across
the sky.... And as time passed the silence became more sinister.... At last the sounds of splashing and rustling and something
resembling a whisper came from the other side of the mole.
Gavrila thought he would die on the spot.

"P'st! Are you asleep? Hold this.... Careful now!" It was
Chelkash's muffled voice.

Something heavy and cube-shaped dropped from the wall.
Gavrila caught it and put it in the bottom of the boat. A second
object of the same kind followed. And then Chelkash's tall figure
appeared over the wall, the oars appeared out of somewhere,
Gavrila's knapsack fell at his feet, and breathing heavily, Chelkash
slipped into the stern of the boat.

Gavrila gazed at him with a pleased but timid smile.

"Are you tired?" he asked.

"Yes, a bit! Now then take to the oars and pull! Pull with
all your might! You've done well, my lad! Half the job's done.
The only thing now is to slip past those devils out there—and
then you can get your share and go home to your Masha. I suppose you have a Masha, haven't you?"

"N-no!" answered Gavrila, pulling at the oars with all his
might. His chest heaved like a pair of bellows and his arms worked

like steel springs. The water swirled from under the boat's
keel, and the blue track at its stern was wider now. Gavrila was
drenched with his own perspiration, but he continued to row with
all his might. Twice that night he had had a terrible fright; he
did not wish to have a third one. All he longed for was to get
over this accursed job as quickly as possible, to go ashore and
run away from this man before he did indeed kill him, or get
him landed in jail. He decided not to discuss anything with him, not
to contradict him, to do all he told him to do, and if he succeeded
in escaping from him, to offer a prayer to St. Nicholas the Miracle-
Worker the very next morning. An ardent prayer was ready to
burst from his breast at this very moment, but he restrained himself.
He puffed like a steam engine and now and again glanced at
Chelkash from under his brows.

But Chelkash, tall, thin, his body bent forward, looking like a
bird ready to take to flight, peered with hawkish eyes into the darkness ahead and twitched his beak like nose. He grasped the steering
oar tightly with one hand and with the other twirled his moustache,
which also twitched from the smiles that twisted his thin
lips. He was pleased with his haul, with himself, and with this
lad who was so terribly frightened of him, and whom he had
converted into his slave. He watched Gavrila putting every ounce
of strength into his oars and felt sorry for him. He wanted to
cheer him up.

"Hey!" he said softly with a laugh. "You were frightened,
weren't you?"

"N-no! Not much," gasped Gavrila.

"You needn't pull so hard now. It's all over. There's only one
spot that we've got to pass. . . . Take a rest. . . ."

Gavrila obediently stopped rowing, wiped the perspiration from
his face with his sleeve and dropped the oars.

"Well, have another go now," said Chelkash after a little while.
"But don't make the water talk. There's a gate we have to
pass. Quietly now, quietly! They're a stern lot here. . . . They
wouldn't hesitate to shoot and bore a hole in your head before you
have time to shout—oh!"

The boat now glided slowly over the water making scarcely a
sound, except for the blue drops that dripped from the oars and

caused small, blue, momentary patches to form on the water where they fell. The night became darker and even more silent. The sky no longer resembled a storm-tossed sea—the clouds had spread and covered it with a smooth heavy blanket that hung low and motionless over the water. The sea became still calmer and blacker, its warm saline odour became still more pungent, and it no longer seemed as broad as it was before.

"I wish it would rain!" whispered Chelkash. "We'd get through as if we were behind a curtain."

On the right and left eerie structures loomed out of the black water—barges, motionless, gloomy, and also black. But on one of them a light was moving; evidently somebody carrying a lantern was walking on the deck. The sea sounded plaintive and hollow, as it lapped against the sides of the barges, and the barges answered with a cold, muffled echo, as if arguing with the sea and refusing to yield to its plaint.

"A cordon!" exclaimed Chelkash in a scarcely audible whisper. The moment Chelkash told him to row more slowly, Gavrila was again overcome by that feeling of tense expectation. He bent forward and peered into the darkness, and he felt as if he were growing, as if his bones and sinews were stretching within him, giving him a dull pain; his head, filled with but one thought, ached; the skin on his back quivered, and small, sharp, cold needles were shooting through his legs. His eyes ached from the tenseness with which he peered into the darkness, out of which, every moment, he expected to hear the cry: "Stop, thief!"

And now, when Chelkash whispered "cordon," Gavrila shuddered; a piercing, burning thought shot through his brain and sent his taut nerves tingling. He wanted to shout and call for help.... He opened his mouth, rose slightly from the seat, stuck out his chest and took a deep breath—but suddenly he was paralysed by fear, which struck him like a whip. He closed his eyes and collapsed in the bottom of the boat.

Ahead of the boat, far away on the horizon, out of the black water, an enormous, fiery-blue sword rose and cleaved the darkness of the night; it ran its edge over the clouds and then lay on the breast of the sea, a broad blue strip. And within this bright strip ships appeared out of the darkness, ships hitherto invisible, black,

silent, and shrouded in the solemn gloom of the night. They looked
as though they had long been at the bottom of the sea, sent there
by the mighty power of the storm, and had now risen at the command of the fiery sword that was born of the sea—had risen to
look at the sky and at everything that was on the water. . . . Their
rigging, clinging to their masts like festoons of seaweed brought
up from the sea bottom together with the black giants who were
enmeshed in their net. The sinister blue sword rose again out of
the depth of the sea, and flashing, again cleaved the night, and
again lay flat on the water, but in another direction. And where
it lay, other ships' hulls, hitherto invisible, appeared.

The boat stopped and rocked on the water as if in perplexity.
Gavrila lay in the bottom of the boat, his face covered with his
hands. Chelkash jabbed at him with his foot and hissed furiously:
"That's the Customs cruiser, you fool. . . . It's an electric lamp!
Get up, you dolt! They'll shine the light on us in a minute
and everything will be all up with you and me! Get up!"

At last a kick from the heel of a heavy top boot heavier than
the first caught Gavrila in the back. He started up, and still
afraid to open his eyes, took his seat, groped for the oars and began to row.

"Quieter! Quieter, or I'll murder you!. . . What a dolt you are,
the devil take you! What frightened you, ugly mug? A lantern,
that's all it is! Quieter with the oars . . . you sour-faced devil!. . .
They're on the lookout for smugglers. They won't see us—they're
too far out. Don't be afraid, they won't see us. Now we. . . ." Chelkash looked round triumphantly. "Of course! We're out of it!
Phew!. . . Well, you're lucky, you thick-headed boob!"

Gavrila said nothing. He pulled at the oars and, breathing heavily, looked out of the corners of his eyes in the direction where
the fiery sword was rising and falling. He could not possibly believe what Chelkash said—that this was only a lantern. The cold
blue radiance that cleaved the darkness caused the sea to sparkle
with mysterious silvery brilliance, and Gavrila again felt hypno-
tized by that soul-crushing fear. He rowed mechanically, crouching
as if expecting a blow from above, and now he was bereft of all
desire—he was empty and soulless. The excitement of this night
had driven everything human out of him.

But Chelkash was jubilant. His nerves, accustomed to shocks, were now relaxed. His moustache twitched voluptuously and a light shone in his eyes. He felt splendid. He whistled through his teeth, inhaled deep breaths of the moist sea air. He looked around, and smiled good-naturedly when his eyes fell upon Gavrila.

The wind swept down and chopped up the sea. The clouds were now thinner and less opaque, but they covered the whole sky. The wind, though still light, was freely sweeping over the sea, but the clouds were motionless and seemed to be absorbed in grey, dull thought.

"Now lad, it's time you pulled yourself together! You look as if all your guts have been squeezed out of your body and there's nothing left but a bag of bones! It's all over now. Hey!"

Gavrila was pleased to hear a human voice at last, even if that voice was Chelkash's.

"I can hear what you say," he said softly.

"Very well, then, milksop. . . . Come and steer and I'll take the oars. I suppose you're tired."

Gavrila mechanically changed places with Chelkash, and as they crossed, Chelkash saw the boy's woe-begone face, and he noticed that his legs were trembling. He felt sorry for him. Patting him on the shoulder, he said:

"Come on, lad! Don't be so down in the dumps. You've earned a good bit tonight. I'll reward you well, my boy. Would you like the feel of a twenty-five ruble bill?"

"I don't want anything. All I want is to get ashore. . . ."

Chelkash waved his hand in disgust, spat, took up the oars and began to row, swinging the oars far back with his long arms.

The sea woke up and began to play with its little waves, giving birth to them, ornamenting them with fringes of foam, dashing them against each other, and breaking them up into fine spray. The foam melted with hisses and sighs, and the air all around was filled with a musical splashing noise. Even the darkness seemed to come to life.

Chelkash began to talk.

"Well now, tell me," he said. "You'll go back to your village and get married, and start grubbing the earth and sow corn. The wife will start bearing children. You won't have enough food for

them. Well, you'll be struggling all your life.... Is there any
pleasure in that?"

"Pleasure! I should say there isn't!" answered Gavrila with a
shudder.

Here and there the wind rent the clouds apart and scraps of
the sky with one or two stars in them peeped between the spaces.
Reflected in the sea, these stars played among the waves, now van-
ishing and now twinkling again.

"Steer to the right!" said Chelkash, "we shall be there soon. . . .
Y-e-ss!. . . . We're finished. It was a nice job! D'you see how it
is?. . . One night's work, and we land a cool five hundred!"

"Fi-v-e hundred?!" drawled Gavrila incredulously. But he at
once caught fright and hurriedly asked, kicking one of the bales
at the bottom of the boat: "What's this?"

"That's worth a lot of money. If we sold it at its proper price
we could get a thousand for it. But I'll ask for less. . . . Clever, ain't
it?"

"Y-e-s?" drawled Gavrila interrogatively. "I wish I could get
a bag like that!" he added with a sigh as he suddenly remembered his village, his wretched farm, his mother, and all that was
distant and dear to him, and for the sake of which he had left
home to earn some money, and had gone through all the horrors
of this night. He was overwhelmed by a wave of recollections of
his little village which scrambled down the steep slope to the river that was concealed by birches, willows, ash, and bird cherry. . . .
"Wouldn't that be fine," he murmured with a mournful sigh.

"Y-e-s!" continued Chelkash. "I'm thinking how nice it would
be for you now to take the train home. . . . Wouldn't you have all
the girls running after you! You could choose any one you liked!
You cou'd build yourself a new house. . . . I don't think you'll
have enough to build a new one though. . . ."

"That's true . . . it won't be enough to build a house. Timber's
dear in our parts."

"Well, you could repair the old one. What about a horse?
Have you got one?"

"A horse! Yes, I've got a horse, but she's too old, the devil."

"Well, you could buy a horse. Ekh, a f-i-n-e horse! And a
cow . . . sheep . . . and poultry. . . . Eh?"

"Oh, don't talk about it!... Good Lord! Wouldn't I live then!"

"Y-e-s, brother, it wouldn't be at all bad.... I've got some idea of what that kind of life is. I had my own little nest once.... My father was one of the richest men in our village...."

Chelkash lazily pulled at the oars. The boat rocked on the waves that were playfully lapping against its sides, barely moving over the dark sea which was becoming more and more boisterous. The two men dreamed as they rocked on the water, thoughtfully gazing around. Wishing to soothe the lad and cheer him up, Chelkash had turned Gavrila's thoughts to his village and had begun the talk in a bantering tone, hiding his smile under his moustache. When questioning Gavrila and reminding him of the joys of peasant life, in which he himself had long been disillusioned, had forgotten and had only recalled now he gradually allowed himself to be carried away by this new train of thought. He stopped questioning the lad about his village and its affairs, and, before he was aware of it, continued in the following strain:

"The main thing in peasant life, brother, is freedom! You're your own master. You have a house. It's not worth much, but it's your own. You have land; only a patch, but it's your own! You are a king on your land!... You have a face.... You can demand respect from everybody.... Isn't that so?" he concluded feelingly.

Gavrila stared at him with curiosity, and he too was carried away by the same feeling. In the course of this conversation he forgot the kind of man he was dealing with and saw before him a peasant, like himself, stuck to the land forever by the sweat of many generations, bound to it by the recollections of childhood, but who had voluntarily run away from it and its cares, and was suffering due punishment for this truancy.

"Yes, brother, what you say is true!" he said. "Oh how true! Look at yourself. What are you now without land? Land is like a mother, you can't forget it so easily."

Chelkash awoke from his musing.... He was conscious of that irritating heartburn which he always felt whenever his pride—the pride of the reckless daredevil—was touched by anybody, particularly by one whom he despised.

"Stop sermonizing!" he said fiercely. "Did you think I was talking seriously?... You must take me for a fool!"

"You're a funny chap!" Gavrila blurted out, feeling crushed again. "I wasn't talking about you, was I? There's lots of men like you. Lots of them! Ekh! How many unhappy people there are in the world!... Roaming around!..."

"Here, come and take the oars, you boob!" commanded Chelkash, for some reason restraining the flood of oaths that came rushing up into his throat.

They changed places again, and as he stepped over the bales in the bottom of the boat to reach the stern, Chelkash felt an almost irresistible desire to give Gavrila a push that would send him tumbling into the sea.

The conversation was not resumed, but Chelkash felt the breath of the village even in Gavrila's silence.... Musing over the past, he forgot to steer, with the result that the boat, turned by current, drifted out to sea. The waves seemed to understand that the boat had lost its way and began to toss it higher and higher, lightly playing with it, causing kindly blue lights to flash under the oars. And before Chelkash's mental vision floated pictures of the past, of the distant past which was separated from the present by a wall of eleven years of hobo life. He saw himself as a child; he saw his village; his mother, a plump ruddy-cheeked woman with kind grey eyes; he saw his father, a red-bearded giant with a stern face; he saw himself as a bridegroom, and he saw his wife, black-eyed Anfisa, a soft, buxom, cheerful girl with a long plait of hair; he saw himself again as the handsome Guardsman; again he saw his father, now grey and bent by toil, and his mother wrinkled and bowed; he also saw the vision of his return to his village from the army, and how proud his father was of his Grigori, of this handsome, sturdy, bewhiskered soldier.... Memory, that scourge of the unhappy, reanimates even the stones of the past, and even pours a drop of honey into the poison that one had once to drink....

Chelkash felt as if he were being fanned by the tender, soothing breath of his native air, which wafted to his ears the kind words of his mother, the grave speech of his earnest peasant father, many forgotten sounds and many fragrant smells of mother earth which has only just thawed, which has only just been ploughed, and is only just being covered with the emerald silken carpet of winter wheat.... He felt lonely, uprooted and isolated forever from the way of life which had produced the blood that now flowed in his veins.

"Hey! Where are we going?" suddenly exclaimed Gavrila.

Chelkash started and looked round with the alert gaze of a bird of prey.

"Christ, look where we have drifted to! Lay to the oars! Pull! Pull harder!"

"You've been dreaming, eh," Gavrila asked with a smile.

"I'm tired. . . ."

"So now we won't get caught with these, will we?" Gavrila asked, kicking at the bales at the bottom of the boat.

"No. . . . You can ease your mind on that score. I'll deliver them and get the money. . . . Y-e-s!"

"Five hundred?"

"No less."

"A tidy sum! Wish I had it! Ekh, wouldn't I play a tune with it!"

"On the farm?"

"I should say so! I'd. . . ."

And Gavrila flew off on winged dreams. Chelkash remained silent. His moustache drooped; his right side, splashed by the spray, was dripping wet. His eyes were now sunken and had lost their brightness. Everything rapacious in him had sagged, subdued by humiliating thoughts, which were reflected even from the folds of his grimy blouse.

He swung the boat round abruptly and steered towards something black that loomed out of the water.

The sky was again overcast and rain fell, a fine, warm rain, which pattered merrily as the drops struck the backs of the waves.

"Stop! Be quiet!" commanded Chelkash.

The boat's nose struck the side of a barge.

"Are they asleep, or what, the devils?" growled Chelkash, catching hold with a boat hook of some ropes that were dangling from the deck. "Drop the ladder! Blast it! It must go and rain now! Why couldn't it have rained before! Hey, you swabs! Hey!"

"Is that you, Selkash?" came a voice from above that sounded like the mewing of a cat.

"Come on, drop the ladder!"

"Kalimera, Selkash!"

"Drop the ladder, you hell-smoked devil!" roared Chelkash.

"Oh how angry he eez tonight.... Eloy!"

"Up you go, Gavrila!" said Chelkash to his mate.

Within a moment they were on the deck, where three dark-bearded figures were animatedly chattering to each other in a strange lisping tongue and looking over the gunwale down at Chelkash's boat. A fourth, wrapped in a long chlamys, went up to Chelkash, silently shook hands with him, and then glanced suspiciously at Gavrila.

"Get the money by the morning," said Chelkash to him curtly. I'll turn in now. Come on, Gavrila! Do you want anything to eat?"

"All I want is to sleep . . ." answered Gavrila, and five minutes later he was snoring, while Chelkash, sitting beside him, was trying on somebody's top boot, pensively spitting on the side and whistling a mournful tune through his teeth. Then he stretched out beside Gavrila, put his hands under the back of his head and lay there, twitching his moustache.

The barge rocked gently on the playful water. Something creaked plaintively. The rain pattered softly on the deck. The waves splashed against the side of the barge.... And it all sounded so sad, like a cradle song sung by a mother who had no hopes of happiness for her son....

Chelkash bared his teeth, raised his head, looked around, whispered something to himself, and lay down again.... He spread out his legs, and this made him look like a huge pair of scissors.

III

He woke up first, looked around anxiously, calmed down at once and looked at Gavrila who was still sleeping, snoring lustily, with a smile spread all over his boyish, healthy, sunburnt face. Chelkash sighed and climbed up a narrow rope ladder. A patch of leaden sky peered down the hatchway. It was already light, but the day was dull and grey, as it usually is in the autumn.

Chelkash returned about two hours later. His face was flushed and his moustaches were dashingly screwed upward. He wore a tunic and buckskin breeches, and a pair of tall, stout top boots. He looked like a huntsman. Although not new, the costume was still sound and suited him well. It made him look broader, concealed his gauntness and gave him a martial appearance.

"Hey, you calf, get up!" he cried, pushing Gavrila with his foot.

Gavrila jumped up. Still half asleep, he failed to recognize Chelkash and stared at him with dull, sleepish eyes. Chelkash burst out laughing.

"You do look fine!" exclaimed Gavrila at last, with a broad smile. "Quite a gentleman!"

"That doesn't take long with us. Well, aren't you a frightened baby! You thought you were going to die a thousand times last night. didn't you?"

"Yes, but judge for yourself. It was the first time I was on a job like that! I might have damned my soul for the rest of my life!"

"Would you come with me again?"

"Again?... Well.... What can I say? What will I get out of it? Tell me that!"

"Well, suppose you'd get two rainbow ones?"

"Two hundred rubles? That's not so bad.... I'd go for that...."

"But wait a minute! What about damning your soul?"

"Well ... perhaps ... it won't be damned!" answered Gavrila with a smile. And if it won't ... I'll be a made man for life."

Chelkash laughed merrily and said:

"All right! Enough of joking, let's go ashore...."

They were in the boat again. Chelkash at the tiller and Gavrila at the oars. Above them was the grey sky, evenly overcast with clouds. The dull green sea played with the boat, boisterously tossing it on its waves, which were still merrily casting bright salty sprays into the boat. Far ahead loomed a yellow strip of sandy shore, and behind them stretched the vast expanse of the sea, furrowed by packs of waves that were ornamented with fluffy white foam. There, too, in the distance, were numerous ships; far on the left was visible a whole forest of masts, and the white houses of the town, whence came a muffled rumble which, mingling with the splashing of the waves, created fine, powerful music.... And over all was cast a thin film of grey mist, which made things seem remote from each other....

"Ekh! There'll be hell let loose this evening!" said Chelkash, nodding in the direction of the sea.

"A storm?" asked Gavrila, ploughing the waves with powerful strokes. He was already drenched from head to foot from the
spray which the wind scattered over the sea.

"That's it!" said Chelkash.

Gavrila looked into his face enquiringly....

"Well, how much did they give you?" he asked at last, realizing
that Chelkash was not inclined to talk.

"Look!" said Chelkash, showing Gavrila something that he drew
from his pocket.

Gavrila saw a roll of coloured bills, and his eyes lit up with joy.

"Ekh!... And I thought you were kidding me! How much have
you got there?"

"Five hundred and forty!"

"My word!" exclaimed Gavrila in a whisper, following the
five hundred and forty rubles with his greedy eyes as Chelkash put
the money back into his pocket. "Ekh! If only I had as much as
that!"—and he heaved a mournful sigh.

"Won't we have a wonderful time, my lad!" exclaimed Chel-
kash cheerfully. "Ekh, we'll go on the spree!... Don't worry!
You'll get your share.... I'll give you forty. Does that satisfy you?
I'll give it to you right now if you want to?"

"If it's not too much for you.... Why not? I'll take it!"

Gavrila trembled with the expectation that gnawed in his breast.

"Oh, you devil's baby! I'll take it, you say! Well, take it,
please! Do me a favour! I don't know what to do with all this
money! Help me to get rid of it. Take it, do!"

Chelkash held out several bills. Gavrila took them with a trembling hand, dropped the oars and tucked the bills inside his blouse,
greedily screwing up his eyes and inhaling noisily, as if he
were drinking something very hot. Chelkash watched him with an
ironic smile. Gavrila again took up the oars and rowed with downcast eyes nervously, hurriedly, as if afraid of something. His shoulders and ears twitched.

"You're greedy!... That's bad.... But it's not surprising....
You're a peasant ..." said Chelkash pensively.

"But look what you can do with money!" exclaimed Gavrila.
aflush with excitement; and he began to talk rapidly, hurriedly,
as if trying to catch up with his thoughts and clutching at words,

about life in the village with money and without money, about the
honour, abundance and pleasure one can acquire with money.

Chelkash listened attentively, with a grave face and eyes screwed
up as if thinking hard. Now and again he smiled with satisfaction.

"Here we are!" he exclaimed, interrupting Gavrila.

A wave lifted the boat and landed it on the sandy beach.

"Well, it's all over now, brother. Pull the boat up higher so
that it won't be washed away. They'll come for it. And now we
must part!.... It's eight versts from here to town. I suppose you
are going back to town, aren't you?"

A shrewd, good-natured smile lit up Chelkash's face, and his
whole bearing indicated that he had thought of something pleasing
to himself and surprising for Gavrila. Thrusting his hands in his
pocket, he rustled the bills that were lying in them.

"No.... I ... won't go ... I ..." gasped Gavrila as if he were
choking.

Chelkash looked at him and asked:

"What's ailing you?"

"Nothing ... only...." Gavrila's face was alternately flushed
and ashen-grey, and he stood there wriggling, whether from a desire to hurl himself upon Chelkash, or because he was torn by
another desire difficult to fulfill, it was hard to say.

Chelkash felt uneasy at the sight of the lad's agitation and he
waited to see what the upshot of it would be.

Gavrila began to laugh in a queer way that sounded more like
sobbing. He hung his head, so that Chelkash was unable to see
the expression on his face; only his ears were visible, and these
grew red and pale by turns.

"Go to the devil!" exclaimed Chelkash, waving his hand in
disgust. "Have you fallen in love with me, or what? Stands there
wriggling like a girl! Or is it that you don't want to part from
me? Now then, you boob! Speak up, or else I'll go away!"

"You'll go away?" shrieked Gavrila.

The sandy, deserted beach shuddered at the sound of this shriek,
and the sandy ridges washed up by the waves of the sea seemed
to heave. Chelkash too shuddered. Suddenly Gavrila darted towards
Chelkash, threw himself at his feet and flinging his arms around
his knees gave a sudden tug. Chelkash staggered and dropped heavily

to the sand. Grinding his teeth, he raised his long arm and was about
to bring his clenched fist down upon Gavrila's head when the blow
was checked by the lad's shy and plaintive whisper:

"Be a good fellow!... Give me that money! For the sake of
Christ, give it to me! It isn't much to you. You got it in one
night.... Only one night, but it would take me years.... Give it
to me, and I will pray for you! Always.... In three churches....
I'll pray for the salvation of your soul!... You will only throw
the money away.... But I, I'd put it in the land! Give me the
money! It isn't much to vou. You can easily get some more. One
night ... and you are rich! Do me a good turn. After all, you're
a lost man.... There's nothing before you.... But I.... Oh....
What couldn't I do with the money! Give it to me!"

Chelkash sat on the sand, frightened, amazed and angry, leaning back and propping himself up with his arms, saying not a
word, but staring with wide open eyes at the lad who was pressing his head against his knees and whispering, gasping and pleading. At last he pushed the boy away, jumped to his feet, thrust
his hand in his pocket, took out several bi'ls and flung them at
Gavrila.

"Here you are! Take them ..." he shouted, trembling with excitement, filled with both intense pity and hatred for this greedy
slave. And having thrown the money at h'm. he felt like a hero.

"I wanted to give you more myself." he said. "My heart was
softened last night, thinking of my village.... I thought to myself:
I'll help the lad. I just waited to see what you would do, whether
you would ask for it or not. But you.... Ekh! You've got no guts!
You're a beggar!... Is it worth while tormenting yourself like
that for money? Fool! Greedy devils!.... They've no self respect.... They'd sell themselves for five kopecks!...

"Angel!... May Christ guard and save you! I'm a different
man now.... I'm rich!" squealed Gavrila, in a transport of joy,
putting the money inside his b'ouse with a trembling hand. "You
are an angel!... I shall never forget you, not as long as I live!...
And I'll tell my wife and my children to pray for you!"

Hearing these rapturous cries and seeing the lad's radiant face
distorted by this paroxysm of greed, Chelkash felt that he, a thief, a
rake, torn from all his kith and kin, would never become a greedy,

low, self-degrading creature like this. No! He would never sink so low!... And this thought and feeling, making him conscious of his own freedom, kept him on the deserted seashore with Gavrila.

"You've made me happy for life!" shouted Gavrila again, seizing Chelkash's hand and pressing it against his own face.

Chelkash remained silent, baring his teeth like a wolf. Gavrila kept on chattering:

"And just imagine! As we were coming here I was thinking to myself: I'll give him, meaning you, one c-rr-a-c-k over the head with the oar ... take the money, and chuck him, meaning you, into the sea.... Nobody would miss him, I thought to myself. And even if he was missed, nobody would worry about him. He's not the kind of man anybody would make a fuss about!... No use to anybody. Who would stand up for him?!"

Chelkash seized Gavrila by the throat and barked:

"Give that money back!"

Gavri'a struggled, but Chelkash's other arm wound round him like a snake.... There was a screech of tearing cloth, and Gavrila lay on the sand kicking his legs, his blouse ripped down to the hem, his eyes staring with wild amazement and his fingers clutching the air. Chelkash stood there, tall, straight, thin, with a rapacious look on his face. Baring his teeth he laughed a staccato, sardonic laugh, while his moustache twitched nervously on his sharp angular face. Never in all his life had he been so cruelly insulted, and never had he been so angry.

"Well, are you happy?" he asked Gavrila amidst his laughter. And then, turning his back on him, he strode off in the direction of the town. But he had barely taken half a dozen paces when Gavrila crouched like a cat, jumped to his feet, and with a wide swing of his arm hurled a large pebble at Chelkash, exclaiming fiercely:

"Take that!"

Chelkash gasped. put his hands to his head, staggered, swung round to face Gavrila and fell prone on the sand. Gavrila gazed at the prostrate man dumbfounded. He saw his leg move. he saw him try to raise his head and then stretch out and tremble like a taut string. And then Gavrila dashed off, as fast as his legs could carry him, into the distance, where a shaggy black cloud hung over the misty steppe, and where it was dark. The waves surged

up on the sandy beach, merged with it and surged back again.
The surf hissed, and the air was filled with spray.

Rain fell at first slowly, but soon in heavy dense streaks,
pouring down from the sky. And the streaks wove an entire net of
water threads, a net which at once covered the expanses of steppe
and sea. Gavrila vanished in this net. For a long time nothing was
visible except the rain, and the long body of the man lying on the
sand on the seashore. But out of the rain Gavrila reappeared,
running as fast as a bird upon the wing. He ran up to Chelkash,
dropped to his knees in front of him and turned him over on the
sand. His hand came in contact with something warm, red and
sticky.... He shuddered and started back with horror written on
his pallid face.

"Brother, get up!" he whispered into Chelkash's ear amidst the
pattering of the rain.

Chelkash came to, pushed Gavrila away and said in a hoarse
voice:

"Go away!..."

"Brother! forgive me! It was the devil who tempted me..."
whispered Gavrila in a trembling voice, kissing Chelkash's hand.

"Go.... Go away ..." gasped Chelkash.

"Take this sin from my soul!... Please! Forgive!..."

"For.... Go away!... Go to hell!" Chelkash suddenly shouted,
sitting up. His face was pale and angry, his eyes were dull and
heavy, and the lids drooped as if he very much wanted to sleep.
"What else do you want? You've done your job.... Now go! Clear
out!"

And he lunged at grief-stricken Gavrila with his foot, but the
effort was too much for him, and he would have sunk back to
the sand had not Gavrila put his arm round his shoulders. Chelkash's face was now on a level with Gavrila's. Both were pale and
horrible to look at.

"Pht!" and Chelkash spat into his hireling's wide-open eyes.

Gavrila wiped his eyes with his sleeve and whispered:

"Do what you like.... I shan't say a word. Forgive me, for
the sake of Christ!"

"Worm!... You haven't got guts for anything!..." shouted
Chelkash contemptuously, and then, tearing his blouse from under

his coat, he began silently to bandage his head, now and again grinding his teeth with pain. At last he said through his clenched teeth, "Did you take the money?"

"No, I didn't take it, brother! I don't want it! It only causes trouble!..."

Chelkash put his hand into the pocket of his coat, drew out the roll of bills, took a rainbow-coloured one from it and put it back in his pocket, and threw the rest at Gavrila, saying:

"Take this and clear out!"

"I won't take it, brother!... I can't! Forgive me!"

"Take it, I tell you!..." roared Chelkash, rolling his eyes horribly.

"Forgive me ... and then I'll take it ..." said Gavrila timidly, dropping down on the rain-drenched sand at Chelkash's feet.

"Liar! You will take it! I know you will, you worm!" said Chelkash in a confident voice. Pulling Gavrila's head up by the hair, he pushed the money into his face and said:

"Take it! Take it! You've earned it! Take it. Don't be afraid! Don't be ashamed of having nearly killed a man! Nobody would punish you for getting rid of a man like me. They would even thank you for it if they got to know of it. Take it!"

Seeing that Chelkash was joking, Gavrila felt relieved. He grasped the money tightly in his hand and enquired in a tearful voice:

"But you do forgive me, brother, don't you, eh?"

"Angel!..." answered Chelkash mockingly in the same tone of voice. Rising and swaying on his feet, he said: "Forgive? There's nothing to forgive! You tried to do me in today, and I might try to do you in tomorrow."

"Ekh, brother, brother!" sighed Gavrila, mournfully shaking his head.

Chelkash stood in front of him with a queer smile on his face; and the rag on his head, gradually becoming red, began to look like a Turkish fez.

The rain was now pouring down in torrents. The sea murmured with a hollow sound, and the waves beat furiously and angrily upon the shore.

The two men remained silent.

"Well, good-bye!" said Chelkash ironically, walking off.

He staggered, his legs trembled, and he held his head in a queer way, as if afraid it would drop off.

"Forgive me, brother!" Gavrila begged once again.

"Never mind!" answered Chelkash coldly, continuing on his way.

He staggered on, holding his head with his left hand and slowly twirling his yellow moustache with the right.

Gavrila gazed after him until he vanished in the curtain of rain, which was now pouring from the clouds more densely than ever, in thin, endless streaks, and enveloping the steppe with impenetrable gloom, the colour of steel.

He then took off his soaking cap, crossed himself, looked at the money that he grasped tightly in his hand, heaved a deep sigh of relief, put the money inside his blouse and strode firmly along the beach, in the direction opposite to that in which Chelkash had gone.

The sea howled and hurled large, ponderous waves upon the sandy shore, smashing them into spray and foam. The rain beat heavily upon the water and the land.... The wind shrieked.... The air all around was filled with whining, roaring, and rumbling.... The rain blotted out both sea and sky.

Soon the rain and the spray from the waves washed away the red stain on the spot where Chelkash had lain, and washed out the tracks that Chelkash and the young lad had made on the sandy beach.... And nothing was left on the deserted seashore to remind one of the little drama in which these two men had been the actors.

AFLOAT

AN EASTER STORY

I

THE LEADEN clouds crept slowly over the sleepy river, seeming
to sink lower and lower; in the distance their grey tatters appeared
to touch the surface of the swift, turbid springtide waves, and
where they touched the water, rose towering to the skies in an impenetrable wall of cloud, blocking the current and barring the way
of the rafts.

And the waves, ineffectually trying to lift this wall, beat vainly
against it in a low, plaintive murmur, recoiling from each impact
to roll back into the damp gloom of the fresh spring night.

But the rafts sailed on, and the distance receded before them
in a wilderness of heavy tumbled cloud masses.

The shores were invisible, hidden by the night, pushed back
by the sweeping surge of the tide.

The river resembled a sea. The sky above it was wrapped in
clouds. Everything was damp, oppressive and dreary.

The rafts glided swiftly and noiselessly over the waters, and in
front of them a steamboat loomed out of the darkness, its funnel
shooting out a merry swarm of sparks and its wheel blades churning the water....

Two red lanterns on the shallows glimmered larger and brighter, and the lamp on the mast swayed gently from side to side and
winked mysteriously at the darkness.

The air was filled with the plash of water and the heavy sighs
of the engine.

"Look ou-oot!" came a deep-chested shout from the rafts.

At the tail-end of the raft two men stood at the helm oars. One
of them was Mitya, the son of the timber-floater, a fair, sickly-look-
ing, thoughtful youth of twenty. The other was Sergei, the hired

workman, a morose-faced strapping fellow with a red beard fram-
ing a set of strong prominent teeth with a bared upperlip drawn
up in a sarcastic expression.

"Put over to larboard!" a loud cry from the head of the rafts
once more rent the darkness.

"We know what to do, what you hollering about?" muttered
Sergei testily, and taking a deep breath he bent his body to the oar.

"Oo-ooch! Get going, Mitya!"

Mitya, with his feet braced against the wet logs, lugged the
heavy pole of the tiller over to him with his thin hands, breaking
into a hoarse cough.

"Put her over... more to port!... Godammit!" cried an anxious infuriated voice in front.

"All you know's to yell! Your weakly son couldn't break a straw
across his knee, and you put him on the tiller and then holler all over
the river. Too stingy to hire another man, damned skinflint—messing
around with your daughter-in-law. Well, yell yourself blue now!..."

Sergei now grumbled aloud, apparently not afraid of being
heard—in fact, as though wanting to be heard. ...

The steamboat raced past the rafts, churning the waters under
its blades into a hissing foam. The logs pitched and tossed from
the surge, and the braces made from twisted branches creaked with
a dreary wet sound.

The steamer's lighted windows gazed out upon the river and the
rafts like a row of huge eyes, casting their reflection in shimmering
bright patches on the turbulent water, then vanished from sight.

The heaving swell threw waves splashing over the rafts, the logs
tossed up and down, and Mitya, swaying on his feet, clung hard to
the tiller for fear of losing his balance.

"Now, now!" Sergei muttered mockingly, "doing a dance! Mind
your father doesn't yell at you again.... Or he'll give you a poke
in the ribs that'll send you dancing properly! Put over to starboard!
Heave-ho, now! Oo-ooch!..."

And Sergei, with brawny arms, powerfully plied his oar, cleaving deep into the waters. ...

Tall and energetic, a trifle morose and sarcastic, he stood as if
rooted to the logs with his bare feet, tensely poised, peering into
the distance, ready at any moment to veer the rafts round.

"Christ, look at the way your dad's cuddling Mashka! The devils! No shame or conscience—the man hasn't! Why don't you go somewhere, away from those foul devils?... eh? D'you hear what I say?"

"I hear!" said Mitya in an undertone, keeping his eyes averted from where, through the misty gloom, Sergei could see his father sitting.

"I hear! Ugh, you sop!" mocked Sergei and burst into a laugh.

"Some goings-on, I tell you!" he went on, provoked by Mitya's apathy. "There's an old devil for you! Marries off his son, then takes his daughter-in-law for himself and doesn't give a rap! The old blighter!"

Mitya said nothing and gazed back at the river where the clouds have closed in another dense wall.

Now the clouds were everywhere, and it seemed that the rafts were not floating down the current but standing motionless in the thick black water, crushed beneath the weight of these dark-grey masses of cloud which had fallen upon it from the heavens and stemmed its progress.

The river looked like a fathomless pool hedged in by towering mountains and clothed in a dense cloak of mist.

An oppressive stillness reigned all around, and the water, gently lapping the sides of the raft, lay as if in a hushed expectancy. There was an infinite sadness, a timid question in that frail sound, the only one amid the night, that seemed only to deepen its stillness....

"A bit of a breeze now wouldn't be bad..." said Sergei. "Though better not—a wind'll bring rain," he debated with himself as he filled his pipe.

There was the flash of a lighted match, the sizzling sound of a clogged pipe, and the broad face of Sergei swum out of the murk in the light of a flickering red flame.

"Mitya!" came his voice. He was less morose now, and the amused tone in his voice was more in evidence.

"What?" answered Mitya in an undertone, his eyes still peering into the distance, staring at something he saw there through his big melancholy eyes.

"How'd the thing happen, my lad, eh?"

"What thing?" retorted Mitya in a tone of annoyance.

"How d'you get married? What a scream! How'd it happen? Now, you went to bed with your wife—and what happened next, eh?!"

"Hey, you fellows there! Look ou-oot!" a warning shout echoed across the river.

"He can yell all right, that damned rip!" Sergei observed in a tone of admiration, and returned to his subject.

"Well, come on, tell us about it! Mitya! Tell us how it happened, eh?"

"Oh, leave me alone. Sergei! I told you already!" said Mitya in a pleading whisper, and, probably aware that he would not shake off the importunate Sergei, he hurriedly began:

"Well, we went to bed. And I says to her—'I can't be your husband, Maria. You're a strong healthy lass, and I'm a sick, weakly man. I didn't want to marry at all, but Dad made me—you've got to, he says, and that's that! I'm not fond of your sex, and still less of you,' I says. 'Too lively by half.... Yes.... And I can't do anything of that kind ... you know.... It's just filthy and wicked.... Children too.... You've got to answer for them before God....'"

"Filthy!" screamed Sergei, rocking with laughter, "Well, and what about her, Masha—what did she have to say, eh?"

"She.... 'Well, what am I to do now,' she says. Sits and cries. 'Why don't you like me?' she says. 'It isn't as if I was ugly,' she says. She's a shameless hussy, Sergei! ... 'What am I to do—go to my father-in-law with my fine health?' I told her—'do just as you please.... Go wherever you want. I can't go against my soul. Grandpa Ivan used to say that thing's a mortal sin. We're not beasts, you and I, are we?' And all she does is cry. 'You've spoiled my life, youth, poor girl that I am.' I was awfully sorry for her. 'Never mind, things'll come round somehow. Or, maybe you'll go into a convent?' I says. She starts swearing at that—'you're a fool, Mitya, a scoundrel, that's what you are....'"

"Well, I'm blowed!" stuttered Sergei in amazement. "D'you actually mean to say you gave her that bit of advice—told her to go into a convent?"

"That's what I told her," answered Mitya simply.

"And she called you a fool?" said Sergei in a rising voice.

"Yes. . . . She swore at me."

"I should think so too! And quite right! I'd have boxed your ears in the bargain if I was her," he added in a sudden change of tone. He now spoke sternly and weightily.

"D'you think a man can go against the law? That's what you've gone and done! It's the way of the world—and that's all there is to it! There's no arguing about it! And what do you do? Crikey, what a thing to say! Go into a convent! Silly ass! What d'you think the lass wants? And you talk about a convent! Good lor', some people make you sick! D'you realize what you've done, you muff? You're no damned good yourself and you've ruined that girl's life, made her that old gaffer's mistress—and led the old fellow into the sin of lechery. Look how much law you've broken! Silly ass!"

"The law's in a man's soul, Sergei. It's the same law for all—don't do anything that goes against the soul and you won't be doing any evil on earth," said Mitya gently and soothingly, with a toss of his head.

"But that's just what you have done!" Sergei countered energetically. "A man's soul! Bah! . . . What's the soul got to do with it? You can't put a ban on everything—it isn't done. The soul. . . . You've got to understand it first, brother, and then talk. . . ."

"No, Sergei, that's not so!" Mitya broke in warmly, seeming to have suddenly kindled. "The soul's always pure, brother, like a dewdrop. It's in a shell, that's where it is! It's deep. And if you hearken to it you won't go wrong. It'll always be God's way if it's done the soul's way. For isn't God in the soul?—and if so, the law's there too. It's God who created it, God who breathed it into man. Only you've got to be able to look into it. Only by forgetting self can a man. . . ."

"Hey, you! Sleepy devils! Look sharp!" a thundering voice echoed over the river.

Judging by its lustiness the voice clearly belonged to a healthy, vigorous man pleased with himself and the world, a man richly endowed with vitality and well aware of it. He shouted not because he was provoked to do so by the raftsmen, but because his heart swelled with a sense of elation and vigour, the sheer joy of living that sought an outlet and found it in that lusty boisterous sound.

"Hear him bark, the old devil!" Sergei noted with pleasure, keeping a vigilant lookout in front of him. "Spooning like a couple of doves! Ain't you envious, Mitya?"

Mitya turned his eyes indifferently to the fore oars where two figures could be seen running across the rafts from side to side, now stopping close to each other, now merging into a dark blur.

"Don't you envy 'em?" repeated Sergei.

"Why should I? It's their sin, and they'll answer for it," answered Mitya quietly.

"So!" drawled Sergei ironically, and refilled his pipe. The darkness was once more lit up by a red glow.

The night grew deeper, and the grey, black clouds descended still lower over the still broad river.

"Where'd you get all that wisdom from, Mitya, eh? Or were you born that way? You don't take after your Dad a bit. He's full o' spunk, your Dad is. Just think—the old fellow's half a century, and look at the peach he's getting off with! She's a regular beauty! And hasn't she fallen for him—you can see that with half an eye. Yes, she loves him, my dear fellow. She's crazy about him. Who wouldn't love a trump like that? The king of trumps, that's what your Dad is, a topnotcher. It does your heart good to see the way he handles his work; he's made a pretty penny too; looked up to plenty, and his head's screwed on right. M'yes. You don't take after your Dad, or after your mother either. Mitya? I wonder what your father'd do if your mother, Anfisa, had been alive? Humph! I can just see it. . . . She was pretty hot stuff too, your Ma was. . . . A match for Silan."

Mitya was silent, leaning on his oar and gazing into the water.

Sergei fell silent too. From the front of the rafts came a woman's rippling laughter, answered by a man's deep laugh. Their figures, woven into the darkness, were barely visible to Sergei, who peered at them with curiosity through the gloom. One could distinguish that the man was tall and was standing by the oar with his legs wide apart half-facing a plump little woman who was leaning her bosom against another oar within ten feet of the first. She wagged a premonitory finger at the man and went into gales of merry laughter. Sergei turned away with a sigh of regret, and after a profound silence, began again:

"Ah, well! They're having a sweet time. Lovely! Nothing for a lonely vagabond like me! Gad, I'd never in my life leave a woman like that if I had her! Hang it, I'd squeeze the life out of her if I got her in my hands. There! That's the way I love you—let her know it.... Hell! I've got no luck with women.... Looks like they don't take to ginger fellows. M'yes. She a capricious bit—that one is. A proper minx! She's out for a good time, Mitya! Hi, are you asleep?"

"No," Mitya answered softly.

"Good for you! How d'you intend to go through life, brother? Come to think of it, you're all alone in the blessed world. That ain't very cheerful! What d'you intend to do with yourself? You won't be able to live among people. You're a poor fish of a man. What's the use of a man who can't stand up for himself! What you need in life, brother, are fangs and claws. Everyone'll try to worst you. Now, tell me, can you stick up for yourself? I'd like to see you doing it! Bah! You're a poor fish!"

"D'you mean me?" Mitya came out of his reveries with a start. "I'll go away. This very autumn—to the Caucasus—and that's all! God! Only to get away from you people! Soulless people! Godless men you are—only to get away from you is salvation! What are you living for? Where's your God? It's a mere word to you.... D'you live according to Jesus Christ? You—you're wolves! People over there are different, their souls live in that of Christ, and their hearts are filled with love and they yearn for the world's salvation.... And you? Oh, you! Beasts, sinks of corruption! There are different people. I've seen them. They've called me. I'll go to them. They brought me the holy book of scriptures. Read it, man of God, they said, dear brother of ours, read the word of truth! ... And I read it, and my soul was reborn by this word of God. I'll go away. I'll run away from you mad wolves, who feed on each other's flesh. May you be damned!"

Mitya uttered all this in a passionate whisper, choking with wrath and withering scorn towards these mad wolves, overcome by a sudden hungering for the people whose souls yearned for the salvation of the world.

Sergei was astounded. He stood silent for a while with his mouth agape and his pipe in his hand. Then, after a moment's thought, he glanced round and said in a hollow, sullen voice:

"Fancy going off the deep end like that! ... You're pretty fierce too You shouldn't ha' read that book. Who knows what kind o'book it is? Oh, well ... go ahead, clear out, or you may get spoilt altogether. Go along with you, before you get real wild. ... What kind of people are they down in the Caucasus? Monks? Or maybe the Old Believers? What are they—Molokans, perhaps? Eh?"

But Mitya had gone out as quickly as he had kindled. He plied his oar, gasping with the effort, and muttered something rapidly and nervously under his breath.

Sergei waited long and in vain for a response. His robust simple nature was oppressed by the grim, deathly-still night. He wanted to be reminded of life, to waken the hushed world with sound, to stir up and frighten the lurking rapt stillness of these ponderous masses of water slowly winding to the sea and those inert mountains of cloud hanging drearily in the air Life was being lived at the other end of the rafts, and that roused him to life.

From there now and again came floating a soft thrilling laugh and snatches of exclamations, muffled by the silence and darkness of a night saturated with the fragrance of spring, a night that stirred a passionate longing to live.

"Stop it, Mitya—what you tacking for? The old man'll start swearing, you watch," he said, no longer able to endure the silence, and noticing that Mitya was stabbing the water with his oar in a desultory fashion. Mitya stopped, wiped the perspiration from his brow, and froze motionless on his oar, breathing hard.

"Very few steamboats about today somehow. ... Been sailing so long and only came across one of 'em."

And seeing that Mitya evinced no intention of replying, he went on argumentatively:

"I suppose that's because navigation hasn't started yet. It's only just beginning. We'll make Kazan in fine time—the Volga's pulling grand. Got a giant's spine, she has—lift anything on earth. What's the matter with you? Got the wind up, Mitya, or what? Eh?"

"What do you want?" answered Mitya irritably.

"Nothing. Funny chap you are. ... Why don't you say something? Thinking all the time? Chuck it. It ain't good for a man. Oh, you wiseacre—you think you're wise. but that you haven't a ha'porth of wisdom—that you can't see! Ha-ha!"

Giving himself a laugh in the knowledge of his own superiority, Sergei followed it up with a deep grunt, then fell silent for a while, broke off a whistle he had started, and pursued his train of thought.

"Thinking! That ain't a pastime for a common man. Look at your father—he doesn't worry his head, yet he lives. Spooning with your wife and making fun o' you, the two of 'em, you wise chump. Yes! That's the stuff! I bet you Masha's pregnant already, what? Don't get scared, the kid won't take after you. He'll be a sturdy bounder like Silan Petrov—you can take that from me. He'll be registered as yours, you know. Some business, let me tell you! Ha! Call you 'daddy.' And you won't be his daddy but his brother, by the looks o' it. His daddy'll be his grandpa! How do you like that! Gad, what a dirty bunch o'sinners! A dare-devil lot! Isn't that so, Mitya?"

"Sergei!" came a passionate. agitated. almost sobbing whisper. "For Christ's sake, don't tear my heart. don't torture me, leave me alone! Be quiet! In the name of God, I beg you not to speak to me; stop tormenting me. stop sucking my blood. I'll throw myself in the river, and a great sin will lie on you. I'll destroy my soul— leave me in peace! I swear by God—please!..."

The silence of the night was rent by a painfully shrill cry, and Mitya dropped on the logs as though struck down by something heavy that had fallen out of the sullen clouds poised above the black river.

"There, there!" muttered a dismayed Sergei, watching the figure of his companion writhing on the logs, as though seared by a burning flame. "You're a funny chap! If you take it so bad why didn't you ... er ... why didn't you say so, silly...."

"You've been tormenting me all the way. Why? What am I— your enemy? eh? your enemy?" Mitya whispered passionately....

"Funny chap you are! Really, you are!" stammered Sergei in a flustered and injured tone. "How's I to know? I don't know what's going on in your soul!"

"I want to forget it all, don't you understand! Forget it for all time! My disgrace ... the terrible anguish.... You're savages! I'll go away! I'll go for ever.... I can't stand it any more!..."

"Yes, go away!..." bellowed Sergei in a voice that reverberated over the river, and followed up the exclamation with a thun-

derous cynical invective. But the words suddenly died on his lips
and he seemed to shrink as he squatted down, apparently stunned
at the human drama that had unfolded before him and to which he
could no longer shut his eyes.

"Hey, you!" the voice of Silan Petrov came floating over the
river. "What's up there? What's the barking about? Eh-ho-o?"

Silan Petrov seemed to like making a noise, wakening the heavy
silence of the river with his deep, powerful lungs. His shouts followed one another in quick succession, rending the warm damp air
with a lusty vitality that seemed to crush the puny figure of Mitya
who was again at his oar. Sergei answered his employer at the top
of his voice, while in an undertone he cursed him in picturesque,
spicy Russian terms. Two voices split the silence of the night, tore
it and shook it in a tumult of sound that now mingled in a deep
rich note like the tone of a brass trumpet, now rose to a shrill
falsetto, floated in the air, faded, and died. Then silence reigned
once more.

Yellow patches of moonlight fell upon the water from out the
rifts in the clouds and vanished with a brief gleam into the smudgy
greyness around.

The rafts drifted on amid the darkness and silence.

                                    II

At one of the fore oars stood Silan Petrov in a red shirt open
at the throat, revealing a powerful neck and a strong hairy chest,
as hard as an anvil. A mop of raven-black hair tumbled over his
brows, and from under them gleamed a pair of smiling hazel eyes.
His sleeves, rolled up to the elbows, bared his muscular hands that
were gripping the oar. Leaning slightly forward, he peered intently
into the murky distance.

Masha stood within three paces of him, sideways to the current,
and regarded the broad-chested figure of her man with a smile.
Both were silent, engrossed with their observations—he gazing into
the distance, she studying the play of his vivacious bearded face.

"A fisherman's campfire, I suppose!" he said at length, facing
her. "It's all right then. We're keeping straight! Oo-ooch!" he puffed,

sending out a column of hot air, as he dipped his oar to larboard and gave a powerful tug.

"Don't overdo it, Masha dear!" he observed, seeing her make the same dexterous movement with her oar.

Plump and round, with black impudent eyes and rosy cheeks, barefooted, wearing only a wet sarafan that clung to her body, she turned her face to Silan and said with a tender smile:

"You take too much care of me. I'm pretty strong, thank God!"

"I don't when I kiss you," said Silan with a shrug.

"You shouldn't!" she whispered provokingly.

They said nothing for a while, devouring each other with hungry eyes.

The water rippled dreamily beneath the rafts. Somewhere far away on the lee the cocks began to crow.

The rafts sailed on with a faint rocking motion towards the thinning, melting darkness, where the clouds now stood out in sharper contours and lighter shades.

"Silan! D'you know what they were squealing about there? I know, honestly I do! Mitya must have been complaining about us to Sergei, and started whining for misery, and Sergei swore at us."

Masha searched his face, which at her words had grown grim, cold and hard.

"Well, what of it?" he asked drily.

"Oh, nothing."

"If it's nothing, there was nothing to talk about."

"Don't be angry!"

"What, at you? I'd like to at times, but I just couldn't."

"Do you love your Masha?" she whispered playfully, bending towards him.

"Oo-ooch!" he ejaculated with an expressive grunt, and holding out his powerful arms to her, he said between clenched teeth:

"Come here. . . . Don't tease. . . ."

She curved her lithe body like a cat and slipped softly into his arms.

"We'll throw the rafts off the course again!" he whispered, kissing her face that flamed under his lips.

"Enough! It's getting light. . . . They can see us from the other end."

She tried to wriggle free, but his arm tightened about her.

"Can they? Let 'em see! Let everybody see! To hell with them all. I'm committing a sin, that's a fact. I know it. What of it? I'll answer for it before God. You haven't been his wife anyway. That means you're free to do anything you like with yourself. It's hard on him? I know it is. What about me? D'you think there's anything flattering in living with a son's wife? Though, it's true, you're not his wife. . . . Still! Taking my social position, what do I look like now? And isn't it a sin before God? It is! I know it all! And I've gone against it all. And damme, it's worth it! We live once on this earth, and may die any day. Ah, Maria! If only I'd have waited another month before marrying off Mitva! Things would ha' been different. As soon as Anfisa died, I'd have sent a matchmaker down to you—and the thing's done! All lawful and proper! No sin and no shame! It was my mistake. It'll eat the heart out o' me for five or ten years, that mistake will. Kill you before you die. . . ."

"Oh, come, drop it, don't worry about it. We've talked it over plenty and enough," whispered Masha, and gently twisting out of his arms, she went back to her oar. He began jerkily and violently plying his oar as if desirous of shaking off the weight that pressed on his chest and cast a sudden shadow across his handsome face.

Day was breaking.

The clouds, growing thinner, straggled across the sky as if reluctant to make way for the rising sun. The water assumed the cold tint of steel.

"He mentioned it again the other day. 'Dad,' he says, 'isn't it a shame and disgrace for both you and me? Give her up'—meaning you," said Silan Petrov with a wry smile. " 'Give her up and come to your senses.' 'My son,' I says, 'my dear son, get out o' the way if you wish to keep a'ive! I'll tear you to pieces like a rotten rag. There'll be nothing left of your virtue. Cursed be the day that I brought such a degenerate like you into the world.' He stood trembling. 'Dad, is it my fault?' he says. 'It is your fault, you whimpering mongrel, 'cause you're a stone in my path. It's your fault 'cause you can't stand up for yourself. You're just carrion, that's what you are—a stinking garbage. At least if you were strong one could ki'l you—but one can't even do that to you, you miserable scarecrow.' He started howling! Ah, Maria! Men haven't got any gumption nowadays! Another fellow in my place—ugh! We'd soon shake off the noose! And we're only putting our heads into it! Who knows but we'll draw it tight about each other."

"What do you mean?" Masha asked timidly, gazing fearfully at the grim face of the man, whose whole personality emanated a cold tremendous force.

"I mean if he died ... that's what I mean. If only he'd die ... wouldn't it be wonderful! Everything'd drop into its rut. I'd give your folks the land—that would keep their mouths shut—and you and I'd go to Siberia ... or to the Kuban! Who's she? She's my wife. D'you get me? We'd obtain the necessary document ... I'd open a shop in some village. And we'd live our lives together, and pray off our sin to God. We don't need much. We'd help people, and they'd help us to ease our conscience.... How'd you like it? Eh? Masha?!"

"Y-yes," she sighed, and with eyes tightly screwed up, she became lost in thought.

They were silent for a while.... There was no sound but the rippling of the water....

"He's a sickly fellow.... Maybe he'll die soon..." said Silan Petrov in a muffled voice.

"I hope to God it happens soon!" murmured Masha in a fervid voice, and made a sign of the cross.

The beams of the spring sun streamed in a flood of sparkling gold and rainbow on the water. A wind rose, and everything quivered into life, stirred and smiled.... The blue sky amid the clouds smiled too at the sun-kissed waters. The clouds were now left behind the rafts.

There, gathered in a dark heavy cluster, they hung irresolute and motionless over the broad river, as if contemplating a way of escape from the living spring sun, rich with joy and lustre, the inveterate enemy of these mothers of winter blizzards who had tarried before the onset of spring.

In front of the rafts the clear blue sky shone brightly, and the sun, still matutinally fresh but vernally brilliant. mounted majestically into the azure depths of the heavens out of the purple-gold waves of the river.

To the right loomed the tawny ridge of the hilly bank in a green girdle of forests, and to the left the pale emerald carpet of the meadows gleamed in a diamond spangle of dew.

The succulent smell of the earth, of new-born grass and the resinous odours of the pine were wafted on the air.

Silan Petrov threw a look at the oarsmen behind.

Sergei and Mitya stood motionless at their oars, but it was too far to discern the expression on their faces.

He shifted his glance to Masha.

She was chilled. Standing by her oar, she shrank into a small round ball. All bathed in sunlight, she gazed before her with wistful eyes, her lips parted in that elusive alluring smile that makes even an unattractive woman seem fascinating and adorable.

"Keep a lookout there, lads! Oho!" roared Silan Petrov with all the power of his lungs, feeling a mighty surge of elation rising in his broad chest.

His shout seemed to send everything rocking, and long did the startled echoes resound over the hilly bank.

TWENTY-SIX MEN AND A GIRL

WE WERE TWENTY-SIX MEN, twenty-six living machines cooped up in a dark hole of a basement where from morn till night we kneaded dough, making pretzels and cracknels. The windows of our basement faced a sunken area lined with bricks that were green with slime; the windows outside were encased in a close-set iron grating, and no ray of sunshine could reach us through the panes which were covered with meal. Our boss had fenced the windows off to prevent any of his bread going to beggars or to those of our comrades who were out of work and starving—our boss called us a bunch of rogues and gave us tainted tripe for dinner instead of meat....

Stuffy and crowded was life in that stony dungeon beneath a low-hanging ceiling covered by soot and cobwebs. Life was hard and sickening within those thick walls smeared with dirt stains and mildew.... We got up at five in the morning, heavy with lack of sleep, and at six, dull and listless, we sat down to the table to make pretzels and cracknels out of the dough our comrades had prepared while we were sleeping. And all day long, from morning till ten o'clock at night some of us sat at the table kneading the stiff dough and swaying the body to fight numbness, while others were mixing flour and water. And all day long the simmering water in the cauldron where the pretzels were cooking gurgled pensively and sadly, and the baker's shovel clattered angrily and swiftly on the hearthstone, throwing slippery cooked pieces of dough onto the hot bricks. From morning till night the wood burned at one end of the oven, and the ruddy glow of the flames flickered on the bakery walls, as though grinning at us. The huge oven resembled the ugly head of some fantastic monster thrust up from under the floor, its wide-open jaws ablaze with glowing fire breathing incandescent flames and heat at us, and watching our ceaseless toil through two sunken air-holes over its forehead. These

two hollows were like eyes—the pitiless impassive eyes of a monster; they looked at us with an invariable dark scowl, as though
weary with looking at slaves of whom nothing human could be
expected, and whom they despised with the cold contempt of wisdom.

Day in, day out, amid the meal dust and the grime that we
brought in on our feet from the yard, in the smelly stuffiness of
the hot basement, we kneaded the dough and made pretzels which
were sprinkled with our sweat, and we hated our work with a
fierce hatred, and never ate what our hands had made, preferring
black rye bread to pretzels. Sitting at a long table facing one
another—nine men on each side—our hands and fingers worked
mechanically through the long hours, and we had grown so accustomed to our work that we no longer watched our movements.
And we had grown so accustomed to one another that each of us
knew every furrow on his comrades' faces. We had nothing to talk
about, we were used to that, and were silent all the time—unless
we swore, for there is always something one can swear at a man
for, especially one's comrade. But we rarely swore at each other—
is a man to blame if he is half-dead, if he is like a stone image,
if all his senses are blunted by the crushing burden of toil? Silence is awful and painful only for those who have said all there
is to say; but to people whose words are still unspoken, silence is
simple and easy.... Sometimes we sang, and this is how our song
would begin: during the work somebody would suddenly heave a
deep sigh, like a weary horse, and begin softly to sing one of
those long-drawn songs whose mournfully tender melody always
lighten the heavy burden of the singer's heart. One of the men
would sing while we listened in silence to the lonely song, and it
would fade and die away beneath the oppressive basement ceiling
like the languishing flames of a campfire in the steppe on a wet
autumn night, when the grey sky hangs over the earth like a roof
of lead. Then another singer would join the first, and two voices
would float drearily and softly in the stuffy heat of our crowded
pen. And then suddenly several voices at once would take up the
song—it would be lashed up like a wave, grow stronger and louder, and seem to break open the damp, heavy walls of our stony
prison....

All the twenty-six are singing; loud voices, brought to harmony by long practice, fill the workshop; the song is cramped for
room; it breaks against the stone walls, moaning and weeping, and
stirs the heart with a gentle prickly pain, reopening old wounds
and wakening anguish in the soul.... The singers draw deep and
heavy sighs; one will suddenly break off and sit listening for a
long time to his comrades singing, then his voice will mingle again
in the general chorus. Another will cry out dismally: "Ach!"
singing with closed eyes, and maybe he sees the broad torrent of
sound as a road leading far away, a wide road lit up by the brilliant sun, and he himself walking along it....

The flames in the oven still flicker, the baker's shovel still
scrapes on the brick, the water in the cauldron still bubbles and
gurgles, the firelight on the wall still flutters in silent laughter....
And we chant out, through words not our own, the dull ache within us, the gnawing grief of living men deprived of the sun, the
grief of slaves. And so we lived, twenty-six men, in the basement
of a big stone house, and so hard was our life. that it seemed as
though the three stories of the house were built on our shoulders....

Besides our songs there was something else that we loved and
cherished, something that perhaps filled the place of the sun for
us. On the second floor of our house there was a gold embroidery
workshop, and there, among many girl hands, lived sixteen-year
old Tanya, a housemaid. Every morning a little pink face with
blue merry eyes would be pressed to the pane of the little window
cut into the door of our workshop leading into the passage, and a
sweet ringing voice would call out to us:

"Jail-birdies! Give me some pretzels!"

We would all turn our heads to the sound of that clear voice
and look kindly and joyfully at the pure girlish face that smiled
at us so sweetly. We liked to see the nose squashed against the
glass, the little white teeth glistening from under rosy lips parted
in a smile. We would rush to open the door for her, jostling each
other, and there she would be, so winsome and sunny, holding
out her apron, standing before us with her little head slightly tilted, and her face all wreathed in smiles. A thick long braid of

chestnut hair hung over her shoulder on her breast. We grimy,
ignorant, ugly men look up at her—the threshold rises four steps
above the floor—look up at her with raised heads and wish her
good morning, and our words of greeting are special words, found
only for her. When we speak to her our voices are softer,
our joking lighter. Everything we have for her is special. The baker draws out of the oven a shovelful of the crustiest browned pretzels
and shoots them adroitly into Tanya's apron.

"Mind the boss doesn't catch you!" we warn her. She laughs
roguishly and cries merrily:

"Good-bye jail-birdies!" and vanishes in a twinkling like a
little mouse.

And that is all. . . . But long after she has gone we talk about
her—we say the same things we said the day before and earlier,
because she, and we, and everything around us are the same they
were the day before and earlier. . . . It is very painful and hard
when a man lives, and nothing around him changes, and if it
doesn't kill the soul in him, the longer he lives the more painful
does the immobility of things surrounding him become. . . . We always talked of women in a way that sometimes made us feel
disgusted with ourselves and our coarse shameless talk. That is
not surprising, since the women we knew did not probably deserve
to be talked of in any other way. But of Tanya we never said a
bad word; no one of us ever dared to touch her with his hand
and she never heard a loose joke from any of us. Perhaps it was
because she never stayed long—she would flash before our gaze
like a star falling from the heavens and vanish. Or perhaps it was
because she was small and so very beautiful, and everything that
is beautiful inspires respect, even with rough men. Moreover,
though hard labour was turning us into dumb oxen, we were only
human beings, and like all human beings, could not live without
an object of worship. Finer than she there was nobody about us,
and nobody else paid attention to us men living in the basement—
though there were dozens of tenants in the house. And finally—
probably chiefly—we regarded her as something that belonged to
us, something that existed thanks only to our pretzels; we made it
our duty to give her hot pretzels, and this became our daily sacri-
fice to the idol, almost a holy rite, that endeared her to us ever

more from day to day. Besides pretzels we gave Tanya a good
deal of advice—to dress warmly, not to run quickly upstairs, not
to carry heavy bundles of firewood. She listened to our counsels
with a smile, retorted with a laugh and never obeyed them, but we
did not take offence—we were satisfied to show our solicitude for her.

Often she asked us to do things for her. She would, for
instance, ask us to open a refractory door in the cellar or chop some
wood, and we would gladly and with a peculiar pride do these
things for her and anything else she asked.

But when one of us asked her to mend his only shirt, she sniffed
scornfully and said:

"Catch me! Not likely!"

We enjoyed a good laugh at the silly fellow's expense, and
never again asked her to do anything. We loved her—and there
all is said. A man always wants to foist his love on somebody or
other, though it frequently oppresses, sometimes sullies, and his
love may poison the life of a fellow creature, for in loving he
does not respect the object of his love. We had to love Tanya, for
there was no one else we could love.

At times one of us would suddenly begin to argue something
like this:

"What's the idea of making such a fuss over the kid? What's
there so remarkable about her anyway?"

We'd soon brusquely silence the fellow who spoke like that—
we had to have something we could love: we found it, and loved
it, and what we twenty-six loved stood for each of us, it was our
holy of holies, and anybody who went against us in this matter
was our enemy. We love, perhaps, what is not really good, but
then there are twenty-six of us, and we therefore want the object
of our adoration to be held sacred by others.

Our love is no less onerous than hate ... and, perhaps, that
is why some stiff-necked people claim that our hate is more flattering than love.... But why do they not shun us if that is so?

In addition to the pretzel bakehouse our boss had a bun bakery.
It was situated in the same house, and only a wall divided it
from our hole. The bun bakers, however, of whom there were
four, held themselves aloof from us, considered their work cleaner

than ours, and themselves, therefore, better men; they never visit-
ed our workshop, and treated us with mocking scorn whenever
they met us in the yard. Neither did we visit them—the boss banned
such visits for fear we would steal buns. We did not like the
bun bakers, because we envied them—their work was easier than
ours, they got better wages, they were fed better, they had a roomy,
airy workshop, and they were all so clean and healthy, and
hence so odious. We, on the other hand, were all a yellow grey-
faced lot; three of us were ill with syphilis, some were scabby,
and one was crippled by rheumatism. On holidays and off-days
they used to dress up in suits and creaking high boots, two of
them possessed accordions, and all used to go out for a stroll in
the park, whilst we were dressed in filthy tatters, with rags or
bast shoes on our feet, and the police wouldn't let us into the park
—now, could we love the bun bakers?

And one day we learned that their chief baker had taken to
drink, that the boss had dismissed him and taken on another in
his place, and that the new man was an ex-soldier who went about in
a satin waistcoat and had a watch on a gold chain. We were curious to have a look at that dandy, and every now and then one
of us would run out into the yard in the hope of seeing him.

But he came to our workshop himself. Kicking open the door
he stood in the doorway, smiling, and said to us:

"Hullo! How do you do, boys!"

The frosty air rushing through the door in a smoky cloud eddied
round his feet, while he stood in the doorway looking down at
us, his large yellow teeth flashing from under his fair swaggering moustache. His waistcoat was indeed unique—a blue affair,
embroidered with flowers, and all glittering, with buttons made of
some kind of red stone. The chain was there too....

He was a handsome fellow, was that soldier—tall, strong, with
ruddy cheeks and big light eyes that had a nice look in them—a
kind, clean look. On his head he wore a white stiffly starched cap,
and from under an immaculately clean apron peeped the pointed
toes of a highly polished pair of fashionable boots.

Our chief baker politely asked him to close the door. He com-
plied unhurriedly and began questioning us about the boss. We
fell over each other telling him that the boss was a skinflint, a

crook, a scoundrel and a tormentor—we told him everything there
was to tell about the boss that couldn't be put in writing here.
The soldier listened, twitching his moustache and regarding us with
that gentle, clear look of his.

"You've a lot of girls around here..." he said suddenly.

Some of us laughed politely, others pulled sugary faces, and
some one informed the soldier that there were nine bits in the
place.

"Use 'em?" asked the soldier with a knowing wink.

Again we laughed, a rather subdued, embarrassed laugh....
Many of us would have liked to make the soldier believe they were
as gay lads as he was, but they couldn't do it, none of us could
do it. Somebody confessed as much, saying quietly:

"How comes we...."

"M'yes, you're a long way off!" said the soldier convincedly,
subjecting us to a close scrutiny. "You're not ... er, up to the
mark.... Ain't got the character... the proper shape ... you
know, looks! Looks is what a woman likes about a man! Give
her a regular body ... everything just so! Then of course she likes
a bit of muscle.... Likes an arm to be an arm, here's the stuff!"

The soldier pulled his right hand out of his pocket, with the
sleeve rolled back to the elbow, and held it up for us to see....
He had a strong, white arm covered with shining golden hair.

"The leg, the chest—everything must be firm.... And then a
man's got to be properly dressed ... in shipshape form.... Now,
the women just fall for me. Mind you, I don't call 'em or tempt
'em—they hang about my neck five at a time...."

He sat down on a sack of flour and spent a long time in telling
us how the women loved him and how dashingly he treated them.
Then he took his leave, and when the door closed behind him with
a squeak, we sat on in a long silence, meditating over him and
his stories. Then suddenly everybody spoke up at once, and it
transpired that we had all taken a liking to him. Such a simple,
nice fellow, the way he came in, sat down, and chatted. Nobody
ever came to see us, nobody talked to us like that, in a friendly
way.... And we kept on talking about him and his future success
with the seamstresses, who, on meeting us in the yard, either
steered clear of us with lips offensively pursed, or bore straight down

on us as though we did not stand in their path at all. And we
only admired them, in the yard or when they passed our windows,
dressed in cute little caps and fur coats in the winter, and in
flowery hats with bright coloured parasols in the summer. But
among ourselves we spoke of these girls in a way that, had they
heard us, would have made them mad with shame and insult.

"I hope he doesn't ... spoil little Tanya!" said the chief baker
suddenly in a tone of anxiety.

We were all struck dumb by this statement. We had somehow
forgotten Tanya—the soldier seemed to have blotted her out with
his large, handsome figure. Then a noisy argument broke out: some
said that Tanya would not stand for it, some asserted that she
would be unable to resist the soldier's charms, and others proposed to break the fellow's bones in the event of him making love to
Tanya. Finally, all decided to keep a watch on the soldier and
Tanya, and warn the kid to beware of him.... That put a stop
to the argument.

About a month passed. The soldier baked buns, went out with
the seamstresses, frequently dropped in to see us, but never said
anything about his victories—all he did was to turn up his moustache and lick his chops.

Tanya came every morning for her pretzels and was invariably
gay, sweet and gentle. We tried to broach the subject of the soldier with her—she called him "a pop-eyed dummy" and other funny names and that set our minds at rest. We were proud of our
little girl when we saw how the seamstresses clung to the soldier.
Tanya's attitude towards him bucked us all up, and under her
influence as it were, we ourselves began to evince towards him an
attitude of scorn. We loved her more than ever, and greeted her
more gladly and kindly in the mornings.

One day, however, the soldier dropped in on us a little the
worse for drink, sat down and began to laugh, and when we asked
him what he was laughing at, he explained:

"Two of them have had a fight over me.... Lida and Grusha....
You should have seen what they did to each other! A regular
scream, ha-ha! One of 'em grabbed the other by the hair, dragged
her all over the floor into the passage, then got on top of her ...

ha-ha-ha! Scratched each other's mugs, tore their clothes. . . . Wasn't that funny! Now, why can't these females have a straight fight? Why do they scratch, eh?"

He sat on a bench, looking so clean and healthy and cheerful, laughing without a stop. We said nothing. Somehow he was odious to us this time.

"Why am I such a lucky devil with the girls? It's a scream! Why, I just wink my eye and the trick's done!"

He raised his white hands covered with glossy hairs and brought them down on his knees with a slap. He surveyed us with a look of pleased surprise, as though himself genuinely astonished at the lucky turn of his affairs with the ladies. His plump ruddy physiognomy shone with smug pleasure and he repeatedly passed his tongue over his lips.

Our chief baker angrily rattled his shovel on the hearth and suddenly said sarcastically:

"It's no great fun felling little fir trees—I'd like to see what you'd do with a pine!"

"Eh, what? Were you talking to me?" asked the soldier.

"Yes, you. . . ."

"What did you say?"

"Never mind. . . . Let it lay. . . ."

"Here, hold on! What's it all about? What d'you mean— pine?"

Our baker did not reply. His shovel moved swiftly in the oven, tossing in boiled pretzels and discharging the baked ones noisily onto the floor where boys sat threading them on bast strings. He seemed to have forgotten the soldier. But the latter suddenly got excited. He rose to his feet and stepped up to the oven, exposing himself to the imminent danger of being struck in the chest by the shovel handle that whisked spasmodically in the air.

"Now, look the—who d'you mean? That's an insult. . . . Why, there ain't a girl that could resist me! No fear! And here are you, hinting things against me. . . ."

Indeed, he appeared to be genuinely offended. Evidently the only source of his self-respect was his ability to seduce women: perhaps this ability was the only living attribute he could boast, the only thing that made him feel a human being.

There are some people for whom life holds nothing better or higher than a malady of the soul or flesh. They cherish it throughout life, and it is the sole spring of life to them. While suffering from it they nourish themselves on it. They complain about it to people and in this manner command the interest of their neighbours. They exact a toll of sympathy from people, and this is the only thing in life they have. Deprive them of that malady, cure them of it, and they will be utterly miserable, because they will lose the sole sustenance of their life and become empty husks. Sometimes a man's life is so poor that he is perforce obliged to cultivate a vice and thrive on it. One might say that people are often addicted to vice through sheer boredom.

The soldier was stung to the quick. He bore down on our baker, whining:

"No, you tell me—who is it?"

"Shall I tell you?" said the baker, turning on him suddenly.

"Well?"

"D'you know Tanya?"

"Well?"

"Well, there you are! See what you can do there. ..."

"Me?"

"Yes, you."

"Her? Easier'n spitting!"

"We'll see!"

"You'll see! Ha-a!"

"Why, she'll. ..."

"It won't take a month!"

"You're cocky, soldier, ain't you?"

"A fortnight! I'll show you! Who did you say? Tanya? Pshaw!"

"Come on, get out, you're in the way!"

"A fortnight, and the trick's done! Oh, you!..."

"Get out!"

The baker suddenly flew into a rage and brandished his shovel. The soldier fell back in amazement, then regarded us all for a while in silence, muttered grimly "All right!" and went out.

All through this argument we had kept our peace, our interest having been engaged in the conversation. But when the soldier left we all broke out into loud and animated speech.

Somebody cried out to the baker:

"That's a bad business you've started, Pavel!"

"Get on with your work!" snapped the baker.

We realized that the soldier had been put on his high ropes and that Tanya was in danger. Yet, while realizing this, we were all gripped by a tense but thrilling curiosity as to what would be the outcome of it. Would Tanya hold her own against the soldier? We almost unanimously voiced the conviction:

"Tanya? She'll hold her ground! She ain't easy prey!"

We were terribly keen on testing our idol; we assiduously tried to convince each other that our idol was a staunch idol and would come out on top in this engagement. We ended up by expressing our doubts as to whether we had sufficiently goaded the soldier, fearing that he would forget the wager and that we would have to prick his conceit some more. Henceforth a new exciting interest had come into our lives, something we had never known before. We argued among ourselves for days on end; we all somehow seemed to have grown cleverer, spoke better and more. It seemed as though we were playing a sort of game with the devil, and the stake on our side was Tanya. And when we had learned from the bun bakers that the soldier had started to "make a dead set for Tanya" our excitement rose to such a furious pitch and life became such a thrilling experience for us that we did not even notice how the boss had taken advantage of our wrought up feelings to throw in extra work by raising the daily knead to fourteen poods of dough. We didn't even seem to tire of the work. Tanya's name was all day long on our lips. And we awaited her morning visits with a peculiar impatience. At times we fancied that when she came in to see us it would be a different Tanya, not the one we always knew.

We told her nothing, however, about the wager. We never asked her any questions and treated her in the same good-natured loving way. But something new had crept into our attitude, something that was alien to our former feelings for Tanya—and that new element was keen curiosity, keen and cold like a blade of steel....

"Boys! Time's up today!" said the baker one morning as he began work.

We were well aware of it without his reminder. Yet we all started.

"You watch her.... She'll soon come in!" suggested the baker. Some one exclaimed in a tone of regret:

"It's not a thing the eye can catch!"

And again a lively noisy argument sprang up. Today, at length, we would know how clean and incontaminate was the vessel in which we had laid all the treasure that we possessed. That morning we suddenly realized for the first time that we were gambling for high stakes, that this test of our idol might destroy it for us altogether. All these days we had been hearing that the soldier was doggedly pursuing Tanya with his attentions, but for some reason none of us asked her what her attitude was towards him. She continued regularly to call on us every morning for her pretzels and was always her usual self.

On that day, too, we soon heard her voice:

"Jail-birdies! I've come...."

We hastened to let her in, and when she came in we greeted her, contrary to our custom, with silence. We looked hard at her and were at a loss what to say to her, what to ask her. We stood before her in a silent sullen crowd. She was obviously surprised at the unusual reception, and suddenly we saw her turn pale, look anxious and stir restlessly. Then in a choky voice she asked:

"Why are you all so ... strange!"

"What about you?" threw in the baker in a grim tone, his eyes fixed on her face.

"What about me?"

"Nothing....."

"Well, give me the pretzels, quick...."

"Plenty of time!" retorted the baker without stirring, his eyes still glued on her face.

She suddenly turned and disappeared through the door.

The baker picked up his shovel, and turning to the oven, let fall calmly:

"Well—she's fixed! The soldier's done it... the blighter!..."

We shambled back to the table like a herd of jostling sheep, sat down in silence and apathetically set to our work. Presently some one said:

"Maybe it isn't...."

"Shut up! Enough of that!" shouted the baker.

We all knew him for a clever man, cleverer than any of us. And that shout of his we understood as meaning that he was convinced of the soldier's victory.... We felt sad and perturbed....

At twelve o'clock—the lunch hour—the soldier came in. He was, as always, clean and spruce and—as always—looked us straight in the eyes. We felt too ill at ease to look at him.

"Well, my dear sirs, d'you want me to show you what a soldier can do?" he said with a proud sneer. "You go out into the passage and peep through the cracks ... get me?"

We trooped into the passage, and tumbling over each other, pressed our faces to the chinks in the wooden wall looking onto the yard. We did not have to wait long. Soon Tanya came through the yard with a hurried step and anxious look, skipping over puddles of thawed snow and mud. She disappeared through the door of the cellar. Presently the soldier sauntered past whistling, and he went in too. His hands were thrust into his pockets and he twitched his moustache....

It was raining and we saw the drops falling into the puddles which puckered up at the impacts. It was a grey wet day—a very bleak day. Snow still lay on the roofs, while on the ground dark patches of slush stood out here and there. On the roofs too the snow was covered with a brownish coating of dirt. It was cold and disagreeable, waiting in that passage....

The first to come out of the cellar was the soldier. He walked leisurely across the yard, twitching his moustache, his hands deep in his pockets—much the same he always was.

Then Tanya came out. Her eyes ... her eyes shone with joy and happiness, and her lips smiled. And she walked as though in a dream, swaying, with uncertain gait....

It was more than we could endure. We all made a sudden rush for the door, burst into the yard and began yelling and whistling at her in a fierce, loud, savage uproar.

She started when she saw us and stood stock-still, her feet in a dirty puddle. We surrounded her and cursed her with a sort of malicious glee in a torrent of profanity and shameless taunts.

We did it unhurriedly, quietly, seeing that she had no way of escape from the circle around her and that we could jeer at her to our heart's content. It is strange, but we did not hit her.

She stood amid us and turned her head from side to side, listening to our insults. And we ever more fiercely, ever more furiously, flung at her the dirt and poison of our wrath.

Her face drained of life. Her blue eyes, which the moment before had looked so happy, were dilated, her breath came in gasps and her lips quivered.

And we, having surrounded her, were wreaking our vengeance on her—for had she not robbed us? She had belonged to us, we had spent our best sentiments on her, and though that best was a mere beggar's pittance, we were twenty-six and she was one, and there was no anguish we could inflict that was fit to meet her guilt! How we insulted her!... She said not a word, but simply gazed at us with a look of sheer terror and a long shudder went through her body.

We guffawed, we howled, we snarled.... Other people joined us.... One of us pulled the sleeve of Tanya's blouse....

Suddenly her eyes blazed; she raised her hands in a slow gesture to put her hair straight, and said loudly but calmly, straight into our faces:

"Oh, you miserable jail-birds!..."

And she bore straight down on us, just as if we had not been there, had not stood in her path. Indeed, that is why none of us proved to be in her path.

When she was clear of our circle she added just a loudly without turning round, in a tone of scorn and pride:

"Oh, you filthy swine.... You beasts...." And she departed—straight, beautiful, and proud.

We were left standing in the middle of the yard amid the mud, under the rain and a grey sky that had no sun in it....

Then we too shuffled back to our damp stony dungeon. As of old, the sun never peered through our window, and Tanya came never more!...

MALVA

THE SEA—was laughing.

Stirred by the light sultry breeze it quivered, and covered with tiny ripples which reflected the sun's rays with dazzling brilliance it smiled at the blue sky with a thousand silvery smiles. The vast space between the sea and the sky rang with the merry sounds of splashing waves as they raced, one behind the other, towards the sloping beach of the spur. The splashing waves and the glint of the sun reflected by the thousands of ripples on the sea merged harmoniously in continuous movement, full of animation and joy. The sun was happy because it was shining, and the sea—because it reflected the sun's jubilant light.

The wind fondly stroked the silky breast of the sea, the sun warmed it with its burning rays, and the sea, sighing drowsily under these tender caresses, filled the hot air with a salty fragrance. The greenish waves breaking on the yellow beach bespattered it with white foam, which melted on the hot sand with a soft sigh and kept it moist.

The long, narrow spur looked like an enormously tall tower which had fallen from the shore into the sea. Its slender spire cut into the limitless expanse of sparkling water, its base was lost in the distant sultry haze which concealed the mainland, whence, wafted by the wind, came a repugnant smell that was inexplicable and offensive here, in the midst of the immaculate sea, under the bright blue dome of the sky.

On the beach, which was strewn with fish scales, a fishing net hung on poles driven into the ground, casting spider-web shadows on the sand. Several large boats and a small one were lying in a row, and the waves, running up the beach, seemed to beckon to them. Boat hooks, oars, baskets and barrels lay scattered in disorder, and among them stood a shack built of willow branches and reeds, and covered with bast matting. Before the entrance of the

shack a pair of felt boots were stuck, soles upward to the sky, on
a couple of gnarled sticks. Above this chaos towered a tall mast
with a red rag at its head, fluttering in the wind.

In the shade of one of the boats lay Vassili Legostyev, the watchman on the spur, which was the outpost of Grebenshchikov's fisheries. Vassili was lying on his stomach, supporting his chin on
the palms of his hands, gazing into the distant sea at the barely
visible strip of shore of the mainland. His eyes were fixed on a
tiny black speck on the water, and it was with infinite pleasure
that he watched it growing larger and larger as it drew near.

Screwing up his eyes to shield them from the dazzling sun rays
reflected in the water, he smiled with satisfaction—this was Malva
coming! She will come and laugh, and her breasts will quiver
enticingly. She will embrace him with her round soft arms, greet
him with a resounding kiss that will frighten the sea-gulls, and
tell him all the news about what is going on over there, on shore.
Together they will cook some excellent chowder, drink vodka,
stretch out on the sand, talk and fondle each other, and then, when
the shadow of evening falls, they will put the kettle on, drink tea
with tasty pretzels and then go to sleep.... That is what happened
every Sunday and on every holiday. Early in the morning he, as
usual, will take her to the mainland, across the still sleepy sea, in
the fresh twilight of the dawn. She will sit dozing in the stern of
the boat and he will gaze at her as he rowed. How funny she looked
at such times, funny and yet lovable, like a well-fed cat. Perhaps she will slip from the seat to the bottom of the boat, curl up
and fall fast asleep. She often did that....

That day even the seagulls were dazed by the heat. Some were
sitting on the sand in a row with drooping wings and open beaks;
others were lazily rocking on the waves, making no sound, and
desisting from their customary rapacious activity.

It seemed to Vassili that there was somebody else in the boat besides Malva. Had that Seryozhka hooked on to her again? Vassili
turned heavily over on the sand, sat up, and shading his eyes with
his hand, peered anxiously across the sea, trying to make out who
else was in the boat. Malva was sitting in the stern and steering.
The man at the oars was not Seryozhka. He was obviously not used
to rowing. Malva wouldn't have to steer if Seryozhka were with her.

"Ahoy!" Vassili shouted impatiently.

Startled by the cry, the sea-gulls on the sand rose to their feet and stood on the alert.

"A-h-o-o-y!" came Malva's ringing voice from the boat.

"Who's that with you?"

A laugh came in reply.

"She-devil!" muttered Vassili, swearing under his breath and spitting in disgust.

He was dying to know who was in the boat with Malva. Rolling a cigarette, he gazed intently at the neck and back of the oarsman. He could distinctly hear the splash of the water at the stroke of the oars; the sand crunched under his bare feet.

"Who's that with you?" he shouted when he discerned a queer, unfamiliar smile on Malva's handsome face.

"Wait and see!" she shouted back with a laugh.

The oarsman turned his face to the beach and glancing at Vassili also laughed.

The watchman frowned, trying to think who the stranger could be. His face seemed familiar.

"Pull hard!" Malva commanded.

The waves carried the boat almost half length up the beach. It heeled over on its side and struck fast while the waves slipped back into the sea. The oarsman jumped out of the boat and said:

"Hello, father!"

"Yakov!" exclaimed Vassili in a choking voice, more amazed than pleased.

The two embraced and kissed each other, three times, on the lips and cheeks. The expression of Vassili's face was a mixture of pleasure and embarrassment.

"... I looked and looked ... and felt a tickling in my heart. I wondered what it was.... So it was you? Who could have thought it? At first I thought it was Seryozhka, but then I saw it wasn't. And it turns out to be you!"

As he spoke Vassili stroked his beard with one hand and ges-ticulated with the other. He was dying to look at Malva, but the smiling eyes of his son were turned on his face and their brightness confused him. The satisfaction he felt at having such a fine, strapping lad for a son was marred by the embarrassment he felt at the presence of his mistress. He stood in front of Yakov, stepping from one foot to the other, and fired question after question at him without waiting for an answer. Everything was mixed up in his head and he almost got a shock when he heard Malva say mockingly:

"Don't stand there jumping for joy! Take him into the shack and treat him to something!"

He turned to her. A mocking smile played on her lips. He had never seen her smile like that before; and her whole body—round, soft and fresh as always—looked different somehow; it looked strange. She shifted her greenish eyes from father to son, cracking melon seeds with her small white teeth. Yakov looked from one to the other with a smile, and for several moments, unpleasant for Vassili, the three remained silent.

"Yes, in a minute!" Vassili said suddenly, starting for the shack. "You get out of the sun while I go and get some water.... We'll cook some chowder.... I'll treat you to some chowder, Yakov, such as you've never tasted before! In the meantime, you two, make yourselves comfortable. I'll be back in a minute."

He picked up a kettle from the ground near the shack, walked briskly towards the net and was soon hidden in its grey folds.

Malva and Yakov stepped towards the shack.

"Here you are, my handsome lad! I've brought you to your father!" said Malva, casting a sidelong glance at Yakov's sturdy figure, at his face framed in a short, brown curly beard, and at his sparkling eyes.

"Yes, we've arrived," he answered, turning his face towards her eagerly. "How good it is here! And the sea! Isn't it fine!"

"Yes, it's a wide sea.... Well, has your father aged much?"

"No, not very much. I expected to find him much greyer. He has only a few grey hairs.... And how hale and hearty he still looks!"

"How long is it you haven't seen him, you say?"

"About five years, I think.... Since he left home. I was getting on for seventeen then...."

They entered the shack. It was stuffy in there and the bast sacks lying on the ground smelt of fish. They sat down—Yakov on a thick tree stump, and Malva on a heap of sacking. Between them stood a sawn off barrel, the upturned bottom of which served as a table. They sat gazing at each other in silence.

"Well ... I don't know.... I'd like to if I could get a job here."

"You'll get a job here all right," said Malva confidently, probing him with her greenish, enigmatically half-closed eyes.

Yakov, keeping his eyes off the woman, wiped the perspiration from his face with the sleeve of his blouse.

Suddenly she laughed.

"I suppose your mother must have sent greetings and a message to your father," she said.

Yakov glanced at her, frowned and answered curtly:

"Of course.... Why do you ask?"

"Oh, just like that!"

Yakov didn't like that laugh—it was so tantalizing. He turned away from the woman and tried to remember the message his mother had given him.

His mother had seen him off to the outskirts of the village. Leaning against a wattle fence she had said, speaking rapidly, and rapidly blinking her dry eyes:

"Tell him, Yasha.... For the sake of Christ, tell him that after all he is a father! ... Your mother is all alone, tell him.... She's been all alone for five long years! Tell him she is getting old! For God's sake, tell him that, Yasha! Your mother will be an old woman soon.... And she's all alone! Working hard. For the sake of Christ, tell him that! ..."

And she had wept silently, hiding her face in her apron.

Yakov had not felt sorry for her then, but he felt so now.

He glanced at Malva and frowned.

"Well, here I am!" exclaimed Vassili, appearing in the shack with a fish in one hand and a knife in the other.

He had got rid of his embarrassment, concealing it deep down his bosom, and now looked at the two quite calmly, except that his movements betrayed a fussiness that was unusual for him.

"I'll go and light the fire and then I'll come in and we'll have a long talk, eh, Yakov?" he said.

With that he left the shack again.

Malva continued to crack melon seeds, quite unceremoniously staring at Yakov; but he, although dying to look at her, studiously kept his eyes off her.

After a time the silence became oppressive to him and he said:

"Oh, I've left my knapsack in the boat. I'll go and get it."

He got up leisurely and left the shack. Soon after Vassili returned. Leaning over towards Malva he demanded in a hurried and angry tone:

"Why did you come with him? What shall I tell him about you? What are you to me?"

"I came, and that's all there is to it!" Malva answered curtly.

"Oh, you ... silly woman! What shall I do now? Tell him right in his face? Spit it right out? I have a wife at home! His mother.... You ought to have understood that!"

"What's it got to do with me? Do you think I'm afraid of him? Or of you?" Malva asked contemptuously, screwing up her greenish eyes. "How funny you looked skipping in front of him! I could barely keep from laughing!"

"It may seem funny to you! But what am I going to do?"

"You should have thought of that before!"

"How was I to know that the sea would throw him up on to this shore like this?"

The crunching of sand underfoot told them of Yakov's approach and they cut the conversation short. Yakov brought in a light knapsack, threw it into a corner and glanced angrily at the woman out of the corner of his eye.

She went on zestfully cracking melon seeds. Vassili sat down on the tree stump and rubbing his knees with the palms of his hands he said with a smile:

"Well, so you're here. . . . What made you think of coming?"

"Oh, just like that. . . . We wrote to you. . . ."

"When? I never got the letter!"

"Is that so? But we wrote. . . ."

"The letter must have gone astray," said Vassili in a disappointed tone. "Devil take it! What do you think of it, eh? Just when you want it it goes astray!"

"So you don't know what's happened at home?" Yakov enquired, glancing at his father distrustfully.

"How should I know? I didn't get your letter."

Yakov then told him that their horse had died, that their stock of grain was all gone by the beginning of February, that he hadn't been able to get any work, that the hay had run out and the cow

had nearly died. They had dragged on somehow until April and
then decided that he, Yakov, should go to his father, after the
ploughing, for about three months, to earn some money. They wrote
to the father telling him of their decision and then they sold three
sheep, bought some grain and hay and ... well ... here he was!

"So that's how it is, is it?" exclaimed Vassili. "Humph....
But ... how's that? I sent you some money, didn't I?"

"It wasn't much, was it? We did some repairs to the house....
Maria got married and that cost us a bit.... We bought a plough....
Why, it's five years since you've been away!"

"Y-e-es! Th-a-at's so! It wasn't enough, you say?... Hey! The
chowder's running over!"

With that Vassili dashed out of the shack.

Squatting down in front of the fire over which the chowder
was boiling, Vassili absent-mindedly skimmed the chowder and threw
the scum into the fire. He was lost in deep reflection. What Yakov
had told him had not moved him very much, but it had roused in
him a feeling of hostility towards his wife and son. In spite of all the
money he had sent them during the five years, they had allowed the
farm to go to rack and ruin. Had Malva not been there he would
have given Yakov a piece of his mind. He had sense enough to
leave home without his father's permission, but he hadn't sense
enough to manage the farm! The farm, which Vassili had thought of
very rarely during the free and easy life he had been leading here,
suddenly leapt into his mind as a bottomless pit into which he had
been throwing his money during the past five years, as something
superfluous in his life, as something he had no use for. He stirred
the chowder with a spoon and sighed.

The small yellow flames of the fire looked pale and feeble in the
brilliant light of the sun. Blue wreaths of transparent smoke stretched
from the fire to the sea to meet the surf. Watching the smoke,
Vassili thought bitterly of the turn for the worse his life would
take now; it would be less free. Yakov had no doubt guessed that
Malva....

Malva was sitting in the shack confusing the lad with her mocking, challenging eyes, in which a smile played all the time.

"I suppose you've left a sweetheart at home," she said suddenly, looking Yakov straight in the face.

"Perhaps I have," answered Yakov reluctantly.

"Is she pretty?" Malva asked in a careless tone.

Yakov made no reply.

"Why don't you answer?.... Is she better-looking than me?"

Involuntarily he raised his eyes and looked the woman in the face. He saw her dark, round cheeks and full, moist, trembling lips, parted in a mocking smile. Her pink cotton blouse fitted her exceptionally well and outlined her well-rounded shoulders and high, supple breasts. But he took a dislike to her sly, half-closed, greenish, laughing eyes. He heaved a sigh.

"Why do you talk like that?" he said in a pleading voice, although he wanted to talk to her sternly.

"What other way should I talk?" she answered with a laugh.

"And you laugh.... Why?"

"I'm laughing at you!"

"Why? What have I done to you?" he asked angrily and cast his eyes down again.

She did not answer.

Yakov guessed what her relations with his father were, and this prevented him from speaking to her freely. His surmise did not surprise him. He had heard that men who go to work away from home have a good time, and he understood that a hale and hearty man like his father would find it hard to live without a woman for long. But for all that, he felt awkward in this woman's presence, and in his father's, too. Then he thought of his mother—a weary, complaining woman, slaving out there, in their village, knowing no rest. ...

"Supper's ready!" announced Vassili appearing in the shack.

"Get the spoons, Malva!"

Yakov glanced at his father and thought to himself:

"She must come here often since she knows where the spoons are kept."

Malva got the spoons and said she must go and wash them. There was also a bottle of vodka in the boat that she said she would go and fetch.

Father and son watched her leave the shack and when she was gone they sat together in silence. After a while Vassili asked Yakov:

"How did you come to meet her?"

"I went to the office to ask about you and she was there. . . . She says to me, she says: 'Why walk all that way along the sand? Let's go by boat. I'm going across to him too.' So we came."

"Aa-a-ah!. . . I often used to think to myself: 'I wonder what Yakov is like now?' "

The son looked into his father's face with a good-natured smile, and this smile lent Vassili courage.

"A nice little woman, isn't she . . . eh?" he asked.

"Not so bad," Yakov answered indefinitely, blinking his eyes.

"What the hell can a man do, little brother?" Vassili exclaimed, waving his arms. "I bore it patiently at first, but I couldn't stand it any longer! It's a habit. . . . I'm a married man! And besides, she mends my clothes, and one thing and another. Dear, oh dear! You can't escape from a woman any more than you can escape from death!" he concluded fervently.

"What's it got to do with me?" said Yakov. "It's your business. It's not for me to judge you."

But to himself he said:

"You can't tell me a woman like that would sit around and mend pants."

"Besides," said Vassili, "I'm only forty-five. . . . I don't spend much on her. She's not my wife."

"Of course not," Yakov agreed, and thought to himself: "But she empties your pockets all the same, I bet!"

Malva came back with a bottle of vodka and a string of pretzels. They sat down to eat the chowder. They ate in silence, sucking the fishbones with a loud noise and spitting them out on the sand near the door. Yakov ate a lot, and ate greedily. Evidently this pleased Malva, for her face lit up with a kindly smile as she watched him blow out his tanned cheeks and rapidly work his thick, moist lips. Vassili ate little, although he tried to appear as if his mind was concentrated on his food. He was obliged to do this so as to be able without interruption, and unperceived by his son and Malva, to think out a plan of action.

The soft music of the waves was interrupted by the rapacious screeching of the sea-gulls. The heat had become less oppressive and now and again a stream of cool air, impregnated with the smell of the sea, blew into the shack.

After the savoury chowder and the vodka Yakov's eyes became heavy. A vacuous smile mounted his lips, he began to hiccough and yawn, and he loked at Malva in a way that compelled Vassili to say to him:

"Go and lie down a bit, Yakov, my boy. Take a nap until the tea is ready. We'll wake you when it is."

"Yes. . . . I think I will," said Yakov, readily dropping down on a heap of sacks. "But . . . where are you two going? Ha-ha-ha!"

Embarrassed by that laugh, Vassili hastily left the shack; but Malva pursed her lips, raised her brows and said in answer to Yakov's query:

"Where we are going is no business of yours! What are you? You're only a boy! You don't understand these things yet!"

"What am I? All right! You wait . . . I'll show you! You think you're smart . . ." said Yakov in a loud voice as Malva left the shack.

He kept on mumbling for a little while longer and then fell asleep with a drunken, sated smile on his flushed face.

Vassili stuck three sticks into the ground, tied them together at the top, threw some bast sacking over them, lay down in the shade thus made with his arms under his head, and gazed into the sky. When Malva dropped down on the sand beside him he turned his face towards her. She saw that he was displeased and offended.

"What's the matter, aren't you glad to see your son?" she asked laughing.

"There he is . . . laughing at me. . . . Because of you!" growled Vassili.

"Oh! Because of me?" Malva asked in mock surprise.

"What do you think?"

"You miserable old sinner! What do you want me to do now? Stop coming to see you? All right, I won't!"

"Aren't you a witch!" said Vassili reproachfully. "Eh! You're all alike! He's laughing at me, and so are you. . . . And yet you are the closest friends I have! What are you laughing at me for you devils?" With that he turned away from Malva and remained silent.

Clasping her knees and slowly swaying her body Malva gazed at the merrily sparkling sea with her greenish eyes and smiled one of those triumphant smiles which women who are conscious of their beauty possess in such abundance.

A sailing boat was gliding over the water like a large, clumsy, grey-winged bird. It was a long way from the shore, and was receding still further from it to where the sea and the sky merged in blue infinity.

"Why don't you say something?" said Vassili.

"I'm thinking," answered Malva.

"What about?"

"Oh, nothing particular," answered Malva twitching her brows. After a pause she added: "Your son's a fine lad."

"What's that got to do with you?" exclaimed Vassili jealously.

"A lot!"

"Take care!" said Vassili casting at her a look of anger and suspicion. "Don't play the fool! I'm a quiet chap, but I'm a devil when I'm aroused. So don't tease me, or you'll be sorry for it!"

Doubling his fists he added through his clenched teeth:

"You were up to something as soon as you got here this morning. . . . I don't know what it is yet. . . . But take care, it'll go hard with you when I find out! And that smile of yours. . . . And everything else. . . . I know how to handle your kind, don't you worry!"

"Don't try to frighten me, Vassya," said Malva in an impassive tone without even looking at Vassili.

"Don't get up to any tricks then. . . ."

"And don't you threaten me. . . ."

"I'll give you a good thrashing if you get up to any of your larks," said Vassili flaring up.

"What? You'll thrash me?" said Malva, turning to Vassili and looking curiously into his excited face.

"Who do you think you are, a duchess? Yes, I'll thrash you!"

"And who do you think I am—your wife?" Malva asked calmly, and without waiting for a reply continued: "Because you're in the habit of beating your wife for no reason at all you think you'll do the same to me, don't you? But you're mistaken. I am my own mistress and I'm not afraid of anybody. But you—you're afraid of your son! It was a disgrace to see the way you danced in front of him this morning. And yet you dare threaten me!"

She tossed her head contemptuously and fell silent. Her cold contemptuous words quenched Vassili's anger. He had never seen her so beautiful before.

"There you go, off the deep end..." he growled. He was angry with her, but he could not help admiring her.

"And I'll tell you another thing!" Malva burst out. "You boasted to Seryozhka that you were like bread to me, that I couldn't live without you! You're wrong!... Perhaps it's not you that I love, and not you that I come to see, but this spot!" and with that she made a wide sweep with her hand. "Perhaps I like this place because it is deserted—nothing but sea and sky, and no disgusting people around. The fact that you are here makes no difference.... It's what I have to pay to come here.... If Seryozhka were here i'd come to him. If your son's here I shall go to him.... It would be better if nobody were here.... I'm sick of you all!... With my beauty I can always get a man when I want one, and I can choose the one I want."

"Is that so?" hissed Vassili, suddenly clutching Malva by the throat. "Is that the idea?"

He shook her, but she did not struggle, although her face was almost livid and her eyes were bloodshot. She merely placed her hands on Vassili's that were squeezing her throat, and stared into his face.

"So that's the sort you are?" said Vassili hoarsely, his rage gaining mastery over him. "You kept quiet about it up till now, you slut.... Cuddled me.... Petted me.... I'll show you!"

He forced her head down and with the utmost zest punched her in the neck—two heavy, swinging blows with his tightly clenched fist; it gave him the greatest pleasure to feel his fist come down upon her soft neck.

"Take that... you snake!" he said triumphantly, flinging her away from him.

She sank to the ground without even a gasp, and lay there on her back, silent and calm, dishevelled, flushed, but beautiful. Her greenish eyes flashed cold hatred at him from under their lashes, but he, panting from excitement, and conscious of a pleasant feeling of satisfaction at having given vent to his anger, failed to catch her glance, and when he looked at her triumphantly she smiled—

her full lips twitched, her eyes flashed, dimples appeared on her cheeks. Vassili looked at her in amazement.

"What is it, you she-devil?" he shouted, roughly pulling her arm.

"Vaska!" said Malva almost in a whisper. "Was it you who beat me?"

"Of course, who else?" answered Vassili, looking at Malva in perplexity, and not knowing what to do. Hit her again? But his anger had subsided, and he could not bear the thought of raising his hand against her again.

"That means you love me, doesn't it?" Malva whispered again, and that whisper sent a hot wave surging through his body.

"All right," he growled. "You didn't get half you deserved!"

"I thought you didn't love me any more. . . . I thought to myself: 'Now his son's come, he'll drive me away.'"

She burst into a queer laugh; it was much too loud.

"You little fool!" said Vassili, also laughing in spite of himself. "What's my son? He can't tell me what to do!"

He felt ashamed of himself and sorry for her, but remembering what she had said he added in a stern voice:

"My son has nothing to do with it. If I hit you, it's your own fault. You shouldn't have teased me."

"But I did it on purpose—to try you," she said, rubbing against his shoulder.

"To try me! What for? Well, now you know!"

"Never mind!" said Malva confidently, half closing her eyes. "I'm not angry with you. You beat me for love, didn't you? Well, I'll repay you for it. . . ."

She lowered her voice, and staring him straight in the face she repeated:

"Oh, how I'll repay you!"

To Vassili these words sounded like a promise, a pleasant one, and it stirred him sweetly. Smiling he asked:

"How? How will you repay?"

"Wait and see," said Malva very calmly, but her lips twitched.

"Oh, you sweet darling!" exclaimed Vassili, grasping her in the tight embrace of a lover. "Do you know," he added, "you've become dearer to me since I beat you! I mean it! I feel we are now of the same flesh and blood!"

The sea-gulls soared over their heads. The wind from the sea caressed them and carried the surf from the waves almost to their feet, and the irrepressible laughter of the sea rolled on and on. ...

"Yes, that's how things are," said Vassili, sighing with relief and pensively caressing the woman pressing against him. "How funny everything in this world is arranged—what is sinful is sweet! You don't understand anything. ... But sometimes I think about life and it scares me! Especially at night ... when I can't sleep. ... You look and you see the sea in front of you, the sky over your head and all around darkness, such black darkness that it gives you the creeps. ... And you are all alone! You feel so small, ever so small. The earth is trembling under your feet and there's nobody on it except yourself. I often wish you were with me then. ... At least, there'd be two of us."

Malva lay silent across his knee; her eyes were closed. Vassili's coarse but kind face, tanned by sun and wind, bent over her, his large, bleached beard tickled her neck. The woman did not move, only her breast rose and fell evenly. Vassili's eyes now wandered out to sea and now tarried on this breast, that was so close to him. He kissed her on the lips, slowly, without haste, smacking his own lips loudly, as if he were eating hot and thickly buttered porridge.

About three hours passed in this way. When the sun began to sink into the sea Vassili said in a dull voice:

"I'll go and put the kettle on for tea. Our guest will wake up soon."

Malva moved away from him, lazily like a pampered cat. He rose reluctantly and went into the shack. The woman watched him go through her slightly raised eyelashes and sighed, as one sighs when throwing off a heavy burden.

Later on the three sat around the fire drinking tea.

The setting sun tinted the sea with animated colours, the greenish waves were shot with purple and pearl.

Vassili, sipping his tea from a white mug, questioned his son about what was going on in their village, and he in his turn gave his recollections of it. Malva listened to their drawling conversation without intervening.

"So the old muzhiks at home are still carrying on, you say?" Vassili enquired.

"Yes, one way or another," answered Yakov.

"We muzhiks don't want much, do we? A roof over our heads, enough bread to eat, and a glass of vodka on holidays.... But we don't even get that. D'you think I'd have left home if we had been able to make a living? At home I'm my own master, the equal to everybody else in the village. But what am I here?... A servant!..."

"But you get more to eat here, and the work's easier...."

"Well, I wouldn't say that! Sometimes you work so hard that all the bones in your body ache. The main thing though, is that you work for a master. At home, you work for yourself."

"But you earn more," retorted Yakov.

In his heart of hearts Vassili agreed with his son. At home, in the village, life and work were harder than here, but for some reason he didn't want Yakov to know that. So he answered sternly:

"Have you counted the money we earn here? Now at home, in the village, my boy...."

"It's like in a pit, dark and crowded." Malva interrupted with a smile. "Especially for us women.... Nothing but tears."

"It's the same for women everywhere... and the light is the same... the same sun shines everywhere!" answered Vassili, looking at Malva with a frown.

"You're wrong there!" exclaimed Malva animatedly. "In the village I've got to marry whether I like it or not, and a married woman is an eternal slave: reap, spin, tend the cattle and bear children.... What's she got left for herself? Nothing but her husband's curses and blows...."

"It's not all blows," interrupted Vassili.

"But here I don't belong to anybody," said Malva, ignoring the interruption. "I'm as free as the sea-gull and can fly wherever I want to. Nobody can bar my way.... Nobody can touch me!"

"And if they do touch you?" asked Vassili with a smile, recalling what happened earlier in the day.

"If they do.... I will repay," Malva answered in a low voice. The light in her eyes died out.

Vassili laughed indulgently.

"Eh!... You're a game cat, but weak! You're a woman, and you talk like a woman. At home, in the village, a man needs a

woman as part of his life ... but here she exists only to play with."
After a slight pause he added: "To sin with."

They stopped talking.... Yakov said with a pensive sigh:
"The sea looks as if there's no end to it!"

All three gazed at the vast expanse of water stretching before
them.

"If only it were all land!" exclaimed Yakov, spreading his
arms out wide. "And black earth! And if we could plough it all!"

"Oh, that's what you'd like, is it?" said Vassili laughing good-
naturedly and looking approvingly at his son, whose face was flushed
with the desire he had expressed. It pleased him to hear the
lad express this love for the land. Perhaps it would soon call him
back to the village, away from the temptations that would beset him
here. And he, Vassili, would then be left alone with Malva, and
everything would go on as before.

"Yes, you are right, Yakov! That's what the peasant wants. The
peasant is strong on the land. As long as he is on the land he's
alive; once he gets off it—he's done for! A peasant without land is
like a tree without roots. It may be useful in some ways, but it can't
live long—it must rot! It has even lost its forest beauty—all bare
and stripped, a miserable looking thing!.... What you said was
right, Yakov."

The sea, taking the sun in its embrace, greeted it with the wel-
coming music of its waves, which the parting rays of the sun had
tinted with the most gorgeous colours. The divine source of light,
the creator of life, bid the sea farewell in an eloquent harmony of
colour in order to waken the slumbering land, far away from the
three who were watching it set, with the joyous rays of the radiant
dawn.

"By God, my heart seems to melt when I see the sun go down!"
said Vassili to Malva.

Malva made no reply. Yakov's blue eyes smiled as they swept
the sea to the distant horizon; and all three sat for a long time
gazing pensively in the direction where the last moments of the day
were passing away. In front of them gleamed the embers of the
fire. Behind, the night was unfolding its shadows around them. The
yellow sand assumed a darker hue. The sea-gulls had vanished.
Everything around became quiet and dreamingly caressing.... Even

the irrepressible waves racing to the beach seemed less merry and noisy than they had been in the daytime.

"Why am I sitting here? It's time to go," said Malva suddenly. Vassili shivered and glanced at his son.

"What's the hurry?" he grumbled. "Wait until the moon rises," he added.

"Why should I? I'm not afraid. This won't be the first time I've gone from here at night!"

Yakov glanced at his father, lowered his head to conceal a mocking smile, and then looked at Malva. She returned his stare, and he felt awkward under her gaze.

"All right then, go!" said Vassili, feeling displeased and sad.

Malva got up, said good night, and walked slowly along the beach. The waves rolled right up to her feet as if they were playing with her. In the sky the stars—its golden flowers—twinkled. Malva's bright-coloured blouse faded in the gloom as she proceeded further and further away from Vassili and his son who were following her with their eyes.

> *Darling, my darling,*
> *Quickly come to me.*
> *How I long to have you pressed*
> *Close against my breast!*

sang Malva in a high-pitched voice. It seemed to Vassili that she had halted and was waiting. He spat angrily and thought to himself: "She's doing that to tease me, the she-devil!"

"Hark at her singing!" said Yakov with a smile.

To them she was only a grey patch in the gloom. Her voice rang over the sea again:

> *Do not spare my breasts,*
> *These two white swans!*

"D'ye hear that!" exclaimed Yakov, starting in the direction from which the tempting words had come.

"So you couldn't manage the farm?" he heard Vassili's stern voice ask.

Yakov looked at his father with bewildered eyes and remained at his side.

Drowned by the sound of the waves only fragments of this
tantalizing song now reached their ears:

> ... *Oh, I cannot close my eyes*
> ... *Alone ... this ... night!*

"It's hot!" said Vassili in a dull voice, lolling on the sand. "It's
night, but it's hot all the same! What an accursed country!"

"It's the sand.... It got hot during the day ..." said Yakov in
a faltering voice, turning over on the other side.

"Here, you! What are you laughing at?" his father demanded
sternly.

"I? What is there to laugh at?" Yakov asked innocently.

"I should say there wasn't!..."

Both fell silent.

Above the noise of the waves sounds reached their ears that
were either sighs or tenderly calling cries.

Two weeks passed. Sunday came again, and again Vassili Legostyev was lying on the sand next to his shack, looking across the
sea and waiting for Malva. The deserted sea was laughing, playing
with the reflection of the sun, and legions of waves were born to
race up the sand, sprinkle it with their spray and slip back into
the sea and merge with it. Everything was the same as it had been
fourteen days ago, except that on the previous occasion Vassili had
waited for his mistress with calm confidence; now he was waiting
with impatience. She had not come on the preceding Sunday—she
must come today! He had no doubt about it, but he was already dying to see her. Yakov would not intrude today. Two days ago he
had come for the net with some other fishermen and had said that
he was going into town on Sunday to buy himself some shirts. He
had got a job as a fisherman at fifteen rubles a month, had been
out fishing several times, and now looked lively and cheerful. Like
all the fishermen, he smelt of salt fish, and, like the rest, he was
dirty and in rags. Vassili sighed as he thought of his son.

"I hope he comes to no harm," he said to himself. "He'll get
spoiled, and then, perhaps, he won't want to go home.... In that
case I'll have to go...."

The sea was deserted except for the sea-gulls. Now and again several tiny black specks moved along the narrow strip of sandy shore that separated the sea from the sky and disappeared, but not a boat came in sight, although the sun's rays were already striking the sea almost perpendicularly. As a rule Malva arrived long before this.

Two sea-gulls were fighting in the air so furiously that their feathers flew, and their fierce screeching introduced a discordant note in the merry song of the waves which merged so harmoniously with the solemn silence of the radiant sky that it sounded like the joyous playing of the sunbeams on the vast expanse of sea. The sea-gulls swooped down into the water, still pecking at each other and screeching from pain and anger, and again rose into the air in pursuit of one another.... And their friends—a whole flock—voraciously hunted the fish, tumbling in the greenish translucent restless waters, as if oblivious to the struggle.

The sea remained deserted. The familiar dark speck failed to appear on the distant shore....

"You're not coming?" said Vassili aloud. "Well, don't! What did you think?..."

And he spat contemptuously in the direction of the shore.

The sea laughed.

Vassili got up and went into the shack with the intention of cooking some dinner, but he felt no desire for food, so he returned to the old spot and lay down again.

"If Seryozhka wou'd come at least!" he mentally exclaimed, and forced himself to think of Seryozhka. "He's a real terror, is that fellow! Laughs at everybody. Always ready for a fight. He's as strong as a bull. Got some learning too. Has been to lots of places ... but he's a drunkard. He's good company, though.... All the women have lost their hearts to him, and although he hasn't been here long, they're all running after him. Only Malva keeps away from him.... She hasn't turned up here! What a stubborn wench she is! Perhaps she's angry with me because I beat her? But was that new for her? Others must have beaten her.... And how! And won't I give it to her now!"

And so, thinking of his son one moment and of Seryozhka another, but most of the time of Malva, Vassili lay on the sand and waited. His anxiety gradually grew into a dark, suspicious thought, but he kept driving it away. And so, concealing this suspicion from himself, he waited until evening, now getting up and pacing up and down the sand, and now lying down again. Darkness had already spread over the sea, but he still gazed into the distance, waiting for the arrival of the boat.

Malva did not come that day.

On turning in Vassili gloomily cursed his fate, which forbade him to go to the mainland. Over and over again, just as he was dozing off, he thought he heard the distant splash of oars. He jumped up and dashed out of the shack. Shading his eyes with his hand he stared out into the dark troubled sea. On shore, at the fisheries, two fires were burning, but the sea was deserted.

"All right, you witch!" he muttered threateningly, and then turned in and fell fast asleep.

But here is what happened at the fisheries that day.

Yakov rose early in the morning, when the sun was not yet so hot and a fresh breeze was blowing from the sea. He went down to the sea to bathe and on the beach he saw Malva. She was sitting in the stern of a fishing boat that was moored to the beach and combing her wet hair; her bare feet were dangling over the boat's side.

Yakov stopped short and gazed at her curiously.

Malva's cotton blouse, unbuttoned at the breast, had slipped down one shoulder, and that shoulder looked so white and tempting.

The waves beat against the stern of the boat causing it to pitch, so that Malva now rose high above the sea and now dropped so low that her bare feet almost touched the water.

"Did you bathe?" Yakov shouted to her.

She turned her face to him, gave him a quick glance and answered, continuing to comb her hair:

"Yes. . . . Why are you up so early?"

"You were up before me."

"Do you have to follow my example?"

Yakov made no reply.

"If you follow my example," she said, "you may lose your head!"

"Oh! Isn't she terrible!" retorted Yakov with a laugh, and squatting down he began to wash.

He scooped up the water in his hands and splashed his face. grunting with pleasure at its freshness. After drying his face and hands with the hem of his blouse he asked Malva:

"Why do you keep trying to frighten me?"

"And why do you keep staring at me?" Malva retorted.

Yakov couldn't recollect having eyed Malva more than he had the other women around the fisheries, but suddenly he blurted out: "You look so tempting, I can't help staring at you!"

"If your father hears about your goings on, he'll wring your neck for you!" said Malva, shooting a sly and challenging glance at him.

Yakov laughed and climbed into the boat. He did not know what Malva meant by his "goings-on," but since she had said it, he must have been staring at her pretty hard. He began to feel quite cocky.

"What about my father?" he said, sitting down beside her on the gunwale. "Has he bought you, or what?"

Sitting beside Malva he ran his eyes over her bare shoulder, her half-exposed breast, her whole body—so fresh and strong, and fragrant of the sea.

"My, aren't you a beauty!" he exclaimed in admiration.

"But not for you!" she answered curtly without looking at him, nor did she trouble to adjust her clothing.

Yakov heaved a deep sigh.

Before them stretched the sea, inexpressibly beautiful in the rays of the morning sun. Small, playful waves, brought into being by the tender breath of the breeze, softly beat against the hull. Far out at sea loomed the spur, like a scar on its silky breast, and against the soft background of the blue sky the mast stood like a thinly drawn line, and the red rag at its head could be seen fluttering in the wind.

"Yes, my lad!" said Malva without looking at Yakov. "I may be tempting, but I'm not for you.... Nobody has bought me, and I'm not beholden to your father either. I live in my own way.... But don't you try to make up to me, because I don't want to stand between you and Vassili... I don't want any squabbling and quarrelling.... Do you understand me?"

"Why do you say that to me?" Yakov asked in amazement. "I haven't touched you, have I?"

"You wouldn't dare!" retorted Malva.

There was such a note of contempt in her voice that Yakov felt humiliated both as a male and a human being. A mischievous almost vicious feeling overcame him and his eyes flashed.

"Oh, I wouldn't dare, eh?" he exclaimed, shifting closer to her.

"No, you wouldn't!"

"But suppose I do?"

"Try!"

"What will happen?"

"I'll give you one in the neck that will send you flying into the water!"

"Go on, do it!"

"Dare to touch me!"

He fixed his burning eyes upon her and suddenly flung his powerful arms around her, crushing her breast and back. The touch of her strong, hot body, set his own on fire, and he felt a choking in the throat as if he were being strangled.

"There you are! ... Go on! ... Hit me! ... You said you would!" he gasped.

"Let me go, Yashka!" said Malva, calmly trying to release herself from his trembling arms.

"But you said you'd give it me in the neck, didn't you?"

"Let go! You'll be sorry for it!"

"Don't try to frighten me! ... Oh! ... Aren't you sweet!"

He held her still tighter and pressed his thick lips against her ruddy cheek.

Malva laughed mischievously, took Yakov's arms in a powerful grip and jerked her whole body forward. The two, held tightly in each other's embrace, shot overboard, plunged into the water with a heavy splash and soon were lost to view amidst a whirlpool of foam and spray. A little later Yakov's head appeared above the surging water with dripping hair and frightened face, and then Malva dived up beside him. Waving his arms desperately and splashing the water around him, Yakov roared and howled, while Malva, laughing heartily, swam round him, splashing the salty water in his face and diving to get out of the way of the broad sweep of his arms.

"You she-devil!" roared Yakov, blowing the water from his nose and mouth. "I'll drown! ... That's enough of it. ... By

God. ... I'll drown! Ah!. ... The water's bitter. ... I'm d-r-o-w-n-i-n-g!"

But Malva had already left him and was swimming to the shore, striking out like a man. On reaching the shore she climbed into the barge with remarkable agility, stood in the stern and laughed as she watched Yakov plunging and gasping in the water, trying to reach her. Her wet clothing clung to her body and outlined its form from her shoulders to her knees, and Yakov, reaching the boat at last and clinging to its side stared hungrily at this almost naked woman who was laughing merrily at him.

"Come on! Get out of the water, you porpoise!" she said between her chuckles, and going down on her knees she extended one hand to Yakov and grasped the gunwale of the boat with the other. Yakov caught her hand and exclaimed excitedly:

"Now look out! I'll give you a ducking!"

With that, standing up to his shoulders in the water, he pulled Malva down towards him. The waves dashed over his head, broke against the hull and splashed into Malva's face. Malva frowned and then laughed. Suddenly she shrieked and jumped into the water, knocking Yakov off his feet with the impact of her body.

And again they began to play in the greenish water like two porpoises, splashing each other, shrieking, spluttering and snorting.

The sun laughed as it watched them playing, and the glass in the windows of the fishery buildings also laughed as it reflected the sun. The water surged and gurgled as it was beaten up by their powerful arms, and the sea-gulls, alarmed by the two people struggling in the water, circled with piercing shrieks over their heads which vanished now and again under the incoming waves. ...

At last, weary and puffed up with the sea water they had swallowed they crawled on the beach and sat in the sun to rest.

"Phew!" ejaculated Yakov, spitting out with a grimace.

"This water is awful stuff! No wonder there's such a lot of it!"

"There's plenty of awful stuff of all kinds in the world. Young fellows, for example. Good Lord, how many' of them there are!" said Malva with a laugh, wringing the water out of her hair.

Her hair was dark and, though not very long, was thick and wavy.

"No wonder the old man fell in love with you," said Yakov with a sly smile, nudging Malva with his elbow.

"Sometimes an old man is better than a young one."

"If the father is good the son must be better!"

"Is that so? Where did you learn to boast like that?"

"The girls in our village often told me that I am not at all bad-looking."

"What do girls know? You ask me."

"But aren't you a girl?"

Malva stared at him, laughed mischievously, and then, becoming grave she said in an earnest tone:

"I had a child once."

"Damaged goods—eh?" said Yakov bursting into a loud laugh.

"Don't be silly!" snapped Malva, turning away from him.

Yakov was cowed. He pursed his lips and said no more.

Both remained silent for about half an hour, basking in the sun to dry their clothes.

The fishermen in the long, filthy sheds which served as their living quarters, awoke from their slumber. From a distance they all looked alike—ragged, unkempt and barefooted.... Their hoarse voices were wafted to the beach. Somebody was hammering on the bottom of an empty barrel and the hollow sounds came over like the beating of a big drum. Two women were quarrelling in shrill voices. A dog barked.

"They're waking up," said Yakov. "I wanted to go to town early today ... but here I am, larking about with you."

"I told you you'd be sorry if you made up to me," answered Malva, half in jest and half seriously.

"Why do you keep frightening me?" Yakov asked with a perplexed smile.

"Mark my words. As soon as your father gets to hear of this. . . ."

Yakov flared up on hearing his father mentioned again.

"What about my father?" he demanded angrily. "Suppose he does hear? I'm not a kid.... He thinks he's the boss, but he can't boss me here.... We're not at home in the village.... I'm not blind. I can see he's no saint.... He does as he likes here.... Let him not interfere with me!"

Malva looked into his face mockingly and asked in a tone of curiosity:

"Not interfere with you? Why, what do you intend to do?"

"I!" answered Yakov, puffing out his cheeks and sticking out his chest as if he were lifting a heavy weight. "What I intend to do? I can do a lot! The fresh air has blown all the village dust off me. I can tell you!"

"Quick work!" said Malva ironically.

"I'll tell you what! I bet I'll win you from my father!"

"Well! You don't say?"

"Do you think I'm afraid?"

"N-o-o?"

"Look here!" Yakov blurted out impulsively. "Don't tease me.... Or else ... I'll...."

"What?" Malva asked coolly.

"Nothing!"

He turned away from her and said no more, but he looked brave and self-confident.

"Aren't you cocky!" said Malva. "The agent here has a black pup. Have you seen it? It's like you. It barks and threatens to bite when you're at a distance. But when you go near it runs away with its tail between its legs!"

"All right!" exclaimed Yakov angrily. "You wait! I'll show you the stuff I'm made of!"

Malva laughed in his face.

A tall wiry man with a tanned face and a thick thatch of unkempt, fiery red hair slowly approached them with a swaggering step. His red cotton blouse, which he wore without a belt, was torn at the back almost up to the collar, and to prevent the sleeves from slipping down he had them rolled up to his shoulders. His pants were nothing but a collection of rents of the most diverse shapes and sizes. His feet were bare. His face was densely freckled, his large blue eyes flashed insolently, and his broad upturned nose gave him an appearance of reckless impudence. On reaching them he halted. The patches of his bare body visible through the innumerable rents in his clothing gleamed in the sun. He sniffed loudly, stared enquiringly at them and pulled a funny face.

"Seryozhka had a drink or two yesterday and today his pocket is like a bottomless basket," he said. "Lend me twenty kopecks! You can be sure I'll not repay you...."

Yakov laughed heartily at this insolent speech. Malva gazed
at the ragged figure with a smile.

"I'll tell you what, you devils! I'll marry you two for twenty
kopecks! Do you want to?"

"Oh you clown! Are you a priest?" enquired Yakov with a
grin.

"Idiot! I worked as a janitor for a priest in Uglich.... Give
me twenty kopecks!"

"I don't want to get married!" said Yakov.

"Never mind—give me the money. I won't tell your father that
you're larking about with his tart," persisted Seryozhka, licking
his dry, cracked lips.

"He wouldn't believe you if you did tell him!"

"He will if I tell him!... And won't he wallop you!"

"I'm not afraid!" said Yakov.

"In that case I'll wallop you myself!" said Seryozhka, calmly
screwing up his eyes.

Yakov begrudged the twenty kopecks, but he had already been
warned to avoid quarrelling with Seryozhka and to yield to his
demands. He never asked for much, but if it was not given him
he would get up to some mischief at work, or give his victim a
thrashing for no reason at all. Yakov remembered this warning
and put his hand to his pocket with a sigh.

"That's right!" said Seryozhka encouragingly, dropping down
on the sand beside him. "Always listen to what I tell you and you'll
become a wise man. And you," he continued, turning to Malva. "Are you going to marry me soon? Make up your mind quickly. I don't intend to wait long!"

"You're nothing but a bundle of rags.... Sew the holes up
in your clothing first and then we'll talk about it," answered
Malva.

Seryozhka gazed at the rents in his pants critically, shook his
head and said:

"It would be better if you gave me one of your skirts."

"What!" exclaimed Malva.

"Yes, I mean it! You surely have an old one you don't want!"

"Buy yourself a pair of pants," Malva advised him.

"No. I'd rather buy drink with the money."

"You'd rather do that!" said Yakov laughing, holding four five-kopeck pieces in his hand.

"Yes, why not? A priest told me that a man must take care of his soul and not of his body, and my soul demands vodka, not pants. Give me the money! . . . Now I'll go and have a drink. . . I'll tell your father about you all the same."

"Tell him!" said Yakov with a wave of the hand, and winking impudently at Malva he nudged her shoulder.

Seryozhka noticed this. Spitting out, he said threateningly:

"And I'll not forget that thrashing I promised you. . . . I'll give you such a thick ear as soon as I get some spare time!"

"What for?" Yakov asked, somewhat alarmed.

"I know what for! . . . Well, are you going to marry me soon?" Seryozhka asked Malva again.

"Tell me what we shall do when we're married, how we're going to live, and then I'll think about it," she answered gravely.

Seryozhka stared out at the sea, screwed up his eyes and licking his lips he said:

"We won't do nothing. We'll have a good time."

"But where shall we get the money from?"

"Ekh!" ejaculated Seryozhka, waving his arm in disgust. "You argue like my old mother—what? and where? and how? How do I know? . . . I'll go and get myself a drink."

He got up and left them. Malva watched him go with a queer smile playing on her lips; Yakov sent hostile glances after him.

"A regular bully, isn't he!" said Yakov when Seryozhka had got out of earshot. "If he lived in our village they'd soon put a curb on him. . . . They'd give him a good licking and that would put a stop to his tricks. But they're afraid of him here!"

Malva looked at him and muttered between her clenched teeth:

"You puppy! You don't understand his worth!"

"What's there to understand? He's worth five kopecks a bunch, and then only if there's a hundred to the bunch!"

"You ought to talk!" exclaimed Malva. "That's no more than you are worth. . . . But he. . . . He's been everywhere, all over the country, and he's afraid of nobody!"

"Am I afraid of anybody?" demanded Yakov boastfully.

Malva did not answer him but pensively watched the play of

the waves that were racing up the beach and rocking the heavy boat. The mast swung from side to side, the stern rose and fell, splashing the water with a loud sound like that of vexation, as if the boat wanted to break away from the beach and slip out into the broad, green sea, and was angry with the cable that was holding it fast.

"Well, why don't you go?" Malva asked Yakov.

"Where to?" he asked in reply.

"You said you wanted to go to town."

"I won't go!"

"Then go to your father."

"What about you?"

"What about me?"

"Will you go too?"

"No."

"Then I won't go."

"Do you intend to hang around me all day long?" Malva asked coolly.

"Oh yes! I need you very much!" answered Yakov contemptuously, getting up and going off in a huff.

But he was wrong in saying that he did not need her. He found things dull without her. A strange feeling had arisen within him since his conversation with her: a vague feeling of discontent with, and protest against, his father. He had not felt this the day before, and he had not felt it earlier that day, before he met Malva. . . . But now it seemed to him that his father was a hindrance to him, although he was far out at sea, on that barely perceptible strip of sand. . . . Then it seemed to him that Malva was afraid of his father. If she were not afraid things would be altogether different between him and her.

He roamed about the fisheries gazing at the people there. Seryozhka was sitting on an upturned barrel in the shade of a hut, strumming a balalaika and singing, pulling funny faces the while:

> *Oh Mr. Policeman*
> *Be very kind to me.*
> *Take me to the station*
> *I've been on the spree. . . .*

He was surrounded by a score or so of people as ragged as himself, all smelling of salt fish, like everything else in the place. Four women, ugly and dirty, were sitting on the sand drinking tea, pouring it out of a large tin kettle. A fisherman, already drunk, although it was still early morning, was rolling on the sand, trying to rise to his feet and falling down again. Somewhere a woman was shrieking and wailing. The strains of an out-of-tune accordion were heard, and everywhere fish scales glistened.

At noon Yakov found a shady spot among a number of empty barrels. He lay down here and slept until the evening. When he awoke he wandered around the fisheries again vaguely conscious that something was drawing him somewhere.

After wandering about for a couple of hours he found Malva lying in the shade of a young willow a long way from the fisheries. She was lying on her side, holding a tattered book of some kind. On seeing him approach she smiled.

"So this is where you got to!" he said, sitting down beside her.

"Have you been searching for me long?" she asked in a tone that suggested that she was confident that he had been searching for her.

"I haven't been searching for you at all!" exclaimed Yakov, suddenly realizing what the vague feeling had been, that he had been longing for her, and he shook his head in perplexity.

"Can you read?" Malva asked him.

"Yes ... but not very well. I have forgotten...."

"I don't read well either.... Did you go to school?"

"Yes, to the village school."

"I taught myself."

"Is that so?"

"Yes.... I served as a cook for a lawyer in Astrakhan. His son taught me to read."

"You didn't teach yourself then!" said Yakov.

She looked hard at him and then asked:

"Do you want some books to read?"

"Me? No.... What for?"

"I love reading. Look! I asked the agent's wife to lend me this book and I am reading it."

"What's it about?"

"It's about St. Alexei."

And she went on to tell him in a pensive voice how a young lad, the son of wealthy and distinguished parents, left home, abandoning all the comforts of life, and later returned, poor and in rags, and lived with the dogs in the courtyard of his parents' house without revealing his identity until the day of his death. When she finished the story Malva asked Yakov in a low voice:

"Why did he do that?"

"Who knows?" answered Yakov in a tone of complete indifference.

The sand dunes swept up by the wind and waves surrounded them. Vague, muffled noises were wafted to them from the distance—the sounds of revelry in the fisheries. The sun was setting, tinting the sand a rosy hue with its rays. The sparse leaves on the stunted branches of the willow trees fluttered feebly in the light breeze that was blowing from the sea. Malva was silent; she appeared to be listening intently for something.

"Why didn't you go over there, to the spur, today?" Yakov suddenly asked her.

"What's that to you?"

Yakov looked hungrily at the woman out of the corner of his eye, trying to think how to say what he was yearning to say.

"When I am alone, and it's quiet," said Malva pensively, "I want to cry ... or sing. Only I don't know any good songs, and I'm ashamed to cry...."

Yakov heard her voice, it was low and tender, but what she said touched no string in his heart, it merely sharpened his desire for her.

"Now listen to me," he said in a low voice, drawing closer, but keeping his eyes away from her. "Listen to what I'll tell you.... I am young...."

"And foolish, very foolish!" said Malva interrupting him, speaking very earnestly, and shaking her head.

"Well, suppose I am foolish?" retorted Yakov in a tone of vexation. "Does one have to be clever for this sort of thing? All right—say I'm foolish! But this is what I've got to say: Would you like...."

"No, I wouldn't!"

"What?"

"Nothing!"

"Here, don't be a fool!" said Yakov, gently taking Malva by the shoulders. "Try and understand. . . ."

"Go away, Yashka!" she said sternly, pushing his hands away. "Go away!"

He rose to his feet and looked around.

"All right. . . . If that's the case, I don't give a damn! There's lots like you around here. . . . D'you think you're better than the others?"

"You're a pup," she said coolly, rising to her feet and shaking the sand from her skirt.

They walked side by side to the fisheries. They walked slowly, because their feet sank in the sand.

Yakov crudely tried to persuade her to yield to his desires, but she coolly laughed at him and parried his pleadings with cruel jests.

Just before they reached the hutments Yakov suddenly stopped, grasped Malva by the shoulders and said between his clenched teeth:

"You are only teasing me . . . working me up . . . aren't you? Why are you doing this? Take care or I'll make you sorry for it!"

"Leave me alone, I tell you!" said Malva, releasing herself from his grasp and walking away.

Seryozhka appeared round the corner of a hutment. On catching sight of them he strode towards them and said with a sinister smile, shaking his unkempt, fiery head:

"Been for a walk, eh? All right!"

"Go to hell, all of you!" Malva screamed angrily.

Yakov halted in front of Seryozhka and gazed at him sullenly. They were about ten paces away from each other.

Seryozhka returned Yakov's stare. They stood for about a minute like two rams ready to charge one another and then silently parted, each going in a different direction.

The sea was calm but was lit up with a lurid glare from the sunset. Muffled sounds came from the fisheries, and above those

sounds was distinctly heard the drunken voice of a woman hysterically screeching the nonsensical words:

> ... *Ta—agarga, matagarga,*
> *My matanichka ... ka!*
> *D-r-unk, and knocked about am I,*
> *Tousled, ruffled and rumpled—ah!*

And these words, as disgusting as lice, overran the fisheries
that were reeking of saltpeter and decaying fish, an offence to the
music of the waves.

The distant sea dozed calmly in the tender light of dawn, reflecting the pearly clouds. On the spur, sleepy fishermen were busy
loading tackle into a fishing boat.

A grey mass of netting crept along the sand to the boat and
lay in folds in its bottom.

Seryozhka, bareheaded and half naked as usual, stood in the
stern hurrying up the fishermen in his hoarse drunken voice. The
wind played among the rents in his blouse and ruffled his red,
unkempt hair.

"Vassili! Where's the green oars?" somebody shouted.

"Vassili, frowning like an October day, was piling the net in
the boat, while Seryozhka stared at his bent back licking his lips—
a sign that he wanted a drink to drive away his hangover.

"Have you any vodka?" he asked.

"Yes," answered Vassili sullenly.

"In that case I won't go out. . . . I'll stay here at the dry
end."

"Ready!" somebody shouted from the beach.

"Cast off! Lively now!" commanded Seryozhka and then
climbed out of the boat. "You go along," he said to the men. "I'll
stay here. See that you spread the net out wide, and don't get it
tangled! And fold it evenly. Don't fasten the loop."

The boat was pushed into the water, the fishermen climbed
into it and picking up their oars held them raised, waiting for
the order to start.

"One!"

The oars struck the water with a single stroke and the boat shot out into the broad expanse of the sea now lit up by the dawn.

"Two!" commanded the man at the tiller and the oars rose and stuck out on each side of the boat like the paws of a gigantic turtle. "One!... Two!..."

Five men remained at the dry end of the net on the beach: Seryozhka, Vassili, and three others. One of them dropped down on the sand and said:

"I'll have a little more sleep!"

Two others followed his example, and three bodies clothed in filthy rags curled up on the sand.

"Why didn't you come on Sunday?" Vassili asked Seryozhka as they walked to the shack.

"I couldn't."

"Why, were you drunk?"

"No. I was keeping an eye on your son, and also on his step-mother," Seryozhka answered coolly.

"A nice job you've found for yourself!" said Vassili with a wry smi'e. "What! Are they little children?"

"Worse.... One's a fool and the other ... a saint. ..."

"What! Malva a saint?" Vassili asked, his eyes flashing anger. "Has she been like that long?"

"Her soul doesn't fit her body, brother!"

"She has a wicked soul!"

Seryozhka glanced at Vassili out of the corner of his eye and snorted contemptuously.

"Wicked! Ekh! You ... dull clodhoppers! You don't understand anything.... All you want a woman to have is fat tits.... You don't give a damn for her character.... But all the spice in a woman is her character.... A woman without character is like bread without salt. Can you get any pleasure out of a balalaika which has no strings? ... Dolt!"

"Gee! What fine talk you drank yourself into yesterday!" sneered Vassili.

He was dying to ask Seryozhka where he had seen Yakov and Malva, and what they were doing, but he was too ashamed.

On entering the shack he poured out a tumblerful of vodka

for Seryozhka, hoping that this dose would loosen his tongue and
that he would tell him about the two of his own accord.

But Seryozhka drained the glass, grunted and, quite sobered up,
sat down at the door of the shack, stretched himself and yawned.

"A drink like that is like swallowing fire," he said.

"And can't you drink!" exclaimed Vassili, amazed at the speed
with which Seryozhka had gulped down the tumblerful of vodka.

"Yes, I can!" said the hobo, nodding his red head and wiping
his moist whiskers with the palm of his hand. "Yes, I can, brother! I do everything quickly, and straight off the bat, without any
higgledy-piggledy. Go straight on, is my motto! What does it
matter where you get to? We've all got to go the same road—
from dust unto dust. . . . And you can't get away from it!"

"You wanted to go to the Caucasus, didn't you?" Vassili asked,
cautiously leading up to his subject.

"I'll go when I feel like it. And when I do feel like it I'll go
straight off—one, two, three, and off! I either get my way or
get a big bump on my head. . . . It's all very simple!"

"Nothing could be simpler! You seem to be living without
using your head."

Seryozhka looked at Vassili with mocking eyes and said:

"You think you're clever, don't you? How many times have
you been flogged at the volost police station?"

Vassili returned Seryozhka's stare, but said nothing.

"Is it good to have the police knock sense into your head
through your backside? . . . Ekh, you! What can you do with your
head? Where do you think it will take you to? What can you
think up with it? Ain't I right? But I push right on without
using my head, and I don't give a damn! And I bet I'll get further
than you," said the hobo boastfully.

"Yes, I believe you will!" answered Vassili with a laugh. "You'll
get as far as Siberia!"

Seryozhka burst into a hearty chuckle.

Contrary to Vassili's expectations the vodka had no effect upon
Seryozhka, and this made him angry. He could have offered him
another glassful, but he grudged the vodka. On the other hand, as
long as Seryozhka was sober he would get nothing out of him. . . .
But the hobo opened the subject without further prompting.

"How is it you're not asking about Malva?" he enquired.

"Why should I?" Vassili answered in a tone of indifference, but trembling from a sort of premonition nevertheless.

"She wasn't here last Sunday, was she? Why don't you ask what she's been doing these past few days?... You're jealous about her, aren't you, you old devil!"

"There's lots like her!" said Vassili with a contemptuous wave of his hand.

"Lots like her!" retorted Seryozhka. "Ekh, you country bumpkin! You can't tell the difference between honey and tar!"

"What are you boosting her up like that for? Have you come here as a matchmaker? You're too late! The match came off a long time ago!" Vassili jeered.

Seryozhka looked at him in silence for a while and then, placing his hand on his shoulder, he said very earnestly:

"I know she's living with you. I didn't interfere—there was no need.... But now Yashka, that son of yours, is hanging round her. Give it to him red-hot! Do you hear what I say? If you don't—I will.... You're a good sort.... Only you're as dense as a block of wood.... I didn't interfere with you.... I want you to remember that."

"So that's how the land lies! You are after her too, is that it?" said Vassili in a hollow voice.

"Too!... If I had wanted to, I'd have gone straight for her, and would have shoved you all out of my way!... But what good am I to her?"

"Then why are you sticking your nose into it?" Vassili asked suspiciously.

This simple question must have astonished Seryozhka, for he looked at Vassili with wide open eyes, laughed heartily and said:

"Why am I sticking my nose in? The devil only knows!... But what a woman she is! Plenty of spice in her!... I like her.... Perhaps I'm sorry for her...."

Vassili looked at him distrustfully, but something in his heart told him that Seryozhka was speaking sincerely.

"If she'd have been an untouched virgin I could understand you being sorry for her. As it is ... it seems funny to me!" he said.

Seryozhka remained silent, watching the fishing boat far out
at sea describing a wide circle as it turned its nose to the shore.
His eyes were frank and wide open, his face was simple and kind.
Vassili softened towards him as he gazed at him.

"Yes, what you say is true. She's a fine woman ... only she's
a bit loose!... As for Yashka, I'll give him hell ... the pup!"

"I don't like him," said Seryozhka.

"And you say he's making up to her?" hissed Vassili through
his clenched teeth, stroking his beard.

"He'll come between you and her, take my word for it! Seryozhka said emphatically.

The rays of the rising sun burst over the horizon like an open
fan. Above the sound of the waves a faint hail reached their ears
from the boat far out at sea:

"A-h-o-o-y!... Pull her in!"

"Get up, lads! Hey! To the net!" commanded Seryozhka.

The men jumped to their feet and soon all five had chosen the
part of the net each was to take. A long cable, taut and as flexible
as steel, stretched from the water to the shore, and the fishermen,
twisting it into loops round their bodies, grunted and gasped as
they hauled it on to the beach.

Meanwhile, the fishing boat, gliding over the waves, was hauld-
ing in the other end of the net.

The sun, bright and magnificent, rose over the sea.

"If you see Yakov, tell him to come and see me tomorrow,"
Vassili requested Seryozhka.

"All right!"

The boat slipped on to the beach and the fishermen, jumping
out of her, grabbed hold of their respective parts of the net and
hauled it in. The two groups gradually drew closer to each other
and the cork floats of the net, bobbing up and down in the water,
formed a perfect semicircle.

Late that evening, when the men at the fisheries were having
their supper, Malva, tired and pensive, was sitting on a damaged
upturned boat and gazing out at the sea, now enveloped in gloom.
Far away a light glimmered. Malva knew that it was the fire that
Vassili had lit. Like a lone spirit lost in the dark expanse of the

sea, the light now flared up brightly and now subsided as if in agony. It made Malva feel sad to watch this red speck lost in the wilderness, flickering feebly amidst the ceaseless booming of the waves. Suddenly she heard Seryozhka's voice behind her:

"What are you sitting here for?"

"What's it to do with you?" she retorted without turning round.

"I'm just interested!"

He said no more, but looked her up and down, rolled a cigarette, lit it, and sat astride the upturned boat. After a little while he said in a friendly tone:

"You're a funny woman! You hide from everybody one minute and hang on nearly everybody's neck the next!"

"I don't hang on your neck, do I?" she said in a dispassionate tone.

"No, not on mine, but on Yashka's."

"And are you jealous?"

"Humph! ... Let's talk straight, from the bottom of the heart, eh?" suggested Seryozhka, patting Malva on the shoulder. She was sitting sideways to him, so he could not see the expression on her face when she said curtly:

"All right!"

"Tell me, have you dropped Vassili?"

"I don't know," answered Malva. After a brief pause she added: "Why do you ask?"

"Just like that."

"I'm angry with him."

"Why?"

"He beat me."

"You don't say!... What, he? And you let him! Oh! oh!" Seryozhka was amazed. He glanced sideways at her and clicked his tongue ironically.

"I wouldn't have let him if I had not wanted to," she said fervidly.

"Why didn't you stop him then?"

"I didn't want to."

"That shows you are head over heels in love with the old tomcat," said Seryozhka mockingly, blowing his cigarette smoke at her. "I'm surprised! I didn't think you were one of that sort!"

"I don't love any of you," she answered in a dispassionate voice, waving the smoke away.

"That's a lie!"

"Why should I lie?" she asked, and by the tone of her voice Seryozhka realized that she really was not lying.

"If you don't love him, why did you allow him to beat you?" he asked her in an earnest tone.

"Do I know?... What are you pestering me for?"

"Funny!" said Seryozhka, shaking his head.

Both remained silent for a long time.

Night drew in. The clouds, moving slowly across the sky, cast shadows on the sea. The waves murmured.

The light from Vassili's fire on the spur had gone out, but Malva was still gazing in that direction. And Seryozhka gazed at her.

"Tell me," he said. "Do you know what you want?"

"If only I knew!" Malva answered in a very low voice, heaving a deep sigh.

"So you don't know? That's bad!" Seryozhka said emphatically. "I always know what I want!" And he added with a touch of sadness in his voice: "The trouble is I rarely want anything."

"I am always wanting something," said Malva pensively, "but what it is... I don't know. Sometimes I feel I'd like to get into a boat and go out to sea ... far, far out, and never see anybody again. And sometimes I feel I'd like to turn every man's head and make him spin like a top around me. And I would look at him and laugh. Sometimes I feel so sorry for them all, and most of all for myself; and sometimes I want to kill them all, and then die a frightful death myself.... Sometimes I feel sad and sometimes happy.... But all the people around me seem so dull, like blocks of wood."

"You are right, the people are no good," Seryozhka agreed. "More than once I've looked at you and thought to myself: 'You're neither fish, flesh nor fowl'... but for all that there's something about you ... you're not like other women."

"And thank God for that!" said Malva with a laugh.

The moon rose up from the dunes on their left and shed its silvery light upon the sea. Large and mild, it floated slowly

across the blue vault of heaven, and the bright light of the stars
paled and vanished in its even dreamy light.

Malva smiled and said:

"Do you know what?... Sometimes I think what fun it would be
to set fire to one of the huts. What a hullabaloo there'd be!"

"I should say so!" Seryozhka exclaimed with admiration, and
suddenly slapping Malva on the shoulder he said: "Do you know
what? I'll teach you an amusing game, and we'll play it. Would
you like to?"

"Rather!" said Malva burning with curiosity.

"You've set Yashka's heart on fire, haven't you?"

"It's burning like a furnace," answered Malva with a chuckle.

"Set him against his father! By God it'll be funny!... They'll
go for each other like a couple of bears.... You tease the old
man up a bit, and the young one too ... and then we'll set them
against each other. What do you think of it, eh?"

Malva turned and gazed intently at Seryozhka's red, jolly smiling face. Lit up by the moon, it looked less blotched than in
the bright light of the sun in the daytime. It bore no trace of
anger, it bore nothing but a good-natured and somewhat mischievous smile.

"What makes you dislike them?" Malva asked him suspiciously.

"I?... Oh, Vassili is all right. He's a good chap. But Yasha ...
he's no good. You see, I dislike all muzhiks.... They're rotters!
They pretend to be poor and destitute ... and get bread, and everything, given them. They have Zemstvo, you see, and the Zemstvo
does everything for them.... They have their farms, their land
and cattle.... I once served as a coachman to a Zemstvo doctor
and I saw quite enough of them.... And later I was on the road
for a long time. Sometimes you'd go into a village and beg for a
piece of bread and they'd nab you in a jiffy!... Who are you?
What are you? Where's your passport?... That's happened to me
lots of times.... Sometimes they take you for a horse thief, and
sometimes they put you in the stone jug just for nothing.... They're
always snivelling and pretending they're poor, but they know how
to live! They have something to hold on to—land. What am I compared to them?"

"Aren't you a muzhik?" Malva asked interrupting him.

"No!" answered Seryozhka with a touch of pride. "I'm town-bred. I'm a citizen of the town of Uglich."

"And I come from Pavlish," Malva told him in a pensive voice.

"I have nobody to stand up for me!" continued Seryozhka. "But the muzhiks ... they can live, the devils! They have the Zemstvo, and all that sort of thing!"

"What's the Zemstvo?" Malva enquired.

"What's the Zemstvo? The devil knows! It was set up for the muzhiks. It's their administration.... But to hell with it.... Let's get down to business—shall we arrange this little joke, eh? It won't do any harm. They'll just have a fight, that's all!... Vassili beat you, didn't he? Well, let his own son pay him out for it."

"It's not a bad idea," said Malva smiling.

"Just think ... isn't it a pretty sight to see other people busting each other's ribs for your sake? And only at a word from you! You wag your tongue once or twice... and they go for each other hammer and tongs."

Speaking half in jest and half in earnest Seryozhka explained to Malva at great length, and with equally great zeal, the attractions of the role she was to play.

"Oh, if only I were a good-looking woman! Wouldn't I cause some trouble in the world!" he exclaimed in conclusion, putting his hands to his head and closing his eyes tight as if in ecstasy.

The moon was already high in the sky when they parted, and with their departure the beauty of the night increased. Now only the limitless solemn sea, the silvery moon, and the blue star-spangled sky remained. There were also the sand dunes, the willow bushes among them, and the two, long, dilapidated buildings in the sand, looking like two, huge, roughly made coffins. But all this seemed petty and insignificant compared with the sea; and the stars which looked down upon this shined with a cold light.

Father and son sat opposite each other in the shack drinking vodka. The son had brought the vodka so that the visit to his father should not be dull, and also to soften his father's heart towards him. Seryozhka had told him that his father was angry with him over Malva, that he had threatened to beat Malva almost to

death, that Malva knew about this, and that was why she was not
yielding herself to him. Seryozhka had said to him mockingly:
"He'll pay you out for your tricks! He'll pull your ears until
they are over a yard long. You had better not let him set eyes on
you!"

The jeering of this red-haired, repulsive fellow had roused in
Yakov's heart a feeling of burning rage against his father, and on
top of this was Malva's behaviour: The way she looked at him
tantalizingly at one moment and longingly another inflamed his
desire to possess her until it was too painful to bear.

And so, on visiting his father, he regarded him as an obstacle
in his path, an obstacle which you could neither climb over nor
go around. But he felt not the slightest trace of fear of his father.
He sat opposite him and looked at him confidently with a sullen
angry stare as much as to say:
"Dare to touch me!"

They had already had two drinks but had not yet said a word
to each other, except for an insignificant remark or two about
things concerning the fisheries. Facing each other alone in the
midst of the sea they sat there accumulating anger in their hearts
against each other. Both were aware that soon this anger would
boil over and scald them.

The bast matting which covered the shack rustled in the wind,
the reeds knocked against each other, the red rag at the masthead
fluttered, making a chattering noise; but all these sounds were subdued and resembled distant whispering voices, incoherently and
timidly begging for something.

"Is Seryozhka still on the booze?" Vassili asked in a glum
voice.

"Yes, he gets drunk every night," said Yakov, pouring out some
more vodka.

"It'll be the death of him.... So that's what it is, this free
life ... without fear! And you'll be like that too...."

Yakov answered curtly:
"No, I won't!"

"You won't?" said Vassili frowning. "I know what I'm talking
about.... How long have you been here? This is the third month.
It'll be time for you to go home soon. Will you have much money

to take with you?" He picked up his cup angrily, shot the vodka
into his mouth, gathered his beard into the palm of his hand and
tugged it so vigorously that his head went down with it.

"I couldn't have saved much in the short time I've been here,"
said Yakov.

"If that's the case, it's no use you gallivanting here. Go back
home to the village!"

Yakov smiled but said nothing.

"What are you pulling a face for?" Vassili exclaimed angrily,
irritated by his son's coolness. "How dare you laugh when your
father is talking to you! Take care! You've started taking liberties
far too early! I shall have to put a curb on you!"

Yakov poured out some more vodka and drank it. His father's
reproaches provoked him to anger, but he restrained himself, trying not to say what he was thinking in order to avoid exciting his
father still more. To tell the truth, he was somewhat frightened
by the stern and even cruel light in his father's eyes.

Seeing that his son had taken another drink without offering
him one, Vassili flared up still more.

"Your father tells you to go home, but you laugh at him, eh?"
he demanded. "Take your discharge on Saturday and ... quick
march home! Do you hear what I tell you?"

"I won't go!" said Yakov firmly, obstinately shaking his
head.

"You won't, eh?" roared Vassili, and resting his hands on the
barrel he rose from his seat. "Who do you think you are talking
to? Are you a dog to bark at your father? Have you forgotten
what I can do to you? Have you forgotten?"

His lips trembled, his face twitched convulsively, the veins
stood out on his temples.

"I haven't forgotten anything," answered Yakov in a low voice
without looking at his father. "But do you remember everything?
You'd better look out!"

"Don't dare teach me! I'll smash you to a pulp! ..."

Yakov dodged his father's arm as it rose over his head and
muttered through his clenched teeth:

"Don't dare touch me.... You're not at home in the village."

"Silence! I'm your father no matter where we are!"

"You can't get me flogged at the volost police station here! There ain't no volost here!" said Yakov laughing in his father's face and also rising from his seat.

Vassili stood with bloodshot eyes, head thrust forward and fists clenched, breathing hot breath mixed with vodka fumes into his son's face. Yakov stepped back and with lowering brow, watched every movement his father made, ready to parry a blow. Outwardly he was calm, but hot perspiration broke out over his whole body. Between them stood the barrel which served them as a table.

"I can't flog you, you say?" Vassili asked hoarsely, arching his back like a cat ready to spring.

"Everybody's equal here. . . . You are a labourer and so am I."

"Is that what it is?"

"What do you think? Why are you mad with me? Do you think I don't know? You started it. . . ."

Vassili emitted a roar and swung his arm with such swiftness that Yakov was unable to avoid it. The blow came down on his head. He staggered and snarled into the angry face of his father.

"Take care!" he warned him, clenching his fists, as Vassili raised his arm again.

"I'll show you take care!"

"Stop, I tell you!"

"Aha! . . . You're threatening your father . Your father! . . . Your father! . . . "

The small shack hemmed them in and hampered their movements. They stumbled over the salt bags, the overturned barrel and the tree stump.

Parrying the blows with his fists, Yakov, pale and perspiring, teeth clenched and eyes blazing like a wolf's, slowly retreated before his father, while the latter followed him up, waving his fists in his blind fury, and suddenly becoming strangely dishevelled, like a bristling wild boar.

"Leave off! That's enough! Stop it!" said Yakov in a calm and sinister voice, passing through the door of the shack into the open.

His father roared still louder and followed him, but his blows only encountered his son's fists.

"Aren't you mad. . . . Aren't you mad," said Yakov teasingly, realizing that he was far more agile than his father.

"You wait. . . . You only wait. . . ."

But Yakov skipped aside and ran towards the sea.

Vassili went after him with lowered head and outspread arms, but he stumbled over something and fell flat on the ground. He quickly rose to his knees and then sat down on the sand, propping his body up with his arms. He was exhausted by the scuffle, and he positively howled from a burning sense of unavenged wrong and the bitter consciousness of his weakness.

"May you be accursed!" he shouted hoarsely, stretching his neck in the direction Yakov had gone and spitting the foam of madness from his trembling lips.

Yakov leaned against a boat and closely watched his father while rubbing his injured head. One of the sleeves of his blouse had been torn out and was hanging by a single thread. The collar was also torn, and his white perspiring chest glistened in the sun as if it had been smeared with grease. He now felt contempt for his father. He had always thought of him as being stronger than himself, and seeing him now sitting on the sand, dishevelled and pitiful, threatening him with his fists, he smiled the condescending, offensive smile of the strong contemplating the weak.

"Curse you! . . . May you be accursed forever!"

Vassili shouted his curses so loudly that Yakov involuntarily glanced out at sea, towards the fisheries, as if afraid that somebody out there might hear these cries of impotence. But out there there was nothing but the waves and the sun. He then spat out and said:

"Go on, shout! . . . Whom do you think you are hurting? Only yourself. . . . And since this has happened between us I'll tell you what I think. . . ."

"Shut up! . . . Get out of my sight! . . . Go away!" roared Vassili.

"I won't go back to the village," said Yakov, keeping his eyes on his father and watching every movement he made. "I shall stay here for the winter. It's better for me here. I'm no fool. I understand that. Life's easier here. . . . At home you'd do as you like with me, but here . . . look!"

With that he doubled up his fist, showed his father a fico
and laughed, not loudly, but loud enough to make Vassili jump to
his feet again mad with rage. He picked up an oar and made a
dash for Yakov shouting hoarsely:
"Your father? Do that to your father? I'll kill you!"
By the time he reached the boat, blind with fury, Yakov was
already far away, running with his torn-out sleeve flapping behind
him.

Vassili hurled the oar after him, but it dropped short, and,
again exhausted, the old man leaned his chest against the side of
the boat and madly scratched at the wood as he gazed after his son.
The latter shouted at him from a distance:
"You ought to be ashamed of yourself! You've got grey hairs
already, and yet you go mad like that over a woman! Ekh, you!
But I'm not going back to the village.... Go back yourself....
You've no business to be here!"
"Yashka! Shut up!" roared Vassili drowning Yashka's voice.
"Yashka! I'll kill you!... Get out of here!"
Yakov strolled off at a leisurely pace.

His father watched him go with dull, insane eyes. He already
looked shorter, his feet seemed to have sunk into the sand....
He had sunk up to the waist... up to the shoulder... to the
neck... he was gone! A moment later, however, somewhat further
from the spot where he had vanished, his head reappeared, then
his shoulders, and then his whole body... but he was smaller
now. He turned round, looked in Vassili's direction and shouted
something.
"Curse you! Curse you! Curse you!" shouted Vassili in reply.
His son made a gesture of disgust, turned round and went off,
and ... again vanished behind the sand dunes.

Vassili gazed for a long time in the direction his son had gone
until his back ached from the awkward posture of his body as he
lay leaning against the boat. He rose to his feet and staggered
from the pain he felt in every limb. His belt had slipped up to
his armpits. He unfastened it with his numbed fingers, brought it
close to his eyes and threw it on the sand. Then he went into
the shack and halted in front of a hollow in the sand and remembered that that was where he had stumbled, and that had

he not fallen he would have caught his son. The shack was in
utter disorder. Vassili looked round for the vodka bottle. He
saw it lying among the sacks and picked it up. The bottle was
tightly corked and the vodka had not been spilt. Vassili slowly
prized the cork out and putting the mouth of the bottle to his
lips he wanted to drink, but the bottle rattled against his teeth
and the vodka flowed out of his mouth on to his beard and chest.

Vassili heard a ringing in his ears, his heart throbbed violently, his back ached unbearably.

"After all I am old!" he said aloud and sank down on the
sand at the entrance of the shack.

The sea stretched out before him. The waves laughed, noisily
and playfully as always. Vassili gazed for a long time at the
water and remembered the yearning words his son had uttered:

"If only all this was land! Black earth! And if we could
plough it all!"

A bitter feeling overcame this muzhik. He vigorously rubbed
his chest, looked around and heaved a deep sigh. His head
drooped low and his back bent as if under the weight of a heavy
burden. His throat worked convulsively as if he were choking. He
coughed hard to clear his throat and crossed himself, looking up
into the sky. Gloomy thoughts descended upon him.

... For the sake of a loose woman he had abandoned his wife,
with whom he had lived in honest toil for over fifteen years ...
and for this the Lord had punished him by the rebellion of his
son. That was so, oh Lord!

His son had mocked at him, had torn his heart.... Death
would be too good for him for having vexed his father's soul in this
way! And what for! For a loose woman who was living in sin....
It had been a sin for him, an old man, to forget his wife and son
and to associate with this woman....

And so the Lord in His holy wrath had reminded him of his
duty and through his son had struck at his heart in just punishment.... That was so, oh Lord!

Sitting huddled up on the sand Vassili crossed himself and
blinked his eyes, brushing away with his eyelashes the tears that
were blinding him.

The sun sank into the sea. The lurid glare of the sunset slowly faded away. A warm wind from the silent distance fanned the muzhik's face that was wet with tears. Absorbed in his thoughts of repentance, he sat there until he fell asleep.

Two days after his quarrel with his father, Yakov, with a number of other fishermen, went off in a large boat towed by a steam tug to a spot thirty versts from the fisheries to catch sturgeon. Five days later he returned to the fisheries alone in a sailing boat—he had been sent back for provisions. He arrived at midday, when the fishermen were resting after dinner. It was unbearably hot, the scorching sand burnt one's feet, and the fish scales and fishbones pricked them. Yakov cautiously made his way to the hutments, cursing himself for not having put his boots on. He felt too lazy to go back to the boat to get them and, besides, he was hurrying to get a bite and also to see Malva. He had often thought of her during the dull time he had spent at sea, and now he wanted to know whether she had seen his father and what he had told her.... Perhaps he had beaten her. That wouldn't be a bad thing—it would knock the starch out of her a bit! As it was, she was far too perky and impudent!

The fisheries were quiet and deserted. The windows of the hutments were wide open, and these large wooden boxes also seemed to be gasping from the heat. In the agent's office, which was hidden among the huts, an infant was bawling with all its might. Low voices were heard behind a pile of barrels.

Yakov boldly stepped up to the barrels, he thought he heard Malva's voice. On reaching them, however, and looking behind them, he started back, frowned and halted.

Behind the barrels, in their shade, red-haired Seryozhka was lying on his back, his hands under his head. On one side of him sat his father, on the other side was Malva.

"What's he doing here?" said Yakov to himself, thinking of his father. "Has he given up his quiet job to come here so as to be nearer to Malva and to keep him away from her? Oh hell! What if mother heard about all his goings-on?... Shall I go to him or not?"

"Well!" he heard Seryozhka say. "So it's good-bye, eh? All right! Go and grub the soil!"

Yakov blinked his eyes with joy.

"Yes, I'll go!" his father said.

Yakov then boldly stepped forward and exclaimed merrily: "Greetings to an honest company!"

His father shot a rapid glance at him and turned away. Malva did not turn an eyelash, but Seryozhka jerked his leg and said in a deep bass voice:

"Lo! Our beloved son Yashka hath returned from distant lands!" And then he continued in his usual voice: "He deserves to be flayed and his skin used for a drum like a sheepskin!"

Malva laughed softly.

"It's hot!" said Yakov sitting down.

Vassili glanced at him again and said:

"I've been waiting for you, Yakov."

Yakov thought his voice was softer than usual and his face looked younger.

"I've come back for provisions," he announced, and then he asked Seryozhka to give him some tobacco for a cigarette.

"You'll get no tobacco from me, you young fool!" said Seryozhka without moving a muscle.

"I'm going home, Yakov," said Vassili impressively, making marks on the sand with his finger.

"Is that so?" answered Yakov, looking innocently at his father. "What about you ... are you remaining here?"

"Yes, I'll remain. . . . There's not enough work for both of us at home."

"Well. . . . I won't say anything. Do as you please. . . . You're no longer a child. . . . Only remember this—I won't last much longer. Perhaps I shall live ... but as for being able to work—I'm not sure about that. . . . I've got unused to the land. . . . So don't forget —you've got a mother back home."

He must have found it hard to talk; his words seemed to stick in his teeth. He stroked his beard and his hand trembled.

Malva stared at him. Seryozhka screwed up one eye and with the other, large and round, looked hard into Yakov's face. Yakov was bubbling over with joy, but fearing to betray it he sat silently staring at his feet.

"So don't forget your mother ... remember you're her only son!" said Vassili.

"You needn't tell me that, I know!" said Yakov shrinking.

"All right, since you know!" said his father, eyeing him distrustfully. "All I say is—don't forget!"

Vassili heaved a deep sigh. For several moments all four remained silent. Then Malva said:

"The bell will go soon!"

"Well, I'll go along!" said Vassili, rising to his feet. The other three did the same.

"Good-bye, Sergei! ... If ever you are on the Volga, perhaps you'll look me up? Simbirsk Uyezd, Village of Mazlo, Nikolo-Lykovskaya Volost."

"All right!" said Seryozhka shaking Vassili's hand, holding it tight in his sinewy paw that was overgrown with red hair and smiling into his sad, grave face.

"Lykovo-Nikolskaya is a fairly large place. . . . It's known all over the countryside, and we live about four versts from it," Vassili explained.

"All right, all right. . . . I'll look in if ever I'm that way!"

"Good-bye!"

"Good-bye, old man!"

"Good-bye, Malva," said Vassili in a choking voice without looking at her.

Malva unhurriedly wiped her lips on her sleeve and placing her white hands on Vassili's shoulders silently and gravely kissed him three times on his cheeks and lips.

Vassili was confused and muttered something incoherently. Yakov dropped his head to conceal an ironic smile, while Seryozhka looked up into the sky and yawned softly.

"You'll find it hot work walking," he said.

"Oh, that's nothing. . . . Well, good-bye, Yakov!"

"Good-bye!"

They stood opposite each other not knowing what to do. The sad phrase "good-bye," which had rung out so often and monotonously during these few seconds, awakened a tender feeling for his father in Yakov's heart, but he did not know how to express it: to embrace him as Malva had done, or to shake hands with him as Seryozhka had done. Vassili was vexed by the irresolution expressed in his son's posture and face, and he still felt something that was

akin to shame in Yakov's presence. This feeling had been roused
by his recollection of the scene on the spur and by Malva's kisses.

"And so—don't forget your mother!" he said at last.

"All right, all right!" exclaimed Yakov with a cordial smile,
"Don't worry... I'll do the right thing!"

He nodded his head.

"Well... that's all! Farewell. May the Lord send you all the
best.... Think of me kindly.... Oh Seryozhka! I buried the tea
can in the sand under the stern of the green boat!"

"What's he want the tea can for?" Yakov enquired hastily.

"He's taken over my job ... out there on the spur," explained
Vassili.

Yakov looked at Seryozhka, glanced at Malva and dropped his
head to conceal the joyous sparkle in his eyes.

"Well, good-bye, friends.... I'm going."

Vassili bowed all round and went off. Malva went with him.

"I'll see you off a little way," she said.

Seryozhka dropped down on the sand and caught hold of
Yakov's foot just as Yakov was about to step out after Malva.

"Whoa! Where you off to?"

"Wait! Let me go!" cried Yakov, trying to tear his foot free.

But Seryozhka caught him by the other foot too and said:

"Sit down next to me for a while!"

"Hey! Stop playing the fool!"

"I'm not playing the fool.... But you sit down!"

Yakov sat down.

"What do you want?" he demanded through his clenched teeth.

"Wait! Shut up for a minute! Let me think and then I'll tell
you!"

Seryozhka looked threateningly at Yakov with his insolent eyes
and Yakov yielded to him.

Malva and Vassili walked on in silence for a little while. She
cast sidelong glances at his face and her eyes glistened strangely.
Vassili frowned and said nothing. Their feet sank in the loose sand
and they walked very slowly.

"Vassya!"

"What?"

He glanced at her and at once turned his eyes away.

"I made you quarrel with Yashka on purpose.... You could have lived here together without quarrelling," she said in a calm and even voice.

"Why did you do that?" Vassili asked after a brief pause.

"I don't know.... Just like that!"

She shrugged her shoulders and laughed.

"A nice thing to do! Ekh, you!" he said reproachfully in an angry voice.

She remained silent.

"You'll spoil that boy of mine, spoil him completely! Ekh! You are a witch, a witch! You don't know the fear of God! You have no shame! What are you doing?"

"What ought I to do?" she asked, and there was a note either of anxiety or of vexation in her voice, it was difficult to say which.

"What you ought to do? Ekh, you!" exclaimed Vassili, feeling anger welling up in his heart against her.

He passionately wanted to strike her, to knock her down at his feet and trample upon her on the sand, to kick her in the breast and face with his heavy boots. He clenched his fist and looked round.

Near the barrels he could see the figures of Yakov and Seryozhka, their faces were turned towards him.

"Go away, go away! I could smash you, you...."

He hissed the abusive word almost in her face. His eyes were bloodshot, his beard quivered and his hands involuntarily stretched towards her hair, which had slipped from under her kerchief.

She, however, gazed at him calmly with her greenish eyes.

"I ought to kill you, you slut! Wait ... you'll get what's coming to you! Somebody'll wring your neck yet!"

She smiled, said nothing, and then, heaving a deep sigh, she said curtly:

"Well, that's enough! Good-bye!"

And turning on her heel she went back.

Vassili roared after her and ground his teeth. But Malva walked on, trying to step into the distinct and deep traces of Vassili's footsteps in the sand, and each time she succeeded she carefully obliterated them with her foot. And so she proceeded, slowly, until she reached the barrels, where Seryozhka greeted her with the question:

"Well, so you saw him off?"

Malva nodded in the affirmative and sat down beside him. Yakov looked at her and smiled tenderly, moving his lips as if he
were whispering something which he alone heard.

"Now that you've said good-bye you feel sorry he's gone, eh?"
Seryozhka asked again, quoting the words of the song.

"When are you going out there, to the spur?" asked Malva by
way of reply, nodding in the direction of the sea.

"This evening."

"I'll go with you."

"You will! Now that's what I like!"

"And I'll go!" said Yakov emphatically.

"Who's inviting you?" Seryozhka asked, screwing up his eyes.

The sound of a cracked bell was heard calling the men back
to work, the strokes hastily following one another and dying away
in the merry surge of the waves.

"She is!" said Yakov, looking at Malva challengingly.

"I?" she exclaimed in surprise. "What do I want you for?"

"Let's talk straight, Yashka!" said Sergei sternly, rising to his
feet. "If you start pestering her ... I'll smash you to a pulp! And
if you put a finger on her ... I'll kill you as I would a fly! One
crack on the head—and you'll be a goner! It's very simple with
me!"

His face, his whole figure and knotty hands stretching towards
Yakov's throat, all very convincingly testified that it was very
simple with him.

Yakov stepped back a pace and said in a choking voice:

"Wait a bit! Why, she herself. . . ."

"Now then—that's enough! Who do you think you are? Mut-
ton's not for you to eat, you dog! Be grateful if you get a bone to
gnaw. . . . Well . . . what are you glaring at?"

Yakov glanced at Malva. Her green eyes were laughing in his
face, an offensive, humiliating mocking laugh, and she pressed against
Seryozhka's side so lovingly that the sweat broke out all over Yakov's body.

They walked away from him, side by side, and when they had
gone a little distance they both laughed out loudly. Yakov dug his
right foot deeply into the sand and stood as if petrified, breathing
heavily.

In the distance, over the yellow, deserted, undulating sand, a small dark human figure was moving. On its right the merry mighty sea glistened in the sun, and on its left, right up to the horizon, stretched the sand—a dreary, monotonous desert. Yakov looked at the lonely figure and blinked his eyes, which were full of vexation and perplexity, and vigorously rubbed his chest with both his hands.

The fisheries were humming with activity.

Yakov heard Malva shouting in a resonant throaty voice: "Who took my knife?"

The waves were splashing noisily, the sun was shining, the sea was laughing. . . .

SONG OF THE STORMY PETREL

O'er the silver plain of ocean winds are gathering the storm-clouds, and between the clouds and ocean proudly wheels the Stormy Petrel, like a streak of sable lightning.

Now his wing the wave caresses, now he rises like an arrow, cleaving clouds and crying fiercely, while the clouds detect a rapture in the bird's courageous crying.

In that crying sounds a craving for the tempest! Sounds the flaming of his passion, of his anger, of his confidence in triumph.

The gulls are moaning in their terror—moaning, darting o'er the waters, and would gladly hide their horror in the inky depths of ocean.

And the grebes are also moaning. Not for them the nameless rapture of the struggle. They are frightened by the crashing of the thunder.

And the foolish penguins cower in the crevices of rocks, while alone the Stormy Petrel proudly wheels above the ocean, o'er the silver-frothing waters!

Ever lower, ever blacker, sink the storm-clouds to the sea, and the singing waves are mounting in their yearning toward the thunder.

Strikes the thunder. Now the waters fiercely battle with the winds. And the winds in fury seize them in unbreakable embrace, hurling down the emerald masses to be shattered on the cliffs.

Like a streak of sable lightning wheels and cries the Stormy Petrel, piercing storm-clouds like an arrow, cutting swiftly through the waters.

He is coursing like a Demon, the black Demon of the tempest, ever laughing, ever sobbing—he is laughing at the storm-clouds, he is sobbing with his rapture.

In the crashing of the thunder the wise Demon hears a murmur of exhaustion. He is certain that the clouds will not obliterate the sun; that the storm-clouds never, never, will obliterate the sun.

The waters roar.... The thunder crashes....

Livid lightning flares in storm-clouds o'er the vast expanse of ocean, and the flaming darts are captured and extinguished by the waters, while the serpentine reflections writhe, expiring, in the deep.

The storm! The storm will soon be breaking!

Still the valiant Stormy Petrel proudly wheels among the lightning, o'er the roaring, raging ocean, and his cry resounds exultant, like a prophecy of triumph—

Let it break in all its fury!

COMRADE

A TALE

I

EVERYTHING in this town was strange and incomprehensible. Its many churches raised their varicoloured cupolas skywards, but the walls and chimneys of the factories rose above the bell towers, and the churches, obscured by the heavy façades of business houses, were submerged in the lifeless labyrinth of stone walls like fantastic blossoms amid a heap of dust and debris. And when the church bells summoned to prayers, their metallic cries fell upon the iron of the roofs and were lost amid the narrow canyons between the houses.

The buildings were immense and frequently handsome, but the people were ugly and always contemptible; from morning till night they bustled about like grey mice, scurrying along the narrow, crooked streets of the town and searching with avid eyes, some for bread, others for amusement. Still others, standing on the crossroads, kept a hostile and watchful eye on the weak to see that they humbly submitted to the strong. The strong were the wealthy and everyone believed that money alone gave man power and freedom. All of them desired power, for all were slaves, the luxury of the rich evoked the envy and hatred of the poor, and for no one was there sweeter music than the clink of gold, and hence every man was another man's enemy and one and all were ruled by cruelty.

Sometimes the sun shone over the town, but the life was always dark and the people were like shadows. At night they lighted a myriad of bright lights, but then the hungry women came onto the street to sell their caresses for money, the odour of diverse rich foods assailed the nostrils and everywhere silently, hungrily blazed the resentful eyes of the starving, and a muffled moan of misery, too weak to cry aloud in anguish echoed faintly over the town.

Life was dreary and full of anxiety, all men were enemies and all men were in the wrong, only a few felt righteous but they were as coarse as animals, they were crueller than all the others. . . .

Everyone wanted to live and no one knew how, no one could freely follow the path of his desires, and every step into the future caused an involuntary glance back at the present, which with the powerful, relentless hands of a greedy monster halted man in his tracks and enmeshed him in its viscid embrace.

Man paused helplessly in pain and bewilderment as he beheld the ugly grimace on life's face. Life gazed into his heart with thousands of sad, helpless eyes and beseeched him wordlessly, whereupon the bright images of the future died in his soul and man's groan of impotence was submerged in the uneven chorus of groans and cries of miserable, wretched people tortured on the rack of life.

There was always dreariness and anxiety, sometimes terror, and the dark gloomy city, with its revoltingly symmetrical heaps of stone that blotted out the temples, stood motionless, surrounding the people like a prison and giving back the sun's rays.

And life's music was a muffled cry of anguish and wrath, a soft hiss of hidden hatred, a menacing roar of cruelty, a sensual scream of violence. . . .

II

Amid the gloomy turmoil of sorrow and misfortune, in the convulsive grappling of greed and want, in the morass of pitiful egotism, a few solitary dreamers went unnoticed about the basements where dwelt the poor who had created the wealth of the city; spurned and derided, yet full of faith in man they preached revolt, they were rebellious sparks of the distant flame of truth. Secretly they brought with them into the basements small but always fruitful seeds of a simple yet great teaching, and now sternly with a cold glitter in their eyes, now gently and lovingly, planted this bright burning truth in the heavy hearts of the slave-men, the men turned by the will of the brutal and avaricious into blind and dumb tools of acquisition.

And these dark, downtrodden people listened distrustfully to the music of the new words, a music their weary hearts had desired dimly for so long, and gradually they raised their heads, extricating themselves from the web of cunning lies with which their powerful and greedy tormentors had entangled them.

Into their lives so full of a dull, suppressed resentment, into hearts poisoned by so many wrongs, into minds muddled by the flashy wisdom of the powerful—into this hard and miserable existence saturated with the bitterness of humiliation—a simple radiant word was flung.

"Comrade!"

It was not new to them, they had heard it and uttered it themselves, but until then it had had the same empty, dull sound as all the familiar, hackneyed words which to forget is to lose nothing.

But now it had a new ring, strong and clear, it sang with a new meaning and there was something as hard, sparkling and many-faceted about it as a diamond.

They accepted it and uttered it cautiously, gently, cherishing it tenderly in their hearts as a mother her babe she rocks in its cradle.

And the deeper they penetrated into the radiant soul of the word, the brighter and finer it seemed to them.

"Comrade!" they said.

And they felt that this word had come to unite the whole world, to raise all men to the summits of freedom and weld them with new bonds, the firm bonds of respect for one another, respect for man's freedom.

When this word took root in the hearts of the slaves, they ceased to be slaves and one day they declared to the city and all its mighty: "Enough!"

Whereupon life stopped, for they were the force that set it in motion, they and none other. The water ceased to flow, the fires died, the city was plunged in darkness and the powerful were as helpless as infants.

Fear possessed the souls of the oppressors and suffocating in the stench of their own excrement, they stifled their hatred of the rebels in fear and amazement at their power.

The spectre of hunger haunted them, and their children wailed piteously in the darkness.

Houses and churches, enveloped in gloom, merged in a soulless chaos of stone and iron; an ominous stillness held the streets in the grip of death; life stood still, for the power that gave it birth had grown aware of itself and the slave-man had found the magic, invincible word to express his will—he had freed himself from oppression and had seen his own power—the power of the creator.

Those were days of misery for the mighty, for those who had believed themselves to be the masters of life; the night was as a thousand nights, so thick was the gloom, so pitifully meagre and timid the lights that flickered in the dead city, and that city built in the course of centuries, the monster that had sucked the blood of men, rose before them in all its abominable ugliness, a pitiful heap of stone and wood. The sightless windows of houses looked out hungrily and gloomily onto the streets, where the true masters of life now walked with a new vigour. They too were hungry, hungrier indeed than the others, but the sensation was a familiar one, and the suffering of their bodies was not as acute as the suffering of the masters of life, nor did it dim the flame that burned brightly in their souls. They burned with a knowledge of their own power, the promise of coming victory shone in their eyes.

They walked the streets of the city, this dismal cramped prison of theirs where they had been scorned and derided, where so many injuries had been heaped upon their souls, and they saw the great significance of their labour, and this made them conscious of their sacred right to be the masters of life, the makers of its laws, its creators. And then with a new force, with a dazzling radiance the life-giving, unifying word sounded:

"Comrade!"

It rang out among the false words of the present as glad tidings of the future, of the new life that awaited all and everyone. Was it far or near, that life? They felt it was for them to decide; they were approaching freedom and they themselves were postponing its coming.

III

The prostitute, but yesterday a half-starved animal, waiting wearily on the squalid street for someone to come to her and cruelly purchase her caresses for a pittance—the prostitute too heard that word, but smiling embarrassedly she did not dare to repeat it. A

man came up to her, one of those who had never crossed her path
before this, he laid his hand on her shoulder and spoke to her as
one would speak to a kinsman:

"Comrade!" he said.

And she laughed softly and shyly so as not to weep with gladness such as her bruised heart had never known before. Tears, the
tears of a pure, new-born joy glistened in her eyes that had yesterday stared brazenly and hungrily at the world. This joy of the
outcasts who had been admitted into the great family of the world's
toilers shone everywhere on the streets of the city, and the dim
eyes of its houses looked on with growing malevolence and coldness.

The beggar to whom but yesterday the sated had flung a miserable coin to rid themselves of him and salve their conscience, he
too heard this word, which was for him the first alms that had
caused his poor poverty-corroded heart to beat with joy and gratitude.

The cabby, an absurd fellow whom customers had prodded in
the back so that he might pass on the blow to his starved, exhausted nag—this man accustomed to blows, his senses dulled by the
rattle of wheels on the stone pavements, he too, smiling broadly,
said to a passer-by:

"Want a lift... Comrade?"

Whereupon, frightened by the sound of the word, he gathered
up the reins ready to drive quickly away, and gazed down at the
passer-by, unable to wipe the happy smile from his broad, red face.

The passer-by returned his look kindly and said with a nod:

"Thanks, Comrade! I have not far to go."

Still smiling and blinking his eyes happily, the cabby turned
in his seat and set off with a loud clatter down the street.

People walked in compact groups on the pavements, and like
a spark the great word that was destined to unite the world was
tossed back and forth among them:

"Comrade!"

A policeman, bewhiskered, grave and important approached a
crowd gathered around an old man addressing them on a street
corner, and after listening to him for a few moments, said slowly:

"It's against the law to hold street meetings... disperse,
gentlemen...."

And, pausing for a second, he lowered his eyes and added softly:

"Comrades. . . ."

On the faces of those who bore this word in their hearts, who had invested it with flesh and blood and the strident sound of a clarion call to unity—on their faces glowed the pride of youthful creators, and it was clear that the strength they so lavishly invested in this word was indestructible, inexhaustible.

Against them grey, blind mobs of armed men were already being mustered, forming themselves silently into even lines—the wrath of the oppressors was about to descend upon the rebels who were fighting for justice.

And in the crooked, narrow streets of the great city, among its chill, silent walls built by the hands of unknown builders, a great faith in the brotherhood of man was spreading and maturing.

"Comrades!"

Here and there fire burst forth that was destined to flare up into the flame that would envelop the earth with the strong bright feeling of the kinship of all men. It will envelop the earth and sear it, reducing to ashes the malice, hatred and cruelty that disfigure us, melting all hearts and merging them in a single heart, the heart of upright, noble men and women linked in a closely-knit friendly family of free workers.

On the streets of the dead city the slaves had built, on the streets of the city where cruelty had reigned, faith in man, in his victory over himself and the evil of the world, grew and gathered strength.

And in the chaos of uneasy, joyless existence, like a bright, merry star, a torchlight into the future, shone that simple, heartfelt word:

"Comrade!"

THE NINTH OF JANUARY

THE CROWD reminded one of the dark swell of the ocean, scarcely roused by the first gust of a storm. It rolled on sluggishly;
the grey faces of the people looking like murky foam on the crest
of a wave.

Eyes sparkled with excitement, but the people looked wonder-
ingly at each other, as if they could not believe their own determination. Words circled over the crowd like tiny grey birds.

They spoke in low voices, gravely, as if trying to justify themselves to each other.

"It's impossible to bear it any longer, that's why we've
come...."

"People wouldn't have come out without a reason...."

"Won't 'He' understand?..."

They talked most of all about "Him," telling each other that
"He" was good and kind-hearted, and would understand everything.... But there was no colour in the words with which they depicted him. One felt that they had not thought of "Him" seriously,
or pictured him as a real live person for quite a long time, if
ever at all; that they did not know what "He" was, and did not
even understand what "He" was for, or what "He" could do. But
today "He" was needed. All were eager to understand him, and not
knowing the one who actually existed, they involuntarily pictured
him as something great. Great were their hopes, and they needed
something great to sustain them.

Now and again a bold voice was heard among the crowd
saying:

"Comrades! Don't let yourselves be deceived...."

But it was self-deception that they wanted, and the voice was
drowned by frightened and angry cries.

"We want to come out openly...."

"You keep quiet, brother...."

"Besides, isn't Father Gapon with us?"

"He knows...."

The crowd flowed sluggishly down the canal-like street, breaking up into eddies, murmuring, arguing and discussing, swerving against the house walls and again filling the middle of the street, a dark, fluid mass. A vague ferment of doubt seemed to pervade it, an obvious, intense expectation of something that would light up the path to the goal with belief in success, so that this belief could bind, merge all the fragments in one, strong and harmonious body. They tried to conceal their lack of belief, but could not do so, and a vague feeling of anxiety, and a particularly acute sensitiveness to sound, was observed among them. They shuffled along cautiously, pricking up their ears, staring ahead, persistently searching for something with their eyes. The voices of those who believed in the strength within them and not in a strength outside of them, imbued the crowd with a sense of fear and irritation far too acute for one who was convinced that he had a right to contend in open dispute against the power he wished to see.

As it poured from street into street, however, the crowd rapidly grew, and this outward growth gradually created a feeling of inner growth, awakened the consciousness that the slave-people had a right to call upon the government to pay attention to its needs.

"Say what you like, but we, too, are human...."

" 'He' will understand that we are only asking...."

"He must understand! ... We are not rebels...."

"Then, again, there's Father Gapon...."

"Comrades! One doesn't ask for freedom...."

"Oh, Lord! ..."

"You wait, brother!"

"Chase him away, the devil!"

"Father Gapon knows best...."

A tall man in a black overcoat with a yellow patch on the shoulder got up on the curb and, removing his cap from his bald head, began to talk loudly and solemnly, with flashing eyes and trembling voice. He talked about "Him," about the tsar.

At first there was an artificial exaltation in his words and tone of voice; they lacked the emotion, which, by infecting others, can almost perform miracles. It seemed as though the man was straining himself in an effort to awaken and conjure up an image that had

long been impersonal, lifeless, and obliterated by time. All his life
"He" had been remote from men; but now men needed "Him," men
were reposing all their hopes in "Him."

And they gradually revived the corpse. The crowd listened attentively—the speaker was expressing what it wished, it felt this;
and although the power which they had fantastically conjured up
in their minds obviously did not merge with "His" image, all knew
that such a power existed, that it must exist. The speaker identified
this power with the being with whom all were familiar from calen-
dar portraits and linked it with the image which they knew from legends; and in the legends this image was human. The words the
speaker uttered, loud and intelligible, clearly depicted a being that
was powerful, benevolent, and just, and who displayed paternal
interest in the needs of the people.

Belief came and enveloped the people, excited them, and drowned
the low whisperings of doubt.... The people hastened to yield
to the mood they had long been waiting for. They pressed close
together, a huge, compact mass of unanimous bodies, and the densi-
ty, the closeness of shoulders and hips, warmed the heart with com-
forting confidence, of hope of success.

"We don't want any red flags!" shouted the bald man. Waving
his cap, he stepped out in front of the crowd, his bald pate glistening dully, swaying before the eyes of the people and attracting
their attention.

"We are going to our father!"

"He'll not do us any wrong!"

"Red is the colour of our blood, comrades!" a determined voice
rang out over the heads of the crowd.

"No power can liberate the people except the power of the
people themselves!"

"Stop that!"

"Agitators! We want none of that!"

"Father Gapon is carrying a cross, but he comes along with a
flag!"

"You're too young to take command yet!"

Those who were the least confident walked in the heart of the
crowd, and from there shouted out angrily and apprehensively:

"Chase him away, that one with the flag!"

They now walked at a more rapid pace, without hesitation, and
with each step they took, they infected each other with this unity
of mood, with the intoxication of self-deception. The "He" which
they had just created persistently roused in their minds the shades
of the ancient, benevolent heroes, echoes of the legends they had
heard in childhood; and absorbing the vital strength of the human
desire to believe, "He" grew and grew in their imagination....
    Somebody shouted:
    " 'He' loves us...."
And there can be no doubt that this mass of people sincerely
believed in the love of the being whom they had just created.
    When the crowd poured from the street onto the embankment
a long, crooked line of soldiers barred its way to the bridge, but
the people were not daunted by this thin grey barrier. There was
nothing menacing in the figures of the soldiers that were distinctly
drawn against the light blue background of the broad river. They
were skipping to warm their frozen feet, flapping their arms, and
pushing each other about. On the other side of the river the
people saw a large, gloomy house. That was where "He," the tsar,
the master of this house, lived. Great and strong, kind and loving,
he could not, of course, have ordered his soldiers to prevent the
people from going to the one they loved, and to whom they wished
to speak about their needs.
    Still, a shadow of perplexity appeared on many faces, and the
people in front reduced their pace. Some looked back, others left
the crowd and stepped onto the sidewalk, but all tried to show
that they were aware of the presence of the soldiers and that it
did not surprise them. Some calmly gazed at the golden angel
that glistened high in the sky above the gloomy fortress, others
smiled. A voice said commiseratingly:
    "It's cold for the soldiers...."
    "Rather...."
    "But still they've got to stand there!"
    "The soldiers are here to keep order."
    "Quiet now, fellows! ... Keep calm!"
    "Three cheers for the soldiers!" somebody shouted.
    An officer, wearing a yellow hood thrown back on his shoul-
ders, drew his sword from its scabbard and, brandishing the curved

steel blade, shouted something to the crowd. The soldiers sprang
to attention and stood motionless, shoulder to shoulder.

"What are they doing?" a rather plump woman asked.

Nobody answered her. Suddenly everybody found it difficult to walk.

"Stand back!" they heard the officer shout.

Some of the people looked behind and saw a dense mass of
bodies into which a dark human river was continuing to flow in an
endless stream. Yielding to the pressure of this river the crowd
moved on and filled the open space in front of the bridge. Several
people stepped forward, and, waving white handkerchiefs, went out
to meet the officer, shouting:

"We are going to our tsar!"

"In a perfectly orderly manner!"

"Go back! If you don't, I shall order my men to shoot!"

When the officer's voice reached the crowd it was echoed by
a buzz of amazement. Some of the people had said that they would
not be allowed to go to "Him," but this threat to shoot at the
people who were going to "Him" in a perfectly orderly manner,
believing in his power and benevolence, distorted the image they
had created. "He" was a power above all powers and had no reason to fear anybody, had no reason to repulse his people with
bayonets and bullets. . . .

A tall, gaunt man, with a starved face and black eyes suddenly shouted out:

"Shoot? You won't dare!"

And turning to the crowd he continued loudly and angrily:

"Well? Didn't I tell you they wouldn't let us through?"

"Who? The soldiers?"

"Not the soldiers, but them, over there. . . ."

And he waved his arm into the distance.

"Those higher up. . . . Ah! I told you so, didn't I?"

"We don't know yet. . . ."

"When they hear what we've come for, they'll let us through!"

The noise increased. Angry exclamations and sarcastic remarks
were heard. Common sense had been shattered against this silly
barrier and was now silent. The gestures of the people became more
nervous and agitated. A raw, cold wind blew from the river. The
rigid bayonets glistened.

Bandying remarks and yielding to the pressure from behind, the people pushed forward. Those who had been waving handkerchiefs turned aside and disappeared in the crowd; but those in front, men, women and children, were all waving white handkerchiefs now.

"Shoot? What are you talking about? Why should they?" said an elderly man with a beard streaked with grey. "It's simply that they won't let us cross by the bridge and want us to go straight over the ice."

Suddenly a dry, uneven rattle broke out, and it seemed as though the crowd had been lashed by scores of invisible whips. For a moment all voices seemed to have been frozen, but the mass of people continued slowly to push forward.

"Blank shot," said somebody in a colourless voice, whether enquiring or stating a fact was not clear.

But here and there groans were heard, and several bodies lay at the feet of people in the crowd. A woman, wailing loudly and holding her hand to her breast, rapidly stepped out of the crowd towards the bayonets which were thrust out to meet her. Several people hurried after her, and then some more, sweeping round her and running ahead of her.

Again came the rattle of rifle fire, louder, but more ragged than before. The people standing near the fence heard the boards crunch, as if they were being fiercely gnawed by invisible teeth. One bullet scraped along the wooden fence and knocked small chips from it, scattering them into the faces of the people. People fell to the ground in twos and threes; some sank to the ground clutching their abdomens, others hastened away limping, still others crawled across the snow, and everywhere bright scarlet patches appeared on the snow, spreading, giving off vapour, and attracting everybody's eyes. . . . The crowd swept back, halted for a moment as if petrified, and then a savage nerve-racking howl rose from hundreds of throats. It rose and floated in the air like a continuous, intensely vibrating and discordant combination of cries of acute pain, horror, protest, mournful perplexity and cries for help.

Groups of people, bending low, ran forward to pick up the killed and wounded. The wounded too were shouting and shaking their fists. The faces of all had suddenly changed, and there was a glint of something akin to madness in their eyes. There were no signs of panic, of that state of universal horror which suddenly overcomes people, sweeps bodies into a heap like dry leaves and blindly drags and drives everybody in an unknown direction in a wild whirlwind of desire to hide. But there was every sign of horror, horror that burned like the touch of frozen iron; it froze the heart, held the body as in a vice, and compelled one to stare with wide-open eyes at the blood that was spreading over the snow, at the blood-stained faces, hands and clothing, and at the corpses which were lying so calmly amidst the pandemonium of the living. There was every sign of burning indignation, of mournful, impotent rage, of much perplexity; there were numerous strangely motionless eyes, brows drawn in an angry frown, tightly clenched fists, convulsive gestures, and anger expressed in strong language. But it seemed as though it was cold, soul-crushing, bewilderment that filled people's breasts most. Only a few short moments before they had marched along, clearly seeing their object before them; before their eyes had hovered that majestic, legendary image which they had admired, had loved, and which had sustained their hearts with great hope. Two volleys, blood, corpses, groans and—they all found themselves standing before a grey vacuum, impotent, and with hearts torn to shreds.

They kept moving about in one spot as if riveted to it with fetters, which they were unable to break. Some silently and mournfully carried away the wounded and picked up the dead, while others watched them doing this as if in a dream, stunned, in a strange state of apathy. Many shouted words of complaint and reproach at the soldiers, swore at them, shook their fists at them, took their caps off and bowed for some reason, and threatened them with the terrible wrath of someone or other....

The soldiers stood motionless, with ordered arms. Their faces were rigid too; the skin on their cheeks seemed taut and their cheekbones stood out prominently. It looked as though all the soldiers had white eyes, and that their lips were frozen together....

Somebody in the crowd cried out hysterically:

"It's a mistake! They made a mistake, brothers! They are taking us for somebody else! Don't believe it! Go, brothers—go and explain it to them!"

A boy who had climbed up a lamppost shouted out:

"Gapon is a traitor!"

"Do you see the reception they are giving us, comrades?..."

"No! It's a mistake! Things like this can't happen! Try and understand!"

"Make way for the wounded!"

Two working men and a woman were leading the tall, gaunt man. He was all covered with snow, and blood was dripping from the sleeve of his overcoat. His face was livid, his nose was sharper, and his dark lips moved feebly as he whispered:

"I told you they wouldn't let us through!... They are keeping him away from us. What do they care about the people!"

"Cavalry!"

"Run!"

The wall of soldiers shook and then opened like the two leaves of a wooden gate; and through the opening, on prancing, snorting horses, filed a troop of cavalrymen. The sharp command of an officer rang out, and above the heads of the horsemen sabres flashed like silver ribbons, cleaving the air and sweeping in one direction. The crowd stood swaying, excited, waiting, not believing.

Silence reigned. Suddenly a frenzied shout was heard:

"M-a-r-ch!"

It seemed as though a whirlwind struck the faces of the people and as if the ground heaved under their feet. Then commenced a mad stampede. People ran, pushing and knocking each other down, dropping the wounded they were carrying, and jumping over dead bodies. The heavy clatter of horses' hoofs reached them. The horsemen yelled, their horses leaped over the wounded, the fallen and the dead, sabres flashed, cries of horror and pain went up and now and again the swish of steel and its impact with bone was heard. The cries of the injured merged in a prolonged, hollow groan....

"A-a-a-h!"

The horsemen swung their sabres and brought them down on the heads of the people, their bodies lurching over their horses' sides with every blow. Their faces were flushed and looked sightless. The horses neighed, bared their teeth ferociously and wildly tossed their heads....

The people were driven back into the street from which they had come, and no sooner had the clatter of horses' hoofs died away in the distance than they began to look at each other, gasping for breath, their eyes bulging with astonishment. A guilty smile appeared on many faces. Somebody laughed and said:

"Oh, didn't I run!"

"It was enough to make anybody run!" answered another.

Suddenly cries of amazement, fright and anger rose on all sides. . . .

"What's the meaning of this, brothers, eh?"

"It's murder, that's what it is, fellow Christians!"

"What for?"

"There's a government for you!"

"Hack us to pieces, eh? Trample upon us with horses. . . ."

And so they stood there in bewilderment, expressing their indignation to each other. They did not know what to do. Nobody went away. They pressed against each other, trying to find a way out of this motley confusion of feeling, they looked at each other with anxious curiosity and yet, more surprised than frightened, waited for something, pricked up their ears, looked around expectantly. But all were crushed and stunned by amazement; this was the feeling that was uppermost in their hearts and prevented their mood from merging into something more natural in this unexpected, frightful, idiotically uncalled for moment, impregnated with the blood of the innocent. . . .

A young voice called out energetically:

"Hey! Come and pick up the wounded!"

Everybody awoke from their torpor and proceeded quickly towards the river. From the opposite direction came injured people covered with blood and snow, some crawling over the snow and others staggering on their feet. These were picked up and carried. Izvozchiks were stopped, their passengers were ordered to get out and the wounded were put in their place and driven away. Everybody became careworn, gloomy and silent. They looked at the wounded with appraising eyes, silently measured things, compared them, and pondered deeply to find an answer to the frightful question which confronted them like a vague, formless black shadow. It obliterated the image of the hero, the tsar, the fount of charity and goodness which they had so recently conjured up. But only a few dared audibly confess that this image was now destroyed. It was hard to confess this, for it meant abandoning one's only hope. . . .

The bald man in the overcoat with the yellow patch passed by. His dully shining skull was now stained with blood. His head and shoulders drooped and his knees seemed to be giving way. He was supported by a broad-shouldered, hatless lad with curly hair, and by a woman in a torn fur coat whose face was dull and lifeless.

"Wait a minute, Mikhailo. How can this be?" mumbled the wounded man. "Shoot the people? That's not allowed! . . . It ought not to be, Mikhailo."

"But that's what's happened!" shouted the lad.

"They shot . . . and they hacked . . ." observed the woman despondently.

"Then they must have had orders to do so. Mikhailo. . . ."

"Of course!" the boy answered angrily. "Did you think they'd come out and talk to you? Bring you out a glass of wine?"

"Wait a minute, Mikhailo. . . ."

The wounded man halted, leaned his back against the wall and shouted:

"Fellow Christians! . . . Why are they killing us? Under what law? . . . By whose orders?"

People walked past, hanging their heads.

Further down, at the street corner, next to a fence, several score of people had gathered, and in the middle of the crowd somebody was saying in an alarmed and angry voice, gasping for breath as he spoke:

"Gapon went to see the Minister last night. He must have known what would happen today. That shows he has betrayed us. Led us to death!"

"What good would that do him?"

"How do I know?"

The excitement spread. Everybody was faced with questions that were still unclear, but everybody felt that these questions were important, profound, stern, and imperatively demanded an answer. In the fire of this excitement, belief in assistance from outside, the hope of a miraculous saviour from want, perished.

A rather stout, poorly-clad woman, with a kind, motherly face and large sad eyes, walked down the middle of the street. She was weeping and supporting her blood-stained left hand with her right.

"How shall I be able to work now?" she wailed. "How shall I feed my children? To whom can I go to complain?... Fellow Christians, who is to protect the people if the tsar. too. is against us?"

Her questions, loud and clear, awakened the people. roused and stirred them. People ran up to the woman from all sides, halted in front of her and listened to what she said, gloomily, but attentively.

"So it means that there is no law for the people?"

Sighs broke from the lips of some of the people around her. Others swore under their breath.

A shrill angry voice shouted out from somewhere in the crowd: "I got assistance.... They broke my son's leg!"

"My Peter was killed!" another voice shouted.

Numerous cries of a similar kind went up. They lashed the ear and more and more often called forth a vengeful echo. whipped up the feeling of rage, and stimulated the consciousness that something had to be done to protect oneself against the murderers. Something like a decision appeared on the people's pale faces.

"Comrades! Let's go into town.... After all, perhaps we'll get some explanation of this.... Let's go, a few at a time!"

"They'll slaughter us...."

"Let's talk to the soldiers. Perhaps they'll understand that there's no law which permits the killing of people!"

"Perhaps there is such a law. How do you know?"

The mob slowly but steadily underwent a change; it became transformed into the people. The young people went away in small groups, but all went in one direction, back to the river. Meanwhile, more and more wounded and killed were being carried away. The smell of warm blood pervaded the air. and groans and exclamations rent the air.

"Yakov Zimin was shot right through the forehead...."

"Thanks to the Little Father, the tsar!"

"Y-e-s! He gave us a nice reception!"

Several strong oaths were uttered. Only a quarter of an hour before the crowd would have torn to pieces anybody who had uttered only one like them.

A little girl ran down the street loudly asking everybody: "Have you seen my mummy?"

The people looked at her silently and made way for her.

Later, the woman with the shattered hand was heard crying out:

"I'm here, I'm here!"

The street became deserted. The young people dispersed more and more quickly, while the older ones moved off in twos and threes, gloomily and unhurriedly, casting furtive glances at the young people who were hurrying away. They spoke little. Only now and again somebody, unable to restrain his bitter feelings, exclaimed in a low voice:

"So they have cast off the people...."

"Damned murderers!"

They expressed pity for those who were killed; and they had an inkling that a certain strong, slavish prejudice was killed too, but they prudently said nothing about it, they no longer pronounced "His" name, which now jarred on their ears, so as not to stir up the sorrow and anger that smouldered in their hearts....

But perhaps they said nothing about it because they feared that another prejudice would come to take the place of the dead one....

...A close, unbroken cordon of soldiers was drawn round the tsar's house. Cavalry were posted in the palace square, right under the windows, to which rose the smells of hay, horse dung and horse sweat, and the sounds of rattling sabres, clinking spurs, commands and stamping feet.

A dense mass of people, tens of thousands, with cold anger gnawing at their breasts, bore down upon the soldiers from all sides. They spoke calmly, but with a new emphasis, new words and with new hope, which they themselves scarcely understood. A company of soldiers, one flank resting against the wall of the building and the other against the iron railings of the park, barred the way to the palace square. Close up against them, face to face, stood the crowd, immeasurably large, mute and black.

"Move along, please!" said the sergeant-major in an under-tone, as he passed down the line, pushing the people away from the soldiers with his arms and shoulders and trying not to look into their faces.

"Why don't you let us through?" he was asked.

"Where to?"

"To the tsar!"

The sergeant-major halted for a moment and in a tone that sounded like boredom he exclaimed:

"But I'm telling you he's not here!"

"What, the tsar's not here?"

"No, I'm telling you he's not. So go away!"

"Do you mean he's gone for good?" enquired a sarcastic voice.

The sergeant-major halted again, raised his hand warningly and said:

"Take care, now! You know what you'll get for saying things like that!"

And then he went on to explain in a different tone:

"He's not in town."

To this came responses from the crowd:

"He's not anywhere!"

"He's dead!"

"You've shot him, you devils!"

"Did you think you could kill the people?"

"You can't kill the people! ... There's too many of us. ..."

"You have killed the tsar—do you understand?"

"Move along, I tell you, and stop that talk!"

"What are you? A soldier? What's a soldier?"

At another part of the line a little old man with a pointed beard was saying animatedly to the soldiers:

"You are human. So are we! Just now you are in uniform, but tomorrow you will be in civvies. You'll want a job, because you have to eat. You'll have no job, and you'll have nothing to eat. And so, boys, you'll have to do what we here are doing now. ... And they'll have to shoot at you, is that it? To kill you, because you are hungry, eh?"

The soldiers felt cold. They hopped from foot to foot, stamped their feet and rubbed their ears, passing their rifles from one hand to the other. Hearing this talk they sighed heavily, looked this way and that, and smacked their frozen lips. Their faces, livid with cold, all bore the uniform impress of despondency, perplexity and stupidity. They blinked their eyelids and lowered their eyes. Only a few of them screwed up an eye as if taking aim at something, and clenched their teeth, evidently finding it difficult to restrain their anger at this mass of people who were compelling them to freeze like this. The entire grey line breathed weariness and boredom.

The people stood opposite the soldiers, breast to breast and, pushed from behind, sometimes collided with them.

"Steady there!" one of the soldiers said in a low voice whenever this happened.

Other people grasped the soldiers' hands and spoke to them ardently. The soldiers listened, blinking their eyes; their faces became distorted by indefinite grimaces, which made them look pitiful, or shy.

"Don't touch the gun!" one of them said to a young lad in a fur cap. The boy was tapping the soldier's chest and saying:

"You're a soldier, not a butcher.... You were called up to protect Russia against her enemies, but they are making you shoot at the people.... But try and understand! The people—that's Russia!"

"We are not shooting!" answered the soldier.

"Look!" said the boy, pointing to the crowd. "This is Russia, the Russian people! They want to see their tsar...."

Somebody interrupted with a shout:

"They don't!"

"Is there anything bad in the people wanting to talk to the tsar about their affairs? Tell me, is there?"

"I don't know!" answered the soldier, spitting.

The man next to him added:

"We have orders not to talk...."

He sighed despondently and lowered his eyes.

One little soldier suddenly brightened up and asked the man in front of him eagerly:

"Hey, you! Aren't you from Ryazan?"

"No, I'm from Pskov.... Why do you ask?"

"Oh, just like that.... I'm from Ryazan...."

He smiled a broad smile and hunched his shoulders from the cold.

The crowd swayed in front of the straight grey wall and beat against it like the waves of a river beating against its rocky banks, receding and rolling forward again. It is doubtful whether many of the people knew why they were here, what they wanted, and what they were waiting for. They had no conscious aim or definite intention. They were conscious only of a bitter sense of wrong, of indignation, and many, of a desire for revenge; this is what bound them all, kept them here in the street. But there was no one upon whom to vent these feelings, no one upon whom to wreak vengeance.... The soldiers did not rouse anger, they did not irritate the people—they were simply stupid and unhappy, they were freezing; many were unable to keep from shivering, and their teeth were chattering.

"We've been here since 4 o'clock this morning!" they said. "It's simply awful!"

"It's enough to make you want to lie down and die...."

"Suppose you went away, eh? We could go back to our warm barracks then...."

"What's the time?"

It was nearly 2 o'clock.

"What are you all excited about? What are you waiting for?" the sergeant-major asked.

The question, his grave face, and the serious and confident tone in which he asked the question, cooled the ardour of the people. There seemed to be a special meaning in everything he said, more profound than the simple words he uttered.

"There's nothing to wait for! You are only keeping the men out in the cold...."

"Will you shoot at us?" a young man in a hood asked the sergeant-major.

The sergeant-major remained silent for a moment and then answered coolly:

"If we are ordered to—we will!"

This caused an outburst of reproaches, oaths, and jeers.

"What for? What for?" asked a tall, red-headed man, louder than the rest.

"Because you are disobeying the orders of the authorities!"
explained the sergeant-major, rubbing his ear.

The men listened to the talk going on among the crowd and
blinked their eyes despondently. One of them softly exclaimed:
"Wouldn't it be nice to have something hot now?"

"Would you like some of my blood?" somebody asked him in
a tone that was both angry and sad.

"I'm not a wild beast." answered the soldier, gloomily and
resentfully.

Many eyes stared at the broad flat faces of the long line of
soldiers with cold, silent curiosity, contempt and disgust. But the
majority tried to warm them with the fire of their own excitement,
to stir something in their hearts, which had been tightly compressed by barrack life, and in their heads, which had been stuffed
with the rubbish of barrack room training. Most of the people
wanted to do something, to put their thoughts and sentiments into
practice somehow, and they kept obstinately beating against this
grey cold wall of men who wished only one thing—to warm their
bodies.

The talk became more ardent, the words more and more
striking.

"Soldiers!" said a thick-set man with a long broad beard and
blue eyes. "Who are you? Aren't you sons of the Russian people?
The people are poor, downtrodden, without protection, without
work and without bread, and so they have come here today to ask
the tsar to help them. But the tsar orders you to shoot, to kill
them! Soldiers! The people—your fathers and brothers—are asking for assistance not only for themselves, but also for you! You
are being put against the people. They are compelling you to
kill your own fathers and brothers! Think of what you are doing!
Don't you understand that you are going against yourselves?"

That voice, calm and even, the fine face and grey-streaked
beard, the whole appearance of the man and his simple and truth-
ful words evidently moved the soldiers. They lowered their eyes
at his glance, they listened to him attentively, some shaking their
heads and sighing, others frowning and looking round. One of
them advised in an undertone:

"Go away—the officer will hear you!"

The officer, tall, fair, with a big moustache, was slowly pacing down the line. Pulling at the glove on his right hand he kept hissing through his clenched teeth:

"Disss-misss!... Get out of here! What? You want to talk? I'll give you talk!"

He had a fat red face and round eyes, bright, but with no sparkle in them. He walked down the line unhurriedly, stepping firmly on the ground. But on his approach time flew more quickly, as if every second was in a hurry to pass in case it should be filled with something offensive and disgusting. It seemed as though an invisible ruler was trailing behind the officer, straightening the line of men. They stood up, drew in their abdomens, pushed out their chests and glanced down at their toes. Some of them drew the attention of the people to the officer with their eyes and made angry faces. On reaching the end of the line the officer commanded:

"'Shun!"

The soldiers drew smartly to attention and stood as if petrified.

"I order you to disperse!" the officer then said, unhurriedly drawing his sword from its scabbard.

It was absolutely impossible for the crowd to disperse, for the whole of the small square was crammed with people, and more and more people were pressing into its rear from the street.

Looks of hatred were cast at the officer, jeers and oaths were hurled at him, but he stood unmoved. He ran his dull eyes down the line of soldiers and his brows twitched slightly. A clamour went up from the crowd. It was irritated by the officer's calmness, which was too inhuman to be appropriate for the present moment.

"That one would give the order!"

"He'd shoot without orders. . . ."

"Yes. Drew his sword, and all. . . ."

"Hey, Mister! Are you ready to kill?"

This bantering tone gradually grew into one of recklessness; the cries became louder and the jeers more biting.

The sergeant-major looked at the officer, shuddered, went pale and also quickly drew his sword.

Suddenly the sinister strains of a bugle were heard. The people turned their eyes in the direction of the bugler—his cheeks were

strangely puffed out and his eyes bulged; the bugle trembled in
his hands and he played much too long. The nasal, brassy sounds
were drowned by an outburst of whistling, shrieking, howling,
curses, reproaches, despairing groans of impotence and shouts of
reckless desperation called forth by the consciousness that death
could follow in an instant, and that it would be impossible to
escape it. There was nowhere to go to escape from it. Several dark
figures dropped to the ground and pressed close to it, others hid
their faces with their hands. The man with the large beard stepped
out in front, tore his overcoat open at his chest and peered with
his blue eyes into the faces of the soldiers. He spoke to them, but
what he said was unheard, for his voice was drowned in the chaotic tumult.

The soldiers whipped their rifles to the "ready," then raised
them to "present," and stood as if petrified, in a uniform, alert
posture, with their bayonets pointing at the crowd.

The line of bayonets suspended in the air was uneven—some
were held too high and others too low; only a few were pointed
straight at the breasts of the people, but all looked soft, and they
quivered, seeming to melt and bend.

A loud voice rang out in horror and disgust:

"What are you doing? Murderers!"

The line of bayonets shook convulsively. A frightened volley
rang out. The people recoiled, hurled back by the sound, by striking bullets and by the falling bodies of the killed and wounded.
Some, without uttering a word, began to jump over the railings of
the park.

Another volley rang out ... and then another.

A boy, who was struck by a bullet as he was climbing the
railings, suddenly bent over and remained suspended with his feet
upwards. A tall graceful woman with fluffy hair gasped and sank
slowly to the ground near the boy.

"May you be accursed!" somebody shouted.

The place became less congested and quieter. The people in the
rear ran back into the street and took refuge in the courtyards. The
crowd slowly retreated as if pushed back by invisible hands. A
space of about twenty feet was left between the crowd and the soldiers, and this space was strewn with bodies. Some got up and ran

quickly towards the crowd. Others got up with great difficulty, revealing patches of blood on the ground, and staggered off, leaving
a trail of blood behind them. Many lay motionless, face upwards,
face downwards, and on their sides, but all stretched in a queer
state of tension, as if death had caught them, and they were trying
to tear themselves out of its clutches. . . .

   The smell of blood pervaded the air, reminding one of the
warm, saline breath of the sea in the evening, after a sultry day;
it was a pernicious smell; it intoxicated one and roused an unhealthy
desire to inhale it long and deeply. It distorted the imagination
in a disgusting way, as butchers, soldiers and others professionally
engaged in killing know.

   The crowd wailed as it retreated. Curses, oaths and cries of pain
mingled with a confused medley of whistling, howling and groans.
The soldiers stood with their feet firmly planted on the ground, as
rigid as the dead. Their faces were ash-grey, their lips were closely
pressed together, as if they, too, wanted to shout and whistle, but
restrained themselves because it was against orders. They stared in
front of them with wide-open eyes; they no longer blinked. There
was nothing human in that stare; it seemed as though those dull, vacant spots on the grey, drawn faces were sightless. Perhaps they did
not want to see, because they were secretly afraid that if they saw
the warm blood which they had spilled, they would want to spill
more. Their rifles trembled in their hands, the bayonets twisting as if
they were boring into the air. But this trembling could not dispel
the dull indifference of the men whose hearts had been hardened
by the violence which had been done to their will, and whose minds
had been thickly plastered with disgusting, putrid falsehood. The
bearded, blue-eyed man rose from the ground and again addressed
the soldiers in a sobbing voice, his whole body twitching as he
spoke:

   "You have not killed me. . . . That's because I told you the sacred truth. . . ."

   The people again slowly and gloomily pressed forward to pick
up the dead and wounded. Several men stood beside the one who was
addressing the soldiers and, interrupting him, also began to plead,
to shout and to rebuke, not angrily, but in tones of sadness and
sympathy. The voices still rang with naive confidence that truth

would prevail, with a desire to prove the absurdity and madness of cruelty and to make the soldiers understand how awful was the mistake they had made. They wanted, and tried hard, to make them understand how shameful and disgusting was the part they were involuntarily playing. . . .

The officer drew his revolver from its holster, carefully examined it, and strode up to the group that was talking to the men. They made way for him, unhurriedly, as one steps aside when a stone is slowly rolling down the mountainside. The blue-eyed bearded man, however, did not budge, but met the officer with ardent words of reproach, and with wide gestures pointed to the blood all round.

"How are you going to justify this?" he asked him. "There is no justification for it."

The officer stood in front of the man, knitted his brows in a preoccupied manner and raised his arm. The shots were not heard, but wisps of smoke encircled the arm of the murderer, once, twice and thrice. After the third time, the bearded man's knees gave way, his head fell back, and waving his right arm he fell to the ground. People rushed at the murderer from all sides. He retreated, brandishing his sword and pointing his revolver at everybody. . . . A boy fell down at his feet, and he plunged his sword into his stomach. He shouted in a grating voice and jumped about like a prancing horse. Somebody threw a cap in his face. He was pelted with clots of blood-stained snow. The sergeant-major and several men ran towards him with out-thrust bayonets, and the attackers ran away. The victor waved his sword at the retreating people threateningly, and then he suddenly lowered it and plunged it once again into the body of the boy, who was crawling at his feet, bleeding profusely.

And again the brassy strains of the bugle rang out. On hearing them the people rapidly deserted the square, but the sounds continued to undulate in the air, as if putting the finishing touches to the vacant eyes of the soldiers, the bravery of the officer, his red-tipped sword and his dishevelled moustache. . . .

The vivid, scarlet hue of the blood irritated the eye and yet fascinated one, rousing a drunken and vicious desire to see more of it, to see it everywhere. The soldiers looked alert, they stretched

their necks this way and that as if searching with their eyes for
more living targets for their bullets. . . .

The officer stood at one end of the line, waved his sword and
shouted something in a choking voice, angrily, savagely.

From all sides came answering cries:

"Butcher!"

"Scoundrel!"

The officer stroked his moustache.

Another volley was fired, and then another. . . .

The streets were packed with people as tightly as a sack with
grain. There were fewer working men here; most of the people
were small shopkeepers, salesmen and clerks. Some of them had
already seen the blood and the corpses, and others had been beat-
en up by the police. They were brought out of their houses into
the street by alarm; and they spread alarm everywhere, magnify-
ing the outward horrors of the day. Men, women and children
looked around anxiously, and listened intently and expectantly. They
told each other about the killing, moaned and groaned, swore,
questioned the slightly wounded working men, and now and again
lowered their voices to a whisper and talked mysteriously to each
other. Nobody knew what was to be done, and nobody went home.
They felt and guessed that something important was going to happen
after this killing, something more profound and tragic for them
than the hundreds of killed and wounded, who were strangers to
them.

Up to this day they had lived almost without thinking, with
vague ideas, heaven knows when or how acquired, about the government, the law, the authorities, and their rights, and these ideas,
being amorphous, did not prevent their brains from becoming enmeshed with a thick, close web, from being covered with a thick,
slimy crust. These people were accustomed to think that there was
a certain power whose function it was to protect them and was
capable of protecting them, namely—the law. This habit gave
them a sense of security and safeguarded them from all troublesome thoughts. Life was tolerable under these conditions, and although these vague ideas were often disturbed by life's pin-pricks,
scratches, jostles and sometimes even heavy blows, they remained

strong and tenacious. The scratches and fissures soon healed, and
the ideas retained their lifeless integrity.

But today, their brains were suddenly exposed, and they shuddered; their breasts were filled with alarm that chilled them like
a cold blast. Everything that had been established and habitual
was upset, was shattered and had vanished. All of them were conscious, more or less clearly, of a sad and frightful loneliness and
defenselessness in face of a cruel and cynical power which recog-
nized no rights and no law. This power held all lives in its hands
and could with impunity sow death among masses of people,
could destroy the living just as its will dictated, and in any numbers
it pleased. Nobody could restrain it. It refused to talk to anybody.
It was all-powerful and coolly proved that its authority was limitless by senselessly strewing the streets of the city with corpses and
flooding them with blood. Its bloody, thirsty, insane caprice was
clearly visible, and it sowed universal alarm, a gnawing, soul-de-
stroying dread. But it also persistently roused the mind, compelling
it to devise new plans for protecting the individual, new methods
for the protection of life.

A short, thick-set man was walking along with lowered head,
swinging his blood-stained hands. The front of his coat was also
profusely stained with blood.

"Are you wounded?" he was asked.

"No."

"What about the blood?"

"It's not my blood," the man answered and passed on. Suddenly he
halted, looked round and said in a loud voice that sounded queer:

"It's not my blood. It's the blood of those who believed . . ." and
he went on his way, lowering his head again, without finishing
what he had to say.

A troop of horsemen rode among the crowd, swinging their
knouts. The people rushed away from them in all directions, col-
liding with each other, and pressing against the walls. The soldiers were drunk. They smiled idiotically, swayed in their saddles,
and now and again, as if reluctantly, struck at people's heads and
shoulders with their knouts. One man was bowled over by a blow and
fell to the ground, but he sprang to his feet again and asked the soldier:

"What was that for? Ekh! You brute!"

The soldier unslung his carbine and without reining in his horse fired at the man. The man dropped to the ground again. The soldier laughed.

"Look what they are doing!" shouted a respectably dressed. horrified gentleman, turning his distorted face in all directions. "Do you see what they're doing?"

The murmur of excited voices continued without interruption, and amidst the torments of fear, the anguish of despair, something was born that slowly and imperceptibly united resurrected. awkward minds, minds which were unaccustomed to work.

But men of peace appeared.

"Why did he abuse the soldier?" demanded one.

"The soldier struck him, didn't he?"

"He should have got out of the way!"

In an archway two women and a student were attending to a working man who had been shot through the arm. The wounded man winced, looked around angrily, and said to those around him:

"We had no secret intentions whatever. It's only skunks and dicks who say we had. We went openly. The Ministers knew why we were going. They had a copy of our petition. If we were not allowed to go, why didn't they say so, the skunks! They had plenty of time to tell us. We didn't arrange this today. . . . They knew—the police and the Ministers—that we were going. The murderers. . . ."

"What did you ask for in your petition?" enquired a short. grey-haired, lean old man, thoughtfully and gravely.

"We asked that the tsar should assemble representatives elected by the people and govern the country with them, and not with the government officials. Those scoundrels have ruined Russia, they have robbed everybody."

"Yes, that's true. . . . We must have control!" observed the little old man.

The working man's arm was bandaged and they carefully rolled down the sleeve of his coat.

"Thank you," he said. "I told my comrades that it was no use going, that nothing would come of it. Now they will see that I was right."

He gingerly inserted his hand into his buttoned overcoat and unhurriedly went off.

"Do you hear how they talk? You know what that means, brother. . . ."

"Y-e-s! Still, they shouldn't have done this slaughter. . . ."

"They shot him today. It may be my turn tomorrow. . . ."

"You're right there. . . ."

At another spot two men were arguing heatedly. One said:

"He might not have known!"

"Then why. . . ."

But there were few now who wanted to revive the corpse, so few that they were hardly noticeable. They only roused anger by their attempts to raise again the ghost which had now been laid. They were attacked as if they were enemies, and they ran away in fright.

A battery of artillery rode into the street. The soldiers sat on their horses and limbers, thoughtfully gazing ahead, over the heads of the people. The crowd pushed back to make way for the guns. Sullen silence reigned; only the rattle of the harness and the clatter of ammunition boxes was heard. The gun barrels, swaying like elephant's trunks, pointed their muzzles to the ground as if smelling it. The cavalcade reminded one of a funeral.

Shots rang out in the distance. The people stood petrified, listening intently. Somebody said:

"Again!"

Suddenly a ripple of excitement swept down the street.

"Where, where?"

"On the Island. . . . On Vassilyevsky Island. . . ."

"Do you hear?"

"You don't say?"

"On my word of honour! They've captured a gunsmith's shop. . . ."

"Aha!"

"They cut down the telegraph poles and built a barricade. . . ."

"Is that so?"

"Is there a lot of them?"

"Plenty!"

"Oh! If only they avenged the innocent blood that has been spilt!"

"Let's go there!"

"Let's go, Ivan Ivanovich, eh?"

"Y-e-ss.... But ... you know...."

The figure of a man appeared above the crowd, and in the twilight an appeal rang out:

"Who wants to fight for freedom? For the people, for man's right to life and labour? He who wants to die in battle for the future—let him go and help!"

Some gathered round the man, and a close-packed knot of bodies was formed in the middle of the street. Other people hurried away.

"You see how angry the people are!"

"Quite legitimately! Quite!"

"But it's madness...."

The crowd melted in the twilight. People dispersed to their homes, carrying with them an unfamiliar sense of alarm, a frightening sense of loneliness, a half-awakened consciousness of the tragedy of their lives, the oppressed, senseless lives of slaves ... and a readiness to adjust themselves to everything that would be advantageous and convenient....

The atmosphere became more tense than ever. Darkness broke the contacts between people—the feeble contacts of external interests. And those who lacked fire in their hearts hastened to their accustomed nooks.

Night was falling fast, but the street lamps were not lit....

"Dragoons!" shouted a hoarse voice.

Out of a side street a squad of cavalry suddenly appeared. The horses stamped their hoofs for a few seconds and then charged down upon the people. The soldiers yelled in a queer way; they roared, and there was something inhuman, dark, blind, an unintelligible something akin to despair in that roar. Both men and horses looked smaller and blacker in the darkness. Sabres glinted dully, there were fewer outcries, but the sounds of numerous blows were heard.

"Hit them with whatever comes to your hands, comrades! Blood for blood!"

"Run!"

"Don't dare, soldier! I'm not a peasant!"

"Hit them with cobble-stones! Comrades!"

Upsetting the tiny dark figures, the horses pranced, neighed and snorted. The clash of steel was heard. A command rang out: "Squad!..."

A bugle rang out, hurriedly and nervously. People ran, pushing each other and falling. The street became deserted, but dark hummocks remained on the ground, and from somewhere. down a side street, came the rapid clatter of heavy hoofs....

"Are you wounded, comrade?"

"My ear's cut off, I think...."

"What can you do with bare hands?"

The sound of rifle fire echoed in the deserted street.

"They haven't grown tired of it yet—the devils!"

Silence. Hurried footsteps. How strange that there were so few sounds and no movement in the street. A subdued, liquid murmur floated from all directions, as if the sea had invaded the city.

Somewhere near, a low moan trembled in the darkness.... Somebody was running and breathing heavily.

An anxious voice enquired:

"Are you wounded, Yakov?"

"It's nothing!" answered a hoarse voice.

From the side street, down which the dragoons had galloped, a crowd reappeared and flowed blackly across the whole width of the street. Somebody, walking in front, but inseparably from the crowd, was saying:

"Today we took a pledge sealed with our blood—henceforth we must be citizens."

Another voice interrupted him and said nervously with a sob:

"Yes—our fathers have shown us what they really are!"

And somebody else said threateningly:

"We shall never forget this day!"

They walked quickly, in a close-packed crowd, many talking at once, and their voices merged chaotically with the dark, angry, murmer. Now and again somebody raised his voice to a shout, drowning all the other voices.

"Christ, how many were killed today!"

"And what for?"

"No! We can never forget this day!"

Somebody on the side. in a strained hoarse voice. made the sinister prophecy:

"You'll forget, slaves! What's other people's blood to you?"

"Shut up, Yakov!"

It became darker and quieter. Passers-by turned their heads in the direction of the voices and growled.

A light from a window threw a faint yellow patch upon the street. In the patch two black figures were seen. One was sitting on the ground, leaning against a lamppost: the other was bending over him, evidently wanting to help him to rise. And again one of them said, softly and sadly:

"Slaves. . . ."

TALES OF ITALY

I

THE TRAM-CAR employees in Naples were on strike: a string of
empty cars stretched the entire length of the Riviera di Chiaia
and a crowd of conductors and motormen, jolly, voluble Neapolitans, as volatile as quicksilver, had gathered on Piazza della Vit-
toria. Above their heads over the park fence sparkled a fountain
jet like the slender blade of a sword, around them milled a large,
hostile crowd of people who had to travel on business to all parts
of the huge city and all these shop assistants, artisans, petty traders
and seamstresses loudly reproached the strikers. Harsh words and
biting jibes were uttered and there was much gesticulating, for the
Neapolitans speak as expressively and eloquently with their hands
as with their indefatigable tongues.

A light breeze was wafted from the sea, the dark green fronds
of the tall palms in the city park swayed gently, their trunks looking strangely like the clumsy legs of some monster elephants.
Urchins, the half-naked children of the Neapolitan streets, romped
about, filling the air with their sparrow-like twitter and laughter.

The city which resembled an old engraving, was bathed in the
generous rays of the blazing sun and seemed to reverberate like
an organ; the blue waves in the gulf plashed against the stone
embankment adding a muffled beat, like the throbbing of a tambourine, to the hubbub and cries of the city.

The strikers huddled gloomily together barely replying to the
irritable outcries of the crowd; some of them climbed onto the
railing of the park peering anxiously down the street over the heads
of the people, like a pack of wolves surrounded by the hounds. It
was clear that these people in their uniformed attire were closely
linked by an unshakable resolve to stand their ground and this
irritated the crowd still more. But the crowd too had its philoso-

phers. Smoking calmly, the latter admonished the more impassioned opponents of the strikers thus:

"Ah, signor! What is a man to do if he can't afford macaroni for his children?"

Sprucely-attired agents of the municipal police stood by in groups of two and three watching to see that the crowd did not obstruct the movement of the carriages. They kept strictly neutral, staring with like equanimity at the censurers and censured and good-humouredly chaffing both sides when shouts and gestures became too heated. A detachment of carabinieri carrying their short, light rifles were lined up against the buildings on a narrow side-street, ready to intervene in the event of serious clashes. They made a rather sinister group in their three-cornered hats, abbreviated capes and the scarlet stripes like two streaks of blood running down their trousers.

Suddenly the wrangling jeers, reproaches and persuasions subsided. Some new spirit swept the crowd, a pacifying spirit it seemed; the strikers moved closer together with set faces as shouts arose from the crowd:

"The soldiers!"

Whistles of mockery and triumph directed at the strikers mingled with shouts of greeting and one stout man in a light grey suit and a panama hat broke into a caper, tapping with his feet against the stone causeway. The conductors and motormen made their way slowly through the crowd to the cars, some climbed aboard. They looked grimmer than before as they forced their way through the crowd snapping retorts to the exclamations from all sides. The hubbub subsided.

Up from the Santa Lucia embankment with a light, dancing step came the little grey soldiers, their feet beating a rhythmic tattoo and their left hands swinging with a mechanical motion. They looked like tin soldiers and as fragile as mechanical toys. They were led by a ta'l handsome officer with knit brows and a contemptuous twist to his lips; beside him hopped a stout man in a top hat chattering volubly and cleaving the air with innumerable gestures.

The crowd fell back from the cars; the soldiers scattered along them like so many grey beads taking up positions at the platforms where the strikers stood.

The man in the top hat and several other respectable-looking citizens with him waved their arms wildly and shouted:

"The last time ... ultima volta! Do you hear?"

The officer stood with his head inclined twirling his moustache with a bored air; a man ran up to him waving his top hat and shout-ing something in a hoarse voice. The officer glanced at him out of the corner of his eye, then drew himself up, threw out his chest and rapped out commands in a loud voice.

Whereupon the soldiers began jumping onto the platforms of the cars, two on each platform, while the motormen and conductors jumped down one after the other.

This struck the crowd as being funny—it roared, whistled and laughed, but all at once the noise subsided and with grim, tense faces and eyes wide with horror the people fell back from the cars in heavy silence, and stampeded toward the front car.

There, within two feet of its wheels, stretched across the rails, lay one of the motormen. His grey head was bared and his face, the face of a soldier with the moustaches bristling angrily, stared up at the sky. As the crowd gaped, a lad, small and agile as a monkey, threw him-self down beside the motorman, and one by one others followed suit.

A low hum rose from the crowd and voices were heard calling fearfully on the Madonna, some cursed grimly, the women screamed and groaned and the urchins, excited by the spectacle, bounced about like rubber balls.

The man in the top hat yelled something in a hysterical voice, the officer looked at him and shrugged his shoulders—his soldiers had been sent to take over the cars from the tram men but he had no orders to fight the strikers.

Then the top hat, surrounded by some officious people, rushed over to the carabinieri—and now they came forward and bent over the men lying on the rails intending to remove them.

There was a brief scuffle; then suddenly the whole grey dusty crowd of on'ookers swayed, bellowed, howled and rushed over to the rails—a man in a panama snatched off his hat, threw it into the air and was the first to lay down beside the end striker, slapping him on the shoulder and shouting words of encouragement in his ear.

One by one people began to drop down onto the rails, as if their feet had given way beneath them—jolly, noisy folk who had not been there at all two minutes ago. They threw themselves on the ground, laughing and pulling faces at one another and shouting to the officer who was saying something to the top-hatted individual shaking his gloves under his nose, chuckling and shaking his handsome head.

And more and more people poured onto the rails, women dropped their baskets and bundles, small boys, shaking with laughter, curled up like shivering puppies, and decently dressed people rolled about in the dust.

The five soldiers standing on the platform of the front car looked down at the heap of bodies under the wheels and shook with laughter, clinging to the bars for support, throwing back their heads and bending forward, convulsed with amusement. They did not look at all like mechanical toys now.

... Half an hour later the tram-cars, scraping and clanging were speeding through the streets of Naples, and on the platforms stood the beaming victors and down the cars walked the victors, asking politely:

"Biglietti?!"

And the passengers handed them the red and yellow slips of paper with many a wink, smile and good-natured grumbling.

II

On the little square in front of the railway station in Genoa a dense crowd was assembled; they were mostly workingmen but there were a good many respectably dressed and well-fed people as well. In front of the crowd stood members of the town council; above their heads waved the heavy and cunningly embroidered silk banner of the city, with the varicoloured banners of the workers' organizations beside it. The golden tassels, fringes, and cords glittered, the tips of the flagpoles shone, the silk rustled and a low hum like a choir singing sotto voce rose from the festive throng.

Above, on its tall pedestal, stood the statue of Columbus, the dreamer who had suffered so much for his beliefs and who won because he believed. Today too he looked down at the people and his marble lips seemed to be saying:

"Only those who believe can win."

Around the pedestal at his feet the musicians laid their instruments and the brass glittered like gold in the sun.

The receding semi-circle of the station building spread its heavy marble wings as though wishing to embrace the waiting throng. From the port came the laboured breathing of the steamships, the muffled churning of a propeller in the water, the clanging of chains, whistling and shouting. But the square was still and hot under the broiling sun. On the balconies and at the windows of houses women stood with flowers in their hands and beside them were children looking like flowers in their holiday garb.

As the locomotive rolled whistling into the station the crowd stirred and several crushed hats flew into the air like so many dark birds; the musicians picked up their trumpets, and several grave, elderly men spruced themselves, hastily stepped forward and turned to face the crowd speaking excitedly and gesturing to the right and left.

Slowly the crowd parted, clearing a wide passage to the street.

"Whom have they come to meet?"

"The children from Parma!"

There was a strike on in Parma. The bosses would not yield and the workers were hard pressed and so they had gathered their children who had already begun to suffer from hunger and had sent them to their comrades in Genoa.

A neat procession of little people emerged from behind the columns of the stations; they were shabbily clothed and their rags gave them the appearance of some queer shaggy little animals. They walked hand in hand, five in a row, very small, dusty and obviously weary. Their faces were grave but their eyes shone brightly, and when the musicians struck up the Garibaldi hymn a smile of pleasure flickered over those gaunt, hunger-pinched little faces.

The crowd welcomed the men and women of the future with a deafening shout, banners dipped before them, the brass trumpets blared out, stunning and dazzling the children; somewhat taken aback by this reception, they shrank back for a moment and then suddenly they drew themselves up so that they looked taller, coalesced into a mass and from hundreds of throats there rose a single shout:

"Viva l'Italia!"

"Long live young Parma!" thundered the crowd, closing in upon them,

"Evviva Garibaldi!" shouted the children, as their grey wedge cut into the crowd and was engulfed by it.

In the hotel windows and from the roofs of houses handkerchiefs fluttered like white birds, and a shower of flowers and gay, lively shouts poured down on the heads of the crowd below.

Everything took on a festive appearance, everything sprang to life, even the grey marble seemed to blossom out in daubs of bright colour.

The banners waved in the breeze, caps and flowers flew into the air, the tiny heads of the children rose above the heads of the throng, small grimy paws stretched out in greeting sought to catch the flowers and the air resounded with the mighty, unceasing shout:

"Viva il Socialismo!"

"Evviva l'Italia!"

Nearly all the children were snatched up, some sat perched on the shoulders of the grown-ups, others were pressed against the broad chests of stern bewhiskered men; the music was barely audible above the hubbub of shouting and laughter.

Women darted in and out of the crowd picking up the remaining newcomers and shouting to one another:

"You'll take two, Annita?"

"Yes. And you?"

"Don't forget one for lame Margaret. . . ."

A feeling of joyous excitement reigned, on all sides were beaming faces and moist kind eyes, and already some of the strikers' children were munching bread.

"No one thought of this in our time!" remarked an old man with a beak-like nose and a black cigar between his teeth.

"And how simple it is. . . ."

"Yes. Simple and wise."

The old man removed the cigar from his mouth, glanced at its tip and sighed as he shook off the ash. Then noticing two little Parma children—brothers obviously—beside him, he assumed an expression of mock gravity, and with the kiddies staring gravely at him, pushed his hat over his eyes, spread out his arms and, as the boys backed away together scowling, suddenly squatted down and crowed like a rooster. The boys roared with laughter, stamping their bare soles on the cobbles; the man rose, righted his hat, and,

feeling that he had done all that was required of him, strolled off
swaying on his unsteady feet.

A humpbacked, grey-haired woman, with the face of a witch
and wiry grey hairs sprouting on a bony chin, stood at the foot
of the statue of Columbus and wept, wiping her reddened eyes
with the end of her faded shawl. Dark and ugly, she looked
strangely forlorn among the excited throng. . . .

A black-haired young Genoese woman came tripping along,
leading by the hand a young man of about seven wearing wooden
clogs and a grey hat so large that it reached down almost to his
shoulders. He tossed his little head to shake the hat back from his
eyes but it kept slipping forward onto his face until the woman
swept it off and waved it high in the air, laughing and singing;
his face wreathed in smiles the child threw back his head to look,
then jumped up to catch the hat as both disappeared from view.

A tall man in a leather apron, with powerful bare arms carrying a little girl of six on his shoulder, a grey mousey little thing
remarked to the woman walking beside him leading a small boy
with flaming red hair:

"See what I mean? If this sort of thing takes root . . . it won't
be easy to get the better of us, eh?"

And with a deep laugh of triumph he threw his little burden
up into the blue air, crying: "Evviva Parma—a!"

The people gradually dispersed carrying or leading the children with them, until the square was empty of all save the crumpled flowers, candy wrappers, a group of jolly facchini and over
them the noble figure of the man who discovered the New World.

And the happy shouts of the people going forward to a new
life echoed through the streets like the fanfare of great trumpets.

III

The calm blue lake is set in a frame of tall mountains crested
by eternal snows, the dark tracery of gardens undulates in luxu-
rious folds down to the water's edge, white houses that seem built
of sugar gaze into the water and the stillness is like the gentle
slumber of a child.

It is morning. The scent of flowers is wafted sweetly from the hills. The sun has just risen, and the dewdrops still glisten on the leaves of the trees and the blades of grass. The road is a grey ribbon flung into the silent mountain gorge, the road is paved with stones yet it seems as if it must be soft as velvet to the touch.

Beside a heap of rubble sits a worker, as black as a beetle; his face expresses courage and kindliness and he wears a medal on his chest.

Resting his bronzed hands on his knees and raising his head, he looks up into the face of the passer-by standing under the chestnut tree.

"This medal, signor," he says, "is for my work on the Simplon tunnel."

And looking down he smiles gently at the shining piece of metal on his chest.

"Yes, all work is hard until it gets into your bones and you learn to love it, and then it stirs you and ceases to be hard. But, of course, it wasn't easy!"

He shook his head faintly, smiling at the sun; then, livening up suddenly, he waved his hand and his black eyes glistened.

"Sometimes it was a bit frightening. Even the earth must feel something, don't you think? When we burrowed deep inside, cutting a great gash into the mountain side the earth there within met us wrathfully. Its breath was hot, and our hearts sank, our heads grew heavy and our bones ached. Many have experienced the same thing! Then it hurled stones at us and doused us with hot water; that was awful! Sometimes when the light struck it, the water would turn red and my father would say that we had wounded the earth, and it wou'd drown and scorch us all with its blood! That was sheer imagination, of course, but when you hear such talk deep down inside the earth, in the suffocating darkness with the water dripping mournfully and the iron grating against the stone, everything seems possible. It was all so fantastic there, signor; we men seemed so puny compared with that mountain that reached up to the clouds, the mountain into whose bowels we were drilling ... you have to see it to understand what I mean. You ought to have seen the yawning gap we little men had made in the mountain side, and when we would enter through the gap at dawn the sun would look sadly after us as we burrowed into the earth's bowels, you ought to have seen the machines, the gloomy face of the mountain, heard the heavy rumble deep within and the echo of the explosions sounding like the laughter of a madman."

He examined his hands, touched the metal tab on his blue overall and sighed faintly.

"Men know how to work!" he continued with pride. "Ah, signor, man, small as he is, can be an invincible force when he wants to work. And, mark my words, the time will come when puny man will be able to do anything he wishes. My father didn't believe that at first.

" 'To cut through a mountain from one country to another,' he used to say, 'is defying God who divided land by walls of mountains, you'll see, the Madonna will forsake us!' He was mistaken, the Madonna never forsakes men who love her. Later on father came to think almost the same way as I have told you, because he felt bigger and stronger than the mountain, but there was a time when he would sit at table on feast days with a bottle of wine in front of him and lecture me and the others.

" 'Children of God,' that was one of his favourite expressions for he was a good, God-fearing man, 'children of God,' he would say, 'you can't fight the earth that way, she will take revenge for her wounds and will remain unvanquished! You will see: we shall bore our way right to the heart of the mountain and when we touch it, we shall be hurled into the flames, because the heart of the earth is fire, everyone knows that! To till the earth to help Nature with her birthpangs, that man is ordained to do, but we dare not disfigure her face or her form. See, the farther we bore into the mountain, the hotter the air and the harder it is to breathe. . . .' "

The man laughed softly, twirling his moustaches with his fingers.

"He wasn't the only one who thought thus, and indeed it was true: the farther we advanced into the tunnel, the hotter it grew, the more of us took ill and died. And the hot springs gushed in an ever more powerful stream, chunks of earth tore loose, and two of our men from Lugano went insane: At night in the barracks many would rave in delirium, groan and leap from their beds in a fit of horror. . . .

" 'Was I not right?' father said, with terror in his eyes and his cough grew worse and worse.... 'Was I not right?' he said. 'You can't defeat nature!'

"And finally he took to his bed never to rise again. He was a sturdy old man, my father, and he batt'ed with death for more than three weeks, stubbornly, uncomplainingly, like a man who knows his worth.

" 'My work is done, Paolo,' he said to me one night. 'Take care of yourself and go home, and may the Madonna be with you!' Then he was silent for a long time, and lay there breathing heavily with his eyes closed."

The man rose to his feet, glanced up at the mountains and stretched himse'f so that his sinews cracked.

"Then he took me by the hand and drew me close to him and said—God's truth, signor!—'Do you know, Paolo my son, I think that it will be accomplished just the same: We and those who are boring from the other side will meet within the mountain, we shall meet, you believe that, don't you Paolo?' Yes, I believed it. 'Very good, my son! That is well: a man must always believe in what he is doing, he must be confident of success and have faith in God who, thanks to the Madonna's prayers helps good works. I beseech you, son, if it should happen, if the men meet inside the mountain come to my grave and say: Father it is done! Then I shall know!'

"It was good, signor, and I promised him. He died five days later. Two days before his death he asked me and the others to bury him on the spot where he had worked inside the tunnel, he begged us to do it, but I think he must have been raving.

"We and those others who were moving toward us from the other side met in the mountain thirteen weeks after my father's death. That was a mad day, signor! Oh, when we heard there underground in the darkness the sounds of that other work, the sounds made by those coming to meet us in the bowels of the earth, you understand, signor, beneath the tremendous weight of the earth that could have crushed us little men, all of us with one blow!

"For many days we heard these sounds, hollow sounds that grew louder and more distinct each day, and the wild joy of victors possessed us, we worked like fiends, like evil spirits, and felt no weariness, needed no urging. Ah, it was good, like dancing on

a sunny day, it was, I swear to you! And we all became as kind
and gentle as children. Ah, if you but knew how powerful, how
passionate is the desire to meet other men in the darkness underground where you have been burrowing like a mole for many long
months!"

His face flushed with excitement at the recollection, he came
closer and gazing deeply with his profoundly human eyes into
those of his listener, he continued in a soft, happy voice:

"And when finally the last intervening layer of earth crumbled
and the bright yellow flame of the torch lit up the opening and
we saw a black face streaming with tears of joy and more torches
and faces behind it, shouts of victory thundered, shouts of joy—oh,
that was the happiest day of my life, and when I recall it I feel
that my life has not been in vain! That was work, my work, holy
work, signor, I tell you! And when we emerged into the sun ight
many of us fell to the ground and pressed our lips to it, weeping;
it was as wonderful as a fairy tale! Yes, we kissed the vanquished
mountain, kissed the earth; and that day I felt closer to the earth
than I had ever been, signor, I loved it as one loves a woman!

"Of course, I went to my father's grave. I know that the dead
cannot hear anything, but I went just the same, for one must respect the wishes of those who laboured for us and who suffered no
less than we did, is that not so?

"Yes, yes, I went to his grave, knocked at the earth with my
foot and said as he had bade me:

"'Father, it is done!' I said. 'Man has conquered. It is done,
father!'"

IV

At a small station between Rome and Genoa the conductor
opened the door of our compartment and with the aid of a grimy
oiler almost carried in a one-eyed little old man.

"Terribly old!" they chorussed, smiling good-naturedly.

But the old man turned out to be quite vigorous. Thanking his
assistants with a wave of his wrinkled hand, he raised his battered hat from his hoary head with an air of polite affability and
glancing sharply at the benches with his one eve enquired:

"Permit me?"

The passengers moved up and he sat down with a sigh of relief, resting his hands on his bony knees, his lips parted in a good-natured toothless smile.

"Travelling far, granpa?" my companion asked him.

"Oh no, only three stations from here!" was the old one's ready reply. "I'm going to my grandson's wedding. . . ."

A few minutes later to the accompaniment of the rhythmic beat of the wheels he was telling us his story, swaying from side to side like a broken branch on a stormy day.

"I'm a Ligurian," he said, "we Ligurians are a sturdy lot. Take me, I've got thirteen sons, and four daughters and I don't know how many grandchildren. This is the second to get married. Pretty good, eh?"

And proudly surveying us all with his single eye, dimmed yet merry still, he chuckled.

"See how many people I've given my king and country!"

"How did I lose my eye? Ah, that happened a long time ago. I was just a bit of a lad then, I was already helping my father though. He was turning the soil in the vineyard. The soil down our way is hard and stony and needs a deal of attention. A stone flew up from under my father's pickaxe and hit me right in the eye. I don't remember the pain now, but that day while I was eating my dinner my eye fell out. That was awful, signori! They stuck it back and put a warm bread poultice on but it was no use, the eye was gone!"

The old man vigorously rubbed his sallow flabby cheek and again smiled his good-humored gay smile.

"In those days there weren't as many doctors as there are now and people lived foolishly. Oh yes. But perhaps they were kinder, eh?"

Now his one-eyed, leathery face covered with deep furrows and greenish-grey mouldy-looking hair, took on a cunning, sly expression.

"When you've lived as long as I have you can judge people rightly, don't you think so?"

He raised a dark, crooked finger gravely as though reproving someone.

"I'll tell you something, signori, about people...."

"I was thirteen when my father died, and was smaller even than I am now. But I was spry and tireless when it came to work. That was all I inherited from my father, for our plot of land and the house were sold to cover our debts. And so I lived with my one eye and my two hands working wherever there was work to be found.... It was hard, but youth is not afraid of hardships. is it?

"When I was nineteen I met the girl whom I was fated to love. She was as poor as I was, but she was a strapping girl and stronger than me. She lived with her old invalid mother and like myself did whatever work came her way. She wasn't especially handsome but she was kind and had a good head on her shoulders. And a fine voice, too. Ah, how she could sing! Just like a professional. And a good voice is worth a great deal. I used to sing quite well myself.

" 'Shall we get married?' I asked her one day.

" 'That would be foolish, one-eyed one!' she replied sadly. 'Neither you nor I have anything. How should we live?'

"That was God's truth: neither she nor I possessed anything. But what does a young couple in love need? You know yourselves how little love requires, I insisted and won my point.

" 'Well, perhaps you're right,' said Ida at last. 'If the Holy Mother helps you and me now that we live apart it will be so much easier for her to help us when we live together!'

"And so we went to the priest.

" 'This is madness!' he said. 'Are there not enough beggars in Liguria as it is? Unhappy people, you are the devil's playthings, resist his temptations or you will pay dearly for your weakness!'

"The young folk in the community laughed at us, the old folk censured us. But youth is stubborn and wise in its own way! The wedding day arrived, we were no richer on that day than before and we did not even know where we would lay us down to sleep on our wedding night.

" 'Let us go to the fields!' said Ida. 'Why not? The mother of God is kind to people wherever they may be.'

"And so we decided—let the earth be our bed and the sky our counterpane.

208

"And now begins another story, signori. I beg your attention. for this is the best story in all my long life!

"Early in the morning the day before our wedding, old Giovanni for whom I had done a good deal of work said to me, muttering under his breath because he disliked to speak of such trifles:

" 'You ought to clean out the old sheep pen, Ugo. Put in some clean straw. It's dry and the sheep haven't been there for more than a year, but you'd best clean it out if you and Ida want to live in it.'

"And there was our house!

"As I was busy cleaning out the sheep pen, singing at my work, I looked up to see Costanzo, the carpenter, standing in the doorway.

" 'So this is where you and Ida are going to live? But where is your bed? I have an extra one at my place. Come over and get it when you've finished cleaning.'

"As I was going to him, Maria, the shrewish shopkeeper shouted:

" 'Getting married, the fools, with not a sheet nor a pillow to their name! You are crazy, one-eyed one, but send your bride to me. . . .'

"And lame, Ettore Viano tortured by rheumatism and fever, cried out to her from his doorstep:

" 'Ask him how much wine he has put by for the guests? Ah, how can people be so thoughtless!' "

A bright tear glistened in one of the deep folds on the old man's cheek, he threw back his head and laughed soundlessly, his bony Adam's apple working and his loose skin trembling.

"Oh, signori, signori," he was choking with laughter and waving his hands in childish glee. "On the morning of our wedding day we had everything we needed for our home—a statue of the Madonna, dishes, linen, furniture, everything, I swear to you! Ida laughed and wept, I too, and everyone else laughed—for it is bad to weep on a wedding day, and all our own folks laughed at us!

"Signori! It is damned fine to have the right to call people your own. And even better to feel them your own, near and dear to you, people, who do not regard your life as a trifle and your happiness a plaything!

"And what a wedding it was! What a day! The whole community attended the ceremony. and everyone came to our stable which

had all at once become a rich mansion.... We had everything!
Wine and fruit, meat and bread, and everyone ate and everyone was
gay.... That, signori, is because there is no greater happiness than
to do good to people, believe me, there is nothing finer and more
beautiful than that!

"And the priest came too. He made a fine speech. 'Here,' he
said, 'are two people who have worked for all of you, and you
have done what you could to make this day the best in their lives.
And that is as it should be for they have worked for you, and work
is more important than copper and silver money, work is always
more important than the remuneration you receive for it! Money
goes but work remains.... These people are gay and modest, their
life has been hard yet they did not complain, their lives will be
harder still and still they will not grumble, you will help them
in their hour of need. They have good hands and stout hearts.'

"And he said many flattering things to me, Ida and the whole
community!"

The old man surveyed us all with an eye that had regained its
lost youth:

"There, signori, I have told you something about people. It was
good was it not?"

V

Let us raise our voices in praise of woman, the Mother, inexhaustible fount of all-conquering life!

This is the tale of the flint-hearted Timur-i-leng, the lame pan-
ther, of Sakhim-i-Kirani, the lucky conqueror, of Tamerlane, as he
was called by the infidels, of the man who sought to destroy the
whole world.

For fifty years he trampled the earth, his iron heel crushing
cities and states as the foot of an elephant crushes an anthill; red
rivers of blood flowed in his wake in all directions; he built tall
towers out of the bones of vanquished peoples, he destroyed life,
pitting his power against the power of Death, for he was avenging
the death of his son Jigangir. A ghastly man, he wished to rob
Death of all her spoils so that she might expire from hunger and
despair!

From the day when his son Jigangir died and the people of
Samarkand, garbed in black and blue raiment and sprinkling their
heads with dust and ashes, met the conqueror of the evil Juts,
from that day until the hour of his encounter with Death in Ottrarre,
where she overpowered him at last, Timur did not smile. He lived
thus with lips compressed, his head unbowed and his heart locked
against compassion—for thirty years!

Let us sing the praises of woman, the Mother, the sole force
before which Death humbly bows her head! Let here be told the
truth about Mother, how Death's servant and slave, the stony-
hearted Tamerlane, the sanguinary scourge of the earth, bowed his
head to her.

It came about thus: Timur-bek was feasting in the lovely valley
of Canigula wreathed in clouds of roses and jasmine, the valley
Samarkand poets named "Vale of Flowers" whence the blue min-
arets of the great city, the blue cupolas of the mosques are visible.

Fifteen thousand circular tents were spread out fanwise in the
valley like fifteen thousand tulips and over each tent hundreds of
silken pennants fluttered in the breeze like flowers.

And in the centre stood the tent of Gurugan Timur, like a
queen among her train. It was four-cornered, each side one hundred
paces in length, three spears in height, the centre was supported
by twelve golden columns each as thick as a man; atop rested a
pale blue cupola while the sides were of black, yellow and blue
striped silk; five hundred scarlet cords kept it fixed firmly to the
ground so that it might not rise into the sky, four silver eagles
stood at its corners; and under the cupola on a dais in the centre
of the tent sat the fifth, the invincible Timur-Gurugan, the king of
kings, himself.

He was garbed in a flowing silken robe of a celestial hue studded with pearls, five thousand large pearls no less. On his terrible hoary brow sat a white peaked cap with a ruby on the tip that
swayed to and fro like a bloodshot eye surveying the world.

The face of the Lame One was like a broad-bladed knife, rusty
from the blood into which it had been immersed thousands of times;
his eyes were narrow slits that missed nothing, and their glitter was
like the cold glitter of the zaramut, favourite gem of the Arabs
which the infidels call emerald and which cures the falling sick-

ness. And from his ears suspended earings of Ceylon rubies, the colour of a lovely maiden's lips.

On the floor of the tent on carpets of unsurpassed beauty stood three hundred golden jugs of wine and everything meet for a kingly feast; behind Timur sat the musicians, beside him no one, and at his feet, his kinsmen, kings and princes and chieftains and closest to him of all drunken Kermani, the poet, who, when the destroyer of the world once asked him:

"Kirmani! How much wouldst thou give for me, were I to be sold?" had replied: "Twenty-five askers."

"But my belt alone is worth as much!" Timur had exclaimed in amazement.

"It is of thy belt that I was thinking," replied Kirmani, "only of thy belt, for thou thyself art not worth a farthing!"

So spake Kermani, the poet, to the king of kings, the man of horror and evil, and may the glory of the poet, friend of truth, be ever exalted above the glory of Tamerlane!

Let us sing the praises of poets who know but one God, the fearless, beautiful word of truth. That is their God forever!

And so in the hour when the revelry and feasting, the proud reminiscences of battles and victories, were at their height, in the midst of the loud music and the popular games played in front of the king's tent, where innumerable piebald jesters bounded up and down, where athletes were wrestling and tight-rope walkers went through such contortions that one would think there was not a bone in their bodies, and warriors crossed swords exhibiting peerless skill in the art of killing, and performances were given with elephants painted red and green which made some appear frightful and others ridiculous—at that hour of rejoicing among Timur's men, who were intoxicated with fear of him, with pride in his glory, with weariness of victories, with wine and koumiss—at that wild hour, suddenly cutting through the hubbub, like a streak of lightning through a thunder-cloud, the cry of a woman, the proud cry of a she-eagle, a sound familiar and in harmony with his wounded soul, the soul wounded by Death and hence cruel toward living men, reached the ears of Sultan Bayezid's conqueror.

He ordered his men to see who it was that had cried out in joyless voice, and he was told that a woman, a mad creature in dust and rags, had come and, speaking the language of the Arabs was demanding, yes demanding, to see him, the ruler of three cardinal points of the earth.

"Bring her in!" said the king.

And so before him stood a woman. She was barefoot and her tattered clothing had faded in the sun, her black tresses were loosened so that they covered her bare breast, her face was the colour of bronze and her eyes imperious, and her dark hand outstretched toward the Lame One did not tremble.

"Is it thou hast vanquished Sultan Bayezid?" she demanded.

"Yes, I have defeated many besides, and am not yet weary of conquests. And what saith thou of thyself, woman?"

"Hear me!" said she. "Whatever thou hast done, thou art but a man. I am a Mother! Thou servest death, I serve life. Thou hast sinned against me and so I have come to demand that thou atone for thy guilt. I have been told that thy device is 'in justice lies strength,' I do not believe it, but to me thou must be just, for I am a Mother!"

The king had wisdom enough to feel the power behind these bold words.

"Sit down and speak. I would listen to thee!"

She seated herself at her convenience upon the carpet amid the intimate circle of kings and began her tale:

"I am from the region of Salerno, far away in Italy, thou knowest not those parts! My father was a fisherman, my husband too, he was as beautiful as only happy men are and it was I who gave him happiness! I had a son, the finest lad in the world...."

"Like my Jigangir," the old warrior murmured.

"The handsomest and the cleverest lad is my son! He was six years old when the Saracen pirates landed on our coast. They slew my father and my husband and many others, and they carried off my boy and for four years now I have been searching the earth for him. Now thou hast him. This I know, for Bayezid's men captured the pirates, and thou hast conquered Bayezid and taken all his possessions. Thou must know where my son is and give him back to me!"

Everyone laughed and the kings, who always consider themselves to be wise, said:

"She is mad!" said the kings and the friends of Timur, the
princes and chieftains, and they laughed.

Only Kirmani gazed at the woman gravely and Tamerlane
looked at her in great wonder.

"She is mad as a Mother is mad," the drunken poet Kirmani
said softly; and the king, the enemy of peace, said:

"Woman! How hast thou come hither from that unknown land
across the seas, the rivers and mountains, through woods and forests? How is it that beasts and men—often more savage than the
most savage of beasts—have not molested thee, how couldst thou
have wandered alone without a weapon which is the only friend
of the defenceless and which will not betray him so long as he has
strength to wield it? I must know this in order that I might believe thee and that my wonder might not prevent me from understanding what thou sayest!"

Let us sing the praises of woman, the Mother, whose love knows
no obstacles, whose breast has nurtured the whole world! All that
is beautiful in man, is derived from the sun's rays and from his
Mother's milk. This it is that imbues us with love of life!

"I encountered but one sea in my wanderings," she replied.
"There were many islands and fishing boats on it, and when one
seeks a loved one the winds are always with one. And for one who
has been born and brought up on the seashore it is no hardship to
swim rivers. Mountains? I did not notice them."

And the drunken Kirmani said gaily:

"A mountain becomes a valley to one who loves!"

"There were forests, yes. I encountered wild boars, bears, lynxes
and fearful bulls with their heads bent low and twice panthers looked
at me with eyes like thine own. But every animal has a heart, and I
spoke with them as I speak with thee, they believed me when I said
I was a Mother, and they went their way sighing, for they pitied me!
Knowest thou not that the beasts too love their children and know
how to fight for their lives and freedom no worse than men?"

"Well said, woman," said Timur. "And often, this I know,
they love more strongly and fight more stubbornly than men!"

"Men," she continued, like a child, for every Mother is a child
a hundredfold at heart, "men are always children to their mothers,
for every man has a Mother, every man is some mother's son,

even thou, old man, wast born of woman, thou canst deny God, but this thou canst never deny!"

"Well said, woman!" exclaimed Kirmani, the fearless poet. "Well said! From a herd of bullocks there will be no calves, without the sun flowers will not bloom, without love there is no happiness, without woman there is no love, without Mothers, there are neither poets nor heroes!"

And the woman said:

"Give me back my child for I am his Mother and I love him!"

Let us bow to woman, who bore Moses, Mohammed and the great prophet Jesus who was put to death by evil men, but who, as Sherifu 'd-Din hath said, shall rise again and bring judgment upon the living and the dead, and this shall come to pass in Damascus, in Damascus!

Let us bow to Her who tirelessly gives birth to the great! Aristotle is Her son, and Firdusi, and Saadi, as sweet as honey, and Omar Khayyam, like unto wine mixed with poison, Iskander and the blind Homer—these are all Her children, all of them imbibed her milk and She led each one of them into the world by the hand when they were no bigger than tulips. All the pride of the world comes from Mothers!

And the hoary destroyer of cities, the lame tiger Timur-Gurugan sat sunk in thought. After a long silence he said to those gathered about him:

"Men tangri Kuli Timur! I, God's servant Timur, do say what must be said! Thus I have lived, for many years the earth has groaned beneath my feet, and for thirty years I have been destroying it in order to avenge the death of my son Jigangir, for extinguishing the sun of life in my heart! Men have fought against me for kingdoms and cities, but never has anyone fought me for man, and never has man had any value in my sight, and I did not know who he was and why he stood in my path! It is I, Timur, who said to Bayezid when I defeated him: 'Oh, Bayezid, it must be that before God countries and men are as nothing, for behold, he suffers them to be possessed by such as we: thou, one-eyed and I, lame!' So spake I to him when he was brought to me in chains and could barely stand under their weight, so spake I, gazing upon him in misfortune and life at that moment was to me as bitter as wormwood, the weed of ruins!

"I, God's servant Timur, say what must be said! Here before me sits a woman, one of myriads, and she has awakened in my soul feelings such as I have never known. She speaks to me as to an equal, and she does not beg, she demands. And I see now, I understand why this woman is so strong—she loves, and love has taught her that her child is the spark of life which can kindle a flame for many centuries. Were not all the prophets children too, and were not all the heroes weak? O, Jigangir, light of mine eyes, perhaps thou wert destined to kindle the earth, to sow it with happiness. I, thy father, have drenched it with blood and it has grown fat!"

Once again the scourge of the nations lapsed into·silence, then at last he spoke again:

"I, God's servant Timur, speak that which must be spoken! Three hundred horsemen shall set out at once to all corners of my land and they shall find the son of this woman and she shall wait here, and I shall wait with her: he who returns with the child in his saddle good fortune shall be his—It is I Timur who speaks. Have I spoken well, woman?"

She tossed her black hair back from her face, smiled to him and replied:

"Thou hast, king!"

Then rose this terrible old man and in silence bowed to her, and the merry poet Kirmani spake up with great rejoicing:

What is more beautiful than the song of flowers and stars?
The answer all men know: 'tis the song of love!
What is more beauteous than the sunlight at noon in May?
The lover replies: She whom I love!
   Ah, beautiful are the stars in the midnight sky,
   And beautiful the sun on a summer's noontide,
   But the eyes of my loved one are lovelier than all the flowers,
   And her smile is more gentle than the sun's rays.
But the song most beautiful of all is yet to be sung,
The song of the beginning of all things on earth,
The song of the world's heart, of the magic heart,
Of her whom on earth we call Mother!

And Timur said to his poet:

"So Kirmani! God was not mistaken when he chose thy lips to extol his wisdom!"

"God is himself a great poet!" spake the drunken Kirmani.

And the woman smiled and all the kings smiled and the princes, and the chieftains smiled, they were all children as they gazed upon her—upon Mother!

All this is true; every word spoken here is the truth, our mothers know it to be so, ask them and they will tell you:

"Yes, all this is the eternal truth, we are stronger than death, we who are forever bringing into the world sages, poets and heroes, we who imbue man with all that makes him glorious!"

VI

One can talk endlessly about Mothers.

For several weeks enemy hosts had encased the city in a tight ring of steel; by night bonfires were lit and the flames peered through the inky blackness at the walls of the city like a myriad of red eyes—they blazed malevolently, and their warning glare evoked gloomy thoughts within the beleaguered city.

From the walls they saw the enemy noose draw tighter; saw the dark shadows hovering about the fires, and heard the neighing of well-fed horses, the clanging of weapons, the loud laughter and singing of men confident of victory—and what can be more jarring to the ear than the songs and laughter of the enemy?

The enemy had thrown corpses into all the streams that fed water to the city, he had burned down the vineyards around the walls, trampled the fields, cut down the orchards—the city was now exposed on all sides, and nearly every day the cannon and muskets of the enemy showered it with lead and iron.

Detachments of war-weary, half-starved soldiers trooped sullenly through the narrow streets of the city; from the windows of houses issued the groans of the wounded, the cries of the delirious, the prayers of women and the wailing of children. People conversed in whispers, breaking off in the middle of a sentence, tensely alert: was that not the enemy advancing?

Worst of all were the nights; in the nocturnal stillness the groans and cries were more distinctly audible; black shadows crept stealthily from the gorges of the distant mountains toward the half demolished walls, hiding the enemy camp from view, and over the black ridges of the mountains rose the moon like a lost shield dented by sword blows.

And the people in the city, despairing of succour, worn out by toil and hunger, their hope of salvation waning from day to day, the people in the city stared in horror at that moon, at the sharp-toothed ridges of the mountains, the black maws of the gorges and at the noisy camp of the enemy. Everything reminded them of death, and not a star was there in the sky to give them consolation.

They were afraid to light the lamps in the houses, and a heavy darkness enveloped the streets, and in this darkness, like a fish stirring in the depths of a river, a woman draped from head to foot in a black cloak moved soundlessly.

When they saw her, people whispered to one another:

"Is it she?"

"It is she!"

And they withdrew into the niches under archways, or hurried past her with lowered heads. The patrol chiefs warned her sternly:

"Abroad again, Donna Marianna? Take care, someone may kill you and none shall hasten to apprehend your assailant...."

She drew herself up and stood waiting, but the patrols passed by, either not daring or else scorning to raise their hand against her; the armed men avoided her like a corpse, and, left alone in the darkness, she continued her solitary wanderings from street to street, soundless and black like the incarnation of the city's misfortune, while all about her, as though pursuing her, melancholy sounds issued from the night: the groans, cries, prayers and the sullen murmur of soldiers who had lost all hope of victory.

A citizen and a mother, she thought of her son and her country: for leading the men who were destroying her town was her son—handsome, gay and ruthless; and yet, not so long ago she had looked upon him with pride, regarding him as her precious gift to her country, a beneficent force she had brought forth to aid the city folk, the nest where she herself had been born, where her

son had been born and reared. Her heart was bound by hundreds
of invisible threads to these ancient stones with which her forefathers had built their homes and raised the walls of the city; to
the soil wherein lay buried the bones of her kinsmen, to the legends,
the songs and the hopes of the people. And now this heart had
lost a loved one and it wept. She weighed in her heart as on scales
her love for her son and her love for her native city, and she
could not tell which weighed the more.

And so she wandered thus by night through the streets, and
many, failing to recognize her, drew back in fear, mistaking her
black figure for the incarnation of Death that was so near to all
of them, and when they did recognize her, they turned silently
away from the mother of a traitor.

But one day in a remote corner by the city wall she saw another woman kneeling beside a corpse; motionless, like a clod of
earth, the woman was praying, her grief-stricken face upturned to
the stars. And on the wall overhead the sentries spoke in low tones,
their weapons grating against the stone.

The traitor's mother asked:

"Your husband?"

"No."

"Your brother?"

"My son. My husband was killed thirteen days ago, my son
today."

And rising from her knees, the mother of the slain man said
humbly:

"The Madonna sees all and knows all, and I am grateful to
her!"

"What for?" asked the first, and the other replied:

"Now that he has died honourably fighting for his country I
can say that I feared for him: he was lighthearted, too fond of revelry and I feared that he might betray his city, as did the son
of Marianna, the enemy of God and Man, the leader of our foes,
may he be accursed and the womb that bore him!"

Marianna covered her face and went on her way. The next morning she appeared before the city's defenders and said:

"My son has come to be your enemy. Either kill me or open
the gates that I may go to him...."

They replied:

"You are a human being, and your country must be precious to you; your son is as much an enemy to you as to each one of us."

"I am his mother, I love him and feel that I am to blame for what he has become!"

Then they took counsel with one another and decided:

"It would not be honourable to kill you for the sins of your son. We know that you could not have led him to commit this terrible sin, and we can understand your distress. But the city does not need you even as a hostage; your son cares nought for you, we believe that he has forgotten you, fiend that he is, and there is your punishment if you think you have deserved it! We believe that is more terrible than death itself!"

"Yes," she said. "It is indeed more terrible."

And so they opened the gates and suffered her to leave the city and watched long from the battlements as she departed from her native soil now drenched with the blood her son had spilt so copiously. She walked slowly, for her feet were reluctant to tear themselves away from this soil, and she bowed to the corpses of the city's defenders, kicking aside a broken weapon in disgust, for all aggressive weapons are revolting to mothers; they recognize only those used to protect life.

She walked as though she carried a precious phial of water beneath her cloak and feared to spill a drop; and as her figure grew smaller and smaller to those who watched from the city wall, it seemed to them that with her went their dejection and hopelessness.

They saw her pause halfway and throwing back the hood of her cloak turn back and gaze long at the city. And over in the enemy's camp they saw her alone in the field and figures dark as her own approached her cautiously. Approached and enquired who she was and whence she had come.

"Your leader is my son," she said, and not one of the soldiers doubted it. They fell in beside her singing his praises, saying how clever and brave he was, and she listened to them with head proudly raised, showing no surprise, for her son could not be otherwise.

And now, at last, she stood before him whom she had known nine months before his birth, him whom she had never felt apart from her own heart. In silk and velvet he stood before her, his weapons studded with precious stones. All was as it should be, thus had she seen him so many times in her dreams—rich, famous and admired.

"Mother!" he said, kissing her hands. "Thou hast come to me, thou art with me, and tomorrow I shall capture that accursed city!"

"The city where thou wert born," she reminded him.

Intoxicated with his prowess, crazed with the thirst for more glory, he answered her with the arrogant heat of youth:

"I was born into the world and for the world, and I mean to make the world quake with wonder of me! I have spared this city for thy sake, it has been like a thorn in my flesh and has retarded my swift rise to fame. But now tomorrow I shall smash that nest of obstinate fools!"

"Where every stone knows and remembers thee as a child," she said.

"Stones are dumb, unless man makes them speak. Let the mountains speak of me, that is what I wish!"

"And what of men?" she asked.

"Ah yes, I have not forgotten them, mother. I need them too, for only in man's memory are heroes immortal!"

She said:

"A hero is he who creates life in defiance of death, who conquers death. . . ."

"No!" he objected. "The destroyer is as glorious as the builder of a city. See, we do not know who it was that built Rome—Aeneas or Romulus—yet we know well the name of Alaric and the other heroes who destroyed the city. . . ."

"Which outlived all names." the mother reminded him.

Thus they conversed until the sun sank to rest; less and less frequently did she interrupt his wild speech, lower and lower sank her proud head.

A Mother creates, she protects, and to speak to her of destruction means to speak against her; but he did not know it, he did not know that he was negating her reason for existence.

A Mother is always opposed to death: the hand that brings death into the dwellings of men. is hateful and hostile to Mothers. But the son did not perceive this. for he was blinded by the chilly glitter of glory that deadens the heart.

Nor did he know that a Mother is as clever and ruthless a creature as she is fearless when the life she creates and cherishes is in question.

She sat with bowed head, and through the opening in the leader's richly appointed tent she saw the city where first she had. felt the sweet tremor of life within her and the anguished convulsions of the birth of this child who now sought to destroy.

The crimson rays of the sun dyed the walls and towers of the city blood-red, cast a baleful glare on the windowpanes so that the whole city seemed to be a mass of wounds with the crimson sap of life flowing from each gash. Presently the city turned black as a corpse and the stars shone above it like funeral candles.

She saw the dark houses where people feared to light candles so as not to attract the attention of the enemy, saw the streets steeped in gloom and rank with the stench of corpses, heard the muffled whispers of people awaiting death—she saw all and everything; so near and dear to her it stood there, dumbly awaiting her decision, and she felt herself the mother of all those people in her city.

Clouds descended from the black peaks into the valley and like winged steeds swooped down upon the doomed city.

"Perhaps we shall attack tonight," said her son, "if the night is dark enough! It is hard to kill when the sun shines in your eyes and the glitter of the weapons blinds you, many a blow goes awry," he remarked, examining his sword.

The mother said to him:

"Come, my son, lay thy head on my breast and rest, remember how gay and kind thou wert as a child, and how everyone loved thee. . . ."

He obeyed her, laid his head in her lap and closed his eyes, saying:

"I love only glory and thee for having made me as I am."

"And women?" she asked bending over him.

"They are many, one tires of them as of everything that is too sweet."

"And dost thou not desire children?" she asked for the last time.

"What for? That they might be killed? Someone like me will kill them; that will give me pain and I shall be too old and feeble to avenge them."

"Thou art handsome, but as barren as a streak of lightning,"
she said with a sigh.

"Yes, like lightning ..." he replied, smiling.

And he dozed there on his mother's breast like a child.

Then, covering him with her black cloak, she plunged a knife
into his heart, and with a shudder he died, for who knew better
than she where beat her son's heart. And, throwing his corpse at
the feet of the astonished sentries, she said addressing the city:

"As a Citizen, I have done for my country all I could: as a
Mother I remain with my son! It is too late for me to bear another, my life is of no use to anyone."

And the knife, still warm with his blood, her blood, she plunged
with a firm hand into her own breast, and again she struck true,
for an aching heart is not hard to find.

VII

The cicadas are humming.

It is as if thousands of metal strings were stretched taut among
the thick foliage of the olive trees, the wind stirs the tough leaves,
they touch the strings and this light, ceaseless contact fills the air
with intoxicating sound. It is not exactly music, yet it seems as if
invisible hands were tuning hundreds of invisible harps, and one waits
in tense expectancy for the tuning to cease, and for a grand string
orchestra to strike up a triumphant hymn to the sun, sky and sea.

The wind blows, swaying the trees so that their waving crowns
seem to be moving from the mountains down to the sea. The surf
beats dully and rhythmically against the rocky shore; the sea is a
mass of living, white daubs of foam looking like great flocks of
birds that have settled on its blue expanse; they all float in one
direction, then disappear into the depths only to rise again with a
faintly audible sound. And as though luring them away in their
wake, two boats, their triple sails raised high, bob up and down
on the horizon, like two grey birds themselves; the whole scene is
as unreal as a distant, half-forgotten dream.

"There'll be a stiff gale by sundown!" says an old fisherman,
sitting in the shadow of the rocks on the small pebbled beach.

Fragrant seaweed, rust-coloured, golden-hued and green, washed up by the tide is spread out on the pebbles; the seaweed withers on the hot stones under the blazing sun filling the salty air with the tangy scent of iodine. Curly wavelets chase one another up the beach.

The old fisherman resembles a bird with his small wizened face, his hooked nose and the round and doubtless very sharp eyes hidden amid the dark folds of the skin. His gnarled, withered fingers lie motionless on his knees.

"About half a hundred years ago, signor," says the old man, in a voice that harmonizes with the murmur of the waves and the hum of the cicadas, "I remember just such a bright and glorious day, when everything seems to laugh and sing. My father then was about forty, I was sixteen and in love, as is only natural for a lad of sixteen under the beneficent sun to be.

" 'Come, Guido,' said my father, 'Let us go out for some pezzoni'; pezzoni, signor, is a very delicate tasty fish with pink fins, it is also known as coral fish because you find it deep down among the coral reefs. You catch it standing at anchor with a heavily weighted hook. A handsome fish.

"And so we set off anticipating nothing but a successful catch. My father was a strong man and an experienced fisherman, but shortly before this trip he had been ill, his chest had ached and his fingers were twisted with rheumatism, the fisherman's disease.

"This is a very treacherous and evil wind that is blowing now so caressingly upon us from the shore, as if gently impelling us toward the sea; out there it comes upon you unawares and suddenly hurls itself at you, as if you had done it an injury. It sends your barque flying, sometimes keel upwards with you in the water. It happens in a jiffy and before you have time to curse or to utter God's name you are sent swirling helplessly into the distance. A robber is more honest than that wind. But then men are always more honest than the elements.

"Well, it was just such a wind that struck us four kilometres from the shore, quite close by, as you see. It took us by surprise like a coward and a scoundrel.

" 'Guido!' cried my father, seizing hold of the oar with his twisted hands. 'Hold on, Guido! Quick, the anchor!'

"But while I was fumbling for the anchor, the wind tore the oar out of my father's hand knocking him a blow on the chest that sent him reeling unconscious to the bottom of the boat. I had no time to help him for every second threatened to consign us to the waves. At first everything happened very quickly: by the time I took up the oars we were being swept along, with the spray surrounding us on all sides, as the wind picked the crests off the waves and sprinkled us like the priest does, only with a great deal more energy and not in order to wash away our sins.

" 'This is serious, my son!' said father regaining consciousness. He looked out toward the shore. 'This is going to last a long time, my boy,' he said.

"When you are young you do not easily believe in danger; I tried to row and did everything that a sailor must do at critical moments at sea with the wind, the breath of wicked devils, busy digging a thousand graves for you, and singing your requiem free of charge.

" 'Calm yourself, Guido,' said my father, smiling and shaking the water from his head. 'What use is it to pick at the sea with matchsticks? Save your strength or else the folks at home will await you in vain.'

"The green waves tossed our little craft as children toss a ball, they climbed over the sides, rose above our heads, roaring and shaking us madly, we dropped down into yawning pits, then climbed to the top of tall white peaks, and the shore sped swiftly farther and farther away and seemed to be dancing along with our barque.

" 'You may return but I shall not!' my father said to me. 'Listen and I shall tell you what you should know about fishing and work....'

"And he began to tell me all he knew about the habits of one or another fish, where, when and how best to catch them.

" 'Had we not better pray, father!' I suggested when I saw how bad our plight was; we were like a couple of rabbits among a pack of white hounds that were baring their fangs at us from all sides.

" 'God sees all!' said he. 'He knows that men whom he created to dwell on land are now perishing at sea and that one of them, having lost hope of salvation, must bequeath to his son all the knowledge he possesses. Work is necessary for the earth and for men. God understands that. . . .'

"And when he had imparted to me all he knew about his craft, he told me what a man must know in order to live in peace with his fellow men.

" 'Is this the time to teach me?' I said. 'On land you did not do it!'

" 'On land death was never so close.'

"The wind howled like a wild beast, and the waves roared so loud that father had to shout for me to hear him.

" 'Always behave as if you were neither worse nor better than your fellow men, and you will be all right! The nobleman and the fisherman, the priest and the soldier are part of the same organism and you are as necessary a part of that organism as all the others. Never approach a man thinking that there is more bad than good in him, believe that there is more good in him and you will always find it to be so. Men behave as one expects them to.'

"He did not say this all at once, of course. His words came to me through the spray and foam as we tossed from wave to wave, now plunging deep down, now climbing high up. Much of what he said was carried away by the wind before it reached me, much I did not understand, for, signor, how can one learn with death staring one in the face? I was afraid, I had never before seen the sea in such a fury or felt so helpless on it. And I cannot say whether it was then or later on when I remembered those hours that I experienced a sensation I shall never forget as long as I live.

"I can see my father, as if it were yesterday, sitting at the bottom of the boat, his poor arms outstretched as he clung to the sides with his crooked, twisted fingers; his hat had been washed away and the waves struck against his head and his shoulders now from the right, now from the left, in front and behind, and each time he would toss his head, snort and shout to me. Drenched to the skin, he seemed to have shrunken in size and his eyes were large with fear, or perhaps with pain. With pain, I suppose.

" 'Hark!' he would cry. 'Do you hear me?'

"Sometimes I would answer:

" 'I hear you!'

" 'Remember, all good comes from man.'

" 'I shall remember!' I would reply.

"Never had he spoken thus to me on land. He had always been gay and kind but I had felt that he regarded me with amusement and distrust and that I was still a child to him. Sometimes this offended me, for youth is easily wounded.

"His shouts allayed my fear, perhaps that is why I remember everything so vividly."

The old fisherman fell silent, his eyes fixed on the foamy sea. Then he smiled and went on with a wink:

"I have observed people for many years, signor, and I know that remembering is the same as understanding, and the more you understand the more good you see, that's the truth, believe me!

"There, I can remember his dear face, all wet and the big staring eyes looking at me gravely and lovingly and in such a way that I knew then I was not destined to die that day. I was afraid but I knew I would not perish.

"Finally, of course, we capsized. There we were both in the seething water, with the foam blinding us, the waves hurling our bodies about, dashing them against the keel of the boat. We had lashed to the thwarts everything that could be tied, in our hands we held the ropes, we would not be cast away from our barque so long as we had the strength to hold on, but it was hard to keep our heads above water. Several times he and I were thrown against the keel and washed off again. The worst of it is that your head swims, you are deafened and blinded, your ears fill with water, and you swallow great quantities of it.

"This lasted for a long time, about seven hours, until the wind suddenly turned, b'owing strongly shoreward, and we were carried swiftly toward the land.

" 'Hold on!' I cried joyfully.

Father shouted something back but I heard only one word:

" '. . . dashed. . . .'

"He meant the rocks, but they were still far off and I did not believe him. But he knew better than I, we were borne along numb and helpless amid the mountains of water, clinging like snails to our boat which knocked us about unmercifully. This went on for a long while but at last the dark crags of the coast came into view. After that everything happened very swiftly. Swaying, they moved toward us, bending over the water, ready to crash down upon us. The white waves hurled our bodies forward once, twice, our boat crunched like a nut under the heel of a boot, I was torn loose, saw the black ribs of the rocks as sharp as knives looming before me, saw my father's head high above mine, then lifted above those devil's claws.

"He was picked up an hour or two later with his back broken and his skull smashed. The wound in his head was so big that part of the brain had been washed out of it, and I can remember the grey chunks of matter in the wound with red veins running through it like marble or foam mixed with blood. His body was terribly mutilated, but his face was clear and calm and his eyes tightly closed.

"I? Yes, I was also badly battered up, I was unconscious when they pulled me ashore. We had been carried away to the mainland beyond Amalfi, a long way from home, but, of course, the folk there are also fishermen and such things do not surprise them but make them kind and gentle. Men who lead a dangerous life are always kind!

"I'm afraid I haven't been able to make you understand how I really feel about my father and what it is I have been carrying in my heart for fifty-one years now. One needs special words for that, not words but music perhaps. But we simple folk, are like fish, we cannot talk as well as we would wish! One always feels and knows more than one can express.

"The whole thing is that he, my father, in his hour of death, knowing that he could not escape it, was not afraid, he did not forget about me, his son, and found the strength and the time to pass on to me everything he thought I should know. I have lived for sixty-seven years and I can say that everything he told me then is true!"

The old man took off his knitted cap that had once been red and was now brown, pulled out his pipe and bending his naked, bronzed skull, said emphatically:

"Yes, it is all true, dear signor! Men are as you wish to see them, look at them in kindness and you will do good both to them and to yourself. They will become better, and you too. It is simple, isn't it?"

The wind blew more and more strongly, the waves mounted higher, became sharper and whiter; the birds on the sea grew bigger and scurried farther and farther into the distance, and the two boats with the three rows of sails had already disappeared behind the blue rim of the horizon.

The steep shores of the island were encased in foam, the blue water splashed noisily and the cicadas kept up their tireless, passionate din.

VIII

A man in a light suit, lean and clean-shaven like an American, sat down at an iron table near the door of the restaurant and drawled lazily:

"Ga-aarçon...."

Acacia blossoms, white and golden, hung in thick profusion all around, there was radiant sunlight everywhere and earth and sky were filled with the gentle gladness of springtide. Down the middle of the street cantered little shaggy-eared donkeys with a pattering of hoofs, heavy draught horses passed slowly by at a walking gait. The pedestrians strolled along and it was clear that everyone desired to stay as long as possible in the sunshine and the air that was filled with the honey-laden scent of flowers.

Children, the heralds of spring, flashed by, the sun tinting their clothes with bright hues; gaily dressed women, as essential to a sunny day as the stars at night, sailed along, swaying slightly as they walked.

There was something curious about the appearance of the man in the light suit: he looked as though he must have been extremely dirty and had only that day been scrubbed clean, but so vigorously that all vividness had been rubbed off him forever. He gazed around him with faded eyes as if he were counting the sun spots on the walls of the houses and on everything that moved along the dark street and over the broad flagstones of the boulevard. His flaccid lips were pursed and he was softly and painstakingly whistling a queer, sad melody, his long white fingers thrumming in time on the edge of the table. His nails gleamed palely and in his other hand he held a tan glove with which he beat time on his knee. His features bespoke intelligence and resolution, it seemed a pity that the glow had been so roughly wiped off his face.

As the waiter, with a deferential bow, placed a cup of coffee, a small bottle of green liqueur and some biscuits before him, a broad-chested man with agate eyes sat down at the next table. His cheeks, neck and hands were smoke-begrimed and he himself was so angular and with such steel-like quality of strength that he seemed part of some huge machine.

When the eyes of the clean man rested wearily on him, he raised himself slightly, touched his cap with his fingers and said through his thick moustache:

"Good day, Mr. Engineer."

"Ah, so it's you again, Trama!"

"Yes, it's me, Mr. Engineer...."

"Well, we may expect something, eh?"

"How is your work getting on?"

"I'm afraid," the engineer said with a faint smile on his thin lips, "that one cannot make conversation with questions alone, my friend...."

His companion pushed his hat onto one ear and laughed heartily.

"Right you are!" he said through his laughter, "but, I swear I'd give a lot to know...."

A piebald, coarse-haired donkey, harnessed to a coal cart in his tracks, stretched out his neck and emitted a mournful cry, but evidently the sound of his own voice did not please him that day for he broke off in confusion on a high note, shook his shaggy ears and, lowering his head, trotted on with a clatter of hoofs.

"I am waiting for that machine of yours as impatiently as I would wait for a new book from which I could derive greater wisdom...."

"I do not quite understand the analogy," murmured the engineer sipping his coffee.

"Don't you agree that a machine frees man's physical energy as much as a good book frees his spirit?"

"Ah!" said the engineer, raising his head. "Perhaps you're right."

"And now, I suppose, you will start your propaganda?" he added, placing the empty cup back on the table.

"I have started already...."

"What is it? Strikes and disturbances again, eh?"

The other shrugged his shoulders, smiling gently.

"If only all that were not necessary...."

An old woman in black, as austere as a nun, silently proffered a bunch of violets to the engineer. He took two and handing one to his companion, said reflectively:

"You have such a good head, Trama, it is a pity you are an idealist...."

"Thank you for the flowers and the compliment. A pity, you say?"

"Yes! You are essentially a poet, and you ought to study to become an efficient engineer."

Trama chuckled, his white teeth gleaming.

"Ah, there you're right!" he said. "An engineer is a poet. Working with you I have learned that...."

"You are very polite...."

"And I was thinking, why should Monsieur the Engineer not become a Socialist? A Social'st must be a poet too...."

They both laughed in complete mutual understanding, these two men so strikingly different in appearance, the one dry, nervous, worn out, with faded eyes, and the other looking as if he had been hammered out in a forge shop only yesterday and had not yet been polished.

"No, Trama, I would prefer to have my own workshop and some three dozen good lads like yourself working for me. Then we would be able to do something...."

He tapped the table lightly with his fingers and sighed as he put the violets in his buttonhole.

"Devil take it," cried Trama growing excited, "to think that trifles can prevent a man from living and working...."

"Oh so you call human history a trifle, master mechanic Trama?" queried the engineer with a subtle smile. The worker snatched off his hat, gesturing with it as he went on heatedly:

"Eh, what is the history of my forefathers?"

"Your forefathers?" queried the engineer, accentuating the first word with a more caustic smile.

"Yes, mine! Insolence you think? Perhaps. But why are Giordano Bruno, Vico and Mazzini not my forefathers, am I not living in their world, am I not enjoying the fruit of their great minds?"

"Ah, in that sense!"

"Everything the departed have given to the world is mine!"

"Of course," said the engineer, knitting his brows gravely.

"And everything that has been done before me, before us, is the ore which we must turn into steel, is it not?"

"Why, of course, that is obvious!"

"After all, you educated men, just as we workers, are reaping the fruit of the minds of the past."

"I do not deny that," said the engineer, bending his head; a boy in grey tatters, as tiny as a ball that has been battered in play, stood beside him holding a bunch of crocuses in his filthy little paws, and urging insistently:

"Buy my flowers, signor. . . ."

"I have some. . . ."

"You can never have too many flowers. . . ."

"Right you are, lad," said Trama, "Bravo, give me two. . . ."

And when the boy had given him the flowers he raised his hat and offered a bunch to the engineer.

"Thank you."

"It's a glorious day, isn't it?"

"Yes, even at fifty I can appreciate its beauty. . . ."

He glanced thoughtfully about him with narrowed eyes and heaved a sigh.

"You, I daresay feel the spring sun in your veins very keenly, not only because you are young, but because, I see, the whole world looks different to you than it does to me. Is that not so?"

"I do not know," replied the other laughing. "But life is good!"

"Because of what it promises?" the engineer asked sceptically. The question appeared to sting his companion, for replacing his cap on his head, he answered impulsively:

"Life is good because of all that I love in it! The devil take it, my dear sir, for me words are not merely sounds and letters; when I read a book, look at a picture or behold something beautiful I feel as if I had created it all with my own hands!"

They both laughed at that, the one frankly and heartily as though proud of his ability to laugh well, throwing his head back and thrusting out his broad chest, the other, almost soundlessly, chokingly, baring his teeth that had gold clinging to them as if he had recently been chewing it and had forgotten to clean the greenish remnants that had stuck to the ivory.

"You're a good lad Trama, it is always a pleasure to see you," said the engineer and added with a wink: "If only you weren't such a trouble-maker...."

"Oh, I'm always making trouble...."

And screwing up his fathomless black eyes in an expression of mock gravity, he enquired:

"I trust our behavior was quite correct that time?"

The engineer shrugged his shoulders and rose.

"Oh yes, quite. That affair cost the concern some thirty-seven thousand lire, you know...."

"It might have been wiser to have added that to the men's wages...."

"H'm! You miscalculate. Wiser, you say? Every beast has his own brand of wisdom."

He held out a dry yellow hand and when the worker shook it, said:

"I still think you ought to study and study hard...."

"I learn something every minute...."

"You would make an engineer with a rich imagination."

"Oh, my imagination comes in quite handy as it is!"

"Well, so long, my stubborn friend!"

The engineer walked off under the acacias through the tracery of sunbeams, taking long strides with his lanky legs and pulling his glove on to the thin long fingers of his right hand. The blue-black waiter moved away from the door of the restaurant where he had been listening to the conversation and said to the worker who was rummaging in his purse for some coppers:

"Getting old, our engineer...."

"Oh, he can still hold his own!" exclaimed the worker confidently. "There's plenty of sparks under that skull of his...."

"Where will you be speaking next time?"

"In the same place, the labour exchange, have you heard me?"

"Three times, comrade...."

Shaking hands warmly they parted with a smile; one walking off in the opposite direction from that the engineer had taken, the other humming softly as he commenced to clear the tables.

A group of school children in white aprons, boys and girls, marched along in the middle of the road bubbling with noise and laughter; the first two were blowing lustily into their paper trumpets and the acacias softly showered them with snowy petals.

Whenever one looks at children, especially in springtime, one feels prompted to call after them loudly and gaily:

"Hey, there, young folk! May the future be yours!"

IX

It had been raining heavily since early morning but by midday the clouds had spent themselves, their dark fabric grew threadbare and dissolved into a host of filmy shreds which the wind wafted over toward the sea, weaving them again into a dense bluish-grey mass that cast a thick shadow on the rain-calmed sea.

In the east the dark sky was rent by flashes of lightning while a magnificent sun threw its blinding light over the island.

Seen from a long distance out at sea the island must have looked like a rich temple on a feast day; everything so radiantly clean, generously decked with bright flowers, and the big raindrops glistening everywhere, like topazes on the yellowish young leaves of the vines, amethysts on the clusters of wistaria, rubies on the scarlet geraniums and like emeralds strewn in rich profusion over the grass, the green underbrush and the leaves of the trees.

The air was still with the hush that comes after rain; the gentle babble of the brook hidden amid the rocks and under the roots of the euphorbia, dewberry and fragrant, twining clematis. Down below, the sea murmured softly.

The golden shafts of the furze pointed skywards and swayed gently, weighted by moisture, which they shook noiselessly from their fantastic blossoms.

Against the lush green background, the light purple wistaria vied with the blood-red geraniums and roses, the rusty yellow brocade of the clematis blossoms mingled with the dark velvet of the irises and gilly flowers and it was all so vivid and glowing that the flowers seemed to be singing like violins, flutes and passionate violoncellos.

The moist air was fragrant and as heady as old wine.

Under a grey rock, jagged and torn by blasting, the stains of oxidized iron showing in the cracks, amid grey and yellow boulders exuding the sourish smell of dynamite, four quarrymen, husky fellows in damp rags and leather sandals, sat partaking of their midday meal.

They ate heartily and slowly, out of a large bowl filled with the tough meat of the octopus fried with potatoes and tomatoes in olive oil, and washed it down with red wine quaffed in turn from a bottle.

Two of the men were clean-shaven and resembled one another sufficiently to be brothers, twins even; the third was a small, bow-legged, one-eyed chap with quick nervous gestures that made him resemble an old scraggy bird; the fourth was a broad-shouldered, bearded, hooknosed man of middle age with an abundant sprinkling of grey in his hair.

Breaking off large chunks of bread he smoothed out his wine-stained whiskers and placed a piece in the dark cavern of his mouth.

"That's nonsense," he was saying, his hairy jaws working method-ically as he chewed his food. "It's a lie. I haven't done anything wrong. . . ."

His brown eyes under their thick brows had an unhappy mock-ing expression; his voice was heavy and gruff, his speech slow and hesitant. Everything about him—his hat, his hairy coarse-featured face, his large hands and his dark blue suit spattered with white rock powder—revealed that he was the one who drilled the holes in the mountainside for blasting.

His three workmates listened attentively to what he was saying; they did not interrupt him but looked up at him from time to time as if to say: "Go on. . . ."

And he went on, his grey eyebrows moving up and down as he spoke:

"That man, Andrea Grasso, they called him, came to our village like a thief in the night; he was dressed in rags, his hat the colour of his boots and as tattered. He was greedy, shameless and cruel. And seven years later our elders were doffing their hats to him while he barely gave them a nod. And everyone for forty miles around was in debt to him."

"Yes, there are such people," remarked the bow-legged one, sigh-ing and shaking his head.

The narrator glanced at him.

"So you've met that kind too?" he enquired mockingly.

The old man made an eloquent gesture, the two clean-shaven men grinned in unison, the hooknosed one took a draught of wine and went on, watching the flight of a falcon in the azure sky:

"I was thirteen when he hired me along with some others to haul stones to build his house. He treated us worse than animals and when my pal Lukino told him so he said: 'My ass is mine while you are a stranger to me, why should I be kind to you?' Those words were like a knife-thrust to me, and from that time on I began to watch him more closely. He was mean and brutal to everybody, even to old men and women, it made no difference to him, I could see that. And when respectable people told him he was behaving badly he laughed in their faces: 'When I was poor,' he said, 'no one treated me any better.' He took up with priests, carabinieri and policemen, the rest of them saw him only when they were in grave trouble and then he could do what he liked with them."

"Yes, there are people like that," repeated the bow-legged one softly and all three glanced at him in sympathy: one of the clean-shaven workers silently handed him the wine bottle, the old man took it, held it up to the light and before putting it to his lips, said:

"I drink to the sacred heart of the Madonna!"

"He often used to say that the poor have always worked for the rich and the fools for the wise, and that is how it must be always."

The story-teller laughed and stretched out his hand for the bottle. It was empty. He threw it carelessly onto the stones alongside the hammers, picks and a length of Bickford fuse curled up like a dark snake.

"I was a youngster then and I resented those words deeply, so did my workmates: they killed our hopes, our desire for a better life. Late one night I and Lukino my friend met him as he was crossing the field on horseback. We stopped him and said politely but firmly: 'We ask you to be kinder to folk.' "

The clean-shaven fellows burst out laughing and the one-eyed one too chuckled softly while the narrator heaved a loud sigh:

"Yes, of course, it was stupid! But youth is honest. Youth believes in the power of the word. You might say that youth is life's conscience. . . ."

"Well, and what did he say?" asked the old man.

"He yelled: 'Let go of my horse, you scoundrels!' And pulling out a pistol he pointed it at us. We said: 'You have no need to fear us, Grasso. And don't be angry. We are merely giving you a piece of advice!' "

"Now that was good!" said one of the clean-shaven men, and the other nodded in agreement; the bow-legged one pursed his lips and examined a stone, stroking it with his crooked fingers.

The meal was over. One of the men amused himself by knocking the crystalline raindrops off the blades of grass with a thin stick, another looked on, picking his teeth with a dry grass stalk. The air grew drier and hotter. The brief shadows of noon were melting rapidly. The sea murmured a gentle accompaniment to the solemn tale:

"That meeting had unpleasant consequences for Lukino. His father and uncle were in debt to Grasso. Poor Lukino grew thin and haggard, he ground his teeth and his eyes lost the brightness that had once attracted the girls. 'Ah,' he said to me once, 'that was a foolish thing we did that day. Words are worth nothing when addressed to a wolf!' 'Lukino is ready for murder.' I thought to myself. I was sorry for the lad and his good family. But I was poor myself and all alone in the world, for my mother had died recently."

The hook-nosed stone-cutter brushed his moustache and beard with his lime-stained fingers, and as he did so a heavy-looking silver ring gleamed on the forefinger of his left hand.

"I might have done a service to my fellowmen if I had been able to carry the thing to the end, but I am soft-hearted. One day, meeting Grasso on the street, I walked alongside him and speaking as humbly as I could, said: 'You are a mean, greedy fellow, it is hard for folks to live with you, you are liable to push someone's hand and that hand may reach for a knife. My advice to you is to go away from here.' 'You're a fool, young man!' he said, but I kept insisting. 'Listen,' he said with a laugh, 'How much will you take to leave me in peace? Will a lira be enough?' That was insulting but I controlled my anger. 'Get out of here, I tell you!' I insisted. We were walking shoulder to shoulder, I on his right. When I wasn't looking he drew out his knife and stuck me with it. You can't do much with your left hand, so it went into my chest only one inch deep. Naturally I flung him to the ground and kicked him the way you would kick a hog."

" 'Now perhaps you will take my advice!' I said as he writhed on the ground."

The two clean-shaven fellows threw an incredulous glance at the speaker and dropped their eyes. The bow-legged one bent over to tie the leather thongs of his sandals.

"The next morning when I was still in bed the carabinieri came and took me to the sheriff who was a pal of Grasso's. 'You are an honest man, Ciro,' he said, 'so you will not deny that you tried to murder Grasso last night.' I said that was not exactly the truth, but they have their own way of looking at things. So they kept me in jail for two months before I was brought to trial and then they sentenced me to a year and eight months. 'Very well,' I told the judges, 'but I don't consider the incident closed!' "

He drew a fresh bottle from its cache among the stones and thrusting its neck under his moustaches took a long draught of the wine; his hairy Adam's apple moved thirstily up and down and his beard bristled. Three pairs of eyes watched him in grave silence.

"It's sickening to talk about it," he said handing the bottle to his workmates and smoothing his moist beard.

"When I returned to the village it was clear that there was no room for me there; everyone was afraid of me. Lukino told me that things had got even worse that year. He was sick to death of it all, the poor lad. 'So that's it,' I said to myself and went to see that man Grasso; he was terribly scared when he saw me. 'Well, I'm back,' I said. 'Now it's your turn to go away!' He snatched up his rifle and fired but it was loaded with bird shot and he aimed at my legs. I didn't even fall. 'If you had killed me I would come and haunt you from the grave, I have sworn to the Madonna that I shall get you out of here. You are stubborn, but so am I.' We got into a scuffle and before I knew it I had accidently broken his arm. I hadn't intended to do him violence and he had attacked me first. A crowd gathered and I was taken away. This time I got three years and nine months and when my term ended, my jailer, a man who knew the whole story and liked me, tried hard to persuade me not to go back home. He offered me a job with his son-in-law who had a big plot of land and a vineyard in Apulia. But I, naturally, could not give

up what I had undertaken. So I went home, this time with the firm
intention not to indulge in any useless chatter, I had learned by then
that nine words out of ten are superfluous. I had only one thing to
say to him: 'Get out!' I arrived in the village on a Sunday and went
straight to Mass. Grasso was there. As soon as he saw me he jumped
up and yelled all over the church: 'That man has come here to kill
me, citizens, the devil has sent him for my soul!' I was surrounded
before I had time to touch him, before I had time to tell him what
I wanted. But it didn't matter for he fell onto the stone floor in a
fit and his right side and his tongue were paralyzed. He died seven
weeks later.... That's all. And folks invented a sort of legend about
me.... It's quite terrible, but a lot of nonsense."

He chuckled, looked up at the sun and said:

"Time to get started...."

In silence the other three rose slowly to their feet; the hook-nosed
worker stared at the rusty, oily cracks in the rock and said. "Let's
get to work...."

The sun was at its zenith and all the shadows had shrivelled up
and vanished.

The clouds on the horizon sank into the sea whose waters had
grown calmer and bluer than before.

X

Pepe is ten, he is as frail, slender and mobile as a lizard, his
motley rags hang from his narrow shoulders, and the skin, blackened
by sun and dirt, peeps through innumerable rents.

He looks like a dried-up blade of grass, which the sea breeze
blows hither and thither. From sunrise to sunset Pepe leaps from
stone to stone on the island and hourly one can hear his tireless
little voice pouring forth:

Italy the Beautiful,
Italy my country!

Everything interests him: The flowers that grow in riotous profusion over the good earth, the lizards that dart among the purpu-
rescent boulders, the birds amid the chiselled perfection of the

olive tree leaves and the malachite tracery of the vines, the fish in
the dark gardens at the sea bottom and the foreigners on the narrow,
crooked streets of the town: the fat German with the sword-scarred
face, the Englishman who always reminds one of an actor in the role
of a misanthrope, the American who endeavours in vain to look like
an Englishman, and the inimitable Frenchman as noisy as a rattle.

"What a face!" Pepe remarks to his playmates, glancing with
his keen dancing eyes at the German who is so puffed out with im-
portance that his very hair seems to stand on end. "Why, he's got
a face as big as my belly!"

Pepe doesn't like Germans, he shares the ideas and sentiments
of the streets, the squares and the dark little saloons where the townsfolk drink wine, play cards, read the papers and discuss politics.

"The Balkan Slavs," they say, "are much closer to us poor south-
erners than our good allies who presented us with the sands of
Africa in reward for our friendship."

The simple folk of the south are saying this more and more
often and Pepe hears everything and forgets nothing.

Here is an Englishman, striding tediously along on scissor-like
legs. Pepe in front of him is humming something like a funeral
dirge or just a mournful ditty:

> *My friend has died,*
> *My wife is sad...*
> *And I do not know*
> *What ails her.*

Pepe's playmates trail along behind convulsed with laughter,
scurrying like mice to hide in the bushes or behind walls whenever
the foreigner glances at them calmly with his faded eyes.

One could tell a host of entertaining stories about Pepe.

One day some signora sent him to her friend with a basket of
apples from her garden.

"I will give you a soldo!" she said, "you can well use it."

Pepe readily picked up the basket, balanced it on his head and
set off. Not until evening did he return for the soldo.

"You were in no great hurry," the woman remarked.

"Ah, dear signora, but I am so tired!" Pepe replied with a sigh.
"You see there were more than ten of them!"

"Why, of course, there were more than ten! It was a full basket!"

"Not apples, signora, boys."

"But what about the apples?"

"First the boys, signora: Michele, Giovanni. . . ."

The woman grew angry. She seized Pepe by the shoulder and shook him:

"Answer me, did you deliver the apples?" she cried.

"I carried them all the way to the square, signora! Listen, how well I behaved myself: At first I paid no attention to their jibes. Let them compare me to a donkey, I told myself, I will endure it all out of respect for the signora, for you, signora. But when they began to poke fun at my mother, I decided I had had enough. I put the basket down and you ought to have seen, good signora, how neatly I pelted those little devils with those apples. You would have enjoyed it!"

"They stole my fruit!" cried the woman.

Pepe heaved a mournful sigh.

"Oh, no," he said, "the apples that missed were smashed against the wall, but the rest we ate after I had beaten my enemies and made peace with them. . . ."

The woman loosed a flood of abuse on Pepe's small shaven head. He listened attentively and humbly, clicking his tongue now and again in admiration at some particularly choice expression. "Oho, that's a beauty! What a vocabulary!"

And when at last her anger had spent itself and she left him, he shouted after her:

"But you really wouldn't have felt that way if you saw how beautifully I lammed the filthy heads of those good-for-nothings with those wonderful apples of yours. If only you could have seen it, why you'd have given me two soldos instead of one!"

The silly woman did not understand the modest pride of the victor, she merely shook her fist at him.

Pepe's sister who was much older, but not smarter than he, went to work as housemaid in a villa owned by a rich American. Her appearance altered at once; she became neat and tidy, her cheeks became rosy, and she began to bloom and ripen like a pear in August.

"Do you really eat every day?" her brother once asked her.

"Twice and three times a day if I wish," she replied proudly.

"See you don't wear out your teeth," Pepe advised.

"Is your master very wealthy?" he enquired after a pause.

"Oh, yes, I believe he is richer than the king!"

"That's nonsense! How many pairs of trousers has he got?"

"That is difficult to say."

"Ten."

"More, perhaps. . . ."

"Go and bring me one pair, not too long in the leg but the warmest you can find," said Pepe.

"What for?"

"Well, just look at mine!"

There was indeed not much to see for little enough remained of Pepe's trousers.

"Yes," his sister agreed, "you really need some clothes! But won't he think we have stolen them?"

"Don't imagine that folks are sillier than we are!" Pepe reassured her. "When you take a little from someone who has a lot that isn't stealing, it's just sharing."

"You're talking foolishness," his sister objected, but Pepe overcame her scruples and she brought a good pair of light-grey trousers. They were, of course, far too large for Pepe but he knew at once how to overcome that difficulty.

"Give me a knife!" he said.

Together they quickly converted the American's trousers into a very convenient costume for the boy; the result of their efforts was a somewhat wide but not uncomfortable sack attached to the shoulders by bits of string that could be tied around the neck, with the trouser pockets serving as sleeves.

They might have turned out an even better and more convenient garment had the wife of the owner of the trousers not interrupted their labours: she came into the kitchen and began to give vent to a string of very ugly words in many languages, pronounced equally badly, as is customary with Americans.

Pepe could do nothing to check the flow of eloquence; he frowned, pressed his hand to his heart, clutched despairingly at his head and sighed loudly, but she did not calm down until her husband appeared on the scene.

"What's up?" he asked.

Whereupon Pepe spoke up:

"Signor, I am greatly astonished by the commotion your signora has raised, in fact I am somewhat offended for your sake. As far as I can see she thinks that we have spoiled the trousers, but I assure you that they are just right for me! She seems to think that I have taken your last pair of trousers and that you cannot buy yourself another pair...."

The American who had listened imperturbably to the speech, now remarked:

"And I think, young man, that I ought to call the police."

"Really," Pepe queried in amazement, "what for?"

"To take you to jail...."

Pepe was extremely hurt. In fact, he was ready to weep but swallowed his tears and said with great dignity:

"If, signor, it gives you pleasure to send people to jail, that is your affair! But I would not do that if I had many pairs of trousers and you had none! I would give you two, perhaps even three pairs; although it is impossible to wear three pairs of trousers at once! Especially in hot weather...."

The American burst out laughing, for even rich men can sometimes see a joke. Then he treated Pepe to some chocolate and gave him a franc piece. Pepe bit at the coin and thanked the donor:

"Thank you, signor! The coin is genuine, I presume?"

But Pepe is at his best when he stands alone somewhere among the rocks, pensively examining their cracks as if reading the dark history of rock life. At such moments his vivid eyes are dilated and filmy with wonder, his slender hands are laced behind his back and his head, slightly bent, sways slightly from side to side like the cup of a flower in the breeze. And under his breath he softly hums a tune, for he is forever singing.

It is good also to watch him looking at flowers, at the wistaria blossoms that pour in purple profusion over the walls. He stands as taut as a violin string as if he were listening to the soft tremor of the silken petals stirred by the breath of the sea breeze.

As he looks he sings: "Fiorino... Fiorino...."

And from afar, like the sound of some huge tambourine, comes the muffled sigh of the sea. Butterflies chase one another over the flowers. Pepe raises his head and follows their flight, blinking in the sunlight, his lips parted in a smile which though tinged with envy and sadness, is yet the generous smile of a superior being on earth.

"Ohi!" he cries, clapping his hands to frighten an emerald lizard.

And when the sea is as placid as a mirror and the rocks are bare of the white spume of the tide, Pepe seated on a stone, gazes with his bright eyes into the transparent water where among the reddish seaweed the fish glide smoothly, the shrimps dart back and forth and the crab crawls along sideways. And in the stillness the clear voice of the boy pours gently forth over the azure waters:

"Sea, oh, Sea. ..."

Adults often shake their heads disapprovingly at Pepe, saying: "That one will be an anarchist!"

But kinder folk, possessed of greater discernment, are of a different opinion:

"Pepe will be our poet. ..."

And Pasqualino, the cabinet-maker, an old man with a head that seems cast in silver and a face like those etched on ancient Roman coins—wise and respected Pasqualino has his own opinion:

"Our children will be far better than us, and their lives will be better too!"

Many folk believe him.

THE ROMANCER

THERE WAS a man named Foma Varaxin, a cabinet-maker, aged twenty-five, a most absurd man with a large skull, flattened at the temples and elongated behind above the nape; this top-heavy skull tilted up his cropped head, and Foma walked the earth with his broad nose stuck up in the air, so that from a distance he gave the jaunty impression of wishing to cry out:

"Here, touch me, you just try!"

A single glance, however, at his nondescript face with its mouth of generous proportions and neutral-tinted eyes showed him to be just a good-natured fellow looking happily embarrassed over something or other.

His comrade, Alexei Somov, who was also a cabinet-maker, once told Foma:

"Your mug looks awful dreary! Why don't you stick on a pair of eyebrows or something. There's nothing on the whole panel except a nose, and that's as bad a job I've ever seen!"

"That is so," agreed Foma, fingering his upper lip. "Features couldn't exactly be called handsome, but then didn't Polly say I had fine eyes!"

"Don't you believe it. She says that to get you to treat her to an extra bottle of beer."

Alexei was two years Foma's junior, but he had spent five months in prison for politics, read many books, and when he was loath or unable or too lazy to understand a comrade he used to say:

"That's a bourgeois prejudice. Utopia. You must know the history of culture. You don't understand the class contradictions."

He introduced Foma into a circle where little sharp-nosed Comrade Mark, waving hands that resembled bird's feet, rattled off an account of the labour movement in the West. These narrations had an instant appeal for Foma, and after several lectures he pressed a varnish-stained hand to his chest and gushed:

"That's the stuff, Alexei! That's just about right! It does exist...."

Dry sardonic Somov, screwing up his greenish eyes and pursing his lips, asked:

"What does?"

"That same attraction people have towards unity—it does! Now take me. It's all the same to me whether it's a fire, or a religious procession, or a public fair—I always feel myself drawn terribly strong to any kind of place where people are gathered. People! Now take the church—why do I like to go to church? A gathering of souls, that's why!"

"You'll get over that!" Alexei assured him with an ironical grin. "When you grasp the idea...."

Foma thumped himself on the chest and cried joyously:

"I have grasped it! Here's where it is! I grasped it from the very first. Now it's a joy to me like Our Lady of all the afflicted...."

"Off he goes!"

"No, wait a minute. 'Come unto me, all ye that labour and are heavy laden, and I will give you rest.' Isn't that it? That's the idea!"

"Don't be silly—that's the Gospel!"

"What of that? The idea is always the same, it strikes me. It may take on different shapes and different forms but the image is the same! It's the Mother of Love! Isn't that so?"

When Alexei was angry his upper lip curled, his sharp nose quivered, and his green pupils grew round like a bird's. In a dry voice that crackled oddly on its high notes, and in words that sounded like snaps, Alexei impressively and at great length tried to prove to his comrade that he was a Utopian, that his class consciousness was dormant and would probably never be awakened because Foma had been brought up in a clergyman's home where his mother served as cook and where his soul was poisoned by bourgeois prejudices and superstitions.

"But Alexei!" Foma exclaimed in an earnest tone, "it wasn't poisoned—so help me God! Quite the contrary! When I was a kid, frinstance, I didn't go to church at all. Good Lord, you don't think I'm lying, do you? That happened afterwards, when I began to read books, and in general was drawn towards people! It isn't a matter of church-going, but a—you know—communion of souls! That's the idea! Now, what's it all about? Brothers, shame on you, how can you live like that? You're not beasts, are you? It's a matter of inspiring love and conscience, Alexei, that's the important thing it seems to me! Isn't that right?"

"No, it isn't right!" snapped Alexei, his anger rising and his cheeks breaking out in patches of red, and Foma often had the impression that Alexei's words rapped his nose like cards in that game people played.

Foma maintained an embarrassed silence, stroking his head and now and then making a timid attempt in a guilty voice to appease his comrade:

"I understand, Alexei, I really do! Of course—there's the struggle! Nobody's denying that—that's where you've got to sit tight!"

Then he would suddenly meander off, and begin to argue in an earnest tone:

"You see, I was only thinking about man. Now, what is man, generally speaking? I'm not a chisel, am I? Now, say some one began using you as a chisel, they'd start using a mallet on you—that's what I mean, don't you see! A man's not a tool, is he? Then, there's the struggle, to be sure—you can't get away from that! By all means—the struggle! But the apostolic, you know, idea—that er ... general er ... universal concord ... peace on earth and goodwill among men. ..."

Sometimes Alexei would say nothing and fix his comrade with a long contemptuous stare. Then he would begin in a cutting voice. as though he were snipping off Foma's ears:

"No you're stupid! It's a muddle-head you are, a hopeless muddle-head!"

Or he would threaten him, icily and impressively:

"You wait—we'll soon begin to read the history of culture—you'll see."

Foma then felt very small. Incomprehensible words always exercised a depressing effect on him, inspired a reverential awe for the people who used them and elicited strange associations of ideas. Utopia he visualized as a hummocky swamp all covered with a stunted overgrowth, while over the chilly knolls, with arms outstretched, walks a woman clad all in white with the face of Our Lady, as always, filled with the vast sadness of the Mother—and she walks in silence with mute tears in her eyes. He had more than once heard the words "religious cult," and culture he envisaged as a divine service, something in the nature of a solemn matins at Easter. It slowly dawned on him that this wise science could untie all the knots of life's tangled problems, reduce all thoughts to proper order and bathe the variegated tints of life in a single steady mellow light. He spoke a lot, rapturously and breathlessly and always looked his interlocutor straight in the face with lack-lustre, tipsy-looking eyes. Every new thought that entered his mind evoked a torrent of words—he would wave his arms and cry in low and delighted tones:

"Wonderful! That's just it! So simple!"

At first his comrades of the circle and workshop lent him an attentive ear out of curiosity, but they soon discovered that Foma was simply a chatterbox, and Yegor Kashin, the dour-faced fitter, advised him more than once:

"Cut your tongue in halves, windbag!"

But this did not cool Foma's ardour—he surveyed everyone with a friendly glance and babbled on like a gushing spring brook.

When he came to the first lesson on the history of culture and found that it was to be given by a plump little blue-eyed young lady with smooth hair and a thick braid hanging down her back he was sadly puzzled, and tried all the time to avoid looking at the young lady.

He noticed, however, that she was ill at ease, trying in vain to impart a serious expression to her childish face, speaking hurriedly, incoherently, and when asked a question her face blushed crimson and her eyes blinked swiftly in confusion. She was so white and dainty that she stirred in him a feeling of pity.

"Clearly the first time," thought Foma, studiously examining the dark damp wall above her head. He was surprised to hear her speak about lightning, the clouds, sunset, the heroes of fables and Greek myths—he could not see the connection and complained about it to Alexei on their way home:

"That was a flop, Alexei! On a subject like that they should have put a different person entirely, a serious man, some one with grey in his hair like... and a deep voice... make it sound like some one was reading the Twelve Gospels!"

Somov too was disgruntled and snorted:

"Fancy appointing that froggish little thing for such a job! A fat lot I care who the Evil Serpent is.... We know who he is all right—tell us better how to destroy him...."

"Better she'd had just read straight off that thick little book!" said Foma deprecatingly, but soon forgetting the unfortunate lesson, he rambled on in his usual tone of benign dreamer: "Isn't it wonderful, brother, a little person like that coming into our rough company—here, see you, this is what I know, will you just listen! Wonderful! By getting closer to each other...."

"Talking drivel again!" Alexei brusquely stemmed the verbal tide.

"Why is it drivel?" Foma persisted gently, kindly. "You talk about class—now what kind of class is she? Simply a generous-hearted little girl. She feels sort of conscious-stricken living among people of our like, and so she...."

"When will all that treacle ooze out of you?" cried Somov in annoyance. "What's conscience got to do with it? Simply necessity—conscience be hanged! If she had another place to go to, she'd find something easier and wouldn't come to us, don't kid yourself!"

Foma looked down the street at the flaming beads of the lamp lights and asked:

"So you think she does it because she's obliged to?"

"Of course...."

"You think so?" said Varaxin with a backward toss of his head. "I don't believe it somehow!"

"Why not?"

"What's the sense in doing a thing because you're obliged to? If I'm a cabinet-maker and used to my job—why should I do the work of a common carpenter? She's kind of whittling logs...."

Alexei spat, saying:

"Let her whittle logs...."

At the second lesson Foma seemed to catch a glimpse of interesting ideas in the girl's words which stirred his heart, and when she had finished he asked:

"Comrade Liza, will you lend me that book until next time?"

"Certainly," she said, looking obviously pleased.

Then Foma walked by her side through the streets of the town, and was careful not to touch her with his elbow. They walked up a hilly street, on both sides of which the little houses of the suburb gazed at them through darkened windows. A lamp burned at the top of the street, casting a trembling patch of dull yellow around, and the damp gloom of the autumn night was filled with the odours of rotting wood and refuse.

Foma, coughing discreetly and trying to express himself elegantly, asked Liza:

"Then, I can take it for granted that in ancient times man spoke a single language—is that so?"

"Yes, the Aryans," a low voice answered him.

"And that's been proved, has it?"

"Definitely proved."

"Fine! That's wonderful! Then all the nations that are now scattered were once devoted to the unity of life, hence in ancient times people were united by a single common idea—y-yes. . . ."

His words, however, shaped themselves laboriously, and he was thinking not of ancient times but of the little figure of the girl hurrying uphill half a pace in front of him on his left. Cloaked in the darkness she looked smaller than she was. Foma noticed that every time she passed a lighted window she bent her head and tried to slip quickly out of the patch of light.

"Wonderful!" he thought, not ceasing to talk and seeming to become a dual personality, as it were. "Such a little person, without fear, amid strange men, at night, in such a lonely spot. . . . Wonderful!"

To keep his hands from gesticulating he thrust them into his pockets. This was uncustomary and constraining.

"Aren't you afraid of drunks?" he asked.

She answered quickly, softly:

"Oh, I'm dreadfully afraid! There are so many of them around here. . . ."

"Yes," said Foma with a sigh, "they drink an unconscionable lot! The point is—life wants filling up, but there isn't anything to fill it with! I mean life in the sense of the soul. Wine, we know, enriches the fancy. You can't blame people harshly—is it a man's fault that he's obliged to sustain life by fancies?"

"I don't blame them!" exclaimed Liza, slowing her pace. "I understand. What you said is so true, so very true!"

That cheered Foma up—he never remembered any one ever having agreed with him. Drawing his hands out of his pockets and slapping the book under his jacket he resumed in earnest confidential tones:

"Now, frinstance, if books were more accessible—that would be a different matter! Generally speaking, there's no reason to be afraid of people, I assure you they deserve the fullest interest and compassion in the empty lives they lead. The fact of the matter is there is very little of everything, as you know, and that's why everybody's wild. No comforts of any kind, a man's only friend is just naked fate with the awful face of poverty and vice, as the poet has it. But then, of course, when people like you will come down in large numbers from the summit—it'll certainly give to life something that'll make it worthy of man...."

Liza walked still more slowly, holding her skirt with one hand, while she passed the other hand across her face, saying with a sigh: "Yes, yes, that's true!"

"Fyodor Grigorievich," Foma went on, interrupting her, "the son of the clergyman in whose place my mother lived—a good woman, my mother was, but she's dead—Fyodor Grigorievich who'll now soon be a professor, he used to say, when arguing with his father: 'To live is to know!' Very simple! Supposing I live and don't know what I am, the why and wherefore and all that—now could you call that living? Just eking out an existence under the exploitation of all kinds of sinister forces originating in man and prejudices created by him—isn't that so?"

"To live is to know!" repeated Liza. "That's just the thing, comrade—you have such a wonderfully broad outlook...."

Foma did not remember what else he said, but this was the first time in his life that he had spoken so much, so boldly and ardently. They parted at the gate of a large two-storied house with columns on the façade, and Liza, shaking his hand, earnestly asked him:

"Thursday and Monday—don't forget! After seven I'm at home, I'll wait till nine—you won't forget?"

"With the greatest pleasure!" cried Foma, stamping his foot on the pavement. "Awfully grateful! Splendid!"

All night long till morning he roamed about the streets with

his head reared in the air, mentally composing ardent invocatory
speeches about the necessity of rendering aid by word and deed
to people who had still failed to grasp the intrinsic ideas: to live
and to know. He felt very happy. The grey sky of autumn seemed
to yawn before him and out of the deep blue gulf words tumbled
like falling stars, beautiful rich words that formed themselves into
shining ranks of good and kindly thoughts on life and men, and
these thoughts left Foma astonished before their unconquerable
simplicity, their truth and force.

Thursday found Foma sitting in Liza's room, seeing nothing
except the tense glance of her blue eyes which, he could see, were
trying to follow the drift of his words, while he looked into their
blue depths and spoke:

"Then it looks, figurely speaking, as if the idea about the
triumph of light over darkness is of heavenly origin?"

"If you like, yes—but—still—why must you have the heavenly?"

"It kind of looks nicer! And so—the main idea is the Sun that
sheds around it the force of life! That's wonderful and quite
right. I went out of town yesterday—to Yarillo,* you know—to
watch the sunset! Quite easy and simple to imagine the way it's all
described—serpent, swords, the struggle, the defeat of darkness and
then the sunrise in a triumphant blaze! There wasn't any sunrise,
though, it was raining, but that doesn't matter. I've seen the sunrise
many a time, and I'll make it a point to see it on a clear day, I
will!"

He looked round and took a liking to the clean cosy little
room with the white bed in the corner chastely screened in a soft
veil of gloom. On a table before Foma lay numerous books,
others stood slanting on a shelf, the walls were hung with familiar photographs of writers and learned men with long hair and
melancholy faces. Rubbing his palms covered with callouses and
stained with varnish, Foma laughed softly to himself and went on:

"Wonderful, comrade, there I was sitting on a steep bank
with my legs over the side, when a dog comes up, kind of beg-
garly looking dog it was, you know, all covered with dirt and

* An allusion to the ancient Slavonic sun-god called *Yarillo.—Trans.*

burs, with grey whiskers on its face. Hungry, old and homeless.
Comes up and sits down near me and also watches: there was
the sky flaming yellow and red, blue figures kept on changing, the
rays broke 'em up and set 'em alight again, golden rivers flowed
past—and we, a man and a dog, sat watching, just like that. Generally speaking, comrade, nobody knows for certain what a dog
really is, you know, and what it's attitude is to the sun? Maybe it
also—mind you, I don't know, it's just fantasy—but why shouldn't
a dog be able to understand what the sun means, if it feels cold
and warmth and can look at the sky? Now, a pig—that's another
matter, of course! D'you know, I even joked with it—d'you understand, says I, who the real creator of life is, eh? It looked at me
out of the corner of its eye and moved off a little.... Surprising
how every living thing on earth is mistrustful and cautious of one
another—very sad, when you come to think of it! Mind you, maybe
it's silly, but when I read those two chapters I all of a sudden,
you know, seemed to realize it for the first time—why, the sun!
The sun—extraordinary simple!"

"You've read two chapters?" Foma heard her ask.

The question struck him as sounding sort of strict.

"Only two," he returned, and for some reason began fingering the
chair on which he sat. "We've got a lot of work just now, you know,
an urgent job. Klobistyaev, the merchant, is giving his daughter
away in marriage—the son-in-law's going to live with them—and
we're touching up a dining room suite. Splendid furniture he
bought, fine antique workmanship—solid oak, you know...."

He saw the girl's eyes close wearily, and that instantly made
him tongue-tied and threw him into confusion. Foma resumed not
without an effort, smiling embarrassedly:

"Maybe I'm chattering too much—pardon me please!"

The young lady exclaimed hastily:

"Oh no! Your talk is so interesting. I've only just started
work, and it's very important for me to study the mentality of
people who ... people of your class."

Foma brightened up again, became emboldened, and, waving
his arms in the air, broke into song, like a bird at sunrise.

"Allow me to say that people of my kind are like little children—timid, you know! Between ourselves, frinstance, we crafts-

men very rarely have heart to heart talks. Yet every one would
like to say something about himself—because—well, you know, a
man sees very little kindness, and ... if you bear in mind that
every one had a mother ... and was used to being caressed, it's ...
a very sad thing!"

He moved up to the little hostess with his chair—something
creaked with a snap and a thick book dropped on the floor.

"I'm sorry," said Foma. "Very little elbow-room in here!"
Dropping his voice, he continued in a mysterious undertone: "I
want to tell you how remarkably true it is that it's no good for
a man to live by himself! Of course, unity of interests among the
workers is a very good thing—I understand that—but interest is
not the whole story—there's a mighty lot in a man's soul besides
that! A man definitely wants to lay bare his soul, show it in full
dress parade, in all its magnitude.... A man's a young creature,
as you know! Not in years, of course, but taking it as life as a
whole—life's not an old story, is it? Eh? And suddenly, there
you are, nobody wants to listen to anything—and there you have
it—loneliness of the soul ... dumbness and death of thought! I
don't agree with it—the unity of people is absolutely necessary,
isn't it? Unity of interests—all right ... but how can one explain
the loneliness and the awful misery at times? You see...."

"I don't quite follow you," said Liza, and her voice once more
sounded teacher-like and strict.

Foma regarded her smilingly, and she, with knitted brows,
returned his look with a very intent stare that once more damp-
ened his enthusiasm. With a lift of her shoulders she drew her
plait over her breast and her fingers moved swiftly twining and
untwining the black ribbon, while she said in an unnaturally deep
voice:

"That's rather a strange argument. While admitting the unity
of interests...."

"You see, the point is," broke in Foma, "if one ray is here,
another there, there won't be any warmth ... all the rays must be
merged into one, isn't that so?"

"Well, yes, but what do you call a ray?"

"My soul and yours—there you have the rays of the sun,
figurely speaking."

When Foma took his leave he thought Liza looked at him suspiciously and shrank back, and when he shook her hand she tried to pull it back.

And again he wandered nearly all night through the deserted streets of the sleepy town, rousing the night watchmen dozing at the house entrances, and exciting the interest of the policemen on their night rounds.

He recalled the things he had spoken and made a wry face, feeling that he had bungled things and had not said what he wanted to.

"Funny!" he thought, "when I went to her I had everything so pat in my head. Next time I'll rehearse it properly...."

He suddenly stopped, remembering that Liza had not told him when he could come again.

"She's forgotten! I've been speaking too much!"

And then again he escorted her home at nights, and all the way he bombarded her with his rapturous speeches, confided to her, before he was aware of it, the secrets of an awakened soul, not noticing that she listened to him in silence, answered his questions in monosyllables and no longer invited him to come to her warm little room.

"Why, I believe you're a romancer!" she once exclaimed with a feeling akin to regret, and looking him squarely in the face she shook her head deprecatingly.

Foma was disconcerted by a word that was reminiscent of romance and love, and he laughed softly while Liza continued:

"How strange! Of course, I understand romanticism, but...."

She spoke long and didactically, and Foma could not understand what it was all about.

And gradually it became a necessity for him to see Liza—her eyes produced on him a heady pleasant sensation and elicited new words, kindled oddly fervent thoughts. Seeing her surrounded by a close ring of workers listening attentively and thoughtfully to her low persuasive voice, seeing her white hands fluttering like little doves in the semi-dusk of the room, her dark brows moving above the blue eyes and rosy lips quivering like budding petals, Foma thought:

"That's the Idea! To all the afflicted I bring joy...."

And he pictured to himself a cool babbling brook meandering
down the hillside to a parched valley where the trees stand forlorn and dusty, their faded leaves drooping wearily, while the living
water makes its way to their roots.

And he recalled the lovely fairy tale of the little girl lost in
the woods—how she wandered into the cave of the dwarfs and
sat among them trustfully, filled with love and goodwill to every
living thing.

Sometimes Liza, warming to her subject, grew excited, stammered, found difficulty in choosing her words, and her eyes darted
anxiously over the faces of her audience. At such moments Foma
sat tense and breathless, he felt an urge to intervene and help her
out with the missing words and—so painful was the ordeal to
him—that he even perspired with the tension.

"Alexei!" he said to Somov, gesticulating. "What a wonderful
thing it is when a pure person like that—almost a child she is!—
comes to people and says: excuse me, that's not so, it's all wrong,
you don't see the main thing—the idea of the world's unity! Extraordinary! Just like a fairy tale, eh?"

Alexei threw him a look out of the corner of his eye and muttered sarcastically:

"Mind you don't melt, you'll make the floor dirty!"

"Don't be silly! Why, you yourself—you believe, you feel it. . . ."

Somov curled his lip and snubbed his comrade with an angry
snort:

"You'd better listen more and chatter less. And don't start
explaining to people what you don't understand yourself. You
just look, you haven't made yourself too popular—you get on
people's nerves with your talk. . . ."

"I get on people's nerves?" queried Foma incredulously.

One day he had a toothache which he assiduously tried to re-
lieve by stuffing cotton wool saturated in varnish into the cavity; he
even bought some creosote, though he considered it injurious, but
the pain was not allayed and he was unable to attend the lesson.

Late in the evening Somov, looking gloomy and disgruntled,
came into the workshop, and calling Foma aside, demanded sternly:

"What were you talking about with Liza the day before yesterday?"

"Me? Oh, various things. Why?"

Alexei, his lips twisted, looked at him askance and, drawing at his cigarette, asked:

"Complained about being lonely, eh?"

"Complained? Me? Nothing of the kind! I just happened to mention it...."

"You ought to take better care of your words!"

"Did you see her home?"

"Sure."

"What did she tell you about me?" asked Foma, stroking his swollen cheek.

"What I'm telling you—you're a muddle-headed fellow."

"No, really?"

Somov studied the smoking tip of his cigarette and said with a sneer:

"You can take it from me! That's what she said!"

"Never mind!" exclaimed Foma, and even his tooth seemed to ache less. "I'll prove to her that...."

"Look here," said Alexei with a sardonic grin, kicking aside the shavings on the floor, "let me give you a bit of advice—or better I'll tell you what happened to me once. When I was in prison I saw a girl, one of the educated sort, during the promenade, and went nuts over her right off the bat, just like you...."

"You don't say!" Foma exclaimed in astonishment.

But Alexei, his face as wry as though he too suffered from toothache, went on without looking at his pal:

"We tapped out messages to each other at night and all that kind of thing.... I started that stuff about loneliness, and it worked out pretty rotten, my dear fellow, let me tell you!"

"You don't say!" repeated Foma in a soft whisper, waving his hands. "What makes you think—who said I was in love? Where did you get the idea?"

"Come on, kid your grandmother! I advise you to drop it...."

"That's nonsense, Alexei!" said Foma, pressing a hand to his heart and feeling that it was beating with astonishing rapidity, as though at once frightened and overjoyed. "Good Lord, who the devil would have thought it? That's extraordinary, that is! The

thing never entered my mind! But what's the use? Though, on
second thought, she's made up her mind to go with us fellows,
and—well, so what? Very simple, I should say! Supposing we put
it like this: let a person melt in our insipid midst like a pinch
of salt, and satiate...."

Somov crushed the cigarette end slowly between his fingers,
stared around and started whistling between his teeth. Seeing that
his comrade had no desire to listen to him Foma sighed and remarked:

"That damned tooth's a nuisance—hurts...."

"Mind something else doesn't start hurting!" Alexei warned
him, concealing his eyes under his lashes, then suddenly resumed
in a tone Foma had never heard him use before:

"Look here, if we're going to talk this thing out—though I'm
not gifted with the gab—let me tell you this. People say that you're
a muddle-headed fellow—I say it myself ... it's only true—sometimes you talk such piffle, fit to make a fellow sick. Still ... I always hear you—I mean listen...."

He sat on a work-bench, his back bent and his shoulders,
elbows and knees sticking out in sharp angularities, and he looked
as though he had been knocked together out of odd fragments
of wood. Stroking his stiff dark hair he continued slowly and
quietly:

"What I like about you is that you're somehow like a little
child—you put faith in everything you know...."

"Alexei—that's just it!" cried Foma, leaning over to him
confidentially. "D'you remember me telling you about Fyodor Grigorievich? He says the same thing. His father's all for faith. But
he says, even behind faith there's a certain amount of knowledge,
for without it no interpretation of life is possible...."

"You chuck that, my boy!" advised Somov. "I don't understand
that...."

"No, but can't you see, it's very simple! First knowledge—
then faith! It's the mother of faith, it gives it birth—you just
think—how can a man have faith unless he has knowledge? Comrade Mark and Vassili, if you ask me—they simply don't believe
in the power of knowledge, that's why they talk against faith in
general...."

Somov regarded him with a sorrowful ironical look and observed with a shake of the head:

"It's hard to talk with you! Crammed yourself chock-full with all kinds of drivel, and it looks to me you'll never get rid of it. . . . Let me tell you—I'm sorry for you! Get me? And take my advice —-leave Liza alone!"

Foma Varaxin forced a reluctant laugh and screwed up his eyes like a stroked cat.

No, I'll see this thing through. I will, right full ahead! I'll ask her—that's a wonderful idea! Now, what'll she say, eh?"

"What are you going to ask her?" enquired Alexei drily.

"Generally, I'll ask her about complete unity. Word and deed —is that it?"

Somov drew out a cigarette with a trembling hand and put it into his mouth the wrong end. He bit off the moistened end, spat it out on the floor, flung the cigarette after it and asked:

"Do you love her, or what? Might as well say it!"

To which Foma replied without a moment's hesitation:

"Yes, of course, very much. . . . I mean, if you hadn't mentioned it—I might not have guessed it perhaps—but now it's clear! When I speak with her I feel so happy and light, as though I really were a child, upon my word!"

"Good-bye," muttered Alexei, thrusting out his hand, and made for the door. He stopped in the depths of the workshop, looking small and dark, and asked in a quiet voice:

"Damn it, maybe you only just made it up?"

"What?"

"That love of yours?"

"You're a funny chap!" exclaimed Foma. "You said it yourself. I didn't make anything up, I simply didn't grasp the fact yet . . . it was you. . . ."

"I'm a fool too!" said Somov and disappeared.

What with excitement and agonizingly anxious visions of his forthcoming meeting with Liza, Foma forgot his toothache and began pacing backwards and forwards among the rustling shavings. An oil lamp burned smokily on the wall, dimly illuminating the yellow strips of boards stacked on racks overhead, a pile of curly shavings in the corner on which lay sprawled the little body of a sleeping boy, the dark work-benches, the curved legs of chairs and boards gripped in vices.

"Wonderful!" thought Foma, rubbing his hands together vigorously.

He conjured up a simple, delightful life with a clever and loving little wife full of understanding and able to find an answer to every question. Around her are dear friends and comrades, and she herself is dear and near.

"Beautiful!"

Then will come exile—that's sure to come! Somewhere far away in a lonely little village snowed up to the roofs and lost amid dark towering forests—forests towering to the very sky—he sits alone with her, studying. The walls are lined with shelves of thick impressive-looking books that tell you everything you want to know, and they both pass mentally from one to another of them by the bright ways of human thought. Outside there reigns a frozen hush, the white snow has wrapped the earth in a downy cloak and above it hangs the low cupola of the northern skies. Inside the room it is warm, clean and cosy, the fire in the stove dances in vivid yellow tongues of flame, the shadows dart silently along the walls and in a little cot by one of them lies another sweet bit of humanity born into the world to fight for the unity of all mankind into a single family of friends, workers, creators. The wintry sky of this cold country is painted by flaming sunsets, reminiscent of the primeval days when the first childish thoughts of men were born, when the invincible idea of uniting all mankind, the idea of the triumph of light was first nourished in men's minds.

Foma Varaxin did not believe in dawdling—Sunday saw him dressed in his best suit, one side of which, for some unaccountable reason, was longer than the other, and the collar of which evinced an inclination to climb to the back of his head; he put on a shirt with a starched front and frayed cuffs, donned a blue necktie with red spots, hunched his shoulders high and went forth to visit Liza.

The bright winter day was bedecked in hoar-frost and velvet draperies of snow, strengthening in Foma's breast a joyous resolve inspiring him with words bright and pure. The telegraph wires, white and shaggy with hoar-frost, stretched prettily in the air

straight towards the street where lived the girl whom Foma had
already more than once and without any shadow of doubt mentally
called his bride and wife. It was a glorious day, a joyous day, re-
splendent with light and silver scintillations.

"Oh, it's you!" said Liza, opening the door of her room.

"Are you coming in or going out?" asked Foma, smiling and
giving her hand a hearty squeeze.

"I'm going out," she said, her face twisted with pain, as she
blew on her fingers and shook them in front of her face. She had
a little sealskin cap on her head and her left hand was gloved.

"Well, I won't keep you long!" promised Foma, settling himself into a chair in his overcoat and slapping his knee with
his cap.

"Why do you look so radiant?" asked Liza, her blue eyes travelling over his figure.

He took his time, regarding her with an affectionate searching
look—she was so like an apple, small, round and rosy.

"A little doll!" it flashed through his mind.

She walked to and fro between the door and the window, her
heels clicking on the floor. She glanced through the window, then
at the visitor with wrinkled brows, and swaying slightly, moved
slowly towards the door. It seemed to him that her face looked
sterner and more preoccupied than usual.

"Perhaps she feels what's coming?" he thought.

"I'll explain why I look radiant," said Foma aloud and invited
her: "Sit down, please!"

She shrugged her shoulders and reluctantly, irresolutely sat
down facing him.

"Well?"

Foma leaned towards her, put out a yellow-nailed varnish-
stained hand, and began in a low, soft, tender voice:

"Do you know, Comrade Liza, I want to tell you just one
word." He rose to his feet, pointed his finger in front of him and
exclaimed in an impressive tone: "Full ahead!"

"What's that?" asked Liza, smiling.

"Let me explain: imagine a steamboat on the river, engines
throttled down because the fairway's unfamiliar. Then the situation becomes clear. 'Half speed!' yells the captain down to the

engine room, and then, when all's plain sailing, the captain commands: 'Full ahead!' "

Liza opened her eyes in a puzzled look, silently biting her lips with little white teeth.

"You don't understand?" queried Foma, moving up closer.

"N-no! Who's the captain?"

"The captain? You! And me—we're both captains of our lives —you and me! We have the right to command our own destiny— isn't that so?"

"Why, yes, but—what's it all about?" exclaimed the girl, laughing.

Foma held his arms out to her and repeated in broken accents:

"Full ahead, comrade! You know us, me and all the rest—come to us, come with us to complete unity!"

Liza stood up. It seemed to him that a shadow passed over her face and chased the bloom from her cheeks, quenched the shining light of her eyes.

"I don't understand," she said, lifting her shoulders. "It goes without saying—of course I am with you.... What makes you speak of it? What is the matter?"

Foma seized her hands in his own hard palms, shook them and almost shouted:

"It goes without saying! Wonderful, comrade! I knew it ... of course you'll—you'll do it!"

"Do what?" she questioned nervously, snatching her fingers away. "Don't shout, there are other people in the house.... Do what?"

Her voice sounded angry and a little indignant. Foma caught the note and hastened to explain:

"Marry me—that's what I propose! Right full ahead! D'you imagine what it'll be like—our life, comrade? What a holiday it'll be...."

Standing before her, with his arms frantically sawing the air, he began to sketch the long pondered scenes of their life together, their work, pictures of life in exile, and as he spoke his voice dropped lower and lower, for Liza seemed to be melting before his gaze, dwindling and shrinking and receding further and further away.

"Good God, how stupid!" he heard a muffled distressed ex-clamation. "How vulgar!"

It seemed to Foma as if somebody had imperceptibly sprung at him and clenched a hand over his mouth so hard that his heart instantly stopped beating and he gasped for breath.

"You ought to be ashamed of yourself, Foma!" he heard a low indignant voice saying. "It's simply—why, it's awful! It's stupid—don't you see? Oh, how disgusting, how silly!"

It seemed to him that the girl was shrinking into the wall, bury-ing herself among the portraits, and her face grew as grey and lifeless as the photographs above her head. She pulled her plait with one hand and fanned the air in front of her with the other, shrinking ever smaller and speaking in a low but sharp voice:

"Aren't you ashamed of yourself to regard me only as a woman?"

Foma spread his hands and stammered:

"Why? Not a woman, but generally ... as people—you and me...."

"What kind of comradeship is this?" she asked. "What am I to think of you now? Why did you have to insult me, why?"

Foma had no recollection of how he left the little room with the many photographs on the walls, how he took his leave of Liza and what she said at parting—she had utterly dwindled and merged into the grey smudge of the rigid tutorial faces, had become one with them, inspiring, as they did, a cold stern deference.

He paced the streets, seeing nothing but misty circles before his eyes, and pulled his cap down low over his head, musing concen-tratedly, obstinately, drearily:

"Why stupid? Of what should I be ashamed? Vulgar? A wom-an? What's wrong with a woman? Does that matter so much? If there are two souls united in a single idea—what if it is a woman?"

And he pulled his cap lower. His head felt cold, as though it had been stocked with ice and the sense of chilliness was so keen that his heart ached with a dull pain, as if he had been breathing asphyxiating fumes in an ill-ventilated room.

He caught up with a funeral procession. A soldier was being buried. Four stalwarts in uniforms, taking broad even strides, car-ried the coffin on their shoulders, and it swung measuredly from side to side in the frosty air. In front walked a drummer, adroitly beating a tattoo with his drumsticks, scattering into the air the impressive roll of his drum. Behind marched a platoon of soldiers with shouldered rifles. The soldiers wore black ear-caps tied under their chins and they all seemed to be wounded with deep gashes.

Alongside the coffin ran a little dun dog with its tail between its legs, and when the drum ceased beating the burial roll, it ran closer to the coffin, and when the drumsticks resumed their music it darted back with a timorous plaintive whimper.

Foma took off his cap with a great effort, leaned against a fence and watched the strange soldiers go by, shuddering with the cold that filled his breast and thinking, as though enquiring of some one:

"Why ashamed?"

THE MORDVINIAN GIRL

On SATURDAYS, when the town's seven belfries ring their bells for Vespers, the deep-toned peals are answered from under the hillside by the husky screech of the factory whistles, and for several minutes there float on the air two warring currents of sound, so oddly incongruous: one gently calling, the other reluctantly dismissing.

And always on Saturdays, when coming out of the factory gates. Pavel Makov, mechanic, experiences a dismal sense of duality and shame. He walks home unhurriedly, letting his comrades overtake him, walks nervously fingering his pointed little beard and looking guiltily at the green carpeted hill, crowned by a luxuriant ridge of orchards. From behind the dark wall of fruit trees peep the grey triangles of the housetops, the dormer-windows, chimney pots, high up in the sky the starling coops, still higher the black top of a lightning-seared pine tree, and beneath it the house of Vasyagin the shoemaker. There Pavel's wife, his daughter and father-in-law await him.

"Do-ong do-ong . . ." floats the impressive swell overhead.

And below, from the hillside, comes the angry blast:

"Oo-oo-oo. . . ."

With hands thrust in his trouser pockets and body bent forward Pavel walks slowly uphill along a cobble-stone drive, while his comrades make a short cut through the back gardens, leaping like black goats from path to path.

Misha Serdyukov, a foundry man, shouts from somewhere overhead:

"Pavel, will you come?"

"I don't know, old chap, I'll see," answers Pavel, stopping to watch the workmen scrambling and stumbling up the steep craggy ascent. There are sounds of laughter and whistling, all are cheered by the prospect of a Sunday rest, grimy faces shine and white teeth flash exultantly.

The wattle fences of the vegetable gardens creak and snap under the assault of the homegoing crowd; old wife Ivanikha, the gardener, greets the factory hands with her customary torrent of snuffling abuse, and the sun as it sinks beyond the river far down by Prince's Grove paints the hag's tatters in purple and her grizzled head in gold.

From below comes a smell of burning, of oil and dank swamps and the hillside is redolent with the spicy odours of young cucumbers, dill, and black currants. The scolding of the old woman is drowned in the merry carillon of the cathedral bells.

"Y-yes" Makov muses drearily. "Such weakness of character is shameful—very shameful! . . ."

He comes to the top of the hill and looks down. Five chimney pots stick out like the claws of a slimy monster submerged in the fetid marsh.

The narrow tortuous river intersected by shifting islets is flaming red, and hectic patches glow amid the puny fir trees in the swamp as the evening sun casts its reflection in the rusty water between the hillocks.

The lovely sunbeams are wasted on the swampy dreariness, swallowed without a trace by the sour putrid waters of the slough.

"Better be moving on!" Makov urges himself.

But—he stands thoughtfully for a minute or two more.

He was met at the house gate by Vasyagin—a skinny, baldheaded man with one eye. To conceal the ugly cavity where his right eye had been, he wears a pair of dark spectacles when going out into the street, for which the people of the workers' suburb nicknamed him "Goggle-eyed Valek." Beneath a hooked nose was a sparse chaotic growth of grey, wiry hairs which he coaxed on holidays into the semblance of a moustache by some sticky arrangement that pursed up his lips and gave the impression that the shoemaker was constantly blowing at something hot.

Just now his mouth was extended in an affable little smile as Valek whispered to his son-in-law:

"Saturday-night's, if you please!"

Pavel thrust a twenty kopeck piece into his hand and passed through a little courtyard overgrown with grass, where in a corner beneath a rowan-tree a table was laid for dinner; under the table sat old Churkin, the dog, picking burs out of his tail; on the porch steps sat his wife, her feet set wide apart; his daughter, three-year old little Olga, tumbled about on the trodden grass, and when she caught sight of her father, held out a pair of grimy little paws with outspread fingers and chanted:

"Dad-da! Dad-da come 'oom!"

"Why so late?" asked his wife eyeing him suspiciously. "All the men are home a long time. . . ."

He sighed, imperceptibly—everything was the same. And snapping a finger under his little daughter's nose he threw a guilty glance at his wife's protuberant abdomen.

"Hurry up, get a wash!" she said.

He went, followed by a hail of querulous words.

"Again you've given father money for a drink? I've told you thousands of times not to do it! But there— what do my words mean to you. . . . I'm not one of your female comrades, you won't catch me knocking about at meetings of a night, like those hussies of yours. . . ."

Pavel washed and contrived to fill his ears with soap suds not to hear the familiar harangue, whose words coiled around him like the dry rustling of wood shavings. It seemed to him that his wife was whittling away his heart with some idiotic blunt plane.

He recalled the days when he had first met his wife—the nightly strolls about the streets of the town in the frosty moonlight, the tobogganing down the hill, the show nights in the gallery and the glorious minutes at the cinema—it was good to sit in the dark pressed close together, while the life of dumb shadows flickered on the screen, so very touching, so wildly comical.

Those had been painful days. He had just been released from prison and found everything wrecked and trampled underfoot. Those who had rapturously applauded now hissed viciously at what had previously excited their rapture. . . .

Little curly, grey-eyed Olga romped about his legs, singing:
"Dadda lubs me, dadda buy me dolly, buy me gee-gee, tomolla,
tomolla. . . ."

He shook the drops of moisture from his finger into the child's
face—the little girl rolled away with a squeal of laughter, and he
said to his wife in a gentle voice:

"Come on Dasha, don't nag!"

Little Olga raised the heavy head of old Churkin with no little
effort and commanded:

' Look! Look, I tell 'oo!"

The dog wagged an unresponsive head—he had seen enough.
Opening his jaws wide he whined briefly.

"When the husband's such a clever fellow that his comrades are
dearer to him than his family," his wife went on, relentlessly whittling away at his heart. Pavel stood in the middle of the yard;
through the open gate he could see the endless vista of the woods.
Once he had sat with Dasha on a bench near the down slope drive,
and gazing at this distant view, had said:

"Gee, aren't we going to be happy together."

"I suppose it's because she's pregnant now," he tried to cheer
himself with the reflection and picked up his daughter.

Makov sat down to the table in silence, and his daughter climbed
to his knees, smoothing out the moist curly hairs of his beard with
baby fingers, prattling:

"Ola go tomolla with Dadda and Mummy far 'way. On cabby
—gee-up!"

"Shut up, Olga! I've enough of you all day long!" said her
mother sternly.

Pavel longed to fetch his wife a whack over her forehead with
the back of his spoon, a resounding whack that would be audible
through the yard and outside on the street. He restrained the impulse
with a scowl and a self-deprecatory thought:

"You ought to know better. . . ."

Father-in-law came in, sat down to the table, and stretching his
thin lips across his skinny face in a beatific smirk, pulled a small
bottle out of his pocket.

"There he goes!" said Dasha with a snort.

Makov lowered his head to conceal a smile—he knew beforehand what Valek's answer would be:

"Unless you go you won't get there!"

The old man's solitary eye rolled comically as he watched the gurgling liquor spouting from the neck of the bottle. Having drained his glass he smacked his lips with relish. Churkin stared unflinchingly into his face, and the shoemaker addressed himself to the dog:

"You won't get any. If you drink vodka you'll get a scolding."

These words too were familiar to Pavel. Everything here was starkly familiar.

His wife complained:

"All day long you haven't a moment you could call your own—sewing, cooking, washing—and all that brat knows is to go shrieking over the fence that somebody steals the cucumbers...."

She was a large buxom woman with a round face and a fine smooth white brow. Her ears were small and sharp and had an engaging way of moving when she spoke.

Just now, however, she was not too attractive. Her uncombed head looked enormous, the untidy hair clotted with many a day's dust and sweat straggled down her forehead and over her ears, her nose dilated in angry sniffs and her large red lips seemed swollen with wrath. When a wisp of hair got into her mouth Dasha tossed it aside with the handle of her spoon. Her soiled blouse was torn under the armpits and carelessly fastened in front. Pink rounded arms. bared to the elbow, were smeared with dirt. And from her chin hung a yellow drop of kvass.

"It wouldn't take her long to comb her hair and wash herself," Pavel reflected.

She will comb her hair tomorrow, after dinner, put on a striped yellow-green blouse and a lilac skirt. The skirt will be hitched up on her stomach, bringing into view a pair of button boots and even a glimpse of stocking—black, with a yellow sheen—they were her favourite stockings, and she had been very pleased with the purchase.

In the evening, walking by his side, she will carry her belly through the main street of the town, her lips severely compressed, her brows knitted in a solemn frown. This imparts to her the air of a shopkeeper—and when they'd meet his comrades Pavel would imagine a mocking, provoking twinkle in their eyes.

He would feel hot all over, as though an invisible but heavy body clutched him in a loathsome warm, suffocating embrace. He preferred to think of something else, think aloud.

"Today during lunch Kuliga, the timekeeper, told us about the French electricians. . . ."

His wife began to eat hurriedly, and his father-in-law more slowly. The latter's lips twitched and his face and bald head were suffused with grim mirth.

"That's an organization for you!" Pavel said dreamily.

"And how are things in Germany?" asked Valek in honied tones, raising his eyes skyward.

"It's all right there—the party machine there works like clockwork. . . ."

"Thank God for that!" said the old fellow. "I was beginning to worry whether everything was all right with the Germans!"

Valek's voice rose on a shrill note and Pavel felt uncomfortable. He knew the words that would come tumbling through the old man's dark loose teeth. The old man had already blown out his cheeks, cocked his head to one side like a crow and fastening his eye on his son-in-law, he commenced in a thin chirp that had an undertone of maliciousness in it:

"So everything's fine in Germany, eh? And what about the home-money?"

And he broke out into a cackle, bouncing up and down on his chair. Little Olga too caught the infection of his mirth, clapped her hands, and dropping the spoon under the table, received a cuff on the back of her head from her mother with a shouted injunction:

"Pick it up, you brat!"

The child began to cry, piteously and softly, and her father, pressing the sobbing girl to him, looked around him: dusk was falling, it was an hour when light and gloom meet and mingle in a grey murk. The carols of some gay bachelors and the annoying sounds of accordions are wafted down on the air. and the words of his father-in-law flit about him like winged bats:

"No, you'd do better to think about your pocket and not about Germany, you take my word! Once you've gone and married you've got to think about your pocket, yes, sir! And if you've started bringing kids into the world—you fix 'em up properly in this world, and

that you can only do on a sound pocket, yes, sir, on a well-filled
pocket!"

Rocking his dozing daughter in his arms Makov was thinking of
his father-in-law. Four years ago he had known a different Valek.
He remembered how, at a meeting in the brickyard shed, the shoemaker had shouted, wiping the small teardrops from his eyes:

"Boys! I'm sorry for you—but all the same! Go straight ahead
with it! March on bravely! Now, we spared ourselves, lived as we
were told to, we endured patiently for your sake—now you must
suffer and go through with it for your children's sake. . . ."

And to him, Pavel, the shoemaker had one day said:

"When I look at you, my boy, and hear you speak I'm sorry I
haven't a son instead of a daughter. What wouldn't I give to have
a son like you! . . ."

But ever since the hooligan "patriots" of the town had knocked
Valek's right eye out for him, the old man had made a sheer change
of front.

"He's not the only one that's turned tail," thought Pavel sorrow-
fully.

His wife began clearing the table with brusque movements, removing the dirty dishes, rattling the plates, dropping spoons and
shouting:

"Pick it up! You know it's hard for me to bend down."

"No, you leave politics to the foreign countries, and look after
your domestic affairs!"

Makov carried the sleeping child indoors. The porch steps
creaked and his wife nagged in the same creaking key:

"If it wasn't for all that nonsense. . . ."

"Yes, yes, yes!" hammered the wooden voice of her father.

The ruddy orb of the moon rose above the dark trees. Pavel
Makov sat on the porch steps next to his wife, stroking her hair
and talking to her almost in a whisper:

"If I get put in prison the comrades will help you. . . ."

"I dare say, not likely!" Dasha snorted.

"We've all got to try and get organized.

"Try! What did you marry for?"

Cherished thoughts flashed through his head and his heart, he did
not hear Dasha's dreary objections and she did not listen to him.

"Don't tell me any more of that drivel. You used to bring home a hundred rubles a month, and now—what?"

"It's not my fault, it's the general situation. . . ."

"Damn the situation . . . drop your comrades and settle down to your work. . . ."

She wished to speak kindly, coaxingly, but she was tired out by the day's drudgery and wanted to sleep. These talks had been dragging on for over three years and nothing had changed—she was sorry for her husband, afraid for his sake, he was almost as kind and unpractical as he had always been, and just as obstinate. She knew that she could not overcome that obstinacy, and ever stronger in her breast grew the fear for her own and her daughter's fate. Pity for her husband waxed into an oppressive ache that, finding no outlet in speech, was lashed into bitterness.

And he sat watching the shadow of the rowan-tree creeping across the courtyard to his feet with its innumerable pointed fingers spread in quivering clutching movements; his thoughts drifting ever more into the future, he confided to his wife in a mysterious whisper:

"There, you see . . . in France already. . . ."

"Oh, shut up!" she blurted out in a sullen tone, and tossing back her head she almost shouted in a choking voice: "But we shan't live to see it . . . don't forget the children. . . ."

He fell silent, knocked from the remote and limpid heights into the little courtyard and the cramped circle of crooked little paths.

She felt like crying, but resentment dried the font of tears and only her voice quivered in her throat as she pulled herself to her feet and said:

"I'm going to sleep. I suppose you're going to your comrades? . . ."

"Yes," he said after a pause.

She grumbled loudly as she went.

"If only they'd round you up quickly, the whole damn lot of you—it's got to happen sooner or later! Maybe that'll knock some sense into your heads. . . ."

The moon was now high in the sky, and the shadows were shortened. Dogs were barking.

Somewhere from the garden plots came the raucous voice of Fenka Lukovitsa, the woman of the town, singing in a maudlin, sobbing voice:

> *My sweetheart sailed on a Volga lighter.*
> *He went and got drowned the dirty blighter....*

Sometimes these talks culminated in stormy scenes. Dasha shouted, choking with passion, waving her arms while her big breasts shook disgustingly beneath her dirty blouse. The sight of her at such moments nauseated Pavel, and while he silently brushed aside the angry torrent of coarse abuse he asked himself in bewilderment:

"How is it I didn't see she was that kind of woman?"

And then, after one of these scenes, had come that thing in his life which had left him with a sense of duality and deception, under which he had been fretting for nearly a year, a thing he was ashamed of but which he could not undo.

One Saturday he had brought home little money and this had thrown his wife into a passion of rage. She had flung the money on the floor and begun shouting at him. And when, touched to the quick, he had said, firmly and sternly:

"Shut your mouth!" she had given him a push towards the door, wildly shrieking:

"Get out, you beggar! This is my father's house—my house! And you're a good-for-nothing, your place is in jail, that's where it is—get out!"

He had understood the reason for this outburst—it was the cabbage pickling season and she did not have enough money for buying cabbage. Deeply hurt, beyond himself with rage, he had rushed into the street, sat for a long time in somebody's vegetable garden, endeavouring to hide his pain and resentment, then he had gone into town where, in a filthy little public house, he had drunk vodka, and suddenly found himself in Cathedral Square—a wretched little garden facing a squat five-domed cathedral.

A wind was blowing, and a dangling rope scraped against the bells, drawing soft sighs from the brass. The lights of the street lamps glimmered fitfully in a ring round the cathedral, and grey ragged clouds sped past over the crosses on the domes, laying bare cold, blue hollows in the sky, and it seemed as if the wind was sweeping from out these heavenly casements in a rushing torrent.

Now and then an affrighted moon showed its face among the clouds which flung themselves on it like a drab mob of beggars on a silver coin, smearing it across the sky with their wet hulk into a dismal lurid smudge. The wind rocked the earth like a cross-grained nurse the cot of an unbeloved child.

Makov sat on a seat holding a fuddled head in his hands, thinking dazedly of life's cruel jests—the more a man hankers after the good things the worse does he get.

Some one sat down beside him. He raised his head—of course it was a girl, and it struck him that this was as it should be. Who, save a thief or a prostitute would accost a lonely man sitting in foul weather in such a desolate spot?

They exchanged words, then walked for a long time about the streets of the town, and all the way Pavel, in a state of intoxication, spoke about his unhappy marriage, about his wife in whom he had failed to find a kindred soul and to whom he could not unburden his heart.

The girl said:

"That often happens...."

"Often?" asked Pavel. "How do you know?"

"Men often complain...."

Pavel glanced at her face—nothing much, the ordinary face of a street girl.

Then, remembering his wife, he thought maliciously:

"You've asked for it! Just watch me going with this here...."

At her lodging he resumed his discourse on life, his thoughts, then he went to bed and fell asleep before she joined him.

In the morning, looking rather sheepish, he drank tea with her, trying to avoid the girl's eyes, and before leaving he offered her thirty-five kopeks—all that he had on him.

But she calmly pushed his hand aside and said very distinctly.

"What for? There's no need."

He did not like the gesture and the words too struck him unpleasantly.

"Come, take it, please!"

"All right!" she agreed, taking only two silver coins. Then. with
a shrug, she repeated:

"Really—there's no need...."

"Now she'll invite me to drop in," thought Pavel, getting into his
coat. "She'll tell me her name, when she's at home...."

Staring at the floor at a spot somewhere under his feet she said
thoughtfully:

"You spoke very well yesterday ... about our sisterhood, us
women...."

These words flattered him, and for a moment stifled the sense of
loathing she had aroused in him. Smiling apologetically he murmured:

"Very glad you think so.... I was drunk—I don't usually drink,
you know.... Good-bye!"

She held out her hand in silence.

Out in the street he thought:

"She did not ask me to come! Didn't want to take the money—I
wonder why?"

He could not recollect what he had been saying and even her face
was a vague blur.

Approaching his house he thought with a mixed feeling of pleasure and regret:

"If I met her again I wouldn't recognize her...."

Rain was falling in a drizzle, his coat was wet and clung heavily
to his shoulders, his head ached and he was overcome by sleepiness.

His wife met him in silence—she did not even glance at him.
He sat long in a corner watching her kneading the dough with
her strong arms, and the engaging dimples coming and going in
her elbows. She was so comely and firm of flesh.

To break the ice he said:

"Where's Olga?"

"Where indeed? Don't you know it's a holiday today with all
good people—she's gone to church with Grandpa...."

Pavel said amicably:

"Really, I don't see the point in that—why take the child out in
the rain to such a stuffy place?"

He stopped as it dawned on him that he had more than once
replied in the very same words to a similar taunt.

The dough squeaked under her hands and the table creaked.

"Should I tell her—this is what you've brought me to, d'you see? See what you are driving me to—should I tell her?"

Under the impulse of a sudden emotion he went up to her and put his hand on her round shoulder.

"Keep your hands off!" she shouted, shaking his hand off and the angry colour swept in a deep flush over her face and neck.

"Go to the devil— or I'll smack your face for you!"

She straightened up and patted her hair with doughy hands making it grey.

Valek came in with Olga in his arms, took off his spectacles, and, with a gleam of his one eye, exclaimed:

"God's blessings. . . ."

"Dadda, dadda!" cried the child.

Pavel wanted to take her, then remembered where he had spent the night, and slouched out of the room to wash his hands.

All day his wife groused and snorted and his father-in-law scoffed and sneered without intermission:

"Well, mister social-politician, why don't you munch some pie? Munch away till the final victory of the working class, when all the beggars'll have pie to eat—that's a good way off yet!"

"At least you might stop nagging!" Pavel demurred. "Nothing'll come of it anyway. . . ."

"That's true!" agreed Valek. "You said it—nothing will come of it. . . ."

After an interval of several minutes he resumed:

"I've mended your boots—did you notice?"

"Yes."

"Are you pleased?"

"Thanks."

"Dasha, pickle the thanks, will you, I'll eat it when there's nothing left in the pantry. . . ."

The rain spattered against the windowpanes, the wind ran riot in the attic, swinging some object with a bang. A pine tree creaked over the house top, somewhere an unfastened wicket slammed loudly, a latch rattled, and the rain sang and sobbed as it dripped into the the water-butt. The room was pervaded by a gloom and the smell of roasted onions, leather and tar.

Makov observed that his daughter sensed the prevailing atmosphere—she gazed at every one with apprehensive, questioning eyes, and her face began to crumple up preparatory to bursting into tears.

"What's going to happen to her?" he thought as he watched the child, feeling himself guilty before her.

"Here, come to me girlie!" he called, holding out his arms. But when Olga jumped up to run to him her mother caught hold of her and shouted·

"Don't you dare!"

Olga burst into tears, her little face buried in her mother's lap, but her mother sprang to her feet and pushed the child away into a corner:

"Go to sleep, you brat! Don't let me see anything more of you. . . ."

Pavel too got up. His face burned, and a sharp chill ran up his spine.

"If you dare," he said, moving up to his wife, "ever again. . . ."

His wife held up her face defiantly and urged him in a whisper full of pain and hatred:

"Hit me, come on! Hit me!"

Her father grabbed a last and danced around, yelling:

"So that's it, eh? There's s-solidarity for yer!"

Pavel thrust his wife aside, and seizing his cap he rushed out.

He ran under the rain, thinking in despair:

"If he hadn't butted in, I'd have. . . ."

Streams of dirty water rushed to meet him, splashing his feet, and the wind drove the cold stinging spray of the autumn rain into his face.

And now he was again in that girl's room, sitting at the table, his sodden jacket thrown on the floor, waving one arm, rubbing his throat with the other and speaking hurriedly:

"I'm not a brute! I understand—she's not to blame. . . ."

The girl darted anxiously about the room like a peg-top whipped into spurts of activity by an invisible hand. She was preparing the samovar, breaking firewood splinters across her knee, making a rustling noise with the charcoal. while behind her floated the ends of a shawl she had thrown over her bare shoulders.

"You see, I've come to you—though I have comrades, but I feel ashamed to tell them about this—though I daresay they too have such days when everyone in the house torments one another—why? Tell me—why?"

"How do I know?" he heard a low reply.

"This rotten life eats into every one's bones, into one's heart—and one day you suddenly find your heart burning with a maddening pain and hatred...."

The girl went up to him, lightly touched his shirt, and said, her eyes blinking:

"You're all wet—and I haven't anything to give you.... What's to be done?"

"Don't worry about it," he said, seizing her hand.

She gently extricated her fingers and went on solicitously:

"You'll catch a cold and get ill! That's a bad thing for a working man!"

She went out into the passage and instantly reappeared with a coloured tattered garment which she warmed up over the samovar, urging the visitor in impersonal tones:

"You change your things... this is a woman's dress, but at least it's dry...."

Throwing the shred of garment on the table she went out again into the passage. Makov followed her with his eyes, and his thoughts were hazy, like in a dream:

"Fate! Fate?—what nonsense. For me it's just a place to go to, and to her—it's all the same."

Bitter reproaches slithered up, squirming into his consciousness like the thin-lipped whispers of his father-in-law:

"Fed up, eh? Comrades? Why didn't you go to your comrades in this difficult hour—why don't you go to them? Aha-a! Ashamed, are you?"

He smoothed down his cropped hair and his lips twisted in a painful smile.

"Why haven't you changed?" asked the hostess in a business-like tone, looking in at the door.

His wet clothes clung to his body with a disagreeable sensation of chilliness. Pavel swiftly tore them off and wrapped himself in the long woman's dress.

"That's right," said the girl, coming in.

"Do I look funny?" he asked.

"You do," acquiesced the girl, but there was not the ghost of a smile on her face.

Pavel for the first time subjected her to a close unceremonious scrutiny. She had a stocky little figure, high cheek bones and slits of eyes.

"It's funny, yet you don't laugh!" he said, taking a look round.

The little room was crowded with a bed, a table, two chairs, a cupboard, and, near the door, a big stove. In the front corner hung a little icon, above it a twig of pussy willow with a paper blossom. Gaudy little pictures looked down from blackened walls and cockroaches crawled over them with a rustling sound. Between the logs hung tufts of oakum. The window was a tiny square of glass, dim with age.

The girl, bending over the samovar, did not answer Pavel. He felt awkward and thought to himself with a feeling of animosity:

"Probably stupid."

Aloud he asked:

"Is this the kitchen?"

"Yes."

"Does any one else live in the house?"

She placed the boiling samovar on the table, cut a big slice of rye bread and poured out the tea, speaking in a voice that was as low and monotonous as the sound of the rain outside:

"Two old women live here—old maids. But they practically do no cooking at home, they make calls on rich acquaintances and have their meals there. Very often they don't come home for the night. I've got nothing but bread—I'm sorry!"

"I'm not hungry," said Pavel, conscious of a growing sense of embarrassment. What had made him come here?

Suddenly, before he realized it himself, he had asked, loudly and sternly:

"Are you registered?"

"Where?"

"At the police?"

She replied calmly:

"Yes, of course, my passport's registered. I'm employed here as cook and housemaid. There's nothing to do all day...."

Pavel felt there was something wrong here, something he could not understand.

"I didn't mean that...."

She guessed. Her face with its high cheek bones darkened, her eyes closed entirely.

"Oh," she murmured, "I see.... My being on the boulevard yesterday? No, I don't do that...."

He didn't believe it. He swung back on his chair, smiling, contemplating her—it amused him that she concealed her calling, he was both amused and sorry for her.

The girl's oblique eyes suddenly opened—they were blue and warm and agreeably lighted up her face with a slightly beautifying effect.

"I went out yesterday just like that," she was saying, breaking off pinches of bread and rolling them into little balls—"I felt so sick of everything, and went out. Maybe I'd have thrown myself in the river, but I caught sight of you. There, I thought, he's a man and also feels miserable! So I went up. And you started talking right away—I could see you were very upset. I had a suspicion you intended to do away with yourself too.... It happens every day—people shoot themselves, hang themselves...."

He listened, still incredulous, making a mental note:

"Went out.... So I went up.... Not much of a talker. Uninteresting girl...."

And the girl went on talking in the same level tone, laconically. She was a Mordvinian, of a well-to-do family, and had received a schooling—had attended the parish school. A fire ruined the family, her father went to Siberia to look for land and never came back. She went to work as maid at the railway station—she lived there for three years. The station-master had a brother, he was the telegraph operator.

"When you speak you remind me of him."

Covering her eyes with her light lashes she repeated with conviction:

"Yes, exactly like him...."

"Where is he?" asked Pavel.

"He's been arrested."

There was no trace of sadness in her voice, but she twisted her neck queerly, her cheek bones looked suddenly drawn and her face puckered up like that of a dog about to whimper.

Pavel no longer speculated whether she was to be believed or not—he did not want to think of it.

Suddenly she said loudly:

"I had a baby too...."

"The telegraph man's?"

"Yes. It was born dead."

"Was the telegraph man a good fellow?"

She smiled broadly.

"Y-yes. He used to speak very interesting, like you, but he was all on his own—every one used to laugh at him. They took him alone. Me they kicked out."

The wind howled in the chimney like a homeless old dog.

Life became an utter falsehood, and the deception, like a canker, gnawed at the roots of Pavel's self-respect.

He loved his wife, loved to take her large, healthy, warm body in his arms. The seductive appeal of her dark eyes exercised an irresistible power over him.

Sometimes, when she was in one of her rare good moods, she spoke to him in a muffled voice, slightly through the nose:

"What about going up to your wife, fondling her and giving her a kiss, you sulky boy!"

There were days and weeks when he almost forgot the dark decrepit little house on the outskirts of the town. The house itself, looking like a mud-hut sunk into the ground, with its two sightless windows, its moss-grown roof and the dark end of a room and its tenant—that mute, timid, nocturnal creature—all these memories melted away, became nothing, and if, at times, they rose to his mind like a cheerless dream, Pavel thought with relief:

"That's all over!"

At first he was strongly tempted to tell his wife about it—tell it to her in a way that would excite her sense of guilt, make her realize the danger which lay for both of them in their spiritual feud.

But he was afraid to broach the subject. The hours when she was sweet-tempered and lovable fled with such imperceptible speed, and whenever he approached a topic that had no immediate bearing on the home, she would yawn languidly, satiated with his caresses, and stem the current of his speech with a drowsy:

"For goodness' sake, don't start harping on that string again...."

She would implore, command:

"Love me without those words of yours...."

If he persisted a sullen furrow would settle between his wife's brows, her eyes would grow bright and dry and she would urge him in a voice of irritation:

"You drop all that, I tell you—remember you have children! Goodness knows we have enough of those books at home—a whole shelf of 'em.... A married man shouldn't have anything to do with comrades and books.... Look how all the men with families have dropped out of it—they're just working quietly, for their wives and children. Only Serdyukov with that Masha of his are still mixed up with your lot—but how comes he to you. Why, last month he only brought home thirty-six rubles, he was fined twice...."

Jealously and zealously picking up all the scandal about the suburb she knew a good deal of bad about people, never spoke a good word about any one, and emptied sackfulls of malicious, very often mendacious rubbish onto her husband's head with avid enjoyment and keen relish.

"It's not true, Dasha!" he hazarded a protest.

She retorted querulously:

"To be sure! Your comrades you believe, I know, but not your wife...."

Under the weight of her speeches all the blood, as it were, was drained out of Pavel's good intentions which, paralyzed and crushed, perished in a heart that had grown increasingly accustomed to remain silent to his wife.

He listened to her speeches without saying anything, merely whistling softly to himself and musing gloomily:

"She doesn't understand. I wonder—won't she ever understand?"

He craved for a woman's exquisite tenderness, something deep and brimming, something that would help kindle the soul into a brighter flame while stirring the blood. But that caress for the soul he

had to seek on the outskirts of the town, from the ugly Mordvinian girl
Liza, who evinced an ability, and obviously a pleasure, in listening to
his stories about life and his dreams of the future. It was pleasant to see
a person sitting opposite you and greedily taking in your every word
like a person gulping air after having recovered from a deep swoon.

In her dry bosom, too, there lived something that was alien and
inscrutable to Pavel—it was as though a little grey bird sang there
at times.

"Do you go to church?" she once asked him, nestling up to him.

"No, you see. . . ."

Pavel explained to her at great length and with warmth why
he did not go to church, but when he had finished the girl said
quietly:

"It works out the same way: you speak about peace on earth and
in church too they pray for 'peace throughout the world. . . .'"

"No, wait a minute! I speak about the struggle. . . ."

"But that's what the struggle's for, to bring peace everywhere. . . ."

He argued with her again, growing excited, waving his arms,
hitting the table with his fist, and waxing more enthusiastic as the
realization dawned on him with a thrill of pleasure that he was
expressing his thoughts with growing ease and eloquence.

The Mordvinian girl retorted with quiet obstinacy:

"No, I love it when the priest says in his deep voice: 'The peace
of the Lord unto ye all.' I don't care who says it, as long as people
hear the words of peace!"

And standing close to him, looking into his eyes, she spoke
softly and fearfully:

"You just look—every one's bad tempered, everywhere people
are fighting! In the pubs and in the markets—everywhere. If they
begin to play, they'll end up by fighting. Even in church people are
touchy, quarrel over places. Little children are beaten. People are
arrested and hung. And how many are killed! The police beat people
terribly! But people beat one another too—it's just purely out of
spite, they beat one another! That time I wanted to do that out of
spite, I got furious with myself—what are you living for, you
wretch? There aren't any good people, and that makes it so awful.
Maybe there are a few—one here, another there—they're hardly
noticeable. . . ."

He laughed at her, but her words were uttered so simply, without a shadow of pretension or presumption that they roused in Pavel's heart a feeling of indulgence towards her and drew them together by a delicate thread of understanding stretched between her unassuming faith and his stern knowledge.

Many times did he revert to this subject, humorously and seriously, but always he met a supple resistance—she neither protested nor let herself be persuaded by his arguments.

"You're looking too far ahead—you want too much!" he said with a laugh. "You and I won't see peace, our lives will pass in struggle. ..."

She pondered this and replied:

"If you know tomorrow's going to be good, the bad things today are not so very frightening, and they don't seem so powerful. ..."

At times, when sitting in Liza's room, Pavel would think of his wife, and his hands would become limp, his heart— suffused with bitterness and gall, and he would grow cold, and reproach himself in shame and anger:

"Call yourself a progressive man and all the rest of it. A denouncer of bourgeois immorality, and here you are. ..."

From this disturbing thought, however, he was diverted by many other thoughts that ran deep and wide, thoughts that were still hazy and which he was eager to speak about. Again and again he unfolded to Liza the burden of his heart and spoke about his wife, of how he loved her and yet how difficult it was for him to get along without her, Liza.

"I can't speak to anybody like I do to you. It seems that there is always something in a man which he can tell only to a woman—yet I can't tell my wife. Neither can I tell my comrades. ... It's awkward somehow, one feels ashamed to talk about himself, but you must get it off your chest!"

She stroked his head with a rough palm and the long fingers of a thin hand, listening to what he said.

"I tried talking about it, but people answer in a bookish way—I can read books myself. People are shy to speak frankly about themselves. ... I suppose many people have the same troubles that I have, things that are not written anywhere except in the heart, things one is ashamed to utter, but which have got to be said, otherwise it's torture!"

He gazed into a pair of shining blue eyes and forgot that those narrow eyes were set at an oblique angle. Liza's hand trembled on his head, on his shoulder, responsive to his agitation.

He sat her on his knees and with a heartache and passion that swept over him in a sudden wave he kissed her rough hot cheeks and lips.

"Never mind, dearest," she whispered with ever widening eyes. "You'll get over it, it'll pass...."

Sometimes he would fall fast asleep with his head on her lap, while she would sit motionless until it was time to waken him, stroking his cropped head softly like a loving nurse.

... Pavel would bring a newspaper with him, unfold the closely printed sheet on the table, and bending over it read with a certain degree of solemnity about the comrades in Europe and the whole world, about their untiring efforts and struggle, would speak about the leaders of the party, and the indefatigable fighters in the daily war.

She sat motionless, quietly and rarely asking him a question, but Pavel was sure the girl understood everything.

He noticed that when heroes or teachers were mentioned her face grew oddly tense and her blue eyes gleamed like those of a child listening to a fairy tale. At times this fixed stare was disconcerting, reminding him of the gaze of a sagacious faithful dog deeply pondering over something that was intelligible only to its own dumb ferine soul. At moments such as these he had the impression that this soft-spoken thick-set girl was quietly capable of doing anything....

Very often she asked:

"What name did you say?"

After a pause she distinctly repeated the name, asking once more: "How will it be in Russian?"

"I don't know. We haven't got such names."

"Didn't we have such holy martyrs?" she queried, incredulous and dejected.

Pavel burst out laughing.

"Holy martyrs are not in our line, my dear girl! We live in hell, they don't breed there...."

"They will!" Liza once declared.

That exclamation sounded very queer, like the first stroke of a bell after midnight heralding the birth of a new day amid the tenebrous night. Pavel looked into his friend's face, but he found nothing unusual there. He remained thoughtful for a moment, then asked: "What makes you ask their names?"

She bent her head without replying. Then he tenderly raised her head and pursued laughingly:

"Maybe you intend to pray for them, eh?"

"What of it," she said, "so I do. Only I pray without the names, just simply: please God help those who are doing good to people! You can laugh, I don't care."

"It's useless, Liza!"

"Every one tries to help good people to the best of his ability."

"That's no good, Liza! No, you've got to learn another way of helping...."

"I will, when I learn...."

And nestling close to him she said:

"It doesn't matter, does it? It can't hurt them, can it?"

Pavel put his arm around her and said nothing, his thoughts dwelling on vague but significant things.

His comrades noticed that he was keeping some of his time from them and his wife and spending it elsewhere, but they held their peace, pretending to believe his explanations.

Only Serdyukov, the jovial foundry man, one day asked him:

"I see you've got yourself a lady-love too Pavel, eh?"

The question took him unawares and in his confusion he asked:

"Who else?"

Pock-marked shaggy-haired Serdyukov threw up his scorched hands with a guffaw.

"I caught you properly there! What do you say to that? Look out, I'll tell your wife now...."

"No, don't say anything!" Pavel said gravely.

"What'll you give me? Give me a book—give me Nekrassov, eh?"

"I won't. But I'll tell her myself...."

Serdyukov stared at him in amazement.

"You'll tell her? Your wife?"

"Well, yes."

"What for?"

"I'd better!"

Serdyukov knitted a furrowed brow, glanced aside and sighed.

"It's that serious, then? Well, that's good! Every one can see she's not your equal. She was born a philistine, it's in her bones. You can't wash a black horse white—and it's not worth wasting time over...."

"He doesn't understand," thought Pavel.

"You don't love her," he said quietly.

"You said it!" retorted Serdyukov with a tinge of irony. "I don't—I love another...."

Then Pavel asked:

"Are you in the same boat?"

"What boat? Oh, yes...."

The foundry man said soberly, with a humourless smile:

"Yes, brother, I'm in the same fix!"

Pavel looked at him in astonishment and offered the comment:

"How is that? Don't you get along together ... isn't your wife a comrade to you...."

"That's just the point—she is a comrade!" said Serdyukov morosely. "That's the trouble—she coughs all the time something terrible, that comrade of mine—she's fading away...."

They were chatting in the factory yard by a soot-covered wall and somewhere above their heads a steam exhaust was spluttering angrily all the time:

"Puff, puff...."

The soot-laden air was filled with groaning, screeching, grating sounds, the roaring of the furnace and the clank of iron.

"Two child-births in three years," Serdyukov was growling moodily, rolling himself a cigarette. "And that, it appears, is a thing that people of our class can't afford. The doctor advises abstinence. Well, I began trying to keep away from her—out of pity. It was the devil to pay, I can tell you brother. Well, I kept away from her so long until I ran into a place I shouldn't have run into! I guess there'll be trouble brewing for me. And there's no turning back—the way is blocked. Turning back!—it means nothing anyway! My wife's got to go to live in the country, not bear children. Children are not for us, it looks like, my dear fellow. What is for us here, anyway?"

He looked round at the piles of scrap iron, the coal blackened earth and the roofs of the factory buildings emitting smoke and steam.

"They've walked off with our ball all right. And we haven't got a single trump to play back—pretty rotten, Pavel!"

He threw his cigarette end over his shoulder and went into his shop. Pavel had never seen him like that before, walking with bent head and looking nervously about him as though fearing a sudden attack. And when he was swallowed in the black jaws of the foundry shop Pavel remembered what a gay lark he had been, a laughter-loving wag, enthusiastic theatre-goer and singer, and Pavel fell deep in thought. It seemed to him that somebody else had been speaking to him just now, somebody more intimate than the Serdyukov of old. This was the first time he had heard a comrade speak so simply of the things that preyed on his mind, and standing at his lathe Pavel thought:

"He'll understand me now, I'll have to get on closer terms with him. It's no good, living the way I do...."

His intentions were not carried out. Within less than a week Serdyukov was picked up among the bushes by the brickyard—he had been cruelly beaten up by somebody and was confined to hospital for a long time.

"What a life!" Pavel was saying, pacing up and down the room in his home. "I'm sorry for him, so terribly sorry you can't imagine, Dasha! He's such a fine chap...."

He sat down beside her, and dropping his voice, continued:

"D'you know he recently spoke to me about his wife...."

"He'd have better kept his mouth shut, the rotter!" muttered Dasha. "D'you think I don't know why he got that beating?"

"Look here, Dasha!"

"Of course, you're ready to find excuses for every scoundrel, once he's a comrade of yours...."

He said sternly:

"Darya! There are no scoundrels among my comrades!"

"Don't shout!"

Despite the resistance of her elbows he put his arms round his
wife and told her about Serdyukov. She was very amused at first,
then pushing her husband away in indignation she began to scold:

"Oh, you miserable devils! D'you mean to say that Marya knew
all about these goings on?"

"Don't you get it into your head to tell her!" Pavel cried in alarm.

"Ah, that I will! Damn it if I won't tell her!" exclaimed Dasha
with a grim smile. "That's where their learning has brought them,
scoundrels! Sorry for his wife, indeed—bears children too often—
what d'you think of that, eh? Ugh!"

When her ire was roused she had a way of throwing her head up,
breathing heavily through her nose, while her nostrils dilated and
quivered like those of a horse. This made her all the more seductive,
but it also repelled Pavel, stirring within him a savage rancour. He
would like to see her ill and wretched and cowed, or a beggar walking the streets in filthy rags, bowing humbly and begging for alms
from Serdyukov's wife—that shrewd subtle woman—from the people
who were so alien to her heart, the dark, heavy oval thing that was
like a ball of iron.

Saturday evening found Pavel in Liza's room, speaking softly:

"They've brought men to such a state when even the good and
human that's in a man is looked on as dirt. A noose has been tied
round my very soul—I don't know how I'll throw it off! I love that
woman, and my daughter, too, of course—but what can she give my
daughter? And I can't live without you, Liza. Ah, Mordvinian lass,
you've a lovely soul, it's my friend you are...."

She listened to him with drooping head, and gravely, quietly
inserted her laconic remarks:

"I don't know what you'll do. I can't think of any way to help
you...."

But she did think of a way.

Once, feeling depressed after a new quarrel with his father-in-
law and his wife, Pavel plodded wearily through the quiet streets
of the town past fences, heavily locked gates and dark windows behind which the spring night lay hid from the cold light of the moon.

"One side, the other side!" he thought to himself, stepping into
the light and back again into the shadows of the trees and houses.

"No, to hell with it all! It's got to be life as I want it, or love as she wants it. I'm for life.... I'm fed up!"

He walked with difficulty, his feet seemed to flounder in the shadows as if they were quicksands or a quagmire. He crossed to the other side of the street that was all bathed in the pale moonlight.

The town dropped reluctantly into the uneasy sleep of vernal night, but dark figures still roamed the streets like men after a hopeless quest. A black rider rode past swaying in his saddle, and the horse's hoofs struck two bluish sparks out of the roadway.

A burly policeman was leading a long-haired workman with a strap on his head. The latter lurched from side to side, raised his hand in a threatening gesture and buzzed like an enormous bumble-bee:

"I'll sh-show you, j-just wait and sh-shee...."

A post office official went by arm in arm with a willowy young lady, leaving a curious train of words in his wake:

"Just a little bit open, and nobody can go through...."

Dogs emitted sleepy little yelps as they thrust their muzzles through the gates; the church watchman leisurely struck the hours: he would strike once and wait until the sound melted in the blue air, like a teardrop in a bowl of cold water.

"Ten," counted Pavel.

He conjured up the little Mordvinian girl in a grey skirt and a yellow blouse with lace in front. She had three blouses, and all were different shades of yellow and all too short for her. When she raised her arms the ends would slip out of her waistband, and when she bent her body one could glimpse a strip of homespun chemise of country linen. Her skirt too sat awkwardly on her, awry.

"Her hair's nice," he reminded himself, feeling a desire to find in Liza something equal to his wife's beauty.

"Lovely hair, so soft. Her eyes too. Very sweet...."

An inner voice protested:

"She's got bony knees. Shoulders too...."

...Darkness gazed at him from the window of Liza's room. He pressed his face against the pane and began drumming on the little ventilator window as he always did. There was a long silence, and then a strange feeble voice came through the ventilator:

"Who d'you want?"

"Is Liza at home?"

There came a muffled reply:

"She doesn't live here."

"What do you mean?"

"She's gone."

"When did she go?"

"Four days ago. Be gone now."

"Wait a minute!" said Pavel loudly, his chest pressed against the wall of the house. "Didn't she leave me any message?"

"Who'll you be?"

"Makov—Pavel Makov."

"There's a note for you—here, I'll push it through the window. ..."

A light flashed for a moment and went out.

There was another flash of light and the window glimmered like a big yellow face marred by a black diagonal scar.

The white corner of a rustling slip of paper was thrust out of the window. Pavel seized it, unfolded it, and by the dim light of the window he read in big sprawling characters:

"Pavel Mitrich, my dear man, I love you very much but it will be bad as it is with your wife just the same. Because I have begun to grow jealous of her and I hate her and it's the same thing for you again therefore I am going away I don't know where Lizaveta."

He crushed the note in his hand, but instantly spread it out again, looked once more at the straggling lines, tore it into shreds and said to himself with a sneer:

"Couldn't think of anything better, ugly bitch. ..."

He slowly let the pieces flutter to the ground as he gazed out at the field, empty and desolate like his heart gripped by a sudden terror.

"Silly girl. ..."

Very quietly he retraced his steps, rubbing the fences with his shoulder, and sadly muttering:

"Oh, Liza, where have you gone?..."

A MAN IS BORN

IT WAS in '92 the famine year, between Sukhum and Ochemchiry, on the river Kodor, not far from the coast—hollow sounding above the merry ripple of the glittering mountain stream I heard the roling sea.

Autumn. Small, yellowed bay leaves were darting hither and thither in the white surf of the Kodor like nimble salmon-trout. I was sitting on the high stony bank overlooking the river and thinking that the gulls and cormorants were also, probably, taking the leaves for fish and being fooled—and that was why they were screaming so plaintively over there, on the right, beyond the trees, where the waves were lapping the shore.

The chestnut trees spreading above me were decorated with gold— at my feet lay numerous leaves that looked like hands severed from human wrists. The branches of the hornbeam on the opposite bank were already bare and hung in the air like a torn net. Inside the net, as if caught in it, hopped a yellow and red mountain woodpecker, tapping at the bark of the trunk with its black beak, driving out the insects, which were at once gobbled up by those guests from the north—the agile tomtits and grey nut-hatches.

On my left, smoky clouds hung low over the mountain tops, threatening rain, and causing shadows to glide across the green slopes on which the boxwood trees grew, and where, in the hollows of the ancient beeches and lindens, one can find the "grog honey" which in the days of old nearly sealed the fate of the troops of Pompeius the Great. It knocked a whole legion of the Roman ironsides off their feet with its inebriating sweetness. The wild bees make this honey from the pollen of bay and azalea blossoms, and "wayfarers" scoop it from the hollows and eat it, spreading it on their *lavash*— flat cakes made from wheat flour.

This is what I was doing, sitting on the stones under a chestnut tree, frightfully stung by an angry bee—I dipped my bread into my tea can, filled with honey, and ate, meanwhile admiring the idle play of the tired autumn sun.

The Caucasus in the autumn is like the interior of a magnificent cathedral which the great sages—being also great sinners—built to hide their shame for their past from prying eyes. They built a vast temple of gold, turquoise and emerald, and hung the mountain sides with the finest carpets embroidered in silk by the Turkmen in Samarkand and Shemaha; they plundered the whole world and brought all their loot here as a gift to the sun, as much as to say:

"Thine—from Thine—to Thee!"

...I saw a vision of long-bearded, hoary giants, large-eyed like merry children, descending from the mountains, beautifying the earth, scattering their multi-coloured treasures with a lavish hand, covering the mountain tops with thick layers of silver and the terraces with the living fabric of a vast variety of trees—and under their hands this patch of heaven-blessed earth was endowed with enchanting beauty.

It's a fine job—being a man in this world! What wonderful things one sees! How the heart is stirred by pleasure almost akin to pain in one's calm contemplation of beauty!

Yes, it's true, sometimes you find it hard. Your breast is filled with burning hatred, and grief greedily sucks the blood from your heart—but this cannot last for ever. Even the sun often looks down on men in infinite sadness: it has laboured so hard for them, and what wretched manikins they have turned out to be! ...

Of course, there's a lot of good ones—but they need repair, or better still, to be made all over again.

... Above the bushes on my left I saw dark heads bobbing; barely perceptible above the murmur of the waves and the rippling sounds of the river. I heard human voices—those were the "starving" on their way from Sukhum, where they had been building a road, to Ochemchiry, in the hope of getting another job.

I knew them—they were from Orel. I had worked with them in Sukhum and we had been paid off together the day before. I had left before them, at night, so as to reach the seashore in time to see the sunrise.

They were four muzhiks and a young peasant woman with high cheekbones; she was pregnant, her huge abdomen protruded upward;

she had bluish-grey eyes, seemingly bulging with fright. I could see her head above the bushes too, covered with a yellow kerchief, nodding like a sunflower in full bloom swaying in the wind. Her husband had died in Sukhum from overeating himself with fruit. I had lived in the same hutment with these people: from the good old Russian habit they had complained about their misfortunes so much, and so loudly, that their lamentations must have been heard a good five versts away.

They were dull people, crushed by sorrow, which had torn them from their native, worn out, barren soil and had swept them like autumn leaves to this place, where the strange, luxuriant clime amazed and dazzled them, and where the hard conditions of labour had finally broken them. They gazed at everything about them, blinking their sad, faded eyes in perplexity, smiling pitifully to each other and saying in low voices:

"Ai-e-e ... what a soil!"

"The stuff just shoots up!"

"Ye-e-es ... but still ... it's very stony."

"It's not so good, you have to admit."

And then they recalled Kobili Lozhok, Sukhoi Gon, Mokrenki—their native villages, where every handful of earth contained the ashes of their forefathers; they remembered it, it was familiar and dear to them, they had watered it with the sweat of their brows.

There was another woman with them—tall, upright, with a chest as flat as a board, a heavy jaw and dull, squinting eyes as black as coal.

In the evening she, together with the woman in the yellow kerchief, would go a little distance behind the hutment, squat down on a heap of stones, and resting her chin in the palm of her hand and inclining her head to the side, would sing in a high-pitched angry voice:

> Beyond the village churchyard,
> Among the bushes green,
> On the yellow sand I'll spread
> My shawl so white and clean
> And there I'll wait....
> Until my darling comes....
> And when he comes....
> I'll greet him heartily....

Usually the one in the yellow kerchief would sit silently looking
down at her abdomen; but sometimes she would suddenly join in
and in a deep, drawling, masculine voice would sing the words of
the sad refrain:

Oh my darling....
My dear darling....
I am not fated....
To see thee more....

In the black, suffocating darkness of the southern night, these wailing voices awakened in me the memory of the snowy wilderness of the
north, of the shrieking blizzard, and the howling of the wolves....
    Later the cross-eyed woman was struck down by fever and she
was carried to the town on a canvas stretcher—on the way she shivered and moaned, and the moaning sounded as if she was continuing her song about the churchyard and the sand.
    ...The head in the yellow kerchief dived below the bush and
vanished.
    I finished my breakfast, covered the honey in my tea can with
leaves, tied up my knapsack and leisurely followed in the track of
the other people, tapping the firm ground with my cornel-wood
walking stick.
    And so, there I was on the narrow, grey strip of road. On my
right heaved the deep blue sea. It looked as though thousands of
invisible carpenters were planing it with their planes, and the white
shavings rustled on the beach, blown there by the wind, which was
moist, warm and fragrant, like the breath of a robust woman. A
Turkish felucca, listing heavily to port, was gliding towards Sukhum,
its sails puffed out like the fat cheeks of the pompous road engineer in Sukhum—a most important fellow. For some reason he
always said "shoot oop" for "shut up," and "mebbe" for "may be."
    "Shoot oop! Mebbe you think you can fight, but in two ticks I'll
have you hauled off to the police station!"
    He used to take a delight in having people dragged off to the
police station, and it is good to think that by now the worms in
his grave must have eaten his body right down to the bones.
    ... How easy it was to walk! Like treading on air. Pleasant
thoughts, brightly-clad reminiscences, sang in soft chorus in my

memory. These voices in my soul were like the white-crested waves
of the sea—on the surface; deep down, however, my soul was calm.
The bright and joyous hopes of youth swam leisurely, like silvery
fish in the depths of the sea.

The road led to the seashore, winding its way nearer and nearer to the sandy strip that was lapped by the waves—the bushes too
seemed to be striving to get a glimpse of the sea and swayed over
the ribbon of road as if nodding greetings to the blue expanse.

The wind was blowing from the mountains—threatening rain.

... A low moan in the bushes—a human moan, which always
goes to the heart.

Pushing the bushes apart I saw the woman in the yellow kerchief sitting with her back against the trunk of a walnut tree; her
head was dropped on one shoulder, her mouth was contorted, her
eyes bulged with a look of insanity. She was supporting her huge
abdomen with her hands and breathing with such unnatural effort
that her abdomen positively leapt convulsively. The woman moaned
faintly, exposing her yellow wolfish teeth.

"What's the matter? Did somebody hit you?" I asked, bending
over her. She rubbed one bare foot against the other in the grey dust
like a fly cleaning itself and, rolling her heavy head, she gasped:

"Go away! ... Ain't you got no shame? ... Go away! ..."

I realized what was the matter—I had seen something like this
before—of course I was scared and skipped back into the road, but
the woman uttered a loud prolonged shriek, her bulging eyes seemed
to burst and tears rolled down her flushed and swollen cheeks.

This compelled me to go back to her. I threw my knapsack,
kettle and tea can to the ground, lay the woman flat on her back
and was about to bend her legs at the knees when she pushed me
away, punched me in the face and chest and turning over, she crept
off on all fours deeper into the bushes, grunting and growling like
a she-bear:

"Devil! ... Beast!"

Her arms gave way and she dropped, striking her face on the
ground. She shrieked again, convulsively stretching her legs.

In the heat of the excitement I suddenly remembered all I had
known about this business. I turned the woman over on her back
and bent up her legs—the chorion was already visible.

"Lie still, it's coming!" I said to her.

I ran to the beach, rolled up my sleeves, washed my hands and returned, ready to act as midwife.

The woman writhed like birch-bark in the flames. She tapped the ground around her with the palms of her hands and tearing up handfuls of faded grass she wanted to stuff it into her mouth; and in doing so she dropped earth on to her frightful, inhumanly contorted face and into her wild, bloodshot eyes—and now the chorion burst and the child's head appeared. I had to restrain the convulsive jerking of her legs, help the child emerge, and see that she did not stuff grass into her distorted mouth. . . .

We swore at each other a bit—she through her clenched teeth, and I in a low voice; she from pain and, perhaps, from shame. I from embarrassment and heartrending pity for her. . . .

"Oh Lord! Oh Lord!" she cried hoarsely. Her livid lips were bitten through, there was foam at the corners of her mouth, and from her eyes, which seemed suddenly to have faded in the sun, flowed those abundant tears of a mother's unbearable pain. Her whole body was taut, as if it were being torn in two.

"Go . . . away . . . you . . . devil!"

She kept pushing me away with her feeble, seemingly dislocated arms. I said to her appealingly:

"Don't be a fool! Try, try hard. It'll be over soon."

My heart was torn with pity for her, it seemed to me that her tears had splashed into my eyes. I felt as if my heart would burst. I wanted to shout, and I did shout:

"Come on! Hurry up!"

And lo—a tiny human being lay in my arms—as red as a beetroot. Tears streamed from my eyes, but through the tears I saw that this tiny red creature was already discontented with the world, kicking, struggling and yelling, although it was still tied to its mother. It had blue eyes, its funny little nose looked squashed on its red, crumpled face, and its lips were moving as it bawled:

"Ya-a-a-ah. . . . Ya-a-a-ah."

Its body was so slimy that I was afraid it would slip out of my arms. I was on my knees looking into its face and laughing—laughing with joy at the sight of him . . . and I forgot what had to be done next. . . .

"'Cut the cord . . . '" the mother whispered. Her eyes were closed. Her face was haggard and grey, like that of a corpse, her livid lips barely moved as she said:

"Cut it . . . with your knife. . . ."

But somebody in the hut had stolen my knife—so I bit the navel cord through with my teeth. The child yelled in a real, Orel bass voice. The mother smiled. I saw her eyes miraculously revive, and a blue flame burned in their bottomless depths. Her dark hand groped in her skirt, searching for her pocket, and her blood-stained, bitten lips moved.

"I've . . . no . . . strength. . . . Bit of tape . . . in my pocket . . . tie up . . . navel," she said.

I found the piece of tape and tied up the child's navel. The mother smiled still more happily; that smile was so bright that it almost dazzled me.

"Put yourself straight while I go and wash him," I said.

"Take care. Do it gently now. Take care," she muttered anxiously.

But this red manikin didn't need gentle handling. He waved his fists and yelled as if challenging me to fight:

"Ya-a-a-ah . . . ya-a-a-ah."

"That's it! That's it, little brother! Assert yourself. The neighbours will pull your head off if you don't," I warned him.

He emitted a particularly savage yell at the first impact of the surf which splashed us both, but when I began to slap his chest and back he screwed up his eyes, and he struggled and shrieked as wave after wave washed his body.

"Go on, yell! Yell at the top of your lungs! Show 'em you come from Orel!" I shouted encouragingly.

When I brought him back to his mother she was lying on the ground with her eyes closed again, biting her lips from the fits of after-pain; but amidst her groaning and moaning I heard her whisper:

"Give . . . give him . . . to me."

"He can wait!"

"No! Give . . . him . . . to . . . me!"

She unbuttoned her blouse with trembling uncertain hands. I helped her to uncover her breast, which nature had made fit to feed

twenty children, and put the struggling Orelian to her warm body.
The Orelian understood at once what was coming and stopped yelling.

"Holy Virgin, Mother of God," the mother muttered with a sigh,
rolling her dishevelled head from side to side on the knapsack.

Suddenly she uttered a low shriek, fell silent again, and then
opened her inexpressively beautiful eyes—the sacred eyes of a mother
who has just given birth to a child. They were blue, and they gazed
into the blue sky. A grateful, joyful smile gleamed and melted in
them. Raising her weary arm the mother slowly crossed herself and
her child....

"Bless you, Holy Virgin, Mother of God.... Oh ... bless you...."

The light in her eyes died out again. Her face again assumed
that haggard hue. She remained silent for a long time, scarcely breathing. But suddenly she said in a firm, matter-of-fact tone:

"Laddie, untie my bag."

I untied the bag. She looked hard at me, smiled faintly, and
I thought I saw a blush, ever so faint, pass over her hollow cheeks
and perspiring brow.

"Go off a little way," she said.

"Take care, don't disturb yourself too much," I warned her.

"All right.... All right.... Go away!"

I retired into the bushes nearby. I felt very tired, and it seemed
as though beautiful birds were singing softly in my heart—and together with the unceasing murmur of the sea this singing sounded
so good that I thought I could listen to it for a whole year....

Somewhere, not far away, a brook was bubbling—it sounded like
the voice of a girl telling her friend about her lover....

A head rose above the bushes, covered with a yellow kerchief,
already tied, in the regular way.

"Hey! What's this? You've got up rather soon, haven't you?"
I cried in amazement.

The woman sat down on the ground, holding on to the branches
for support; she looked as if all the strength had been drained
from her. There was not a hint of colour in her ashen-grey face,
except for her eyes, which looked like large, blue pools. She smiled
a tender smile and whispered:

"Look—he's asleep."

Yes, he was sleeping all right, but no different from any other kid as far as I could see; if there was any difference it was only in the surroundings. He was lying on a heap of bright autumn leaves, under a bush, of the kind that don't grow in the Orel Gubernia.

"You ought to lie down for a bit, mother," I said.

"No-o-o," she answered, shaking her head weakly. "I've got to collect my things and go on to that place ... what do they call it?"

"Ochemchiry?"

"Yes, that's right! I suppose my folks are a good few versts from here now."

"But will you be able to walk?"

"What about the Virgin Mary? Won't she help me?"

Well, since she was going with the Virgin Mary—I had nothing more to say!

She gazed down at the tiny, puckered, discontented face, warm rays of kindly light radiating from her eyes. She licked her lips and slowly stroked her breast.

I lit a fire and heaped some stones near it on which to place the kettle.

"I'll give you some tea in a minute, mother," I said.

"Oh! That will be fine.... My breasts feel dried up," she answered.

"Have your folks deserted you?"

"No! Why should they? I dropped behind. They had had a drink or two.... And a good thing, too. I don't know what I'd have done if they were around...."

She glanced at me, covered her face with her arm, spat out with blood and then smiled shamefacedly.

"Is he your first?" I asked.

"Yes, my first.... Who are you?"

"It looks like I'm a man...."

"You're a man all right! Are you married?"

"I haven't had the honour."

"You are fibbing, aren't you?"

"No, why should I?"

She cast her eyes down in reflection. Then she asked:

"How is it you know about this women's business?"

Now I did tell a fib. I said:

"I learned about it. I'm a student. Do you know what that is?"

"Of course, I do! Our priest's eldest son is a student. He's learning to be a priest...."

"Well, I'm one of those.... I had better go and fill the kettle."

The woman inclined her head towards her baby to hear whether he was breathing. Then she looked in the direction of the sea and said:

"I'd like to have a wash, but I don't know what the water's like.... What kind of water is it? It's both salty and bitter."

"Well, you go and wash in it. It's healthy water!"

"What!"

"I'm telling you the truth. And it's warmer than the water in the brook. The brook here is as cold as ice."

"You ought to know."

An Abkhazian, wearing a shaggy sheepskin hat, rode past at a walking pace, his head drooped on his chest. He was dozing. His little wiry horse, twitching its ears, looked at us askance with its round black eyes and snorted. The rider raised his head with a jerk, also glanced in our directon, and then allowed his head to droop again.

"They're funny people here. And they look so fierce too," the Orel woman said softly.

I went to the brook. The water, as bright and volatile as quicksilver, bubbled and gurgled over the stones, and the autumn leaves were merrily tumbling over and over in it. It was wonderful! I washed my hands and face and filled the kettle. Through the bushes, on my way back, I saw the woman on her hands and knees crawling over the ground, over the stones, looking back anxiously.

"What's the matter?" I enquired.

The woman stopped short as if she were scared, her face became ashen grey, and she tried to conceal something under her body. I guessed what it was.

"Give it to me, I'll bury it," I said.

"Oh, my dear! What are you talking about? It's got to be taken to a bathhouse and buried under the floor...."

"Do you think they'll build a bathhouse here soon?"

"You are joking, but I am afraid! Suppose a wild beast eats it.... Still, it's got to be buried...."

And with that she turned her face away and handing me a moist, heavy bundle, she said shamefacedly, in a soft imploring voice:

"You'll do it thoroughly, won't you? Bury it as deep as you can, for the sake of Christ ... and my little one. You will, won't you?"

...When I returned I saw her walking from the seashore with faltering steps and outstretched arm. Her skirt was wet to the waist. Her face had a touch of colour in it and seemed to be shining with an inner light. I helped her to the fire, thinking to myself in amazement:

"She has the strength of an ox!"

Later, as we were drinking tea with honey, she asked me quietly:

"Have you stopped your book learning?"

"Yes."

"Why? Did you take to drink?"

"Yes, mother. I went to the dogs!"

"That was a nice thing to do! I remember you, though. I noticed you in Sukhum when you had a row with the boss over the food. I said to myself then: He must be a drunkard. He's not afraid of anything...."

Licking the honey from her swollen lips she kept turning her blue eyes to the bush where the latest Orelian was sleeping peacefully.

"How's he going to live?" she said with a sigh, looking into my face. "You helped me. For that I thank you.... But whether it will be good for him ... I don't know."

When she had finished her meal she crossed herself, and while I was collecting my things she sat drowsily swaying her body and gazing at the ground with eyes that seemed to have faded again, evidently engrossed in thought. A little later she got up.

"Are you really going?" I asked.

"Yes."

"Take care of yourself, mother."

"What about the Virgin Mary?... Pick him up and give him to me!"

"I'll carry him."

We argued about it for a bit and then she yielded, and we set out, walking side by side, shoulder to shoulder.

"I hope I won't stumble," she said, laughing guiltily and placing her arm on my shoulder.

The new inhabitant of the land of Russia, the man of unknown destiny, was lying in my arms, snoring heavily. The sea, all covered with white lace trimmings, splashed and surged on the shore. The bushes whispered to each other. The sun shone as it passed the meridian.

We walked on slowly. Now and again the mother halted, heaved a deep sigh, and throwing her head back she looked around, at the sea, at the woods, at the mountains, and then into the face of her son—and her eyes, thoroughly washed with the tears of suffering, were again wonderfully clear, again they shone with the blue light of inexhaustible love.

Once she halted and said:

"Lord! Dear, good God! How good it is. How good! Oh, if I could go on like this, all the time, to the very end of the world, and he, my little one, would grow, would keep on growing in freedom, near his mother's breast, my darling little boy...."

...The sea murmured and murmured....

THE BREAK-UP

ON THE RIVER opposite the city, seven carpenters were hurriedly repairing an ice apron the townsfolk had taken apart for firewood during the winter.

The spring was late that year—the stripling March looked more like October; only around midday, and not every day at that, a pale, wintry sun would appear in a sky shot through with sunbeams, and diving through the blue rents in the clouds, squint down ill-naturedly at the earth.

It was already Friday of Passion Week and still at night the dripping eaves froze into blue icicles a good half-arshin long, the ice on the river, now bare of snow, had the same bluish tint as the wintry clouds.

While the carpenters worked, the church bells in the town rang out their mournful, metallic appeal. The workers raised their heads and gazed into the murky haze that enveloped the town, and often an axe poised for a blow would hang for a moment in mid air as though reluctant to cleave the gentle sound.

Here and there on the broad surface of the river fir branches, stuck into the ice to mark the paths, cracks and fissures, pointed skywards like the hands of a drowning man twisted with the ague.

The river presented a dreary spectacle; deserted and bare, its surface a scabrous mass, it spread desolately away into the gloomy space from which a dank, chill wind breathed lazily and dismally.

... Foreman Osip, a neat well-built little chap with a tidy silver beard that clung in tiny curls to his pink cheeks and mobile neck, old Osip always in the fore, was shouting:

"Get a move on there, you hen's spawn!"

And turning to me, he said mockingly:

"Now then, overseer. What're you standing there mooning for? What do you think you're supposed to be doing? Didn't Vassil Sergeich, the contractor, put you here? Well, then it's your job to keep

us at it, 'Get a move on you so-and-so!' You're supposed to yell at
us. That's what you're here for, and you stand there blinking like a
fish. You're not supposed to blink, you're supposed to keep your
eyes open, and do some shouting too. You're a sort of boss
around here. Well, then, go ahead and give orders, you cuckoo's
egg!"

"Get moving there, you demons!" he yelled at the men. "We've
got to finish the work today, don't we?"

He himself was the laziest of the lot. He knew his business quite
well, and could work with dexterity and zeal when he had a mind
to, but he didn't care to take the trouble and preferred to entertain
the others with tall stories. And so when work would be forging
ahead and the men would be at it in silent absorption, suddenly
obsessed by the desire to do everything well and smoothly, Osip
would begin in his purring voice:

"Did I ever tell you about the time...."

For two or three minutes the men would appear to pay no heed
to him, engrossed in their sawing and planing, and his soft tenor
would flow dreamily on, meandering around them and claiming their
attention. His light-blue eyes half-closed, Osip fingered his curly
beard and, smacking his lips with pleasure, mulled happily over
each word.

"So he catches this here carp, puts it away in his basket and goes
off into the woods, thinking about the fine fish soup he's going to
have.... And all of a sudden he hears a woman's voice pipe up, he
can't tell from where: 'Yelesy-a-a, Yelesy-a-a!...'"

Lyonka, the lanky, angular Mordvinian, nicknamed Narodets, a
young man with small eyes full of wonderment, lowered his axe
and stood gaping.

"And from the basket a deep bass voice answers: 'Here I am!'
And that very same minute the lid of the basket snaps back and out
jumps the fish and darts straight back into the pool...."

Sanyavin, an old discharged soldier and a saturnine drunk who
suffered from asthma and had a grudge of long-standing against
life, croaked hoarsely:

"How could a carp move about on land?"

"Have you ever heard of a fish that could talk?" Osip retorted
sweetly.

Mokei Budyrin, a dull-witted muzhik whose prominent cheekbones, jutting chin and receding forehead lent his face a canine
appearance, a silent unprepossessing fellow, gave vent to his three
favourite words in his slow nasal drawl:
"That's true enough. ..."
His unfailing response to any story—incredible, horrible, filthy
or malicious—would be those three words uttered in a low voice
that rang with conviction.
"That's true enough."
Each time I heard them it was as though some heavy fist struck
me thrice on the chest.
Work stopped because lame and stuttering Yakov Boyev also
wanted to tell a fish story, in fact he had already begun his tale, but
no one listened to him; instead everybody laughed at his painful
efforts to speak. He cursed and swore, brandished his chisel and foaming at the mouth yelled to everyone's amusement:
"When one man lies like a trooper you take it for gospel, but
I'm telling you a true story and all you can do is cackle like a lot
of numbskulls, blast you. ..."
By now the men had dropped their tools and were shouting and
gesticulating, whereupon Osip took off his cap, baring his venerable
silver head with its bald pate, and sternly admonished:
"Hey that'll do now! You've had your breathing spell, now get
back to work!"
"You started it," croaked the ex-soldier spitting disgustedly on
his hands.
Osip began nagging at me:
"Now then, overseer. ..."
I felt that he had some definite purpose in distracting the men
from their work with his chatter, but what I did not understand was
whether he did it to conceal his own laziness or to give the workers
a breather. When the contractor was around, Osip behaved with the
utmost servility, acting the simpleton in front of the boss, contriving
every Saturday to wheedle a little extra money out of him for the
artel.
On the whole he was devoted to the men, but the old workers had
no use for him—they considered him a clown and a good-for-nothing
and had little respect for him; and even the young folk who enjoyed

listening to his stories did not take him seriously, regarding him
rather with ill-concealed mistrust and often with hostility.

I once asked the Mordvinian, an intelligent chap with whom I
often had some heart-to-heart talks, what he thought of Osip.

"I dunno..." he replied with a grin. "Devil knows... he's all
right, I suppose...." Then after a pause he went on:

"Mikhailo, the chap who died a sharp-tongued fellow he was,
and clever too, quarrelled with him once, with Osip, that is, and
lammed into Osip something fierce. 'What kind of a man are you?'
says he. 'As a workingman you're finished and you haven't learned
to be a boss, so you'll spend your days dangling like a forgotten
plummet on a string.' That's pretty near the truth, and no
mistake...."

Then after another pause he added uneasily:

"But he's all right, a good chap on the whole...."

My own position among these men was an extremely embarrass-
ing one. Here I was, a lad of fifteen, put there by the contractor to
keep accounts, to see that the carpenters did not steal the nails or
turn the boards in at the saloon. Of course, they filched nails right
under my nose, going out of their way to show me that I was quite
superfluous, a downright nuisance, in fact. And if any opportunity
afforded itself to bump me with a board or to do me some other
minor injury, as if by accident, they would not hesitate to make
the most of it.

I felt awkward and ashamed in their midst; I would have liked
to say something to reconcile them to my presence, but I could not
find the words and the oppressive sense of my own uselessness
weighed heavily upon me.

Whenever I entered in my book the materials taken, Osip would
walk over to me in his deliberate way and say:

"Got it? Now then, let's have a look...."

And he would screw up his eyes and scrutinize the entry.

"You don't write clearly enough," he would comment somewhat
vaguely.

He could read only printed lettering and he wrote in church
Slavonic letters, too. Ordinary writing was unintelligible to him.

"What's that funny-looking curlicue there?"

"It's the letter 'D.'"

"Ah, D! What a fancy loop.... And what've you written on that line?"

"Boards, nine arshin, five."

"Six, you mean."

"No, five."

"What do you mean, five? Look, Soldier cut up one...."

"He shouldn't have...."

"Who says he shouldn't? He took half to the pub...."

He looked straight at me with his eyes as blue as corn-flowers, twinkling merrily, and, fingering his beard, said with shameless imperturbability:

"Come on, now, put down six! Look here, you cuckoo's egg, it's wet and cold and the work's hard; a fellow's got to have a little drink now and again to warm his soul, don't he? Don't be so upright, you won't bribe God that way...."

He talked long and earnestly, his gentle, caressing words seemed to engulf me like a shower of sawdust until I felt dazed and blinded by them and found myself altering the figure without protest.

"Now that's more like it! Why, the figure even looks nicer, sitting there on the line like a nice, fat kind-hearted wench...."

I saw him triumphantly reporting his victory to the carpenters and knew that they all despised me for my weakness, and my fifteen-year-old heart wept with humiliation and ugly, dreary thoughts whirled in my head.

"How strange and stupid all this is. Why is he so sure that I won't go and change the six back to a five, and that I won't tell the contractor they sold the board for drinks?"

Once they stole two pounds of eight-inch spikes and clamps.

"Listen here," I warned Osip, "I'm going to put that down!"

"Go ahead!" he replied lightly, his grey eyebrows twitching. "It's time to put a stop to all this nonsense! Go ahead, write it down, that'll teach the sons of bitches...."

And he shouted to the men:

"Hey you, loafers, you'll be paying a fine for those spikes and clamps!"

"What for?" the ex-soldier demanded grimly.

"You can't get away with that sort of thing all the time," Osip calmly explained.

The carpenters grumbled and looked askance at me, and I was
not at all sure that I would carry out my threat and whether, if I
did, I would be doing right.

"I'm going to quit this job," I said to Osip. "You can all go to
the devil! I'll be taking to thieving myself if I stay with you fellows much longer."

Osip pondered this for a while, stroking his beard thoughtfully.
Then he squatted down beside me and said softly:

"You know, lad, you're quite right!"

"Eh?"

"You've got to clear out. What sort of a foreman or overseer are
you? In a job like this a man must have respect for property,
he's got to have the soul of a watchdog to guard his master's belong-
ings like his own hide. . . . A pup like you's no good for a job like
this, you haven't any feeling for property. If Vassil Sergeich knew
how you let us carry on he would take you by the scruff of your
neck and throw you right out, he would! Because you're not an asset to him, you're a liability and a man has to be an asset to his
master. See what I mean?"

He rolled a cigarette and handed it to me.

"Have a smoke, penpusher, it'll clear your head. If you weren't
such a smart, handy lad, my advice to you would be: take the holy
orders! But you haven't got the character for that; you're a stubborn, hard sort of chap, you wouldn't give in to the abbot himself.
With a character like yours you'll never get on in the world. And
a monk's like a jackdaw, he don't care what he pecks; so long as
there are seeds he don't care where they come from. I'm telling you
all this from the bottom of my heart because I can see that you're
out of place here, a cuckoo's egg in a strange nest. . . ."

He took off his cap, as he always did when he was about to say
something particularly important—stared up at the bleak sky and
observed piously:

"God knows we're a thieving lot and he won't forgive us for it. . . ."

"That's true enough," Mokei Budyrin trumpeted.

From that moment silver-haired Osip with his bright eyes and
dusky soul had a pleasant fascination for me; a sort of friendship
sprang up between us, although I noticed that his good relations
with me embarrassed him somehow; in front of the others he looked

at me vacantly, his corn-flower blue eyes darting this way and that,
and his lips twisted in a false, unpleasant grimace as he addressed me:

"Now then, keep you eyes peeled, earn your living, can't you see
Soldier over there chewing nails for all he's worth. . . ."

But when we were alone he spoke with a gentle wisdom and a
clever little gleam played in his bright blue eyes as they looked
straight into mine. I listened carefully to what this old man had to
say, for his words were true and honestly weighed, although sometimes he spoke strangely.

"A man ought to be good," I remarked once.

"Yes, indeed!" he agreed. Then he chuckled and with downcast
eyes, he went on softly:

"But what exactly do you mean by 'good'? The way I see it,
people don't care a hang about your goodness or honesty so long as
it doesn't benefit them. No, it pays to be nice to them, amuse them,
humour them ... and someday perhaps it will bring you good
returns! Of course, I don't deny it must be a fine thing to look at
yourself in the mirror and know you're a good man. But as far as
I can see it's all the same to folks whether you're a ruffian or a
saint so long as you're nice to them. . . . That's about the size of it,
lad!"

I am in the habit of observing people carefully for I feel that
each individual I come in contact with might help me fathom the
secret of this mysterious, muddled, painful business called life; moreover, there is one question that has never ceased to torment me:

What is the human soul?

It seems to me that some souls must be like brass globes fixed
rigidly to the breast so that the reflection they cast back is distorted,
ugly and repulsive. And then there are souls that are as flat as mir-
rors. Such souls might just as well not be there at all.

But most human souls I imagine to be formless as clouds, of an
indeterminate opaqueness like the fickle opal always ready to change
its hue to conform to whatever colour comes in contact with it.

I did not know, nor could I imagine what comely old Osip's
soul was like; it was something my mind could not fathom.

I pondered these things as I gazed out over the river to where
the town clung to the hillside, vibrating with the peal of bells from
all of its belfries that soared skywards like the white pipes of my

beloved organ in the Polish church. The crosses on the churches,
like blurred stars captured by the dreary sky, winked and trembled
and seemed to be reaching out toward the clear sky behind the grey
blanket of wind-torn clouds; but the clouds scurried along, effacing
with dark shadows the gay colours down below, and each time the
sunbeams emerged from the bottomless abysses between them
to bathe the town in bright hues, they hastened to blot them out
again, the dank shadows grew heavier, and after one instant of
gladness all was gloomy and dreary again.

The buildings of the town were like heaps of soiled snow, the
ground beneath them was black and bare, and the trees in the gardens were like clods of earth; the dull gleam of the windowpanes
in the grey house walls reminded one of winter, and the poignant
sadness of the pale northern spring spreads softly over the whole scene.

Mishuk Dyatlov, a tow-headed, broad-shouldered, gawky lad with
a harelip, essayed a song:

> She came to him in the morning,
> But he died the night before. . . .

"Shut up, you bastard," the ex-soldier shouted at him, "have you
forgotten what day it is?"

Boyev was also angry. He shook his fist at Dyatlov, hissing:
"S-swine!"

"We're a hardy, tough lot," Osip said to Budyrin as he sat astride
the top of the icebreak measuring its slant with narrowed eyes.
"Slip it out an inch to the left ... that's it! A savage lot, that's what
we are: Once I saw a bishop come along and the people crowded
around him, fell on their knees and begged and implored him:
'Your Reverence,' they said, 'drive away the wolves, the wolves are
ruining us!' And he towered over them and thundered: 'You're
supposed to be Orthodox Christians? I'll have you all severely punished!' Very wrathful he was, why he even spat in their faces. A
little old chap he was, with a kindly face, bleary-eyed...."

About fifty yards down the river from the ice aprons some boatmen and tramps were chopping the ice around the barges; the crow-
bars cracked into the ice, crushing the brittle, greyish-blue crust of
the river, the slender handles of the boat-hooks swayed back and
forth pushing the broken pieces under the solid ice, the current

gurgled and from the sandy beach came the murmur of streamlets. On the ice apron planes cut into wood, saws screeched and hammers pounded, driving clamps into the yellow, smoothly planed wood—and all these sounds mingled with the ringing of the bells which, softened by the distance, stirred the soul. It was as if all the labour of the bleak day had been a paean to spring, urging her to descend upon the thawing but still naked and wretched earth. . . .

"Call the German!" someone yelled hoarsely, "we need more men. . . ."

From shore came the response:

"Where is he?"

"Look in the pub. . . ."

The voices floated heavily in the moisture-laden air and echoed drearily over the broad river.

The men worked feverishly but carelessly; everyone was anxious to get to town, to the bathhouse and then to church as quickly as possible. Sashok Dyatlov a well-built, agile lad with a shock of curly hair bleached white like his brother's was particularly worried. He kept glancing up-stream, saying softly to his brother:

"Don't you hear it crackling?"

The ice had stirred the night before and the river police had been keeping the horses off the river ever since the morning before; a few pedestrians were still slipping across over the foot-bridges, like beads sliding on strings, and you could hear the boards smacking against the water as they bent under the weight.

"It's cracking up," said Mishuk, blinking his white lashes.

Osip, who had been scanning the river his eyes shaded with his hand, cut him short.

"It's the sawdust in your noodle cracking!" he said. "You get on with the job, son of a sorceress! Overseer, take your nose out of your book and keep them at it!"

There was about two hours' work left; the sides of the icebreak were already covered with gleaming planks as yellow as butter, and only the thick iron bands remained to be spiked on. Boyev and Sanyavin had cut out the grooves for the strips of iron but it was now discovered that they had made them too narrow.

"You blind bat, you!" Osip scolded the Mordvinian, clasping his head in despair. "Call that work?"

Suddenly a voice raised in a joyful shout was heard from the shore.
"It's moving! Hoorray!"

As if in accompaniment to the howl, a faint crunching rustling
sound came down the river; the gnarled claws of the pine-bough markers trembled and seemed to clutch at the air for support, and, waving their boat-hooks, the boatmen and tramps noisily clambered up
rope ladders to board their barges.

It was strange to see the deserted river suddenly become crowded
with people; they seemed to have popped up from under the ice
and were now rushing back and forth like jackdaws scared by a
gunshot, running hither and thither hauling boards and poles, dropping them and picking them up again.

"Get your tools together!" roared Osip. "Lively there, you. . . .
We're going ashore!"

"There goes Easter Sunday!" exclaimed Sashok bitterly.

To us it seemed as if the river stood still, while the city shuddering and swaying, with the hill under it, began to sail slowly up the
river. The grey sandy landslip about seventy feet ahead of us also
stirred and floated away.

"Get moving!" Osip shouted, giving me a push. "What're you
gaping at?"

A dread sensation of danger gripped me, and my feet, feeling
the ice shift underneath, mechanically propelled my body to the
sand spit where the willow wands broken and bent by the winter
winds jutted up naked and bare. Boyev, Soldier, Budyrin and the
two Dyatlovs got there ahead of me. The Mordvinian ran beside me
swearing angrily while Osip brought up the rear.

"Stop your howling, Narodets . . . " I heard Osip shout.

"But what are we going to do, Uncle Osip. . . ."

"Everything's all right, you'll see."

"We'll be stuck here for a couple of days."

"Then you'll sit it out. . . ."

"What about the holiday?"

"They'll manage this year without you."

"Bunch of cowards," sneered Soldier, sitting on the sand and
smoking his pipe. "It's only a hop skip and a jump to the shore
and you're ready to run like mad."

"You were the first to take to your heels," Mokei put in.

"What're you afraid of?" Soldier continued. "Christ was the Saviour and even he had to die...."

"But he was resurrected, wasn't he?" the Mordvinian muttered, hurt by the other's remarks.

"Shut up, you pup!" Boyev shouted at him. "Sure he was resurrected. Today's Friday, not Sunday!"*

The March sun broke through a blue gulf between the clouds, and the ice glistened as if mocking at us. Osip scanned the deserted river, shading his eyes with his hand.

"She's stopped," he said. "But not for long...."

"No holiday for us," Sashok muttered sullenly.

Angry furrows cleft the Mordvinian's beardless, moustacheless face, as dark and rough-hewn as an unpared potato.

"So we can sit right here," he muttered, blinking, "with nothing to eat and no money. People are enjoying themselves, but we.... Victims of greed, that's what we are...."

"It's a matter of need, not greed!" Osip, his eyes glued to the river and his thoughts apparently far away, spoke as if talking in his sleep. "What are these ice breakers for? To protect the barges and everything else from the ice. The ice hasn't any sense, it'll just pile up on the string of boats—and good-bye property...."

"Spit on it. It isn't ours, is it?"

"No use reasoning with a fool...."

"Ought to've fixed them earlier...."

Soldier twisted his face in a frightful grimace.

"Shut up, Mordvinian!" he shouted.

"It's stopped," Osip repeated.

The boatmen were shouting on board their vessels. From the river a chill breath and an evil, ominous silence were wafted. The pattern of the markers scattered over the ice altered, and everything seemed altered, pregnant with tense expectation.

"Uncle Osip, what are we going to do?" one of the young lads asked timidly.

"Eh?" he responded absently.

"Are we going to stay here?"

---

* Sunday in Russian is "voskresenye" which also means resurrection.—*Trans.*

"Maybe the Lord doesn't want you sinners celebrating his holiday, eh?" Boyev said, in a mocking nasal twang.

Soldier came to the assistance of his comrade and pointing to the river with his pipe muttered:

"Want to go to town, eh? Who's stopping you? The ice'll go too. Maybe you'll get drowned—it'd save you from getting hauled to the clink anyway."

"That's true enough," said Mokei.

The sun slipped out of sight, the river grew dark, and the town was now more clearly visible. The young men gazed at it with impatient, longing eyes, silent and still.

I had that oppressive feeling which comes with the realization that everyone around you is concerned with his own thoughts and that there is no single purpose that might unite all into an integral, stubborn force. I wanted to get away from them and set off down the ice alone.

With a movement so sudden that he might have just awakened from a deep sleep, Osip got up, removed his cap and, making the sign of the cross in the direction of the town, said in a simple, calm tone of authority:

"Well, lads, let's go, and God be with us...."

"To town?" cried Sashok, jumping to his feet.

Soldier made no effort to move.

"We'll drown!" he declared.

"Stay here, then."

Casting his eye over the men around him, Osip cried:

"Come on, let's get going!"

Everybody was now on his feet and gathered in a huddle. Boyev, who was rearranging the tools in his basket complained:

"Once you're told to go, you might as well go.... But the one who gives the orders will have to answer...."

Osip seemed to have grown younger and stronger. The crafty, good-natured expression had faded from his rosy face, his eyes grew darker, graver and more matter-of-fact. The indolent swagger too disappeared and he now walked with a firm, confident tread.

"Pick up a board, each of you, and hold it cross-wise in front. In case the ice cracks, which God forbid, the ends will hit the solid ice and stop you from going under. They'll help in crossing the cracks too. Anybody got a rope? Here, you, give me the level.... Ready? I'll go ahead, and after me ... who's the heaviest? I suppose you, Soldier. Then Mokei, Mordvinian, Boyev, Mishuk, Sashok. Maximych, being the lightest, will bring up the rear.... Off with your caps and let's pray to the Virgin. Here comes the sun to give us a send-off...."

With one accord the grey and brown heads of matted hair were bared, and the sun glanced down at them through a thin white cloud, only to hide again as if loth to raise unwarranted hopes.

"Let's go!" said Osip in a dry, strange voice. "God be with us! Keep your eyes on my feet. And no crowding. Keep at least a sagene apart and the more space the better. Come on, lads!"

Shoving his cap inside his coat and carrying the level, Osip stepped on the ice, cautiously sliding his feet along its surface. No sooner had he done so than a wild cry came from the river bank behind.

"Where're you going, you ... sheep."

"Keep going, no looking behind!" the leader commanded crisply.

"Get back, you devils!"

"Come on, lads, and keep God in your mind! He's not going to invite us for the holidays...."

A policeman's whistle was heard.

"Now we're in for it!" Soldier grumbled aloud. "They'll let the police know over on the other side—and if we get through alive we'll be locked up for sure.... I'm not going to take any responsibility for this...."

The string of men on the ice followed Osip's ringing voice as if it were something tangible to cling to.

"Watch the ice in front of your feet!"

We were crossing the river diagonally upstream, and being the last I had a good view of small, dapper Osip with his white, fluffy head as he skilfully slid along, barely lifting his feet from the ice. Behind him, as if threaded on an invisible string, filed six dark figures, doubled over and unsteady on their feet; now and then their shadows appeared next to them, then disappeared underfoot only to spread out on the ice once more. Their heads were bent low, as if they were coming down a mountainside and were afraid of stumbling.

On the shore behind us a crowd evidently had gathered, for the outcry had risen to an unpleasant roar and you could no longer make out what they were shouting.

The cautious procession resolved itself into mechanical, tiresome work. Accustomed to walking fast, I now found myself sinking into that somnolent, detached frame of mind when the soul seems to grow void and all thought of self is forgotten, while vision and hearing become inordinately sharp. Underfoot was the bluish-grey, leaden ice worn thin by the current; its diffused glitter was blinding. Here and there it had cracked and jammed into hummocks, ground by the movement of the river into fragments porous like pumice-stone and as jagged as broken glass. Blue fissures yawned coldly, ready to trap the unwary foot. The wide-soled boots shuffled along and the voices of Boyev and Soldier, continually harping on the same theme, tried my patience.

"I'm not going to answer for this. . . ."

"Neither will I. . . ."

"Just because a man has the right to order you about doesn't mean someone else mightn't be a thousand times smarter. . . ."

"You think being smart means anything—it's a glib tongue that counts around here. . . ."

Osip had tucked the hem of his sheepskin jacket under his belt and his legs, encased in pants of grey army cloth, strode along with the ease and resilience of a spring. It was as if some creature visible to him alone were dancing in front of him, preventing him from walking straight ahead, and he was doing his best to circumvent it, slip away from it, darting to the left or the right, sometimes doubling sharply in his tracks, and doing it all at a dance-step describing loops and semicircles on the ice. His voice rang out clearly and resonantly, and it was pleasant to hear it merge with the ringing of the church bells.

We were half-way across the four-hundred-sagene strip of ice when an ominous rumble came from upstream and at the same moment the ice shifted under my feet; taken by surprise I lost my balance and fell down on one knee. I looked up the river and terror gripped me by the throat, throttled me and made the world turn black in my eyes: the grey crust of ice had sprung to life, it was buckling up, sharp angles appeared on the even surface, and a strange crunching like heavy boots walking over broken glass, filled the air.

With a quiet rush, clear water appeared next to me, somewhere splintering wood whined like a living thing, the men shouted huddling together, and through it all rang the voice of Osip:

"Scatter, there.... Get away from each other.... What are you crowding together for! She's going good and proper now.... Get a move on, lads!"

He leapt about as if attacked by wasps, jabbing the air around him with the level as though it were a gun and he were holding off some invisible assailant, while the town swam jerkily past him. Under me the ice crunched and crumpled into fine slivers, water washed against my feet and, springing up, I made a wild dash toward Osip.

"Where d'you think you're going!" he shouted, swinging the level. "Stop, you bloody fool!"

The man before us was not the old Osip; the face had grown strangely young, all the familiar features had gone, his blue eyes were now grey, and the man seemed to have grown a half-arshin taller. Straight as a brand-new nail, his feet firmly planted, he was shouting with his mouth wide open:

"If you don't stop running around and getting into a huddle I'll smash your skulls in!"

Again he swung at me with the level.

"Where're you going?"

"We'll drown!" I said in a whisper.

"Hush!" Then, observing my sorry plight, he added softly:

"Any fool can drown, you make it your business to get out of here!"

Again he began shouting encouragements to the others, his chest thrust out and his head thrown back.

The ice crackled and crunched as it broke up lazily. In the meantime we were slowly being carried past the town. Ashore it seemed some fabulous titan had awakened and was rending the earth asunder; the shoreline below us was stationary while the bank opposite was slowly moving upstream—it could only be a matter of moments before it was ripped apart.

This ominous, creeping movement seemed to cut off our last link with land; the familiar world was receding into oblivion and my breast was laden with grief and my knees quaked. Red clouds slowly sailed across the sky and the jagged chunks of ice catching their reflection turned red too as if with the strain of reaching out for me. All the vast earth was in the throes of the birth pangs of spring, racked by convulsions, its shaggy, moist breast heaving and its joints cracking; and in the massive body of the earth the river was a vein pulsating with thick, warm blood.

It hurt to realize one's insignificance and helplessness in the midst of the calm, irresistible movement of the mass, and deep in the soul a bold dream took shape fed by this sensation of humiliation: if only I could reach out and lay my hand on the hill on shore and say:

"Stop until I reach you!"

The resonant pealing of the bells was now waning to a melancholy sigh, but I remembered that the next night they would once more speak out gaily to proclaim the resurrection.

If only I could live to hear them ringing!

... Seven dark figures danced before my eyes as they leapt from one foothold to another and paddled in thin air with the boards they were carrying; and ahead of them the old man turned and twisted like a groundling, reminiscent of Nicholas the Miracle-Maker, his imperative voice ringing out ceaselessly:

"Keep your eyes op-e-n!"

The ice buckled and the living back of the river shivered and heaved underfoot like the whale in the "Hunch-Backed Horse"; and with increasing frequency the fluid body of the stream gushed from under the armour of ice—the cold, murky water that greedily licked at the men's feet.

We moved along a narrow perch overhanging a deep abyss. The quiet, luring splash of the water conjured up visions of bottomless depths, of my body settling slowly, slowly into the dense icy mass, saw my eyes grow blind, my heart ceasing to beat. I recalled the drowned bodies I had seen, with their slimy skulls, bloated faces and glassy, bulging eyes, the fingers jutting out from swollen hands and the sodden skin that hung on the palms like a rag.

The first to get a ducking was Mokei Budyrin; he had been ahead of the Mordvinian, as silent and retiring as always; he had been calmer than the others and yet he disappeared as suddenly as if he had been pulled in by the legs, only his head and his hands gripping the plank remained above the ice.

"Lend a hand!" Osip cried. "Not all of you, one or two'll be enough."

"Never mind, boys," said Mokei to the Mordvinian and me, as he blew the water out of his mouth. "I'll manage ... myself."

He clambered onto the ice and shook himself.

"Damn it anyway, it looks as if you really might drown down here."

His teeth chattering, he licked his wet moustache with his large tongue, his resemblance to a big, genial dog more marked than ever.

A transient recollection flashed in my mind; I remembered how a month before he had chopped off the thumb of his left hand at the first joint and picking up the pallid, blue-nailed joint had looked at it darkly, with wondering eyes, and addressed it in a low, apologetic tone:

"I've hacked at the poor thing so many times I've just lost count.... It was out of joint anyway, didn't work properly.... So now I suppose I've got to bury it." He carefully wrapped the amputated thumb into some shavings and put it in his pocket. Only then did he proceed to bandage the wound.

The next to get a ducking was Boyev; it looked as if he had purposely dived under the ice. He let out a frenzied cry at once.

"O-ow, help! I'm drowning! Save me, brothers, don't let me go down...."

He thrashed about so hard out of sheer terror that we barely managed to haul him up, and in the fuss we almost lost the Mordvinian who went right under, head and all.

"That was pretty nearly a trip straight to the devils," he said with an abashed smile as he clambered back on the ice, looking lankier and more angular than ever.

A minute later Boyev went down again with a shriek.

"Shut up, Yashka, you soul of a goat!" Osip shouted, threatening him with the level. "Why must you scare everybody out of their wits? I'll teach you a lesson! Loosen your belts, boys, and turn your pockets inside out, it'll be easier that way...."

Every dozen paces or so the ice, crunching and spuming, opened wide, sharp-fanged jaws dripping a murky froth and the jagged blue teeth reached out for our feet; the river seemed anxious to suck us down as a snake swallows a frog. The sodden boots and clothes

hampered our movement and pulled us down; we were all clammy
as if we had been licked down; clumsy and speechless, we plodded
along slowly and submissively.

Osip, as wet as the rest of us, seemed to divine where the fissures were and leapt like a hare from floe to floe. After each leap
we would pause for a moment, look around and give a resonant
whoop:

"That's how it's done, see?"

He was playing with the river; the river stalked him, but so
light and nimble on his feet was he that he easily dodged its passes
and avoided the pitfalls. One might have thought he was steering
the course of the ice and driving the large, solid floes for us to
walk on.

"Keep your chin up, you children of God! Ho! ho!"

"Good for Uncle Osip!" the Mordvinian said in quiet admiration. "There's a man for you! The real sort...."

The closer we got to the shore the finer the ice was chopped
and men kept falling through it more and more frequently. The
town had already practically floated by and the Volga was not far
ahead; there the ice had not moved yet and we were in danger of
being sucked under.

"Looks like we'll drown," the Mordvinian said quietly, looking
over his left shoulder at the blue haze of evening.

Suddenly, as if out of pity for us, a huge ice floe ran end on
against the shore, climbed up it shivering and crunching, and then
stopped.

"Run!" Osip shouted frenziedly. "Leg it for all you're worth!"

He jumped for the floe, slipped and fell down, and sitting on
the edge of the ice where the water lapped up to him he let the rest
of us pass. Five of us dashed for the shore jostling one another in
an effort to get there first; the Mordvinian and I stopped to lend
Osip a hand.

"Run, you pig's progeny, d'you hear me!"

His face was blue and trembling, his eyes had lost their lustre,
and his jaw hung queerly.

"Come on, Uncle...."

His head dropped.

"Must have broken my leg.... Can't get up...."

We picked him up and carried him while he kept on mumbling through chattering teeth, clinging to our necks.

"You'll drown yourselves, you fools.... We'd better thank the Lord for pulling us through.... Look out, it won't carry three, step easy there! Follow the spots where there's no snow ... it's more solid there.... Better drop me, though...."

Osip screwed up an eye and looked me in the face.

"That ledger of yours where our sins are recorded must've gotten all soaked up, or maybe you've lost it, eh?" he said.

As we stepped off the end of the ice floe that had piled up on the bank, smashing a boat into smithereens in the process, the other end of the floe which was still afloat scrunched, broke off and sailed away, rocking in the current.

"Well, well," the Mordvinian said approvingly. "It knew what it was about!"

Soaking wet and chilled to the marrow but in high spirits, we were now ashore surrounded by a crowd of townsfolk. Boyev and the ex-soldier were already having an altercation with them.

"Well boys," Osip cried gaily as we lowered him onto some timbers, "the book's all mucked up, soaked right through...."

The book, tucked away inside my coat, weighed like a brick; I pulled it out when no one was looking and threw it far out into the stream where it plunked into the dark water like a frog. The Dyatlovs were racing up the hillside to the saloon for some vodka, pounding each other with their fists as they ran and shouting:

"R-r-rah!"

"Ekh, you!"

A tall old man with the beard of an apostle and the eyes of a thief was speaking earnestly right into my ear.

"You ought to have your mugs bashed in for scaring peaceable folk, you anathemas, you ... " he was saying.

"What the hell did we do to you?" shouted Boyev, who was busy pulling on his boots.

"Christian folk were drowning and what did you do?" Soldier complained, his voice hoarser than ever.

"What could we have done?"

Osip was lying on the ground, his leg stretched out, going over his jacket with trembling hands.

"Soaked all the way through. Oh mother mine," he moaned. "Done for, these clothes are, and I didn't wear them a year!"

He had shrunk and his face was wrinkled and he seemed to be growing smaller and smaller as he lay there on the ground.

Suddenly he raised himself, sat up, groaned and was off in an angry, high-pitched voice:

"So you had to get to the bathhouse and the church, you bloody fools. Devil's spawn! You can go straight to hell! As if the Lord couldn't celebrate his day without you.... Pretty nearly lost our lives.... And clothes all mucked up.... Hope you croak...."

Everybody else was draining the water from shoes and wringing clothes, wheezing and groaning from exhaustion and arguing back and forth with the townsfolk, but Osip went on still more vehemently:

"Of all the things to do, damn their hides! Had to get to the bathhouse—the police station is where they belong, that's where you'd get your backwashing...."

"They've sent for the police," one of the townsmen said in a placating tone.

"What're you trying to do?" Boyev turned on Osip. "Why put on the act?"

"Me?"

"Yes, you!"

"Wait a minute! What do you mean?"

"Who started this business of coming across, eh?"

"Well, who?"

"You!"

"Me?"

Osip started as if a spasm had seized him.

"Me-e?" he repeated, his voice breaking.

"That's true enough," Budyrin said in a level, distinct voice.

"Honest, it was you, Uncle Osip," the Mordvinian bore out the others, but quietly, apologetically. "You must've forgotten...."

"Of course you started it," the ex-soldier ejaculated sullenly and emphatically.

"Forgotten eh!" Boyev cried in fury. "Tell me another one! I know him, he's trying to shove the blame onto somebody else!"

Osip fell silent and narrowing his eyes surveyed the dripping, half-naked men.

Then emitting a strange whimper—I could not make out whether
he was laughing or sobbing—twitching his shoulders and spreading
out his arms, he muttered:

"That's right ... true enough, it was my idea ... now what do
you make of that!"

"Aha that's better!" Soldier cried triumphantly.

Gazing at the river, which was now seething like a millet gruel
coming to a boil, Osip puckered up his face and guiltily looked
away.

"My mind must have gone blank like that, by God!" he continued. "How we ever made it I don't understand.... Makes me sick
to think of it. Anyway, boys, I hope you won't hold it against me—
after all, there was the holiday coming, wasn't there? You'll forgive
me. I must have sort of gone off a bit or something.... True enough,
I started it ... old fool that I am...."

"You see?" said Boyev. "And what'd you say if I got drowned?"

It seemed to me that Osip really was stricken by the uselessness
and foolishness of what he had done as he sat there on the ground,
looking as slippery as a new-born calf licked by its dam; he shook
his head, passed his fingers through the sand around him and continued mumbling penitently in a strange voice, all the while avoiding
everyone's eyes.

I looked at him and wondered what had happened to the captain
of men who had taken his place at the head of his fellows and led
them so considerately, ably and imperiously.

An unpleasant emptiness welled up in my soul. I dropped down
beside Osip and, hoping to salvage something from the wreckage,
spoke to him in a low voice.

"Don't, Uncle Osip...."

"Ever see anything like it?" he responded in the same tone,
giving me a sidelong glance while his fingers were busy untangling
his matted beard. Then he went on as loudly as before for everybody's benefit: "What a to-do, eh?"

... The dark stubble of the tree-tops on the crest of the hill
was silhouetted against the extinguished sky, and the hill itself
pressed against the shore like some huge beast. The blue shadows of
evening appeared from behind the roofs of the houses that clung
scab-like to the dusky hide of the hillside, and looked out from the

wide-open rusty-red, moist maw of a clayey gully creating the illu-
sion that it was reaching out thirstily for the river.

The river grew black and the rustle and crunching of the ice
became duller and more regular; every now and then an ice floe
dug end on into the shore as the hog roots the earth, remained motionless for a moment, then rocked, broke loose and sailed on farther while the next floe crept into its place.

The level of the water rose rapidly, sweeping against the bank
and washing away the mud, and the silt spread a dark stain in the
murky blue water. Strange noises filled the air—a scrunching and
champing as if some tremendous beast were devouring its meal and
licking its chops with a giant tongue.

From the direction of the town the sweet and pensive melody
of the pealing bells, now muted by distance, floated down.

Like two romping puppies the Dyatlovs dashed down the hillside
carrying bottles in their hands while at right angles to them, along
the river front, came a grey-coated police officer and two policemen
in black.

"God Almighty!" Osip groaned, tenderly rubbing his knee.

As the police approached, the townspeople cleared a passage for
them and an expectant silence fell. The police officer, a lean little chap
with a small face and a waxed reddish moustache, strode up to us.

"So you were the devils..." he began sternly in a rather hoarse
affected bass.

Osip threw himself back on the ground and began hastily to
explain:

"It was me, Your Honor, who started the business.... Begging
your pardon, Your Honor, it was because of the holidays...."

"You old devil," the police officer yelled, but his shouting was
lost in the avalanche of humble entreaties.

"We live here in town and on the other bank we've got nothing;
didn't even have money to buy bread and, Your Honor, the day
after tomorrow's Easter—got to take a bath and go to church like all
good Christians, so I says, let's go, fellows, and take a chance; we
weren't doing anything wrong. I've been punished for my fool idea
though—leg's broken, see.

"That's all very well and good!" the police officer shouted
sternly. "But what if you had drowned?"

Osip heaved a deep, tired sigh.

"What would have happened, Your Honor? Begging your pardon, probably nothing...."

The policeman swore, and everybody listened to him in attentive silence as if the man was uttering words of wisdom to be heard and remembered instead of mouthing obscene, brazen insults.

After taking down our names he left. We had drunk down the fiery vodka and feeling warmed up and in better spirits were getting ready to head for home when Osip, chuckling and throwing a look after the receding policeman, jumped lightly to his feet and fervently crossed himself.

"Thank God that's the end...."

"Why... looks like your leg's all right!" Boyev said in his nasal twang, astonished and disappointed. "D'you mean you didn't break it?"

"You wish I had, eh?"

"Oh, you old comedian! You miserable clown...."

"Come on, boys!" Osip commanded, pulling his wet cap on his head.

... I walked alongside him behind the others, and as we went, he spoke to me in a quiet, tender way as if sharing a secret known only to him.

"No matter what you do and how you try, you just can't live unless you're crafty and cunning—that's life for you, damn it anyway.... You would like to climb to the top of the hill but there's always some devil tripping you up...."

It was dark, and in the gloom, red and yellow lights burst forth as if signalling the message:

"This way!"

We walked up the hill toward the ringing of bells. At our feet rivulets rippled, drowning Osip's caressing voice in their babble.

"Got around the police neatly, didn't I? That's how you've got to do it, so that nobody knows what it's all about and everybody thinks he's the main spring. Yes... it's best to let everyone think he's the one who did it...."

I listened to him, but found it hard to understand what he was saying.

Nor did I want to understand him; as it is my heart was light and at ease. I did not know whether I liked Osip or not, but I was ready to follow him to the ends of the earth, even across the river once more, over ice that would be constantly slipping away from under my feet.

The bells pealed and sang, and the joyous thought came to my mind: How many more times shall I be able to welcome spring!

"The human soul's got wings," Osip sighed. "It soars in your dreams...." A winged soul? Wonderful!

HOW A SONG WAS COMPOSED

THIS IS HOW two women composed a song to the accompaniment of the mournful ringing of church bells, one summer's day. It was in a quiet street in Arzamas, just before sundown, on a seat outside the house in which I lived. The town was dozing in the sultry silence of a June day. Sitting at the window with a book, I was listening to my cook, plump, pock-marked Ustinya, talking quietly to the housemaid of my neighbour, the rural prefect.

"And what else do they write?" she asked in her masculine, but very flexible voice.

"Oh, nothing else," answered the housemaid in a low, pensive drawl. She was a dark, thin girl, with small, fixed, frightened eyes.

"And so—accept our greetings and send us money—is that it? "That's it. . . ."

"As for how you're living—who cares? Ekh!. . ."

In the pond, beyond the back gardens of our street, the frogs were croaking, emitting queer glassy sounds. The ringing of the church bells came floating over with annoying persistence, disturbing the sultry silence. Somewhere in a backyard a saw was snorting, and it seemed as though my neighbour's old house had fallen asleep and was snoring, gasping for breath in the heat.

"Relations," said Ustinya in a sad tone mingled with anger. "But go only three versts away from them and you feel like a twig broken off a tree! It was the same with me the first year I lived in town. I was awfully homesick. I felt as if I was only half alive; as if half of me was here and half had remained in the village. And day and night I used to think and worry: How are they getting on? How are they managing?"

Her words seemed to be accompanied by the church bells, and she seemed to be deliberately speaking in the same key in which they were ringing. The housemaid sat clasping her angular knees. and swaying her head in its white kerchief from side to side and biting her lips, she seemed to be listening intently to something far away. Ustinya's deep voice now sounded scornful and angry and now soft and sad.

"Sometimes the longing for my village was so fierce that I could neither see nor hear what was going on around me and yet I have nobody there. Father was burnt to death when the house caught fire. He was drunk at the time. My uncle died of cholera. I have two brothers, but one has remained in the army—he was made a corporal; the other is a bricklayer and lives in Boigorod. It seems as though they've all been swept away by a flood. . . ."

The lurid sun, sinking to the west, hung in the misty sky suspended from golden rays. The low voice of the woman, the tinkling of the bells and the glassy croaking of the frogs were the only sounds that disturbed the silence of the town at that particular moment. They floated low over the ground, like swallows before the coming rain; and above and around them there was stillness, all-absorbing, like death.

An absurd idea entered my head. It seemed to me that the town had been inserted into a large bottle that was lying on its side and was closed with a fiery cork, and that somebody was lazily and softly beating the heated glass on the outside.

Suddenly Ustinya said in a cheerful but businesslike way:

"Now, Mashutka, help me. . . ."

"Help you with what?"

"To make up a song."

Heaving a loud sigh, Ustinya began to sing in a hurried tone:

> *In the daytime when the sun shines bright*
> *And at night in the light of the moon. . . .*

Hesitantly picking up the tune, the housemaid continued the song in a low timid voice:

> *Lonely I feel and all forlorn. . . .*

Ustinya confidently, but in a very moving tone, capped the verse with:

My heart by longing is torn.

Then she said merrily, and a little boastfully:

"There, that's the beginning! I'll teach you how to make up songs, my dear, as easy as spinning yarn.... Now, then, let's go on."

Remaining silent for a moment as if listening to the mournful croaking of the frogs and the lazy ringing of the church bells, she once again deftly picked up words and music:

Neither fierce winter's storms
Nor rippling streams in the spring....

The housemaid shifted close up to Ustinya, and resting her white kerchiefed head on Ustinya's plump shoulder, she closed her eyes and, now more boldly, continued the verse in her thin and tremulous voice:

A word of tiding from home
To console me doth bring....

"There you are!" said Ustinya triumphantly, slapping her knee. "When I was younger I could make up even better songs than this! The girls used to say: 'Go on, Ustyusha, start a song!' Ekh, didn't I let myself go! Well, how is it to go now?"

"I don't know," said the housemaid, opening her eyes and smiling.

I looked at them through the flowers on the window sill. The singers could not see me, but I could very well see Ustinya's rough, deeply-pitted cheek, her small ear, which her yellow kerchief failed to cover, her grey, animated eye, her straight nose like the beak of a jay, and her square, masculine chin. She was a sly, talkative wench, a confirmed tippler and fond of hearing the lives of the saints read. She was the biggest gossip in the street and, moreover, she seemed to be the repository of all the secrets of the town. Beside her, plump and well-fed, the lean, angular housemaid looked like a child. And the housemaid's mouth was like that of a child; she pouted her small full lips as if she had just

been scolded, was afraid she would be scolded again, and was
ready to burst into tears.

Swallows were darting back and forth in the street, their curved
wings almost touching the ground. It was evident that the
gnats were flying low—a sure sign that it would rain at night. A
crow was sitting on the fence opposite my window, motionless, as
if carved out of wood, watching the flitting swallows with its black
eyes. The church bells had stopped ringing, but the frogs were
croaking more sonorously than before; the silence seemed denser,
hotter.

> *The lark is singing in the sky,*
> *The corn-flowers bloom in the corn,*

sang Ustinya plaintively, looking up at the sky, her arms crossed
over her breast. The housemaid followed her up boldly and tune-
fully,

> *Oh for a glimpse of my native fields,*

and Ustinya, skilfully supporting the girl's high-pitched tremulous
voice, added in a velvety tone the moving words:

> *And with my laddie in the woods to roam!...*

They stopped singing and sat silently for a long time, pressing
close against each other. At last Ustinya said in a low pensive
voice:

"It's not a bad song we made up, is it? Quite good, I think...."

"Look!" said the housemaid softly, interrupting Ustinya.

They looked across the street to the right. There, bathed in
sunshine, a tall priest in a purple cassock was striding down the
street with an important air, tapping the pavement with his long
staff in a measured beat. The silver crook of the staff and the
golden cross on his broad breast glistened in the sun.

The crow glanced sideways at the priest with its black beady
eye, lazily flapped its heavy wings and flew to a branch of an ash
tree, from which it dropped like a grey clot into the garden.

The women rose to their feet and bowed low to the priest. He
did not even notice them. They remained standing, following him
with their eyes until he turned the corner.

"Yes, little girl," said Ustinya, adjusting the kerchief on her head. "If only I were younger, and had a prettier face...."

Somebody called angrily in a sleepy voice:

"Maria!... Mashka!..."

"Oh, they're calling me...."

The housemaid ran off like a frightened rabbit, and Ustinya, sitting down again, smoothed her gaudy cotton frock over her knee, lost in thought.

The frogs croaked. The stifling air was as still as the water in a forest lake. The day was passing away in a riot of colour. An angry rumble came across the fields from beyond the river Tesha— it was the distant thunder growling like a bear.

THE PHILANDERER

AT ABOUT 6 o'clock in the morning I felt a living weight thrust itself upon my bed, and somebody shook me and shouted right into my ear:

"Get up!"

This was Sashka the compositor, my chum. An amusing fellow, about nineteen years of age, with a mop of tousled red hair, greenish eyes like a lizard's, and a face smudged with lead dust.

"Come on, get up!" he shouted, pulling me out of bed. "Let's go on the spree today. I have some money, six rubles twenty kopecks, and it's Stepakha's birthday! Where do you keep your soap?"

He went to the wash basin in the corner and fiercely scrubbed his face. In the midst of his puffing and snorting he asked me:

"Tell me: 'star'—is that 'astra'—in German?"

"No, I think it's Greek."

"Greek? We have a new proof-reader at our place who writes poetry, and she signs herself 'Astra.' Her real name is Trushenikova, Avdotia Vassilievna. She's nice little lady—good-looking, only—rather stout.... Where's your comb? ..."

As he forced the comb through his red mop of hair, he wrinkled his nose and swore. Suddenly he broke off in the middle of a word and closely examined the reflection of his face in the murky windowpane.

Outside the sun was playing on the brick wall opposite. The wall was wet from the previous night's rain and the sun tinted it red. A jackdaw was sitting on the funnel of the rain pipe, preening itself.

"What an awful mug I've got!" said Sashka, and then he exclaimed: "Look at that jackdaw! How all dressed up she is! Give me a needle and cotton, will you; I'll sew a button on my coat."

He pirouetted round and round, as if he were dancing on hot bricks; so much so that the draught he caused blew some scraps of paper from my table.

Then, standing at the window and clumsily plying the needle, he asked:

"Was there ever a king named Lodir?"*

"You mean Lothar. Why do you ask?"

"That's funny! I thought his name was Lodir, and that all lazy people descended from him! Let's go to a tavern first and have some tea. After that we'll go to the nunnery church for late matin and have a look at the nuns—I'm fond of nuns!... And what does 'prospectives' mean?"

He was as full of questions as a rattle with peas. I began to tell him what "prospects" means, but he went on talking without waiting for me to finish.

"Last night that feuilleton writer, Red Domino, came to the printing office, drunk, of course, as usual, and kept pestering me with questions about my prospectives."

After sewing on the button, higher than he should have done, he nipped the cotton with his white teeth, licked his red puffy lips and mumbled plaintively:

"Lizochka is quite right. I ought to read books, otherwise I shall die a boor and never know anything. But when can I read? I never have any time!

"Don't waste so much time courting the girls...."

"What am I—a corpse? I'm not an old man yet! Wait! When I get married, I'll give it up!"

Stretching himself, he mused:

"I'll marry Lizochka. That's a fashionable girl for you! She has a frock made of... what do you call it?... barege, I think. Well! She looks so lovely in it that my legs tremble when I see her wearing it. I feel I could gobble her up!"

In the tone of a grave mentor I said:

"Take care you are not gobbled up yourself!"

He smiled self-confidently and shook his head.

"The other day two students had an argument in our newspaper. One said that love was a dangerous business, but the other said no, it's quite safe! Aren't they clever? The girls like students. They are as fond of them as they are of military men."

We left the house. The cobble-stones, washed by the rain, glistened like the bald pates of government officials. The sky was

* Literally—lazybones. *Trans.*

almost shut out by banks of snow-white clouds, and every now and
again the sun peeped through the spaces between these cloudy
snow-drifts. A strong autumn wind was blowing people down the
street like withered leaves. It buffeted us and rang in our ears.
Sashka shrivelled up and thrust his hands deep down into the
pockets of his greasy trousers. He wore a light summer jacket, a
blue blouse, and brown top boots, down at heel.

At midnight on angel flew across the sky,

he declaimed in rhythm with our footsteps. "I love that piece! Who
wrote it?"

"Lermontov."

"I always mix him up with Nekrassov."

And long she languished in the world,
Filled with strange desires.

And screwing up his greenish eyes he repeated in a low and
pensive voice:

Filled with strange desires. . . .

"Good Lord! How well I understand that! I understand it so
well that I would fly myself. . . . Strange desires. . . ."

A girl walked out of the gate of a gloomy house in holiday
attire—a "claret-colour" skirt, a black blouse with jet trimmings,
and a golden-yellow silk shawl.

Sashka pulled his crumpled cap from his head, and bowing
respectfully, said to the girl:

"Many happy returns of the day, Miss!"

The girl's pretty round face first lit up with a tender smile,
but she immediately drew her thin brows together in a stern frown
and said in an angry, and half-frighened voice:

"But I don't know you!"

"Oh, that's nothing!" answered Sashka cheerfully. "It's always
like that with me. They don't know me at first; but when they do
they fall in love with me. . . ."

"If you wish to be impudent. . ." said the young lady, glancing
round. The street was deserted, except for a cart laden with cab-
bages at the very far end.

"I'm as gentle as a lamb!" said Sashka, walking beside the girl and glancing at her face. "I can see it's your birthday...."

"Please leave me alone."

The girl stepped out faster, clicking her heels determinedly on the brick sidewalk. Sashka halted and mumbled:

"By all means. There! I've dropped behind. Isn't she proud! What a pity I haven't a costume in which to play the part! If I had another suit on, she would have taken an interest in me, don't you worry."

"How do you know that it's her birthday?"

"How do I know? She comes out in her best clothes and is going to church. I'm too poor. That's what's the matter. Ekh! If only I had lots of money! I'd buy myself a little estate in the country and live like a gentleman.... Look!"

Four rough-bearded men were carrying a plain deal coffin out of a side street. In front of them, carrying the coffin lid on his head, walked a boy, and behind them walked a tall beggar, carrying a shepherd's staff. His face was stern, and looked as if it were hewn out of stone; and as he walked he kept his red-rimmed eyes fixed on the greyish nose of the corpse that was visible above the edge of the open coffin.

"The carpenter must have died," surmised Sashka, removing his cap. "Lord rest his soul and keep him far away from his relations and friends!"

A broad smile lit up his face, and his bright eyes flashed merrily.

"It's lucky to meet a corpse," he explained. "Come on!"

"We went to the 'Moskva' tavern, and entered a small room crowded with chairs and tables. The tables were covered with pink cloths. The windows were hung with faded-blue curtains. Flower pots were ranged on the window sills, and above the flower pots canaries in cages were suspended. The place was bright and warm and cosy.

We ordered some fried sausage, tea, half a bottle of vodka, and a dozen cigarettes of the "Persian" brand. Sashka sat down at a table near the window, spread himself out like a gentleman and launched into a discourse:

"I like this polite and genteel life," he said. "You are always complaining that this is bad and the other is bad, but why? Everything is as it should be. Your character is not human, it lacks

harmony. You are like the letter 'yer.'* The word can be understood without it, but they stick it on the end for form's sake, or
perhaps because they think it looks better."

While he was criticizing me I looked at him and thought to
myself:

"How much verve there is in that lad! A man who has so much
in him cannot pass out of this life unobserved."

But he had grown tired of sermonizing by this time. He took
up his knife and scraped it on his plate to tease the birds. At once
the room rang with the shrill trilling of the canaries.

"That set them going!" said Sashka, extremely pleased with
himself. Then, putting down the knife, he ran his fingers through
his red hair and thought aloud:

"No! Lizochka won't marry me. That's out of the question.
But who knows? Perhaps she'll learn to love me. I'm madly in
love with her!"

"But what about Zina?"

"Oh, Zinka is so plain. Lizochka—she's smart, she is," Sashka
explained.

He was an orphan, a foundling. At the age of seven he was
already working for a furrier. Then he worked for a plumber. For
two years he worked as a labourer at a flour mill that belonged
to a monastery, and now, for over a year, he had been working
as a printer's compositor. He liked the work on the newspaper
very much. He learned to read and write in his spare time, hardly noticing it himself, and the mysteries of literature had a great
fascination for him. He was particularly fond of reading poetry,
and he even wrote verses himself. Sometimes he would bring me
scraps of lead-smudged paper with formal lines scribbled on them
in pencil. The subject of these verses was always the same. and
they ran approximately as follows:

> I loved thee at first sight when
> On Black Lake my eyes met thine,
> And all my thoughts have been since then
> Of thee and of thy face divine.

* The hard sign formerly placed after consonants at the end of a word, now
obsolete.—*Trans.*

When I told him that this was not poetry, he would ask in surprise: "Why not? Look! It ends with 'en' here and here, and with 'ine' here and here!"

"But then, remember how Lermontov's verses sound."

"Oh, well! He had lots of practice, whereas I have only just begun! Wait until I get used to it!"

His self-confidence was amusing, but there was nothing repellent about it. He was simply convinced that life was in love with him, as the laundress Stepakha was; that he could do whatever he pleased, and that success awaited him everywhere.

The church bells were ringing, calling for late matin. The canaries, listening to the sound, which made the windowpanes rattle, stopped singing.

Sashka mumbled:

"Shall we go to matin or not?"

And then he decided.

"Let's go!"

On the way he said in a tone of complaint blended with self-condemnation:

"Tell me, how do you explain it? I always feel bored in church, but I love to go! The nuns there are so young. I'm sorry for them!"

In the church he stood at the gates where the beggars and other supplicants were gathered. His greenish eyes opened wide with wonder as he gazed at the choir where a crowd of choiristers were assembled, pale-faced and in pointed hoods, all standing stiff and straight as if they were carved out of black stone. They were singing harmoniously, and their silvery voices sounded amazingly pure. The gold on the icons glittered and the glass cases reflected the lights of the candles, which looked like golden flies.

The beggars sighed and muttered their humble prayers, raising their faded eyes to the dome. This was a week day, and there were few people in the church; only those had come who had nothing to do and did not know what to do with themselves.

In front of Sashka, telling her beads, stood a nun, rather a large woman, wearing a cowl. Sashka, who reached only up to her shoulder stood on tiptoe to peep into her round face and eyes, which were hidden by the cowl; and he stood like that, insolently staring at the nun with his lips pursed, as if for a kiss.

The nun slightly bent her head and gave him a side-long glance, like a well-fed cat looking at a mouse. He collapsed at once, pulled me by the sleeve and hurried out of the church.

"Did you see the look she gave me?" he said, closing his eyes with fright. Then he drew his cap out of his pocket, wiped his perspiring face with it and wrinkled up his nose.

"Gee! The way she looked at me ... as if I were the Devil! It made my heart sink!"

Then he laughed and said:

"She must have had some bad experiences with us fellows!"

Sashka was kind-hearted, but he had no pity for people. Probably, he gave more money to beggars, and gave it more willingly, than many a rich man, but he gave it because he hated poverty. The little daily tragedies of life touched him not at all. He used to talk about them and laugh.

"Have you heard? Mishka Sizov has been sent to prison!" he said to me one day with animation. "He walked and walked about, looking for work, and one day he stole an umbrella and was caught. He didn't know how to steal. They hauled him before the beak. I was walking along and suddenly I saw him being led like a sheep by a policeman. His face was pale and his lips were parted. I shouted out to him: 'Mishka!' but he didn't answer, as if he didn't know me."

We went into a shop and Sashka bought a pound of marmalade sweets.

"I ought to buy Stepakha some pastries," he explained, "but I don't like pastries.. This marmalade is better !"

In addition to the sweets he bought some cakes and nuts, and then we went to a wine shop and he bought two bottles of liqueur, one the colour of red lead and the other the colour of vitriol. Walking down the street with the packages under his arm, he composed the following story about the nun:

"A buxom woman, isn't she! She must have been a shopkeeper's wife. Probably a grocer. I suppose she was unfaithful to her husband! He must have been a puny fellow.... Aren't those women cunning! Take Stepakha, for example..."

By this time we had reached the gates of a house, painted brown, with green shutters. Sashka kicked the wicker gate open as if he were at home, set his cap jauntily on the side of his head and strode into the yard, which was strewn with yellow birch, poplar and elder leaves. At the other end of the yard, built against the garden wall, stood a wash-house, banked with turf right up to the window sills. Its roof was covered with yellowish-green moss, and the treetops swayed over the roof, reluctantly shedding their leaves. With its two windows the wash-house seemed to be gazing at us mournfully and suspiciously, like a toad.

The door was opened for us by a big woman, about forty years of age, with a large pock-marked face, merry eyes and thick red lips, which were stretched in a pleasant smile.

"What welcome guests!" she cried in a singsong voice. And Sasha, placing his hands on her ample shoulders and bringing his face close to hers, said:

"Many happy returns of the day, Stepanida Yakimovna, and congratulations on receiving the holy mysteries!"

"But I didn't go to communion!" protested Stepakha.

"It's all the same!" answered Sashka, kissing her three times on the lips, after which both wiped away the traces of the kisses, Stepakha with the palm of her hand and Sashka with his cap.

In the dark anteroom, encumbered with pokers, baskets and wash tubs, they found Stepakha's daughter, Pasha, busy with the samovar. Pasha was a young girl with large, bulging eyes that stared with stupid astonishment, typical of children who suffered from rickets. She had a wonderfully thick plait of hair of a soft golden colour.

"Many happy returns, Panya!"

"All right," answered the girl.

"You dummy!" exclaimed Stepakha. "You should say 'Thank you.'"

"Oh, all right!" retorted the girl angrily.

A third of the laundress' habitation was taken up by a large oven, and where the shelves for the bathers used to be there was now a wide bed. In the corner, under the icons, stood a table, laid out for tea, and at the wall stood a wide bench, on which it was convenient to place the wash tub. A shaggy dog looked through the open window like a beggar, resting his heavy paws with their broken claws upon the window sill. On the window sills there were flower pots with geraniums and fuchsias.

"She knows how to live," said Sashka, looking round the squalid room and winking to me, as much as to say: "I'm joking!"

The hostess carefully drew a pie from the oven and flipped its rosy crust with her fingernail. Pasha brought in the samovar, glistening like the sun, and cast an angry glance at Sashka. But he said, licking his lips:

"Hell! I must get married! I do love pie!"

"One doesn't marry for the sake of pie," observed Stepakha, gravely.

"Oh, I understand that!"

The buxom laundress laughed merrily at this, but her eyes were grave when she said:

"You'll marry one day and forget me."

"But how many have you forgotten?" retorted Sashka with a grin.

Stepakha also smiled. Dressed as she was, too gaudily for her age, she resembled not a laundress, but a matchmaker, or a fortune teller.

Her daughter, looking like a silent gnome out of a sad fairy tale, was unwanted here, and indeed seemed to be totally unwanted on earth. She ate very carefully, as if she were eating not pie, but fish that was full of bones. And every now and again she slowly turned her large eyes towards Sashka and gazed into his thin mobile face in a queer way, as if she were blind.

The dog whined pitifully at the window. The brassy strains of martial music, the steady tramp of hundreds of heavy marching feet, and the beat of a base drum keeping them in step, came floating in from the street.

Stepakha said to her daughter:

"Why don't you run out and look at the soldiers?"

"I don't want to."

"This is fine!" exclaimed Sashka, throwing the dog a piece of pie crust. "I don't think I need anything more!"

Stepakha looked at him with motherly eyes, and straightening her blouse over her high breast she said with a sigh:

"No, that's not true. There's a lot more things you need."

"What I just said was quite true," answered Sashka. "I don't need anything more now, if only Pashka would stop boring through me with her eyes."

"A fat lot I care about you," the girl retorted softly and contemptuously. Her mother angrily raised her eyebrows, but pursed her lips and said nothing.

Sashka moved in his seat uneasily and looking sideways at the girl said ardently:

"I feel as though I have a hole in my soul. So help me God! I would like my soul to be full, and calm, but I cannot fill it! Do you understand me, Maximich? When I feel bad I want to feel good. And when I get a happy hour I begin to feel bored! Why is that?"

He was already "feeling bored." I could see that. His eyes were roaming restlessly round the room as if taking in its squalor; a critical and ironical spark flashed in them. Obviously, he felt out of place here, and had only just realized it.

He talked warmly about the wrongs that were done in the world, and about the blindness of men who had grown accustomed to these wrongs and failed to see them. His thoughts flitted about like frightened mice, and it was difficult to keep pace with their rapid changes.

"Everything is all wrong—that's what I see! You have a church in one place and next to it you have the devil knows what! Innokenti Vassilievich Zemskov writes poetry like this:

Thanks for those few flashes
Which lit up the gloom of my heart,
For those sweet moments of contact
With your body divine.

But it did not prevent him from cheating his sister out of her house by a lawsuit; and the other day he pulled his parlour maid Nastya by the hair."

"What did he do that for?" asked Stepakha, glancing at her rough hands, which were as red as the feet of a goose. Her face had suddenly become hard and she lowered her eyes.

"I don't know.... Nastya wanted to take him to court for it, but he gave her three rubles and she let it drop, the fool!"

Suddenly Sashka jumped up and said:

"It's time for us to go!"

"Where to?" the hostess asked.

"We have some business to do," said Sashka untruthfully. "I'll look in in the evening."

He offered Pasha his hand, but the girl looked at his fingers for a moment or so, not daring to touch them, and then she took Sashka's hand and shook it in a way that seemed as if she were pushing it away.

We went out. In the yard Sashka mumbled as he pulled his cap tightly over his head:

"The devil! That girl doesn't like me ... and I feel ashamed in her presence. I won't go there tonight."

Unpleasant thoughts appeared on his face, like a rash. He blushed.

"I must give Stepakha up," he said. "It's not a nice business! She's twice my age, and...."

But by the time we turned the corner he was already laughing and saying to himself cheerfully, without a trace of boastfulness:

"She loves me. She tends me like a flower. So help me God! It makes me feel ashamed. Sometimes I feel so good being with her ... better than with my own mother! It's simply wonderful. I tell you, brother, they are troublesome things, are women. But they're a good lot for all that. They deserve all our love.... But is it possible to love them all?"

"It would be good if you loved at least one well," I suggested.

"One, one," he mumbled pensively. "But try loving only one!..."

He gazed into the distance, beyond the blue strip of the river, at the yellowing meadows, at the black bushes stripped by the autumn wind and sparsely clothed with golden leaves. Sashka's face looked kind and thoughtful. It was evident that he was full of pleasant recollections, which played upon his soul as sunbeams played upon a river.

"Let's sit down," he suggested, halting at the edge of a gully near the nunnery wall.

The wind was driving the clouds across the sky. Shadows were flitting across the meadow. On the river a fisherman was tapping away, caulking his boat.

"Listen," said Sashka. "Let's go to Astrakhan."

"What for?"

"Oh, just like that. Or else, let's go to Moscow."

"But what about Liza?"

"Liza. . . . Y-e-ss. . . ."

He looked straight into my eyes and asked me:

"Have I fal'en in love with her yet, or not?"

"Ask a policeman," I answered.

He laughed freely and heartily, like a child. He glanced up at the sun and then at the shadows flitting across meadow, and jumping to his feet he said:

"Those confectionary girls will be coming out soon, come along!"

He strode rapidly down the street. There was a look of concern on his face, he had his hands in his pockets, and his cap was drawn low over his forehead. From the gates of a one-story, barrack-like building, girls came running, one after another, in kerchiefs and grey aprons. One of them was Zina, a dark, graceful girl with Mongolian features and almond eyes, wearing a red blouse fitting tightly round her bust.

"Come and have some coffee," said Sashka to her, clutching her by the arm. Then he went on to say hurriedly:

"Do you mean to tell me you intend to marry that mangy cur? Why, he'll be jealous of you. . . ."

"Every husband ought to be jealous," answered Zina gravely. "Do you want me to marry you?"

"No. don't marry me either!"

"Drop that," the girl said, frowning. "Why aren't you at work?"

"I've taken a holiday."

"Ekh, you!. . . I don't want any coffee."

"What do you mean?" exclaimed Sasha, pulling her into a pastry shop.

When they sat down at a small table by the window, he asked her:

"Do you believe me?"

"I believe every animal, the fox and the hedgehog. As for you—I'll wait a bit," the girl answered slowly.

"Well, without you I shall go to the dogs!"

At that moment Sashka really believed that he was passing through a tragedy—his lips trembled, his eyes were moist. He was sincerely moved.

"Well, I'm a lost man, drowned in my own tears. But it serves me right, since I can't catch fortune by the hem of her cloak. But it won't be easy for you either! I shall give you no rest. Let him have a business and own horses, but you'll not be able to eat a thing, thinking of me. Mark my words. . . ."

"It's time I stopped playing with dolls," the girl said softly but angrily.

"Oh, so I am a doll to you, eh?"

"I wasn't speaking of you."

"There, look at them, Maximich! They are a race of snakes. They have no feeling. She stings me in the heart, and I suffer. But she says: Oh, you are a doll!"

Sashka was indignant. His hands trembled, and his eyes grew dark with anger.

"How can one live with creatures like that?" he demanded.

"A fine actor," I thought to myself, watching him almost with admiration.

His acting obviously captivated the girl, touched her. Wiping her lips with a corner of her kerchief, she asked in a kindly voice:

"Will you be free on Sunday?"

"Free from what? From you?"

"Don't play the fool. . . . Come over here. . . ."

They went over to a corner, and Sashka, with flashing eyes, talked long and ardently to the girl in an undertone. Finally, she exclaimed with sad vexation:

"Good Lord! What kind of husband will you make?"

"I?" shouted Sashka. "This kind!"

And without being in the least embarrassed by the presence of the fat pastry cook, he tightly hugged the girl and kissed her on the lips.

"What are you doing, are you mad?" the girl exclaimed in confusion, tearing herself out of his arms.

She fled out of the door like a bird, and Sashka, wearily sitting down at the table shook his head and said disapprovingly:

"What a temper! She's a wild animal, not a girl!"

"What do you want of her?"

"I don't want her to marry that bald droshky driver. It's a scandal. I won't allow it. I can't bear it!"

Finishing his coffee, now quite cold, he seemed to have forgotten the tragedy he had just passed through and began to reflect lyrically:

"Do you know? On holidays, or even on week days, when a lot of girls are out together strolling, or going home from work, or from high school, my very heart trembles. Good Lord! I think to myself. What a lot of them there are! Each one must love somebody; and if they don't they certainly will love someone tomorrow, or within a month, it makes no difference. Now this is what I understand. This is life! Is there anything better in life than love? Just think—what is night? Everybody is embracing and kissing—oh, brother! that's something, d'you know.... It's something you can't even find a name for! It is really a heaven-sent joy."

Jumping up he said:

"Come along, let's go for a walk!"

The sky was overcast with grey clouds, the rain was coming down in a fine drizzle, like dust. It was cold, raw and miserable. But Sashka, oblivious to everything, strolled along in his light summer jacket and chattered without ceasing about everything in the shop windows that caught his greedy eye—about neckties, revolvers, toys, and ladies' frocks, about machines, confectionary and church vestments. He caught sight of the bold type of a theatrical poster.

"Uriel Acosta! I have seen that! Have you? Those Jews talk well don't they? Do you remember? Only it's all lies. There's one kind of people on the stage and another kind in the street, or in the market place. I love jolly people—Jews and Tatars. Look how heartily the Tatars laugh.... It's a good thing they don't show you real life on the stage, but something remote—boyars and foreigners. As for real life—thank you very much. We have quite enough of our own! But if they do show you real life, let it be all true, and without pity! Children ought to play on the stage, because when they play, it's real!"

"But you don't like what is real?"

"Why not? I do if it's interesting."

The sun peeped out again, reluctantly lighting up the rain-drenched town. We roamed through the streets until vespers, when the church bells called for prayers. Sashka pulled me to a waste lot, to the fence of an orchard that belonged to a stern government official named Renkin, the father of beautiful Liza.

"Wait for me here, will you?" he begged of me, leaping onto the fence like a cat. He sat down on a post and whistled softly. Then, raising his cap with a pleased and polite gesture, he began to talk to a girl, who was invesible to me, wriggling so restlessly that he was in danger of falling off the fence.

"Good evening, Elizaveta Yakovlevna!"

I did not hear what the answer was on the other side of the fence, but through a chink between two boards I saw a lilac skirt, and the thin wrist of a white hand holding a large pair of garden-er's clippers.

"No," Sashka went on to say sadly, but untruthfully. "I haven't managed to read it yet. You know how hard I work. And I work at night. In the daytime I have to sleep—and my chums give me no rest. As I set the type, letter by letter, I think only of you.... Yes, of course! Only I don't like full lines of type; verse is much easier to read.... May I come down? Why not? Nekra-ssov? Yes ... very, only he doesn't write much about love.... Why are you angry? Wait a minute—is there anything offensive about that? You asked me what I liked, and I said that most of all I liked love—everybody likes it.... Elizaveta Yakovlevna ... wait...."

He stopped talking, hung over the fence like an empty sack, and then, sitting up straight, he sat there for several seconds like a mournful raven, tapping his knee with the peak of his cap. His red hair was beautifully lit up by the setting sun and tenderly ruffled by the wind.

"She's gone!" he said angrily, jumping to the ground. "She's offended because I didn't read some book—a book, the devil take it! She gave me something that was more like a flat iron than a book! It was about an inch and a half thick.... Let's go!"

"Where to?"

"What does it matter."

He walked on slowly, barely dragging his feet along. His face looked tired, and he glanced with vexation at the windows that were lit up by the slanting rays of the sun.

"After all, she must love somebody," he said plaintively. "Why doesn't she love me? But no! She wants me to read books! Thinks I'm a fool! Her eyes are brighter than the light of day—and she wants me to read books! It's ridiculous. Of course, I'm no match for her ... but good Lord, you don't always fall in love with your equal!"

After remaining silent for a moment, he softly muttered:

> And long she languished in the world,
> Filled with strange desires,

and remained an old maid, the fool!"

I laughed. He looked at me in surprise and asked:

"What, am I talking nonsense? Ekh, brother Maximich! My heart is swelling and swelling without end, and I feel as if I am all heart!"

We reached the edge of the town, but the other side this time. Before us spread a field, and in the distance loomed the Young Ladies Institute, a tall white building surrounded by trees, standing behind a brick wall, and with brick columns running along the porch.

"I'll read books for her, it won't kill me," mused Sashka. Prospectives... like hell! I'll tell you what, brother. I'll go and see Stepakha.... I'll put my head in her lap and go to sleep. Then I'll wake up, we'll have a drink, and then go to sleep again. I'll stay the night with her. We haven't spent a bad day, the two of us, have we?"

He squeezed my hand tightly and looked tenderly into my eyes.

"I like to walk with you," he said. "You are by my side, and yet you seem not to be there. You don't hinder me in the least. Now that's what I call being a real chum!"

Having paid me this doubtful compliment, Sashka turned on his heel and rapidly walked back to town. His hands were thrust into his pockets, his cap was balanced precariously on the back of his head. and he went along whistling. He looked so thin and sharp, like a nail with a golden head. I was sorry he was going back to Stepakha, but I understood that he had to give himself to somebody, he had to spend the richness of his soul on someone!

The red rays of the sun struck his back and seemed to be pushing him along.

The ground was coldish, the field deserted, the town seemed to murmur softly. Sashka stooped down, picked up a stone, and swinging his arm threw it far away.

Then he shouted to me: "So long!"